MEG CABOT

remembrance

A MEDIATOR NOVEL

wm

WILLIAM MORROW

An Imprint of HarperCollins Publishers

REMEMBRANCE. Copyright © 2016 by Meg Cabot, LLC. All rights reserved. Printed in the United States of America. No part of this book may be used or reproduced in any manner whatsoever without written permission except in the case of brief quotations embodied in critical articles and reviews. For information address HarperCollins Publishers, 195 Broadway, New York, NY 10007.

HarperCollins books may be purchased for educational, business, or sales promotional use. For information please e-mail the Special Markets Department at SPsales@harpercollins.com.

FIRST EDITION

Library of Congress Cataloging-in-Publication Data has been applied for.

ISBN: 978-0-06-237902-3 (trade paperback)
ISBN: 978-0-06-246578-8 (library hardcover)

16 17 18 19   DIX/RRD   10 9 8 7 6 5 4 3 2 1

Dear Reader,

I'm sure you've seen lots of movies and TV series and maybe even reality shows about people with the same ability as my heroine, Suze Simon: so-called "mediators" who can communicate with the dead, helping them resolve whatever issues they've left behind in this world, so they can cross over to the next.

But the "reality" of Suze's gift isn't at all the way they portray it in the movies or on TV. That's because—though she's kept notes on her cases for some time—Suze hasn't shared them, since doing so might risk someone's physical or emotional safety. That's why only a few of her closest family and friends (and now you) are aware of her secret.

But don't worry if you missed any of Suze's previous "progress reports." After all, they took place in high school. And who wants to relive high school?

Except that it was in high school when Suze first encountered the love of her life, Jesse de Silva. It took a miracle to bring them together, and they've sworn that nothing will ever tear them apart. Or will it?

If there's one thing I've learned since high school, it's that life is full of miracles . . . and secrets. . . .

And surprises, like that a character I created in the year 2000 would have such a lasting impact on the lives of so many, including my own.

For that, I'll never stop being thankful, especially to all of you.

Meg Cabot

remembrance

uno

It started while I was in the middle of an extremely heated online battle over a pair of black leather platform boots. That's when a chime sounded on my desktop, letting me know I'd received an e-mail.

Ordinarily I'd have ignored it, since my need for a pair of stylish yet functional boots was at an all-time high. My last ones had met with an unfortunate accident when I was mediating a particularly stubborn NCDP (Non-Compliant Deceased Person) down at the Carmel marina, and both of us had ended up in the water.

Unfortunately, I was at work, and my boss, Father Dominic, frowns on his employees ignoring e-mails at work, even at an unpaid internship like mine.

Muttering, "I'll be back," at the screen (in what I considered to be a pretty good imitation of Arnold Schwarzenegger as the Terminator), I clicked my in-box, keeping the screen to the auction open. With their steel-reinforced toes and chunky heels, these boots were perfect for dealing with those who needed a swift kick in the butt in order to encourage them to pass on to the afterlife, though I doubt that's why the person who kept trying to outbid me—Maximillian28, a totally lame screen name—wanted them so badly.

But if there's anything I've learned in the mediation business, it's that you shouldn't make assumptions.

Which is exactly what I realized when I saw the name of the e-mail's sender. It wasn't one of my coworkers at the Mission Academy, let alone a parent or a student. It wasn't a family member or friend, either.

It was someone I hadn't had any contact with in a long, long time—someone I'd hoped never to hear from again. Just seeing his name in my in-box caused my blood to boil . . . or freeze. I wasn't sure which.

Forgetting about the boots, I clicked on the e-mail's text.

To: suzesimon@missionacademy.edu
Fr: paulslater@slaterindustries.com
Re: Your House
Date: November 16 1:00:02 PM PST

Hi, Suze.

I'm sure you've heard by now that my new company, Slater Industries, has purchased your old house on 99 Pine Crest Road, as well as the surrounding properties.

You've never been a sentimental kind of girl, so I doubt you'll have a problem with the fact that we'll be tearing your house down in order to make way for a new Slater Properties development of moderately sized family homes (see attached plans). My numbers are below. Give me a call if you want to talk.

You know, it really bothers me that we haven't stayed in touch over the years, especially since we were once so close.

Regards to Jesse.

Best,

Paul Slater

P.S.: Don't tell me you're still upset over what happened graduation night. It was only a kiss.

I stared at the screen, aware that my heart rate had sped up. Sped up? I was so angry I wanted to ram my fist into the monitor, as if by doing so I could somehow ram it into Paul Slater's rock-hard abs. I'd hurt my knuckles doing either, but I'd release a lot of pent-up aggression.

Did I *have a problem*, as Paul had so blithely put it, with the fact that he'd purchased my old house—the rambling Victorian home in the Carmel Hills that my mom and stepdad had lovingly renovated nearly a decade earlier for their new blended family (myself and my stepbrothers Jake, Brad, and David)—and was now intending to tear it down in order to make way for some kind of hideous subdivision?

Yeah. Yeah, I had *a problem* with that, all right, and with nearly every other thing he'd written in his stupid e-mail.

And not because I'm sentimental, either.

He had the nerve to call what he'd done to me on graduation

night "only a kiss"? Funny how all this time I'd been considering it something else entirely.

Fortunately for Paul, I'd never been stupid enough to mention it to my boyfriend, Jesse, because if I had, there'd have been a murder.

But since Hispanic males make up about 37 percent of the total prison population in California (and Paul evidently had enough money to buy the entire street on which I used to live), I didn't see a real strong chance of Jesse getting off on justifiable homicide, though that's what Paul's murder would have been, in my opinion.

Without stopping to think—huge mistake—I pulled my cell phone from the back pocket of my jeans and angrily punched in one of the numbers Paul had listed. It rang only once before I heard his voice—deeper than I remembered—intone smoothly, "This is Paul Slater."

"What the hell is your problem?"

"Why, Susannah Simon," he said, sounding pleased. "How nice to hear from you. You haven't changed a bit. Still so ladylike and refined."

"Shut the hell up."

I'd like to point out that I didn't say *hell* either time. There's a swear jar on my desk—Father Dominic put it there due to my tendency to curse. I'm supposed to stick a dollar in it for every four-letter word I utter, five dollars for every F-bomb I drop.

But since there was no one in the office to overhear me, I let the strongest weapons in my verbal arsenal fly freely. Part of my duties in the administrative offices of the Junípero Serra Mission Academy (grades K–12)—where I'm currently trying to earn some of the practicum credits I need to get my certification as a school counselor—are to answer the phone and check e-mails while all of my supervisors are at lunch.

What do my duties not include? Swearing. Or making personal phone calls to my enemies.

"I just wanted to find out where you are," I said, "so I can drive to that location and then slowly dismember you, something I obviously should have done the day we met."

"Same old Suze," Paul said fondly. "How long has it been, anyway, six years? Almost that. I don't think I've heard from you since the night of our high-school graduation, when your stepbrother Brad got so incredibly drunk on Goldschläger that he hurled all over Kelly Prescott's Louboutins. Ah, memories."

"He wasn't the only one who was drunk, if I recall," I reminded him. "And that isn't all that happened that night. You know what I've been doing since then, besides getting my counseling degree? Working out, so that when we meet again, I can—"

I launched into a highly anatomical description of just where, precisely, I intended to insert Paul's head after I physically removed it from his body.

"Suze, Suze, Suze." Paul feigned shock. "So much hostility. I find it hard to believe they allowed someone like you into a counseling training program. Have the people in charge there ever even *met* you?"

"If they met you, they'd be wondering the same thing I am: how a manipulative freak like you isn't locked up in a maximum-security penitentiary."

"What can I say, Simon? You've always brought out the romantic in me."

"I think you're confusing the word *romantic* with sociopathic sleazebag. And you're lucky it was Debbie Mancuso and not Jesse who came along when you were pawing at me that night like an oversexed howler monkey, because if it had been, he'd—"

"—have given me another one of those trademarked beatings

of his that I so richly deserve. Yes, yes, I know, Suze, I've heard all this before."

Paul sighed. He and my boyfriend have never gotten along, mainly because Jesse had been an NCDP for a while and Paul—who, like me, was born with the so-called "gift" to communicate with those trapped in the spirit world—had been determined to keep him that way, mostly so that Paul could get into my pants.

Fortunately, he'd failed on both accounts.

"Could we move on, please?" Paul asked. "This is very entertaining, but I want to get to the part about how I now own your family home. You heard the news, right? Not about your house—I can tell by your less than graceful reaction that you only just found out about that. I mean about how Gramps finally croaked, and left me the family fortune?"

"Oh, no. Paul, I'm—"

I bit my lip. His grandfather had been cantankerous at times, but he'd also been the only person in Paul's family—besides his little brother, Jack—who'd genuinely seemed to care about him. I wasn't surprised to hear that he'd passed on, however. The old man had already been in pretty bad shape when I'd met him from "shifting" back and forth too often through time, a skill mediators possess, but are warned not to use. It's considered hazardous to their health.

Still, it felt wrong to say *I'm sorry for your loss* to Paul, considering he was acting like the world's biggest jackhole.

It didn't end up mattering. Paul wanted something from me, but it wasn't my condolences.

"Yeah, you're talking to one of *Los Angeles* magazine's most eligible bachelors," he went on, oblivious. "Of course my parents aren't too happy about it. They had the nerve to take me to court to contest the will, can you believe that?"

"Uh . . . yes?"

"Funny. But justice prevailed, and I'm now the president and CEO of Slater Industries. I've got a home on both coasts and a private jet to fly between them, but—as the magazine put it—no one special with whom to share them." I could hear the mocking tone in his voice. "Interested in being that special someone, Suze?"

"I'll pass, thanks," I said coolly. "Especially since you can't think of anything more creative to do with your new fortune than knock down other people's houses. Which I don't think you can even do legally. Mine's nearly two hundred years old. It's still got the original carved newel post on the staircase from when it was built in 1850. It has stained-glass windows. It's a historic landmark."

"Actually, it isn't. Oh, it's quaintly charming in its own way, I suppose, but nothing historic ever occurred there. Well, except for what happened between you and me," he smirked, "and considering the way you've been avoiding me these past few years, I guess I'm not the only one who remembers that as being historically significant."

"Nothing ever happened between us, Paul," I said. He was only trying to get under my skin, the same way he'd tried to get under my bra at graduation. That's how he operated, much like a chigger, or various other bloodsucking parasites. "Nothing good, anyway."

"Ouch, Simon! You sure know how to hurt a guy. I distinctly recall one afternoon in my bedroom when you did not seem at all repulsed by my advances. Why, you even—"

"—walked out on you, remember? And no one can tear down a house that old. That has to be a violation of some kind of city code."

"You slip enough money to the right politicians, Simon, you can get permits to do anything you want in the great state of California. That's why they call it the land of opportunity. Congratulations, by the way, on your stepfather's success. Who would have thought that little home-improvement show of Andy Ackerman's would become an international sensation. Where'd your parents move to with all the money he's raking in from the syndication rights? Bel Air? Or the Hills? Don't worry, it happens to everyone. I'm sure they haven't let fame go to their heads. Your mother is a lovely woman with such gracious manners, which is more than I can say for her only daughter—"

"You say one more word about my mother," I snarled, "and I will end you, Paul, like I should have done years ago. I will find you, wherever you are, remove your head from your body, and stuff it up your—"

"You already used that one," Paul reminded me. "So I take it that you *do* have a sentimental side, Suze. How surprising. I always knew you had a soft spot for that undead boyfriend of yours, of course, but I never expected it to extend to real estate. Oh, wait—Jesse must be more than just a boyfriend now that you managed to reunite his body with his soul. I'm afraid I've been a bit out of the loop lately—and who has time to read their alumni newsletter anyway? Have you two tied the knot? Wait, silly me— of *course* you have. It's been six years since high school! I know a love as passionate as the one you and that necromantic cholo shared couldn't *possibly* wait six years to be consummated. And from what I remember, Hector 'Jesse' de Silva respected you far too much ever to try to get into your pants without the sanctity of holy matrimony."

I felt my cheeks begin to burn. I told myself it was indignation at his racism—*necromantic cholo*? Really?—but I knew some of it was due to a different emotion entirely. I was happy Paul wasn't in the same room with me, or he'd surely have noticed. He'd always been discomfortingly sharp-eyed.

"Jesse and I are engaged," I said, controlling—with an effort—

my impulse to swear at him some more. In the past, anytime Paul was able to evoke any kind of emotion from me at all—even a negative one—it pleased him.

And the last thing I'd ever wanted to do was please Paul Slater.

"Engaged?" Paul crowed. "What is this, the 1950s? People still get *engaged*? Do people even get *married*? I mean, straight people?"

I really should have thought before I acted and never called him in the first place, I thought miserably, eyeing a poster Ms. Diaz, the Mission Academy guidance counselor, had stuck on the wall over by the entrance to her office. It was one of those posters ubiquitous to the profession, a blown-up photo of a kitten struggling to hang on to a tree branch emblazoned with the words *Aim High!*

Too late, I realized I ought to have aimed high and approached Paul with cool dispassion, not let my emotions get in the way. That was the only way to handle him.

But he'd always been good at pushing my buttons.

All my buttons.

"Isn't an engagement a little old-school for a modern girl like you, Simon?" he went on. "Oh, wait, I forgot . . . Walking Dead Boy likes to do things the old-school way, doesn't he? Does that mean"—he sounded more pleased with himself than ever—"you two are *waiting for marriage?*"

I felt another overwhelming urge to lash out and punch something, anything, maybe even the tabby kitten in the poster. But the wall behind it was three feet thick, built in the 1700s, and had withstood many a Northern California earthquake. It would definitely withstand my fist.

"That is none of your business," I said, so icily that I was surprised the phone in my hand didn't freeze to my face.

I was trying hard not to clue Paul in to how annoyed I was with my boyfriend's prehistoric notion that we not only couldn't marry until he was in a financial position to support me and whatever children we might have (even though I'd assured him I was on the pill and planned to stay on it until I'd finished my MA and had a job with full dental, at least), we couldn't move in together.

Even worse, Jesse insisted we had to wait until we'd formally exchanged vows—in a church, with him in a suit, and me in a white dress and veil, no less—before we could enjoy conjugal relations. It was the least he could do, he insisted, out of "respect" for all that I had done for him, not only bringing him back to life, but providing him with a life worth living.

I'd let him know many, many times, and in no uncertain terms, that I could live without that kind of respect.

But what else could you expect from a guy who'd been born during the reign of Queen Victoria? Not to mention murdered in—then buried behind, then spent 150 years haunting—the very same house Paul was threatening to tear down?

This had to have something to do with *why* Paul was tearing it down. I'd always suspected Paul of being jealous that in the end I'd chosen the ghost instead of him.

But how could I not? Even in the days when Jesse hadn't had a pulse, he'd had more heart than Paul.

"Waiting for marriage," Paul repeated. He was hooting with laughter that bordered on tears. "Oh, God. That is so sweet. It really is, Simon. I think your stepdad's TV show is about the wrong person. They should be filming you and that boyfriend of yours, and call it *The Last Virgins*. I swear it'd be the highest-rated show since *Ghost Mediator*."

"Go ahead," I said, lifting my heels to my desk and crossing my feet at the ankles. "Laugh it up, Paul. You know what Jesse's doing right now? His medical residency."

That hit home. Paul abruptly stopped laughing.

"That's right," I went on, beginning to enjoy myself. "While you've been out being named one of LA's most eligible bachelors for doing nothing but inheriting your grandfather's money, Jesse passed the MCATs with one of the highest scores in California state history and got a medical degree at UCSF. Now he's doing a pediatrics fellowship at St. Francis Medical Center in Monterey. He just has to finish up his residency there, and he'll be fully licensed to practice medicine. Do you know what that means?"

Paul's voice lost some of its laughter. "He stole someone else's identity? Because that's the only way I can see someone who used to be a walking corpse getting into UCSF. Except as a practice cadaver, of course."

"Jesse was born in California, you idiot."

"Yeah, before it became a state."

"What it means," I went on, tipping back in my chair, "is that next year, after Jesse's board-certified, and I've gotten my certification, we'll be getting married."

At least, if everything went according to schedule, and Jesse won the private grant he'd applied for to open his own practice. I didn't see the point in mentioning any of these "if"s to Paul . . . or that I didn't know how much longer I could go on swimming laps in the dinky pool in the courtyard of my apartment building, trying to work out my frustration about my fiancé and his very nineteenth-century views about love, honor, and sex . . . views I'm determined to respect as much as he (unfortunately) respects my body.

Things have gotten steamy between us enough times for me to know that what's behind the front of those tight jeans of Jesse's will be worth the wait, though. Our wedding night is going to be *epic*.

Unless one of those many "if"s doesn't work out, or something happens to get the groom thrown in jail. Of all the obstacles I'd envisioned getting in the way of our very much deserved wedding night, Paul popping around again was the last thing I'd expected.

"But more important, it means someday we'll be opening our own practice, specializing in helping sick kids," I went on. "Not that helping other people is a concept I'd expect *you* to understand."

"That's not true," Paul said. There was no laughter in his voice at all now. "I've always wanted to help you, Suze."

"Is that what you call what you did to me graduation night, when you said you had a present you had to give to me in private, so I followed you outside and you threw me up against the mission wall and shoved your hand up my skirt?" I asked him, acidly. "You consider that *helping* me?"

"I do," he said. "I was trying to help teach you not to waste your time on formerly deceased Latino do-gooders who consider it a sin to get nasty without a marriage license."

"Well," I said, lowering my feet from my desktop. "I'm hanging up now. It was not at all a pleasure speaking to you again after all these years, Paul. Please die slowly and painfully. Buh-bye."

"Wait," Paul said urgently before I could press End. "Don't go. I wanted to say—"

"What? That you won't tear down my house if I take lessons from you in how to be a more effective mediator? Sorry, Paul, that might have worked when I was sixteen, but I'm too old to fall for that one again."

He sounded offended. "The thing with your house is just business. I only told you about it as a courtesy. What I wanted to say is that I'm sorry."

Paul Slater had never apologized for anything before . . . and meant it. He caught me off guard.

"Sorry for what?"

"Sorry for what I said about Jesse just now, and sorry for what happened that night. You're right, Suze, I'd had way too much to drink. I know that's no excuse, but it's the truth. Honestly, I barely remember what happened."

Was he kidding? "Let me remind you. After you tried to nail me against that wall, I gave *you* a present. It was with my knee, to your groinal area. Does that refresh your memory?"

"A man doesn't forget that kind of pain, Simon. But what happened after that is a bit hazy. Is that when Debbie Mancuso came along?"

"It was. She seemed eager to tend to the wound I gave you."

"Then you should be the one apologizing to me. Debbie's ministrations were far from tender. She straddled me like she thought I was a damned gigolo—"

"Watch it," I growled. "Debbie's married to my stepbrother Brad now. And obviously I didn't knee you nearly as hard as I should have if you were still able to get it on with Debbie afterward. The last thing you're ever going to hear from me is an apology."

"Then accept mine, and let me make it up to you. I have a proposal."

I barked with laughter. "Oh, right!"

"Simon, I'm serious."

"That'll be a first."

"It could save your home."

I stopped laughing. "I'm listening. Maybe."

"Give me another chance."

"I said I'm listening."

"No, that's the proposal. Give me another chance."

dos

The school office was air-conditioned, but the shiver I felt down my spine had nothing to do with the fact that my supervisors (some of whom dress in religious habit) liked to keep the thermostat at a crisp sixty-five degrees.

"I'm sorry," I said, glad the shiver didn't show in my voice. "I'm actually very busy and important and don't have time for rich jerks from my past who want to make amends. But I wish you luck on your path toward transformative enlightenment. Bye now."

"Suze, wait. Don't you want to save your house?"

"It isn't mine anymore, remember? It's yours. So I don't care what happens to it."

"Come on, Suze. This is the first time in six years you've actually called me back when I've reached out to you. I know you care—about the house."

He was right. I'd been upset when Mom told me she and my stepdad, Andy, were selling it—much more upset than Jesse when he heard the news.

"It's only a house, Susannah," he'd said. "Your parents haven't lived there in years, and neither have we. It has nothing to do with us."

"How can you say that?" I'd cried. "That house has everything to do with us. If it weren't for that house, we'd never have found one another!"

He'd laughed. "Maybe, *querida*. Then again, maybe not. I have a feeling I'd have found you, and you me, no matter where we were. That house is only a place, and not our place, not anymore. Our place is together, wherever we happen to be."

Then he'd pulled me close and kissed me. It had been hard to feel bad about anything after that.

I guess I could understand why the big, rambling Victorian on 99 Pine Crest Road meant nothing to him. To Jesse, it's the house in which he was killed.

To me, however, it was the house in which we'd met and slowly, over time and through many misunderstandings, fell in love—though it had seemed for years like a doomed romance: he was a Non-Compliant Deceased Person. I was a girl whose job it was to rid the world of his kind. It had ended up working out, but barely.

While the so-called "gift" of communicating with the dead might sound nifty, believe me, when a ghost shows up in your bedroom—even one who looks as good with his shirt off as Jesse does—the reality isn't at all the way they portray it in the movies or on TV or the stupid new hit reality show *Ghost Mediator* (which is, I'm sorry to say, based on a best-selling video and role-playing game of the same name).

The "reality" is heartbreaking and sometimes quite violent . . . as my need for new boots illustrated.

Except, of course, that in the end it was my "gift" that had enabled me to meet and get to know Jesse, and even help return his soul to his corporal self, though my boss and fellow media-tor, Mission Academy principal Father Dominic, likes to think that was "a miracle" we should be grateful for. I'm still on the fence about whether or not I believe in miracles. There's a rational and scientific explanation for everything. Even the "gift" of see-ing ghosts seems to have a genetic component. There's probably a scientific explanation for what happened with Jesse, too.

One thing there's no explanation for—at least that I've found so far—is Paul. Even though he's the one who showed me the nifty time-jumping trick that eventually led to the "miracle" that brought Jesse back to the living from the dead, Paul didn't do it out of the goodness of his heart. He did it out of a desire to get in my pants.

"Look, Paul," I said. "You're right. I do care. But about people, not houses. So why don't you take your amends and your fancy new housing development and your private jet and stick them all up your external urethral orifice, which in case you don't know is the medical term for dick hole. Adios, muchacho."

I started to hang up until the sound of Paul's laughter stopped me.

"Dick hole," he repeated. "Really, Simon?"

I couldn't help placing the phone to my ear again. "Yes, really. I'm highly educated in the correct medical terms for sexual or-gans now, since I'm engaged to a doctor. And that isn't just where you can stick your amends, by the way, it's also what you are."

"Fine. But what about Jesse?"

"What *about* Jesse?"

"I could see you not caring about me, or about the house, but I think you'd be at least a little concerned about your boyfriend."

"I am, but I fail to see what your tearing down my house has to do with him."

"Only everything. Are you telling me you really don't remember all those Egyptian funerary texts of Gramps' that we used to study together after school? That hurts, Suze. That really hurts. Two mixed-up mediators, poring over ancient hieroglyphics . . . I thought we had something special."

When you're a regular girl and a guy is horny for you, he invites you over to his house after school to watch videos.

When you're a mediator, he invites you over to study his grandfather's ancient Egyptian funerary texts, so you can learn more about your calling.

Yeah. I was real popular in high school.

"What about them?" I demanded.

"Oh, not much. I just thought you'd remember what the *Book of the Dead* said about what happens when a dwelling place that was once haunted is demolished . . . how a demon disturbed from its final resting place will unleash the wrath of eternal hellfire upon all it encounters, cursing even those it once held dear with the rage of a thousand suns. That kind of thing."

I swore—but silently, to myself.

Paul's grandfather, in addition to being absurdly wealthy, had also been one of the world's most preeminent Egyptologists. When it came to obscure, ancient curses written on crumbling pieces of papyrus, the guy was top of his field.

That's why I was swearing. I'd been wrong: Paul wasn't calling to make amends. This was something way, way worse.

"Nice try, Paul," I said, attempting to keep my voice light and my heart rate steady. "Except I'm pretty sure that one was about mummies buried in pyramids, not ghosts who once haunted residential homes in Northern California. And while Jesse was never exactly an angel, he was no demon, either."

"Maybe not to you. But he treated me like—"

"Because you were always trying to exorcise him out of existence. That would make anyone feel resentful. And 99 Pine Crest

Road wasn't his final resting place. Even before he became alive again, we found his remains and moved them."

I couldn't see Jesse's headstone from my desk, but I knew it was sitting only a few dozen yards away, in the oldest part of the mission cemetery. On holy days of obligation, it's the fifth graders' job to leave carnations on it (as they do all the historic gravestones in the cemetery), as well as pull any weeds that might have sprouted from it.

The fact that there's nothing buried under Jesse's grave—since he happens to be alive and well—is something I don't see any reason to let the fifth graders know. Kids benefit from being outdoors. Too much time playing video games has been shown to slow their social skills.

"So tearing down the place where he died isn't going to hurt him," I went on. "I'm not personally a fan of subdivisions, but hey, if that's what floats your boat, go for it. Anything else? I really do have to go now, I've got a ton of things to do to get ready for the wedding."

Paul laughed. Apparently my officious tone hadn't fooled him.

"Oh, Suze. I love how so much in the world has changed, but not you. That boyfriend of yours haunted that crummy old house forever, waiting around for . . . just what *was* he waiting for, anyway? Murder victims are the most stubborn of all spooks to get rid of." He said the word *spooks* the way someone in a detergent commercial would say the word *stains*. "All they want is justice—or, as in Jesse's case, revenge."

"That isn't true," I made the mistake of interrupting, and got rewarded by more of Paul's derisive laughter.

"Oh, isn't it? What was it you think he was waiting around for all those years, then, Suze? You?"

I felt my cheeks heat up again. "No."

"Of course you do. But that love story of yours may not have such a happy ending after all."

"Really, Paul? And why is that? Because of something written on a two-thousand-year-old papyrus scroll? I think you've been watching too many episodes of *Ghost Mediator*."

His voice went cold. "I'm just telling you what the curse says—that restoring a soul to the body it once inhabited is a practice best left to the gods."

"What are you even talking about? *You're* the one who—"

"Suze, I only did what people like you and me are supposed to—attempt to help an unhappy soul pass on to his just rewards."

"By sneaking back through time to keep him from dying in the first place so I'd never meet him?"

"Never mind what I did. Let's talk about what *you* did. The curse goes on to say that any human who attempts to resurrect a corpse will be the first to suffer its wrath when the demon inside it is woken."

"Well, that's ridiculous, since there's no demon inside Jesse, and I didn't resurrect him. It was a miracle. Ask Father Dom."

"Really, Suze? Since when did you start believing in miracles?" I hated that he knew me so well. "And when did you start believing that you could tinker around with space and time—and life and death—without having to pay the consequences? If you help to create a monster, you should be prepared for that monster to come back and bite you in the ass. Or are you completely unfamiliar with the entire Hollywood horror movie industry?"

"Fiction," I said, my mouth dry. "Horror movies are fiction."

"And the concept of good and evil? Is that fiction? Think about it, Simon. You can't have one without the other. There has to be a balance. You got your good. Ghost Boy's alive now, and giving back to the community with his healing hands . . . which makes me want to puke, by the way. But where's the bad? Have you not noticed there's something missing from this little miracle of yours?"

"Um," I said, struggling to come up with a flippant reply.

Because he was right. As any Californian worth his flip-flops could tell you, you can't have yin without yang, surf without sand, a latte without soy (because no one in California drinks full dairy, except for me, but I was born in New York City).

"I assume the bad is . . . you." This was weak, but it was the best I could come up with, given the feeling of foreboding slowly creeping up my spine.

"Very funny, Suze. But you're going to have to come up with something better. Humor doesn't work as a defense against the forces of evil. Which are dwelling, as you very well know, inside your so-called miracle boy, just waiting for the chance to lash out and kill you and everyone you love for what you did."

Now he'd gone too far. "I do *not* know that. How do *you* know that? You haven't even seen him in six years. You don't know anything about us. You can't just come here and—"

"I don't *have* to have seen him to know that he didn't escape from having lived as a spook for a century and a half without having brushed up against some pretty malevolent shit. De Silva didn't just walk through the valley of the shadow of death, Simon. He set up camp and toasted marshmallows there. No one can come out of something like that unscathed, however many kids he's curing of cancer now, or however many wedding-gift registries his girlfriend's signing up for in order to assure herself that everything's just fine and dandy."

"That's not fair," I protested. "And that's not fair. You might as well be saying that anyone who's ever suffered from any trauma is destined never to overcome it, no matter how hard they try."

"Really? You're going to fall back on grad school psychobabble?" His voice dripped with amusement. "I expected better from you. Can you honestly tell me, Simon, that when you look into de Silva's big brown telenovela eyes, you never see any shadows there?"

"No. No, of course I do, sometimes, because he's human, and human beings aren't happy one hundred percent of the time."

"Those aren't the kind of shadows I'm talking about, and you know it."

I realized I was squeezing my phone so hard an ugly red impression of its hard plastic casing had sunk into my skin. I had to switch hands.

Because he was right. I did see occasional glimpses of darkness in Jesse's eyes . . . and not sadness, either.

And while I hadn't been lying when I'd told Paul about Jesse's desire to help heal the sick and most downtrodden of our society—it was an integral part of his personality—I did worry sometimes that the reason Jesse fought so desperately against death when he saw it coming for his weakest patients was that he feared it was also coming back for him . . .

Or, worse, that there was still a part of it inside him.

If what the *Book of the Dead* said was true, and Paul really did tear down 99 Pine Crest Road, there was no telling what that destruction might unleash.

And it didn't seem likely we could count on yet another miracle to save us. A person is only given so many miracles in a lifetime, and it felt like Jesse and I had received more than our fair share.

If miracles even exist. Which I'm not saying they do.

As if he'd once again sensed what I was thinking, Paul chuckled. "See what I mean, Simon? You can take the boy out of the darkness, but you can't take the darkness out of the boy."

"Fine," I said. "What do you want from me, exactly, in order to keep you from tearing down my house and releasing the Curse of the Papyrus, or whatever it is? Forgiveness? Great. I forgive you. Will you go now and leave me alone?"

"No, but thanks for the offer," Paul said, smooth as silk. "And it's called the Curse of the Dead. There's no such thing as the Curse of the Papyrus. Curses are written on papyrus. They're not—"

"Just tell me what you want, Paul."

"I told you what I want. Another chance."

"You're going to have to elaborate. Another chance at what?"

"You. One night. If I can't win you over from de Silva in one night, I'm not worthy of the name Slater."

"You have got to be kidding me."

If I hadn't felt so sick to my stomach, I'd have laughed. I tried not to let my conflicting feelings—scorn, fear, confusion—show in my voice. Paul fed off feelings the way black holes fed off stars.

"I'm not, actually," he said. "I told you, it's never a good idea to joke when the forces of evil are involved."

"Paul. First of all, you can't win back something you never had."

"Suze, where is this coming from? I really thought you and I had something once. Are you honestly trying to tell me it was all in my head? Because I've had a lot of time to think it over, and I have to say, I don't agree."

"Second of all, I'm engaged. That means I'm off the market. And even if I wasn't, threatening to tear down a multimillion-dollar house and release some kind of evil spirit that may or may not live inside my boyfriend is beneath even—"

He cut me off. "What do I care if you're engaged? If Hec*tor* doesn't put enough value on your relationship to bother consummating it"—Paul put an unpleasantly rolled trill on the second syllable of Jesse's given name—"which I know he doesn't, you're still fair game as far as I'm concerned."

"Wait." I could hardly believe my ears. "That isn't fair. Jesse's Roman Catholic. Those are his *beliefs*."

"And you and I are non-believers," Paul pointed out. "So I don't understand why you'd want to be with a guy who believes that—"

"I never said I was a non-believer. I believe in *facts*. And the fact is, I want to be with Jesse because he makes me feel like a better person than I suspect I actually am."

There was a momentary silence from the other end of the phone. For a second or two I thought I might actually have gotten through to him, made him see that what he was doing was wrong. Paul did have some goodness in him—I knew, because I'd seen it in action once or twice. Even complete monsters can have one or two likable characteristics. Hitler liked dogs, for instance.

But unfortunately the good part of Paul was buried beneath so much narcissism and greed, it hardly ever got a chance to show itself, and now was no exception.

"Wow, Simon, that was a real Hallmark moment," he snarked. "You know I could make you feel good—"

"Well, you've gotten off to an excellent start by threatening to turn my fiancé into a demon."

"Don't shoot the messenger, baby. I'm not the bad guy here. If I weren't the one tearing down your house, it was going to be some other filthy-rich real-estate developer."

"I highly doubt that."

"What the hell, Simon? You should be grateful to me. I'm trying to do you a solid. Where is all this hostility coming from?"

"My heart."

"This is bullshit." Now Paul sounded pissed off. "Why should I have to respect some other guy's beliefs? It's called free enterprise. Since when can't a man try to win something that's still on the open market?"

"Did we just travel back through time again to the year 1850? Are women something you believe you can actually *own*?"

"Funny. I'll give you that, you've always been funny, Simon. That's the thing I've always liked best about you. Well, that, and your ass. You still have a great ass, don't you? I tried to look up photos of you on social media, but you keep a surprisingly low profile. Oh, shit, wait, never mind. You're a feminist, right? You probably think that ass remark was sexist."

"*That's* what you're worried about? That I'm going to think you're sexist? Not that I'm going to report you to the cops for trying to blackmail me into going out with you?"

"I'm afraid you're going to find any wrongdoing on my part a little difficult to prove to the cops, Suze, even if you've been recording this phone call, which I'm guessing you only thought of doing just now. No monetary sums have been mentioned, and even if you call it coercion, I'm pretty sure you're going to have a hard time explaining to the cops exactly how my tearing down a property I legally own is threatening you. Though if you mention the stuff about the ancient Egyptian funerary texts, it will probably give the po-po a good laugh."

Unfortunately, he was right. That was the part that burned the most. Until he added, "Oh, and I'm going to expect a little more than you merely *going out* with me. Not to be crude, but virtue is hardly something *I* value. Unlike Hec*tor*, I'm not particularly marriage minded. But I guess being married to you might be fun ... like being a storm chaser. You'd never know what to expect from day to day. But I'm getting ahead of myself. First, our date—it will definitely have to include physical intimacy. Otherwise, how else will I be able to show you I've changed?"

I was so stunned, I was temporarily unable to form a reply, even a four-letter one, which for me was unusual.

"Don't worry," he said soothingly. "It's been a long time since

I've touched Goldschläger. I've vastly improved my technique. I won't throw you against another wall."

"Wow," I said, when I could finally bring myself to speak. "What *happened* to you? When did you become so hard up for female company that you had to resort to sextortion? Have you ever thought of trying Tinder?"

He laughed. "Good one! See, I've missed this. I've missed us."

"There was never any us, you perv. What happened between you and Kelly, anyway?"

"Kelly?" Paul hooted some more. "Kelly *Prescott*? I guess you haven't been reading the online alumni newsletters, either."

"No," I admitted guiltily. The guilt was only because my best friend, CeeCee, wrote the newsletter for our graduating class, and I paid no attention to it.

"Well, let's just say Kelly and I weren't exactly meant for each other—not like you and me. But don't worry about old Kel. She's rebounded with some guy twice her age, but with twice as much money as I have—which is saying a lot, because as I mentioned, I'm flush. Kelly Prescott became Mrs. Kelly . . . Walters, I think is what it said on the announcement. She had some huge reception at the Pebble Beach resort. What, you weren't invited?"

"I don't recall. My social calendar's pretty full these days."

I was lying, of course. I'd been invited to Kelly's wedding, but only because I'm related through marriage to her best friend Debbie, who'd been the maid of honor. I'd politely declined, citing a (fake) prior commitment, and no one had mentioned missing me.

Weddings aren't really my thing, anyway. Large gatherings of the living tend to attract the attention of the undead, and I usually end up having to mediate NCDPs between swallows of beer.

My own wedding is going to be different. I'll kick the butt of any deadhead who shows up there uninvited.

"So when are we having dinner?" Paul asked. "Or, more to the point, what comes after dinner. And I'm not talking about dessert."

"When Jupiter aligns with planet Go Screw Yourself."

"Aw, Suze. Your sexy pillow talk is what I've missed most about you. I'll be in Carmel this weekend. I'll text you the deets about where to meet up then. But really, it doesn't sound like you're taking anything I've just told you about the potential threat to your boyfriend's life very seriously."

"I do take it seriously. Seriously enough to be looking forward to seeing you as it will allow me to fulfill my long-held dream of sticking my foot up your ass."

"You can put any body part of yours in any orifice of mine you please, Simon, so long as I get to do the same to you."

I was so angry I suggested that he suck a piece of anatomy I technically don't possess, since I'm female.

It was unfortunate that Sister Ernestine, the vice-principal, chose that particular moment to return from lunch.

"*What* did you say, Susannah?" she demanded.

"Nothing." I hung up on Paul and stuffed my phone back into the pocket of my jeans. I was going to have to deal with him—and whether or not there was any truth to this "curse" he was talking about—at another time. "How was lunch, Sister?"

"We'll discuss how much you owe the swear jar later, young lady. We have bigger problems at the moment."

Did we ever. I figured that out as soon as I saw the dead girl behind her.

tres

I've been seeing the souls of the dead who've left unfinished business on earth for as long as I can remember. I "mediated" my first ghost—*mediate* is what we pros call it when we help a troubled spirit cross from this world to the next, which, unless you happen to be Paul Slater, we do without charge—when I was just a toddler.

I can remember it like it was yesterday: I think that old lady ghost was more frightened of me than I was of her.

But this was the first time I'd ever seen a ghost clutching a wad of paper towels to a wound to staunch the blood flowing from it.

Forgetting to keep my cool, let alone my secret (that I see dead people), I leapt from my office desk chair, crying, "Oh, my God!"

It took me a few seconds to realize that if she was recently deceased, this girl wouldn't still be gushing blood.

Nor would the full-bosomed, gray-haired figure of the vice-principal be steering her toward me, saying with forced cheer,

"It's all right, Becca, dear. Everything's going to be all right. Miss Simon will get that little cut bandaged up, and this will all be straightened out."

In that instant I knew:

This girl was very much alive.

Also that Sister Ernestine was crazy. That "little cut" on Becca's arm didn't look so little to me, judging from the amount of blood pumping out of it. It looked like a full-on gusher. And none of this was going to be "straightened out" anytime soon, especially since the phone in my back pocket was buzzing.

Paul was calling back, of course, to make sure I'd be showing up for our "dessert."

"Susannah." There wasn't the faintest trace of cheer in Sister Ernestine's voice when she addressed me.

This was not unusual. I'd never been one of Sister Ernestine's favorite students back when I'd attended school here, and six years later she'd been appalled at the idea of hiring me. She had preferred the former full-time administrative assistant, Ms. Carper, but due to cutbacks, dwindling enrollment, Father Dominic's insistence that I'd make a fine, read: free, intern, and Ms. Carper's sudden decision to run off to India with her married Bikram Yoga instructor, the nun had had no choice.

"Where is Father Dominic?" Sister Ernestine demanded.

"He's at that conference in San Luis Obispo," I reminded her, my fingers hovering over the phone. Not my cell—I let Paul's call go to voice mail—but the office phone. "He won't be back until tonight. Sister, I really think we should call 911, don't—"

The nun cut me off, her gaze darting to the open doorway to the guidance counselor's office on the other side of my desk.

"Becca's fine. Put that phone down. Where is Miss Diaz?"

"Lunch," I said. "Ms. Diaz said she'd be back in half an hour."

What Ms. Diaz *actually* said was that she was going down to

Carmel Beach to "split a footlong" with Mr. Gillarte, the track coach and PE instructor, but as they were trying to keep their sizzling affair with cold cuts and one another on the down-low from the higher-ups, I obviously couldn't mention this.

What I also couldn't mention to Sister Ernestine was the second emergency I could now see blooming on the horizon. That's because my initial assessment of the situation had been correct:

There *was* a dead girl in the room.

It just wasn't Becca, the student Sister Ernestine had escorted into the office, who was barely managing to keep the blood flow from her left wrist under control with paper towels someone—I was guessing the good sister—had seized from one of the restrooms.

Younger than Becca by about six or eight years, the dead girl was peeping out from behind Becca's skirt. She seemed to be trying to make herself as transparent and unnoticeable as possible.

It wasn't working, though. Her otherworldly glow was bright enough that I could see it even with the sunlight streaming through the office's tall, wide casement windows. It was as noticeable to me as the blood on the living girl.

No one else could see it, however. No one but me.

There wasn't time to deal with a dead girl, though. Not when there was a living one in the same room, dripping blood down her own shirt.

I went into Ms. Diaz's office and grabbed the first-aid kit. Since the Junípero Serra Mission Academy lacks not only a full-time (paid) administrative assistant but a school nurse, I've been filling in as both.

My cell phone chimed again. I knew without looking that this time it wasn't Paul, but Jesse calling from St. Francis, the newly renovated medical center in Monterey where he'd been lucky enough to win his fellowship . . . although I sometimes wondered, in spite of Jesse's being a brilliant medical student, how much luck had to do with it. St. Francis had at one time been a Catholic hospital, and Father Dominic's influence over the local archdiocese is considerable.

The ringtone I'd assigned Jesse was Elton John's oldie but still goodie "Someone Saved My Life Tonight." Jesse had saved my life so many times—and I his—that it was pretty much a no-brainer that this was our song, especially given the line about butterflies being free to fly away. We'd given each other the freedom to fly away, but we'd chosen instead to stay together, despite what had seemed, at times, like insurmountable odds against us.

Now, even though Jesse and I no longer shared a mediator/non-compliant-deceased-person bond, he still always seemed to know when my life needed saving, or even when I was merely feeling uneasy . . . like because there were a couple of very distressed girls—one living, one not so much—standing in my office.

I told myself that's why he was calling, anyway, and not because he'd sensed, from a half dozen miles away, that Paul Slater was trying to sextort me.

"Hi," I whispered into the phone. "I can't talk right now. Things here at work are a little crazy. Can I call you back?"

"Of course, *querida*."

Simply hearing that deep, smooth tone made the tight muscles in the back of my neck loosen, my shattered nerves begin to heal. Jesse's voice was a soothing elixir, whipped cream floating on rich steaming cocoa on a cold winter morning.

"I wanted to make sure you were all right," he said. "I got the strangest feeling a few minutes ago that something was wrong. I'd have called then, but I was with a patient."

"Wrong? Nope, everything's fine."

What was I doing? Jesse and I were engaged. We were supposed to be completely honest with each other.

Except I couldn't afford to be honest with Jesse. Not about one thing. Well, one *person*, anyway.

"Sister E brought a student in here who's a little banged up, that's all," I said. "Everything else is totally copacetic."

Don't let him sense I'm lying, don't let him sense I'm lying, don't let him sense I'm lying . . .

"I see," Jesse said. "Well, you know where you can bring her if it gets to be too much for you to handle. Not that there's much you can't handle, Susannah."

Jesse's always insisted my nickname, Suze, is too ugly and diminutive for a girl of my strength and beauty. With Jesse it's always been Susannah or—later, when he got to know me better—*querida*, which means *sweetheart* or *my darling*. It still sends a thrill through me when he says it, just like when he says my name.

Let's face it, I'm warm for the boy's form. Which is good, since I fully intend to marry that form. I don't care how many Egyptian curses I have to break in order to do it.

"I think I've got things under control for now," I said. "I'll call you later when I can talk more."

"Yes, you will. Because there is very definitely something going on that you're not telling me. Am I right, Susannah?"

"Damn, Jesse," I said, hoping my lighthearted tone would disguise the fact that I really was unsettled by his seeing through my lie. "You may not be a ghost yourself anymore, but you sure as hell can sense when one's around. How do you do that?"

"A ghost? Is that all? I thought at the very least you'd found out you'd won the Powerball."

"Ha! I wish. I'd buy you that cool new PET scanner you've been wanting."

I knew Jesse was only acting as if he wasn't concerned. He's protective by nature, and when it came to the supernatural, he's more than simply protective. He was what we call in the counseling trade *hypervigilant*.

Considering what he'd been through, however, this was only natural.

"Look out for yourself, then, all right, *querida*? The last thing I want is my fiancée being brought in to the ER as a patient."

"You know that's never going to happen. I can't stand doctors, remember? They think they know everything."

"Because we *do* know everything, actually. *Te amo, querida.*"

Thankfully he hung up before he could do any more extra-sensory percepting (or turn me into a puddle of desire right there on the phone).

I hung up, too. There was no way on earth I was going to tell Jesse about Paul's threat, let alone his proposition. It would only make him angry.

Angry? It would set off a thermal nuclear explosion inside his head.

And now—despite Paul's assertions otherwise—Jesse was a gainfully employed, full-blooded citizen. Unlike before, if he was caught attempting to kill a fellow citizen, he had a lot to lose, what with his fellowship and our planned wedding next year in the basilica at the Carmel Mission. True, the invitations hadn't gone out yet, but there were two hundred guests and counting on the list . . . none of them family from the groom's side, of course, all of Jesse's relatives having died over a century earlier, something Jesse pretended not to mind. But who wouldn't be bothered by it?

It would be awkward to have to pay back all those deposits due to the groom having been indicted for murder.

And what about the private grant Jesse had applied for that, if he won it, would help pay back a substantial chunk of what he owed in student loans, and also help finance his own practice after he became certified? (As long as he agreed to serve uninsured and low-income patients, something he'd planned on doing anyway. One in five American households lives below the poverty line, even in a community as outwardly glitzy as Carmel.)

Jesse's chances of winning it out of so many hundreds of applicants would be another miracle that I didn't think we could count on.

I came out of Ms. Diaz's office and waved the first-aid kit at the bleeding girl. "Let me take a look at that."

"No, it's okay," Becca protested, backing away from me and pulling her arm close. "I'm fine."

She was so far from fine this statement was almost hilarious—except no one was laughing. Besides the blood dripping from her arm, some had spilled down the front of her school uniform—the school had reinstituted a uniform policy after having relaxed it in the years I'd been there (I tried not to take the reinstitution personally). Now all students were required to wear a navy blue sweater over a white shirt, with either gray trousers or a blue plaid skirt. This girl had opted for the skirt.

Her mouse brown hair looked as if it had never met conditioner . . . or a brush. Her skin was pale and unhealthily blemished, her uniform a size or two too big on her. She was wearing glasses with frames that appeared to have been purchased in the early 2000s, or perhaps were hand-me-downs from the nineties.

To use the phrasing of a (soon-to-be) professional school counselor, this kid was a hot mess, and that's not even mentioning the Non-Compliant Deceased Person hanging on to one of the pleats of her too-big navy plaid skirt, dragging it even further askew.

I was the only person in the room who could see it, but I was sure Becca could feel the extra weight. She probably had chronic back or neck pain for which her doctor could find no medical cause.

I knew the cause. It was a ghostly parasite, and I was staring right at it, and at the miserable expression it was provoking from its human host.

Then again, that misery might have been because Becca had just jacked up her wrist so badly, and was being hauled around by one of the state of California's biggest busybodies.

"You sit down right here, Becca," Sister Ernestine said, all but shoving the bleeding girl into the mission-style chair across from my desk. Only it wasn't a chair designed to *look* mission style, it was a chair likely dating back to the 1700s when Father Junípero Serra, a Franciscan friar from Spain who had recently been sainted by Pope Francis, had run up and down the coast of California, frantically building missions so he could beat the Lord's word into the Native Americans he had captured and held there. Judging by their extreme creakiness, I wouldn't doubt most of the school's office furniture has been around since old Father Serra's time. "Let Miss Simon bandage those cuts. I'm going to telephone your parents."

"No!" Becca cried, trying to leap back up from the chair. "I told you, Sister, I'm fine! This is stupid. My compass slipped in geometry, is all. You don't have to call my parents. Mr. Walden was way overreacting—"

"Mr. Walden?" I raised a skeptical eyebrow as I snapped on a pair of latex gloves.

It's completely humiliating that after nearly six years of post-secondary education, the only place in the entire state of California where I could find employment (and not even paying employment) is my former high school. But there are a few upsides. At least here I can tell when kids are lying to my face about the teachers.

"Mr. Walden doesn't overreact," I said. "I had him for my junior *and* senior years. If he says there's a problem, there's a problem. So show me your arm, please."

The girl stared at me through her overlarge, brown plastic frames.

"Wait," she said, registering what the nun had called me. "Miss *Simon*? Are you *Suze Simon*? The one who knocked the head off the Father Serra statue in the courtyard?"

My gaze slid quickly toward Sister Ernestine, who'd fortunately bustled into her office and was already on the phone, presumably with Becca's parents.

"Nope," I said, turning back to Becca. "Never heard of her."

The girl dropped her voice so the nun couldn't overhear us. "Yes, you are. Everyone says you knocked Father Serra's head off with your bare hands during a fight, and that you had to work here in the office to pay to get the statue's head soldered back on." Her eyes widened. "Oh, my God. Are they *still* making you work here to pay it off? Didn't you graduate, like, ten years ago?"

"Six. Six years ago. How old do people think I am, anyway? Arm, please."

Reluctantly, the girl stretched her wrist toward me and I plucked the wad of paper towels from it . . . then inhaled almost as sharply as she did, but not for the same reason. Her blood had finally coagulated, and my ripping the paper towels from the wound had torn it open afresh, causing her to cry out in pain.

I gasped because now that I could finally see the injury, I could tell it hadn't been the result of any accident, though it had definitely been done with a sharp instrument—maybe even like she said, a geometry compass. Carved into the pale flesh of the back of her left wrist were the red letters:

STUP

35

Whoever—or whatever—had done it had been stopped before getting to what I had to assume were the last two letters, *ID*.

Stupid.

Someone—or some*thing*—had tried to carve the word *stupid* in the flesh of this girl's arm.

cuatro

I looked from the scratches—which went from artificial cuts to deep gouges. The V would leave a scar if not properly attended to—to the girl's face. She was glancing nervously in Sister Ernestine's direction, then down at the wounds, then at me. Her lips were pale and chapped. She wore no makeup, though she was sixteen, and makeup isn't against the dress code for high school girls at Junípero Serra Mission Academy.

Something made me doubt Becca had ever applied makeup to her face in her life, however. Her entire look—lank hair, oversize uniform, untidy skin—screamed, *Don't look at me, please.*

"Who did this?" I demanded. My mind was awhirl. The NCDP? Had the ghost done it? Whoever it was, he or she was going to get the ass kicking I'd promised Paul earlier. "Who did this to you, Becca? There's nothing to be afraid of. I won't hurt them."

Much.

"What? Who—?" Her eyes filled with tears behind the lenses

of her glasses, and she shook her head. "No. Oh, no. No one did this to me. I did it . . . I did it to myself."

"*What?*" The word came bursting out of my mouth before I could stop it. But I should have known. We'd covered self-injury in my courses on juvenile and adolescent psychology. But seeing it in real life was entirely different from seeing it in photos, and I couldn't hold back my second question, either. "*Why?*"

"I . . . I don't know," Becca whispered. I could tell by the color rushing into her cheeks—and the fact that she wouldn't meet my gaze—that she was telling the truth. Liars—such as Paul—usually have no problem looking you in the eye. "I just . . . I just hate myself sometimes. This is the first time I've ever done anything like this, though, I swear."

Now she was lying. She looked me full in the face, sweet as pie, lying for all she was worth.

"I'll never do it again, I promise. Please, *please* don't tell. My dad will be so disappointed in me, and my stepmother . . . well, my stepmother won't like it, either. Please, I'm begging you—don't tell. Come on. You know what it's like."

I did not. But apparently, because she'd heard I'd had troubles of my own in my day, she thought I did.

My kind of trouble had never involved gouging myself with sharp objects, though. Only other people trying to gouge *me* with them.

I tried to remember what I'd studied about individuals who self-harm. They don't do it to get attention—in fact, they almost always try to keep their cutting a secret, and usually succeed, except in cases like Becca's, where something goes wrong and they get caught. The brief release of endorphins from the physical pain serves as a balm for whatever emotional trauma or stress they're suffering.

That's why in the long run, cutting doesn't work: the balm is temporary, lasting just as long as the pain itself. Only by getting to the root of the emotional pain (usually through talk therapy with a trained professional) can the patient truly begin to heal.

Obviously something was tormenting Becca. The pitiful ghost child clinging to her—the one that only I could see—was a pretty big clue, and one I could easily handle.

Self-harm, though? Way over my nonexistent pay grade.

And now I couldn't toss it over to Sister Ernestine, because Becca had asked me not to tell. School counselors can't do their jobs effectively if students think they can't trust them not to violate their right to privacy. We're not allowed to inform parents what's going on unless there's a clear threat to their child's safety (or the safety of others).

I didn't have any proof—yet—that Becca's life was in danger, only that she was hurting—and badly—both inside and out.

So all I could say was, "Fine," and reach into the first-aid kit for a disinfectant pad. "But your first time, Becca? Really? That line might work on Sister Ernestine, but unlike her, I just *work* in a rectory, I don't actually live in one. I'm not that gullible. What's going on? Why do you, uh, hate yourself so badly that you'd want to hurt yourself like this?"

Bringing up the elephant—or NCDP—in the room is never easy. I've been doing it for years, and I still haven't figured out the best method. The subtle approach tends to go right over people's heads—"Has there been a death in the family recently?"—but bluntly stating, "There's a ghost behind you," can lead to ridicule or worse.

I wasn't sure which strategy to take with Becca. She was in crisis, but it looked as if she'd been that way for some time. I didn't know if the spook was a symptom or the cause.

"Look," I said when she only stared down into her lap. "Don't worry, you can tell me. I'm an expert on self-hatred."

Becca made a noise that was somewhere between a laugh and a snort of disgust. "You? What have *you* got to hate yourself for? Look at you, with all that hair. You're perfect."

It's true, my hair is pretty amazing. But that wasn't the point.

"No one's perfect, Becca," I said. "And don't try to tell me that you did this because you hate the way you look. You're a smart girl, and smart girls know how to change their look if they're unhappy with it. You obviously don't want to. So what's really going on?"

In a perfect world, this should have led to her blurting, "My little sister died last year, and I miss her so much!"

Then I'd have said, "I'm so, so sorry to hear that, Becca. But, wow, what a coincidence. I happen to be able to see the dead, and your little sister's spirit is standing right next to you! She misses you, too. But your clinging to her memory is causing her to cling to your love, and that's keeping her from being able to pass on into the afterlife. So both of you need to say good-bye now so she can go into the light, and I can go to lunch with my awesome boyfriend. Okay? Okay."

But of course this isn't a perfect world. And considering the day I was having, it was crazy of me to have thought even for one second that there was a possibility this was going to happen.

Instead, Becca pressed her lips together and stubbornly refused to reply to my question.

So I said, "Fine, suit yourself," and laid the disinfectant-soaked pad I'd opened over her arm.

This was a huge mistake—a lot like my having called Paul. But I didn't realize it then.

Becca gave a little squeak and tried to yank her wrist from me as the alcohol seeped into her wounds, but I held on, keeping the pad pressed to the cuts so the disinfectant could do its work.

"Sorry, Becca," I said. "I should have warned you it was going to sting. But we can't let you risk an infection. Anyway, I would have thought you'd enjoy it, hating yourself so much, and all."

I knew Dr. Jo, my school-appointed therapist—everyone getting a master's in counseling has to undergo a few semesters of personal counseling themselves—would disapprove. Counselors (and mediators) are supposed to show compassion toward their clients. We aren't supposed to hurt them, even while cleaning their wounds with disinfectant pads.

But sometimes a little pain can help. Radiation kills cancer cells. Skin grafts heal burns.

I told myself that Becca's reaction was good. It showed spirit. Her ghost-barnacle hadn't completely sucked the will to survive out of her . . . yet.

"My God," Becca whispered. Another good sign—she still didn't want Sister Ernestine overhearing our conversation, even though the nun would definitely have put a stop to my unorthodox nursing methods. "You *did* knock the head off that statue, like everyone says. You're crazy!"

"Yeah," I whispered back. "I am. Be sure to complain to your parents about the crazy woman in the office. That way you'll have to show them your arm to explain how you got sent here in the first place. Then they'll know that you've been hurting yourself, and maybe get you the help you—"

"*Get away from her!*"

Becca wasn't the only one showing some spirit. For the first time the little ghost girl showed some, too, lifting her blond head and taking an interest in what was happening around her.

And she definitely didn't like what she saw . . . namely, me.

Stepping out from behind the shadow of Becca's chair, she drew her brows together in a pout, and, hugging the stuffed animal she was holding—a threadbare horse—she pointed at me and said in a low, guttural voice, "Stop. You're hurting Becca."

It could have been comical, being bossed around by such a tiny sprite.

Except that where ghosts are concerned, size doesn't matter. I've had my butt kicked by some NCDPs who seemed completely harmless . . . until their hands were wrapped around my throat.

Plus, there was nothing comical about the burning hatred in her eyes, or the throaty anger in her voice.

"I'm not hurting Becca," I explained to the dead girl in my most reasonable tone. "Becca's been hurting herself, and I'm trying to help her."

Becca, perplexed, glanced in the direction I was speaking, but didn't see anyone standing there. "Uh . . . Miss Simon? Are you all right?"

I didn't have time for Becca's concern that I'd jumped on the train to Crazy Town.

"I'm trying to help you, too, kid," I said to the ghost. "Who are you, anyway?"

Big mistake. Really, my third biggest mistake of the morning, after calling Paul, then slapping the disinfectant pad on Becca.

Though in my defense, you really shouldn't let the undead run around unsupervised, any more than you should let wounds go too long without cleaning them.

The tiny ghost reacted by reeling backward, so stunned that after however many years she'd been dead someone could finally see her—let alone had communicated with her. She landed with a thump on the cool stone floor . . . a thump that left her looking shocked and humiliated.

But what followed was no girlish tantrum. She may have seemed cute with her blond bangs, stuffed horse, and riding boots and jodhpurs—apparently she'd been an aspiring equestrian in life—but she was by no means an angel (certainly not yet, as something was keeping her earthbound). She leveled me with a menacing stare.

"Lucia," she screamed, with enough force that my hair was lifted back from my face and shoulders and the panes in the windows shook. "And no one hurts Becca!"

And that's when the simple mediation I'd been planning went to complete hell.

The stone tiles beneath my feet began to pitch and buckle ... which was some feat, because they were stone pavers, each more than two feet wide. They had been laid there three hundred years earlier by true believers at the behest of Father Serra. They'd never shown so much as a crack despite all the earthquakes that had since shaken Northern California.

And now some little girl ghost venting her wrath at me had the ancient floors splitting, and the three-foot-thick mission walls trembling, and the fluorescent lights overhead swaying, even the glass in the casement windows tinkling.

"Stop!" I cried, reaching out to grab the arms of the chair in which Becca sat, both to steady myself as well as to shield her from any glass that might start falling. Becca's eyes were wide with terror. She still couldn't hear or see Lucia, and so had no idea what was going on.

I knew, and not only was I as scared as Becca—my heart felt as if it was about to jackhammer out of my chest—I couldn't have been more mad at myself. I'd been so distracted by the potential curse on my boyfriend I'd forgotten one of the most important rules of mediation:

Never, ever underestimate a ghost.

"I'm sorry," I shouted at Lucia's spirit. "I swear I was only trying to help—"

"Shut up!" the little girl thundered in a voice that seemed

to come from straight from the depths of hell itself. "*Shutupshut-upshutup!*"

Each syllable was emphasized by another jolt to the floor and walls, sending drawers from the file cabinets slamming wildly, files—as well as the pages within them—flying like a blizzard of eight-by-eleven-inch paper snowflakes, and the wooden Venetian blinds that had never in my memory been lowered over the windows suddenly came crashing down.

"What's happening?" Becca shouted. It was hard to hear anything above the tinkling of the glass and, above our heads, the groaning of the rafters in the pitched wooden ceiling that tourists loved snapping photos of so they could tell their architects back home, *I want the living room to look just like* this. "Is this an earthquake?"

I *wished* it were an earthquake. A geological explanation for what was happening would be so much simpler than, *Actually, it's a ghost.* No one ever goes for that one.

Instead I said, "Crap," because I noticed my computer had begun to slide from my desk. The huge monitor—not a flat screen because the school couldn't afford anything that fancy—was sliding in our direction.

Becca, hearing my curse, followed the direction of my gaze, then screamed and ducked her head. I hunched over her so my back would take most of the weight of the computer if things didn't work out, then kicked backward, relieved when I felt the sole of my platform wedge meet with a chunk of hard plastic.

This is why I needed a new pair of boots. You never knew when you were going to have to keep a ghost from using your computer to crush you (and a student) to death.

cinco

The shaking stopped.

Sister Ernestine raced from her office, clutching the only adornment to her otherwise sensible attire, a plain silver crucifix that gleamed against her massive chest.

"Good heavens," she cried. "What happened?"

"Uh," I said. "Earthquake."

I looked around for the NCDP. She was gone, of course. What would she stick around for? Her work was done for the day. I imagined she was off wherever baby ghosts go after hours, enjoying some Disney Horror Channel, learning some snappy new rude comebacks and ways to dispose of the living.

"Are you all right, dear?" Sister Ernestine asked Becca solicitously, not giving me so much as a glance.

Becca nodded, looking uncertain. "I . . . I th-think so."

Oh, sure. Ask the kid who just tried to off herself with some school supplies if she was okay. Don't worry about me, the girl doing the splits to keep a piece of computer equipment from killing us both.

Slowly, I lowered my leg, steadying the computer monitor with my hand. The only reason it had stayed in place was because of the cord, still plugged into the wall—and the fact that I was holding it. I shoved it back to its proper position on my desk, straightening my in-box and penholder as well. Not that it did much good. They'd disgorged their contents all over the floor.

The pavers beneath us were back in place, though, not a crack in them. The glass in the windowpanes was fine, too.

The office itself, however, was a mess, which was truly upsetting since I'd only just gotten it organized after the chaos Ms. Yoga Pants Carper had left in her wake. It was going to take me hours—no, days—to get all those folders back into alphabetical order, and then refile all the papers that now blanketed every surface like snow.

When I got my hands on Lucia, however tragically she might have passed, I was going to kill her all over again.

"Oh, dear," Sister Ernestine said as the phone began to ring—not just the one in her office, but the one in Ms. Diaz's, the one half hanging off my desk, and the cell phone in my back pocket, as well.

"Someone Saved My Life Tonight." Jesse.

I pulled my cell phone from my pocket and pressed Ignore. Jesse was going to have to wait a little while longer to find out what was going on. I knew he'd understand. That's the nice thing about soul mates.

Well, for as long as he continued to have a soul, anyway.

"Oh, dear. This is a disaster. I can only imagine what's going on in the classrooms," the nun was murmuring. "I hope there aren't any injuries—"

"Oh, I'm pretty sure we got the worst of it right here." I

leaned down to retrieve the first-aid kit, which had also spilled all over the floor. "I'm guessing this was the epicenter, in fact."

Sister Ernestine threw me a curious glance as she hurried back into her office to answer the phone. She knew my BA was in psychology, not seismology. "Becca, I spoke to your stepmother. She said she's on her way, but now with this quake, who knows how long it will take her to—yes, hello, this is Sister Ernestine."

I peeled the back from a large stick-on bandage and held it toward Becca. "Arm out, please."

She looked up at me, still dazed from the "earthquake." "What?"

"We should probably cover that up before your stepmom gets here." I pointed to her arm. "Don't you think? Unless your near brush with death just now caused you to change your mind, and you've decided to take my advice about fessing up to the 'rents about what you've been doing to yourself. Parents can surprise you, you know."

She glanced down at her arm. "Oh. No. Thanks."

She held the wounded limb toward me, and I applied the large bandage as gently as I could . . . not because I was afraid of her little banshee friend coming back, but because I really did feel sorry for the kid. I knew what it was like to be sent to the principal's office, and also to be picked up by a stepparent—though with Andy, I'd lucked out in that department.

I also knew what it was like to be haunted. The only difference between Becca and me, really, was that I'd been able to see my personal specter, and he'd turned out to be the best thing that ever happened to me.

Becca didn't notice that I was trying to be nice to her—or if she did, she gave no sign. She gave no sign of noticing that her otherworldly albatross was gone, either. She slumped in the chair, looking as defeated as ever, except for one thing: she pulled a silver chain from inside the collar of her too-big white blouse and began to finger the pendant hanging from the end of it in much the same way Sister Ernestine had fingered her cross for comfort a moment earlier.

Only Becca's pendant wasn't a religious icon. It was shaped like a small rearing stallion.

Hmmm. Lucia had been holding a stuffed horse and was dressed in riding clothes. Becca wore a silver pendant of a rearing horse that she twisted when she was nervous. The two girls didn't look too much alike. The dead one had blond hair and a Spanish first name.

But that didn't mean they weren't related somehow. Stepsisters, maybe? Or cousins? It would explain the strong bond.

This mediation was going to be a snap—well, except for the part where the kid had tried to kill me. Too bad that wouldn't count toward my practicum.

Sister Ernestine came bursting from her office.

"Susannah, what are you doing? You're supposed to be answering the phone."

"Oh, I'm so sorry, Sister." Gritting my teeth, I lifted the receiver. "Oh, gee, it's dead. The quake must have knocked out my line." I'm certain when I die, if there actually is some kind of higher power sitting in final judgment of all our souls, mine's going to take a really long time to read off all my sins, considering all the lying I've done, especially to people of the cloth.

But I like to think most of those lies were for a higher purpose. I'm sure whoever (or whatever) is in charge will understand.

"I'd better go check on the kindergarten," Sister Ernestine said, not sounding too happy about it.

"Oh, no. I hope the children are all right."

The nun glared at me. "The *children* are fine. It's Sister Monica who is in hysterics, as usual. And I'm certain you can guess why: the girls are acting up again." There was an accusing note in her voice.

I tried to look innocent, but it wasn't easy. "They're not related to me by blood."

"Sometimes I find that very hard to believe," Sister Ernestine said, and looked pointedly around the office at all the student reports and files scattered on the floor—as if the "earthquake" had been my fault. Which of course it had been, but she didn't know that. "Please stay with Becca until her mother arrives."

"Stepmother," Becca quickly corrected her.

"Sorry, dear, of course." Sister Ernestine gave her the kind of smile I'd never earned once from the nun in all the years I'd known her. "What a day for Father Dominic to be away," she muttered as she exited the office.

As soon as the nun was gone, I whirled back to my computer, but it was no good. It had fritzed out, and I couldn't get it to turn back on. Now I was going to have to call IT. Which at the Junípero Serra Mission Academy meant getting Sean Park, the most tech-savvy of the tenth graders, over to look at it, because there was no budget for an IT department.

I guess I must have verbally expressed my disappointment over losing the online auction for my kickass boots, since Becca said, "You sure do swear a lot."

I shrugged and pointed at the swear jar. "I'm supposed to put a dollar in it every time I curse. But I don't think I'm that bad." I didn't add that at the apartment my roommate, Gina, and I shared, she'd installed a swear jar, too.

"You're that bad," Becca said. "You said the F-word, like, five times in a row."

I tried not to sound indignant. "Swearing is a proven stress reliever. You should try it instead of doing *that* to yourself." I nodded toward her bandaged arm. "When I'm under a lot of stress, dropping a couple of f-bombs makes me feel a lot better."

"What have *you* got to feel stressed about?" She looked around the office. "This doesn't seem like such a hard job."

"Oh, yeah? You don't know the half of it." My job wasn't the problem. It was my personal life that was currently going down the toilet. "I'm not even getting paid for this."

"What?" Becca came out of her daze a little, seeming genuinely surprised, but not enough to let go of the horse pendant. "How come?"

"Because there are, like, nine hundred applicants with way more experience than people my age for every job that comes available. We all have to work for free just to get some experience so we can put it on our résumés so we can maybe get a paying job someday, but there's no guarantee we will. Oh, right. I forgot they don't mention this in high school. You're still brimming with hope and joie de vivre." I looked at her. "Well, maybe not you, particularly."

She didn't seem to get my meaning.

"What did Sister mean by 'the girls'? Do you have kids in this school?"

"No, I don't have kids in this school." I stared at her, horrified. "Seriously, how old do you think I am?"

"I don't know. About thirty-sev—"

"Forget I asked. The kids are my brother Brad's. Stepbrother's, I mean." Brad and I were actually the same age, but had always had vastly different tastes and attitudes. "He knocked up his girlfriend with triplets right after high school, and now their daughters are in kindergarten here. See what can happen if you don't practice safe sex?"

I widened my eyes at Becca dramatically, but she didn't look very scared. The truth is when you're a girl who's miserable enough to carve the word *stupid* in your arm with a compass, the idea of having three kids in kindergarten by the time you're twenty-five probably seems like awesome sauce . . . or maybe so unimaginable, it's not even in the realm of possibility.

I decided to change the subject.

"Do you have siblings, Becca?"

"No."

I eyed the horse pendant she was clutching again. "None at all? Ever?"

"No."

"Not even stepsisters? Half sisters? Adopted?"

She gave me a look that made it clear she thought I'd not only jumped aboard the train to Crazy Town, I was the engineer. "No. Why?"

This mediation might prove to be even tougher than the one that had ruined my boots. The problem with my job is that in reality—unlike on TV shows such as *Ghost Mediator*, which are completely scripted while purporting to be "reality"—if you simply come out and say, "Oh, hey, I'm in touch with the spirit world and your dead relative wants you to know such-and-such," people do not really burst into tears of gratitude and thank you for setting their conscience at ease.

They run away, and then sometimes, if they're of a litigious nature, they come back with a team of lawyers and sue you for causing them emotional distress.

"No reason. I notice you like horses—"

She instantly dropped the pendant, then tucked it away inside her shirt. "Not really."

"Oh. I thought maybe you did because of that necklace. It's pretty. Did someone important to you give it to you?"

She shrugged, looking away. "No. I saw it in a store in New

York this one time. My mom moved there after . . . after she and my dad split up. I said I liked it, so she bought it for me."

"That was nice of her." One of the things they're always drumming into our heads in class is when in doubt, look to the patient's home life, especially the mother. It always goes back to the mother. Thanks, Freud. "Are you and your mom close?"

She shrugged again, looking out the office windows at the sunshine. "I guess."

"Do you get to see her very much?"

Another shrug. "A few weeks in the summer. Holidays."

I could tell there was something going on with the mother. Why else had she moved all the way to New York from the West Coast? It wasn't unheard of for a father to get primary custody, but it wasn't the most common thing, either, even in kooky California.

And what was with the horse thing? Who was Lucia to her? Her bond with Becca had to be a strongly emotional one. I hadn't seen a reaction that violent from a spirit in a long, long time, not since . . . well, a certain spirit I'd laid to rest by putting it back in its living body, which wasn't something I was ever, ever going to do again, thanks to apparently having stirred up the ire of some ancient Egyptian gods . . .

I really needed to get my computer back up and running, so I could look up the veracity of Paul's threat. I never had much success looking things up on my phone.

I tried again, keeping my voice cheerfully neutral. "It must be hard not having your mom around. How long has she been gone?"

"It's fine," she said. Thank God she didn't shrug again, or I might have knocked over a few file cabinets myself in frustration. "Why are you asking me all these questions? She left when I was little, okay, right after the accident—"

She broke off after the word *accident* as if she'd said something she shouldn't have, then looked down at the bandage I'd put on her wrist. "How long will I have to wear this thing?" she whined. "It's starting to itch."

I ignored the question, pouncing on her previous statement. "Right after what accident, Becca?" This was it, I knew. In therapy, they called it the Breakthrough. In Non-Compliant Deceased Person mediation, we called it the Key. "What accident? Did something happen to your mother?"

But before Becca could reply, my cell phone rang once more. "Someone Saved My life Tonight."

I couldn't hit Ignore a second time. Jesse would abandon his patients, get in his car, drive over, and strangle me. Well, not literally, but metaphorically.

"I have to take this," I said to Becca. "It's important. But we're going to get back to that accident you were talking about. Okay?"

"Whatever," Becca said with another one of her infernal shrugs. "It's no big deal. I don't know why you're asking me all this stuff. I said I'd never do it again, and I won't, okay? God." Then she dug out her own phone, slumping even further in her chair as she began to text someone.

So she had friends. Interesting.

"Hey, Jesse," I said, swiveling around in my desk chair so my back was to the haunted girl. "How's your day going?"

"How's *my* day going?" He sounded incredulous. "What's happening over there?"

"Here?" I asked casually. "Nothing. It's work. You know. Boring. Why?"

"Don't, Susannah."

Susannah. Susannah. Susannah. I loved the way he said my name. The truth was, I loved everything about him.

"You know I can tell when you're lying. Even over one of these *things*."

Except the way he always knew when I was lying, and his impatience with modern technology. Those things I didn't love so much.

This had made our separation when he'd gone away to medical school and me to college—though we'd only been four hours away from each other—extremely challenging. He'd insisted on letters.

"We may no longer have a mediator-ghost connection, Susannah," Jesse went on, "but I can still tell when you're feeling something strongly, and earlier, you were afraid. I felt it. I was dealing with a four-year-old with a bee in her ear, or believe me, I'd have driven over there."

"And what, precisely, would you have driven over here to do?" I lowered my voice so Becca couldn't overhear me. "Spank my naughty bottom? Please do not get my hopes up."

I found that joking often worked as a means to distract him when he was being a little too extrasensory perceptive.

"Susannah." He didn't sound very amused.

"You know it gets me hot when you're mad. What are you wearing right now under your stethoscope?"

"You're not funny."

"Oh, come on. I'm a *little* funny."

"Not as funny as you think you are. Tell me what happened."

Crap. This was one of the many problems of being in a relationship with a former ghost.

"There was a little incident here at work involving an NCDP," I said. "Nothing I couldn't handle. But she did turn out to be a little more aggressive than I expected."

Out of the corner of my eye, I saw Becca lift her head to glance at me. She was eavesdropping, of course, and thought I was talking about her. She didn't know what NCDP stood for. She was probably wondering why I'd said she was aggressive.

"At the school?" Jesse sounded surprised. "The one you told me about earlier? A tourist?"

"Student."

"Father Dominic must be slipping," he said, sounding concerned. "I would think he'd have taken care of all of those when the semester first started, well before you got there."

"I'm not sure he'd have noticed this one," I said, carefully guarding my words, both because I was speaking in front of Becca and because I felt defensive on behalf of Father Dominic. "It seemed harmless at first, and barely perceptible."

It was getting hard not to notice that one of Jesse's other prejudices, in addition to cell phones, was against his own kind— well, what *used* to be his own kind, anyway. The closer he came to acquiring his medical license, the less interested he seemed in helping the dead.

I guess I could understand this. Having spent a century and a half as a deceased person wasn't listed as one of the *official* causes of post-traumatic stress disorder in the DSM (*Diagnostic and Statistical Manual of Mental Disorders*), the bible of mental health professionals, but I figured it was pretty much a given that Jesse was suffering from it.

I *hoped* it was this, rather than what Paul was insisting, that there was a part of Jesse that was still haunted . . . and that, if his original grave was destroyed, might be unleashed.

"Are you on call until tomorrow morning?" I asked, figuring it was best to change the subject.

"Fortunately," he said. Unlike normal people, Jesse preferred the overnight shifts at his rotation in the ER. According to him, that's when all the really interesting cases came in. People went to their primary physicians during the daytime. Only people in desperate straits—or who didn't have primary-care physicians—went to the ER in the middle of the night.

That Jesse preferred seeing these people as patients wasn't at all an indication that the curse was true, I told myself.

You can take the boy out of the darkness. But you can't the darkness out of the boy.

Shut up, Paul.

"I'll tell you about it when I see you tomorrow," I said. "*Te amo.*"

He laughed as he always did when I attempted to say anything to him in his native tongue, even though I've been taking Spanish for more than four years. My accent is hopeless, according to both Jesse and my various language instructors.

"I love you, too, *querida*," he said. As always, the word sent warming rays of delight down my spine . . .

Almost enough to cancel out the sense of impending doom that Paul's phone call had caused to settle there.

"Who was that?" Becca demanded rudely as I hung up. "Your boyfriend?"

"Fiancé," I said, looking down at my phone. I'd gotten two text messages. The first was from Jesse.

> **Jesse** Estoy contando las horas hasta que nos encontremos, mi amor.
> Nov 16 1:37 PM

After all the long hours I'd spent wearing earphones in the language lab, I should have been able to translate it on sight. But I had no idea what it said (except that *mi amor* meant my love). Later I was going to have to cut and paste it into my Spanish-to-English translation app.

Damn! Why did he have to torture me like this? A part of me suspected he did it on purpose, to keep me on my toes. As if he had to.

The second text—which I'd received earlier from a number with a Los Angeles area code—needed no translation.

> Dinner is Friday night @8PM, Mariner's, the Carmel Inn. Be there or else.

> It was only a kiss, for chrissakes, Simon. Stop being such a girl.
> Nov 16 1:30 PM

Stop being such a girl. How like Paul to think being called a girl was an insult.

"You're engaged?" Becca seemed super interested. "Can I see your ring?"

I held out my left hand and waggled my ring at her without really thinking about it. I was too busy debating what to text back to Paul.

The last time I'd been foolish enough to agree to meet Paul Slater somewhere alone, I'd ended up with a nasty scrape across my back that had been extremely difficult to explain to my mother (she'd been the one who'd had to slather on the antibacterial cream, since I hadn't been able to reach it, and of course I'd had to hide it entirely from Jesse).

There had to be another way.

But short of killing Paul myself to keep him from knocking my old house down, I couldn't think of one.

"Why's your diamond so small? I can barely see it."

I jerked my hand out from under Becca's nose. I'd forgotten she was there. "What do you mean?" I demanded defensively. "It's not small. It's perfectly normal sized. This ring is vintage. It's been in my boyfriend's family for years." Two hundred, actually, but she didn't seem like the kind of person who'd be impressed by that, or how Jesse had managed to hang on to it for so long, especially after having been murdered over it, sort of. Not that I was going to tell her that.

"Everyone knows that anything less than five carats means the guy isn't really invested in the relationship," she said.

"That's ridiculous. Who told you that, your boyfriend?" I narrowed my eyes at the phone in her lap. "Who were *you* texting just now?"

"No one." A pink flush suffused her cheeks.

"Oh, sure, no one, I can tell. What's Mr. No One's name?"

Her blush deepened. "Seriously, no one. I was playing a video game." She flashed me a look at the front of her screen to prove it. *Ghost Mediator.*

I frowned. "Really?"

"Sorry. I know we're not supposed to play games in school, but it's totally addictive."

"I don't care if you play games. I think it's cool that you're a gamer. I just don't understand why you like *that* game. It's really stupid."

"*Ghost Mediator* isn't stupid. It's really cool. Have you ever played it?" For the first time, her eyes showed some life in them. "See, what you do is, you have to kill all these ghosts in order to get out of the haunted mansion and into the nightclub, but first you have to be able to tell which ones are normal people and which ones are the ghosts, and if you accidentally kill a normal person, you go *down* a level, into the cemetery of doom, so then there are even *more* ghosts—"

"You can't kill a ghost," I said, feeling my blood pressure rising. "They're already dead. That game is inherently flawed. Ghosts are the souls of deceased people who need help moving on to their next plane of existence. They shouldn't be killed, they should be pitied, and whoever invented *Ghost Mediator* needs to be stopped—"

"Oh, my God." She blinked at me. "Calm down. It's just a game."

She was right. What was wrong with me? I'd missed a perfect opportunity to ask her about Lucia, and instead used it to vent about my hatred for a stupid franchise—

"And my stepmom is the one who told me the five-carats thing," Becca added. "That's how I knew it. I don't have a boyfriend. I don't even like anyone."

"Right," I said. "Sorry." I needed to get a grip. "But your stepmother is wrong. The size of the diamond doesn't matter; it's the ring itself that's the symbol of the guy's commitment to—you know what? It's as stupid as the game, actually. The whole thing is a dumb, antiquated practice that I don't even believe in. I'm only doing it because my boyfriend is really old-fashioned. Otherwise, we'd just be living together. So back to what we were talking about earlier. You said something about there having been an accident?"

Becca wasn't going for it.

"My stepmother said no way would she have married my dad if he hadn't committed to at least five carats."

Who the hell was this girl's stepmother, anyway?

It's kind of ironic that at that exact moment the door to the administrative office was thrown open, and a tall, attractive blond woman strode in. She was wearing dark Chanel sunglasses that she lifted to glance in dismay from the mess on the floor to the mess in the chair seated beside me.

I, however, was what she seemed to deem the biggest mess of all.

"Suze Simon?" she said in distaste.

"Kelly Prescott?" I could hardly believe my eyes. "What are *you* doing here?"

Becca sighed. "That's my stepmom."

seis

"Kelly Prescott married Lance Arthur Walters, of Wal-Con Aeronautics, last summer," CeeCee said, licking a bit of foam off the top of her chai latte. "Hey, wasn't Debbie a bridesmaid in that wedding, or something? I thought you got invited."

"Yeah," I said, still feeling a little numb from my shock back at the school. "I blew it off."

Because I'm not a fan of weddings. Or of Kelly.

But if I hadn't been such a fool and gone, I'd have met Becca there, seen her tiny ghost companion, and maybe been able to prevent what had happened earlier that day.

I was a loser who pretty much deserved all the terrible things that were happening to me. I also needed a drink. But it was my friend CeeCee's turn to choose the place we were stopping for after-work libations, and cocktails didn't appear to be on the menu.

"Well, Lance Arthur Walters is one of the richest men in America, and twenty-five years our senior," CeeCee went on as we slid into seats at a table at the Happy Medium, her aunt's coffee-slash-holistic-healing shop. "Obviously, it's a love match."

"Man, Kelly's taken gold digging to a whole new level." I sighed. "She's basically gone pro."

"It's antifeminist to judge another woman for her choices, no matter how crappy they might be. And if you'd bother to read my online alumni newsletters, you'd already know all this."

"Hey," I protested. "You're one of my best friends. You're supposed to *tell* me this stuff, not wait for me to read about it in some newsletter."

"*That I write.*" CeeCee shook her head, her asymmetrically chopped white bob—CeeCee is an albino—bouncing. "Honestly, Suze, you're the worst. Do you ever even go online?"

"Of course. To buy things." I thought wistfully of my boots. "Not always successfully."

"I meant to connect with people socially."

"Why should I, when all the people I want to socialize with are right here in town?" Then I remembered my youngest step-brother, who'd just started his junior year at Harvard. "Oh, except David, of course. But we make it a point to talk on the phone every Sunday."

"You're so weird," CeeCee said. She flipped open her laptop. "But don't worry. I'm setting up you and Jesse with a nice Web page for when you open your practice. Drs. Hector J. and Susannah S. de Silva, Carmel Pediatrics Center, specializing in your child's complete health. Licensed to diagnose and treat the physical, emotional, and developmental needs of children. No gold diggers allowed."

"God, I was kidding about that, okay? I don't think Kelly *literally* married for money. Although considering what her step-daughter told me about her views on engagement rings, one could argue the fact."

CeeCee ignored me. "What do you think of this?" She spun her laptop around to face me. "I've been playing around with your last names as a logo. See how the two S's curl around the staff like the snakes in the symbol for medicine? Well, technically the caduceus is the symbol for commerce, but enough people have misused it over the years that I figured no one realizes it anymore. And of course, even if you don't end up taking Jesse's name when you two tie the knot, we don't have to change it. The two S's still work. Dr. Susannah Simon, or Dr. Susannah de Silva, either is—"

I thought it best to cut her off. The topic of Jesse and me marrying was becoming painful. Nothing ruins a wedding faster than the groom going on a murderous demonic rampage and killing the bride, then her family. Boy, did I need a cocktail.

"So what else has Kelly been up to since graduation?" I asked, trying to sound casual. "I see Debbie with Brad once in a while at family functions, and we talk, and sometimes she mentions Kelly, but I seem to have missed the fact that she's a stepmom."

CeeCee glanced worriedly around the nearly empty coffee shop. "Shhh. Not so loud. Kelly's more the yacht club type, but you never know. She might pop in here once in a while."

I smiled. Once called the Coffee Clutch, the shop had been our hangout all through high school, until a well-known corporate coffee chain had attempted to purchase it from the previous owners.

This did not sit well with the Carmel-by-the-Sea town council, which had managed successfully to ban all chain restaurants, big-box stores, and even traffic lights and parking meters since the town was incorporated in 1916. The goal was to maintain Carmel's position as *Travel + Leisure* magazine's Most Romantic City in America (it was currently number three in the world, after Paris and Venice), and keep it looking like the same charming beach village (atop a cliff overlooking a white sandy beach) it had been for a century.

The council—with the help of people like CeeCee's aunt, who'd stepped in and bought the Clutch herself, in order to prevent it from going corporate—had resolutely met that goal year after year, to the point of not allowing homeowners even to chop down trees.

So how had Paul Slater gotten permission to tear down my old house?

I didn't know, but he had it, all right. I'd seen the forms attached to his e-mail, since the ghost girl's paraspectacular aftershocks hadn't scrambled them from my computer (Sean Park, one of Becca's classmates, had managed to rescue my hard drive, though not in time for me to keep Maximillian28 from winning my boots, and for well under what I'd have been willing to pay. I hoped he or she enjoyed them . . . in hell).

Not only were all of Paul's plans for the destruction of 99 Pine Crest Road—and most of the homes on the rest of my old block—in order, but he hadn't been lying about the Curse of the Dead. With the help of the Internet, I'd been able to find a translation of it posted on the blog of some Egyptology student specializing in the study of ancient languages.

What the blog didn't tell me—either because it wasn't part of the student's assignment or because it wasn't written on the papyrus—was whether or not there was a way to break the curse.

I'd fired off an e-mail to the blog's owner—Shahbaz Effendi—and crossed my fingers that he'd believe my little white lie that I was a fellow Egyptology enthusiast.

I know how pesky those papyruses (*papyri?*) can be. Sometimes they break off midsentence. (Did they? I wasn't even sure what papyrus was.)

Really, though, if there's any chance at all that there's more to the curse, I'd love to know. It would be very helpful to my current research.

God, this guy was going to think I was insane. Or twelve. But until I heard back from him, Jesse and I were screwed.

"Well," CeeCee was saying, "after she graduated from the Mission Academy, Kelly went on to get a degree in fashion merchandising."

I looked up from the cup of coffee I'd been scowling into. "Wait, are you shitting me? *Fashion merchandising?* Like Elle Woods in *Legally Blonde?*"

"I heard that," called my other best friend (and current roommate), Gina, from behind the counter. CeeCee's aunt had hired her to work the four-to-midnight shift, Monday through Friday. Gina ominously tapped a large glass jar with a pen. "Dollar to the swear jar. Two dollars, actually, because I overheard you call Kelly a ho earlier."

"That's a tip jar, not a swear jar," I said, but reached into my messenger bag for my wallet anyway. I didn't want to be a bad sport. "And I said *pro*, not *ho*. You guys are oppressing my right to free speech."

"You should be thanking us," Gina said as I approached the counter. "A future doctor should be classy, not trashy. Not to mention a future doctor's wife."

"Jesse says he loves me the way I am." I shoved two dollars into the already stuffed tip jar. "And shouldn't you be working instead of eavesdropping on my private conversation?"

"Yeah," Gina said, waving a hand at the whimsically painted café tables. Aunt Pru was big on whimsy. "Because it's so packed in here."

"It'll pick up after six," CeeCee said. "The after-work caffeine hounds."

"Getting back to Kelly?" I nudged.

"Oh," CeeCee said. "Right." She glanced back down at the laptop screen. "Apparently things didn't work out with the degree, since she moved home with Mom last year."

"Whoa. Debbie never mentioned *that*." I slid back into my seat. "Probably Kelly never posted about it on Instagram."

"You guys suck," Gina said. "What's wrong with fashion merchandising? And do I need to point out that *both* of you are college graduates who moved back to your hometown? You shouldn't be making fun of this poor Kelly girl for doing the same thing."

"Um, first of all," I said, "if I were to make fun of her, it wouldn't be for her choice of degree or for moving back home, it would be because Kelly is a really mean, terrible person. Did you know she used to refer to CeeCee as 'the freak'? To her face."

Gina threw CeeCee a quick glance—quick enough to catch the way CeeCee's scalp, plainly visible beneath the white strands of her hair, turned a deeper shade of pink with embarrassment at the reminder.

"Oh, CeeCee," Gina said, laying a brown-skinned hand across CeeCee's almost translucently pale one. "I'm so sorry. I didn't know."

"It's okay." CeeCee reached for her latte and took a big gulp. "It's cool to be a freak now. Even if I do still live at home."

Gina bit her lip. "I'm sorry I said that, too. And you're not a freak. It's just . . . I can relate to Kelly's not being able to hack it in the big city. That's why *I'm* here, sleeping on Suze's couch."

"That's totally different," I pointed out quickly. "You're from New York, like me. You're used to public transportation. Navigating all those freeways in LA had to suck. And you're only taking a break from the Hollywood thing until you have some money saved up and your shit together—"

Both CeeCee and Gina pointed at the "swear" jar, which I'd

intended for them to do. I'd sworn on purpose, to lighten the mood. Whenever Gina began to dwell on why she'd taken a detour from her dream of movie stardom, and ended up in my apartment in Carmel, her voice caught, and her eyes filled. She'd been crashing at my place for several months, though none of us—not even Jesse, who was the most soothing of souls—had learned why, except that life in Hollywood had been harder than she'd expected.

"For now," Jesse had advised, after one late-night chat by the backyard fire pit at the house he and my stepbrother Jake shared had left her looking particularly pensive, "leave it alone. She'll tell you what happened when she's ready. Just let her heal."

So Gina was healing on my futon couch and earning minimum wage, plus tips, at the Happy Medium.

Getting up to stuff another dollar in the "swear" jar, I went on, "I don't think Kelly's changed much since high school."

Becca's new stepmother had barely glanced at Sister Ernestine as she'd explained why she'd called.

"So it was just another one of Becca's accidents?" Kelly had asked. "She's so clumsy." Her tone suggested, *So why do you people keep calling me?*

The fact that Becca had had more than one of these kinds of "accidents" alarmed me—this family seemed to dwell a lot on the word *accident*.

But before I could say anything, Sister Ernestine butted in.

"Well, yes, Mrs. Walters, but this time you may want to take Becca to see her pediatrician. Miss Simon and I aren't trained medical professionals, and as you can see by Becca's uniform, there was quite a lot of blood—"

"Becca, you keep a spare shirt in your locker for PE, don't you?" Kelly asked.

Becca nodded, looking cowed by her glamazon of a stepmother.

"Great," Kelly said. "No need for me to take her home then." She'd given us one of her patented Kelly Prescott Look-at-me, I'm-a-real-California-blonde, capped-teeth-and-all smiles. "Well, thanks for calling, Sister. Suze, it was, uh, good to see you again. Buh-bye."

"Not so fast, Kelly," I'd called just as she'd spun around on a red-soled Louboutin, her long, honey-gold curls leaving behind the delicate odor of burnt hair that had spent too long in a curling iron. "I'd definitely have a doctor look at your stepdaughter. In fact, I'd take her over to the emergency room at St. Francis in Monterey right now and ask for a Dr. Jesse de Silva. He's excellent. Here, let me write it down for you."

I'd scrounged around for a pen and notepad, which hadn't looked too professional, since all the pens and notepads had been flung to the floor by Becca's still-absent guardian angel.

"The ER?" Kelly had pushed her sunglasses up onto her forehead. "You can't be serious. It was just a cut. She says she's got an extra shirt. She's fine."

"Yeah." Becca had nodded vigorously. "I'm fine."

"She's not fine, Kelly." I'd shoved Jesse's name and number into Kelly's manicured hand. "Take her to see him. She *needs* to get that cut looked at, and by a professional. Do you understand what I'm saying, Kelly?" I'd wanted to add, *You dumb cow*, but of course I couldn't.

Kelly looked down at the hastily scrawled note in her hands.

"Jesse de Silva," she read aloud. "Why is that name familiar to me?" Then a lightbulb seemed to go off in her dim, beautiful head. "Oh, my God, isn't that your boyfriend? Wait, yes. It is! I read in the online alumni newsletter you two got engaged. Marrying your high-school sweetheart. Isn't that cute?"

I'd felt myself turning red.

"Yes," I'd said. "Jesse is my fiancé. But that doesn't mean he isn't a terrific pediatrician—"

Kelly had crumpled the note in her fist, then thrown it to the floor with all the other detritus. It was apparent her *Isn't that cute?* had been sarcastic.

"You should be ashamed of yourself," she'd said, her perfectly made-up eyes flashing. "Using your job here to drum up business for your boyfriend. I know things are bad in the medical industry, but honestly, Suze. I'd think you of all people would know better. Funny how I used to think you were sort of smart, coming from New York City, and all. I remember some of us in school even looked up to you, once upon a time, and thought you were going to go places. Well, that was a long time ago, *obviously*."

She'd smirked, then stepped over a collapsed Venetian blind and added, "Sister Ernestine, you might want to rethink hiring this person. My husband is a major donor to the academy, you know. I doubt you'd want to do anything to upset him."

Then she'd tossed her hair and left, her high heels ringing on the mission paving stones.

siete

"Geez," CeeCee said, after I'd relayed this story to her and Gina—not the part about Lucia, of course, or the details about Becca's wound. That would have been a violation of student-counselor—and mediator-NCDP—privilege.

"So basically what you're saying is that this Kelly Prescott is the worst person in the world to be parenting a child." Gina tugged on one of her short black dreadlocks. "Worst. Person. In. The. World. Got it."

"Well," I said. "Maybe worst *step*parent. She could just be having a hard time bonding with a kid who isn't her own."

I felt a little bad for Kelly, since I knew she'd dated Paul. If he'd treated her in any way like the way he was treating me . . .

That wasn't any excuse for the way she was treating her step-daughter, though.

CeeCee had sunk her chin into her hand and was regarding me dejectedly. "I'm good with kids, you know. But God forbid a guy—even an old dude like Lance Arthur Walters—would go for a girl like *me*. No, they always go for girls like Kelly. Girls with *pigment*."

Gina had had to get up then because, true to CeeCee's prediction—though her aunt was the only one in the family who professed to be psychic—customers had begun coming in, as it was after six.

So that left only me to say, "Oh, come on, CeeCee. You wouldn't want to be married to some old rich dude anyway. Isn't it better to wait until you can be with someone you actually like, and support yourself?"

"Like you, you mean? Yeah, well, too bad I don't have your luck," CeeCee grumbled, her tone only slightly bitter. Then her violet eyes widened. "Not . . . I didn't mean—with your dad . . ."

I smiled at her. "No. I get it. It's true. I *am* lucky, in a way."

CeeCee didn't mean I was lucky because my dad was dead. He went out jogging one day when I was very young, and never came back (at least, not physically. He hovered at my side spiritually for years, offering unsolicited advice).

CeeCee meant what happened after that.

I didn't find out about it until after my college graduation. That's when Mom told me she'd invested all the Social Security benefits the government had been sending to me in Dad's name, in addition to my portion of his surprisingly hefty life insurance policy. Mom hadn't needed the money to raise me, since she'd had a great job as a local television news journalist, and now she'd gotten herself named as an executive producer of my stepfather Andy's dorky home improvement show.

Or maybe it wasn't so dorky, considering it had gone into international syndication and you couldn't go anywhere without seeing Andy's big handsome face on the side of a bus, urging you to try his new brand of drill bits.

After I'd graduated from college, I'd inherited the money.

Mom said I could do whatever I wanted with it, except spend it "on drugs, designer clothes, or a boob job" (which I found insulting: I don't do drugs, designer clothes are for people lacking in fashion imagination, and my boobs are as amazing as my hair).

"And don't even think about spending it on a wedding," Andy had added. "I know you and Jesse want to get married soon, but we'll pay for it."

I'd decided the wisest thing to do was keep the money where it was, invested in a combination of bonds and blue chip stocks (it turns out there is something about which I'm almost as conservative as Jesse: finances).

I did cash in a little to use for grad school, and to rent my one-bedroom apartment in Carmel Valley, not too far from where my oldest stepbrother, Jake, had bought a house with the money he'd made off an entrepreneurial venture of his own, the house he shares with Jesse.

And of course when I found the perfect couture wedding gown (but with a vintage feel) while on a girls' weekend in San Francisco with CeeCee and our mothers two summers ago, I'd thought it worth the splurge. It's been sitting in my closet ever since, already fitted and ready to go.

Jesse, of course, won't let me use a penny of it to help him with his debt. He has too much pride (or overprotective nineteenth-century macho man bullshit, as I like to call it, often to his face).

CeeCee was right: I *am* lucky—if you can call losing your dad at a young age lucky. Yeah, I lost him, but I still got to visit with him for nearly a decade afterward.

And now I support myself while working an unpaid internship at my alma mater.

But when Jesse and I get married next year, my dad won't be there to walk me down the aisle. I'm not a sentimental girl, but that seems kind of unlucky. I'd give all the money back if I could have my dad alive again, just for a few hours.

Or Paul dead. Either one would be great.

"What about your career?" I asked CeeCee, trying to change the subject. "At least you've got your dream job. Not many new college grads can say that."

CeeCee snorted. "Oh, right. I'm finally full time at the paper, and they've stuck me on the police beat. Do you know what that's like around here? Some old lady over on Sandy Point Way says this is the third day in a row tourists have taken pictures of the front of her house. She called the cops because tourists keep stopping in front of her beachfront bungalow to take photos of it! What does she expect them to do, not look at it? It's her own fault, for living in such a freaking adorable house."

"Be careful what you wish for, CeeCee," I said. "You don't want juicier crimes around here to report on, believe me. Speaking of the paper, I was wondering if you'd mind—"

"Oh, no," CeeCee interrupted with a groan. "Not again."

"—searching the archives," I went on. "I tried to do it myself, but—"

"—the search function on the paper's online edition only lists obituaries by last names," she finished for me in a bored voice. "And you only have the first name. Or wait, let me guess: You don't know what year the person died."

"Um . . . both?"

"Really, Suze? Because I have nothing better to do all day?"

"CeeCee, I wouldn't ask, if it weren't really, really important. Her first name is Lucia, and I'm pretty sure she died in the state of California in the past ten years."

"Oh, that narrows it down," CeeCee said, sarcastically.

"She's six to ten years old, tops. And I think she liked horseback riding, if that helps."

CeeCee stared. "Wait . . . she's a *kid*? Oh, Suze, I didn't know. That's terrible."

I'd never explained my gift to CeeCee. Over the years, however, she—and my youngest stepbrother, David—had caught on. It had made my job a little easier, though the ludicrous story Father Dominic made up to explain Jesse's sudden appearance in Carmel—that he was a "young Jesuit student who'd transferred to the mission from Mexico, then lost his yearning to go into the priesthood" after meeting me—nearly blew my credibility.

My mom and Andy fell for it, though, hook, line, and sinker. It's amazing what people will believe if they want to enough.

"I know," I said. "It's so sad. Don't you want to help now, Cee? Especially knowing you might keep the restless soul of a child from wandering aimlessly between life and death for centuries. And maybe even get to meet the man of your dreams, Mr. Lance Arthur Walters."

CeeCee slammed down the lid of her laptop.

"Excuse me, but I thought I made it abundantly clear that I am not attracted to Kelly Prescott's husband. What does he even have to do with any of this?"

I realized I'd just violated my mediator-NCDP confidentiality. "Uh . . . nothing. Sorry. I've had way too much caffeine. How's Adam anyway? Have you heard from him lately?" I always used my most soothing tone, the way we'd been instructed to in our counseling practicum (part of our required core, worth three whole units), when bringing up CeeCee's on-again, off-again boyfriend.

"Adam?" CeeCee laughed bitterly before folding her arms and slumping down in her chair. "Whatever. We hooked up a few times over the summer, and he said he was going to try to stay in touch, but that things were going to be super busy for him at school this year. And yeah, I get that he just made Law Review, and yeah, I'm happy for him. But it's like he's forgotten I exist. He never returns my texts or even likes my status updates anymore."

She looked as sad-eyed as a puppy in one of those late-night commercials asking for donations for starving and abandoned animals.

"Well, he's a jerk," I said loyally, even though Adam was my friend, too, and there are always two sides to the story. "Screw him. But honestly, Cee, you can't expect a guy to like all your status updates. Come on. If we held everyone to that standard, there'd be no hookups ever in the history of mankind. You know Adam. He adores you—"

CeeCee shook her head at me sadly. "I knew you wouldn't understand. You found the perfect guy. You and Jesse don't have a problem in the world."

"Uh," I said. Where to begin? "That is so far from true, CeeCee, I can't even—"

Fortunately, at that moment, my cell phone chimed.

"I have to take this," I said, getting up from my seat. I'd hoped it was the blogger, Shahbaz, since I'd given him my cell number in my e-mail, but it was someone almost as important. "It's my mom. But hold that thought, CeeCee. I want to talk about this. Your feelings matter to me. They really do."

CeeCee rolled her eyes and reopened her laptop. "You think I can't tell when you're using your stupid thera-speak on me? Say hi to Mrs. S from me anyway."

My mom had kept my dad's name, instead of taking Andy's, because Simon was the name under which she'd become known professionally. More important, it's *my* last name. It rocks.

On the other hand, de Silva rocks, too. If I changed my name when Jesse and I get married—*if* we get married, which was beginning to look less and less likely unless I figured out a way to stop Paul—I won't have to change my initials, as CeeCee had pointed out, just add a *de*.

"I'll tell her," I assured her. "And thanks in advance for anything you can do regarding the, uh, dead kid situation."

CeeCee gave me the finger, which caused more than a few people in the café to raise their eyebrows. You don't often see an albino in an asymmetrical haircut giving a hot brunette the finger.

I was going to have to do better than a mere thank-you. A generous gift card to CeeCee's favorite online store was probably going to be in order to placate her for this one.

I stepped outside the café—CeeCee's aunt Pru doesn't allow cell phone use inside the Happy Medium since she's convinced the electromagnetic radiation they give off interferes with her psychic flow and also kills bees—and answered my cell. "Mom?"

"Oh, Suzie."

My mother is the only person in the world who's allowed to call me Suzie. When I was a kid, I didn't like the name Suzie because I was a tomboy who saw dead people, and didn't think a name ending in a babyish *ee* sound suited me. Then as I got older, it reminded me too much of the old song "Suzie Q," which my dad liked to sing to me. It's a perfectly good song, except for the part where my dad was dead, and hearing it always makes me a little sad for what might have been.

"How are you, honey? Listen," Mom went on, before I could reply. "This isn't really the best time. We're at a shoot. But you sounded so frantic in your message. I hope there isn't anything wrong."

"Well, there is. I need to—"

"If it's about Thanksgiving, Andy and I are still planning to be there next week. We're staying at the Carmel Inn downtown, by the beach. Debbie says she's making dinner, but God only knows how that's going to turn out—I'm sure you remember the fight she and Brad had last time—so I managed to get a table for all of us at Mariner's, just in case. Oh, did Jesse get that grant he applied for?"

"Uh, no," I said. "Not yet. I didn't call about Thanksgiving. I'm wondering why you guys didn't tell me that you sold the old house to Slater Industries?"

"Slater Industries?" Mom sounded confused. "We didn't sell it to Slater Industries. We sold it to a man named Mitchell Blumenthal. He seems like a wonderful—"

"Mitchell Blumenthal is the president of Slater Properties, a subsidiary of Slater Industries, which is owned by Paul Slater," I interrupted her. I'd looked it up earlier in the day, after my computer was fixed. "I got an e-mail from Paul today saying his company bought the place. He's got it scheduled for demo later this month."

"Oh, honey, that's terrible." My mother sounded genuinely upset. "Are you sure? The same Paul Slater from your class? I didn't think you two kept in touch."

"Yes, I'm sure, and we don't."

Through the phone, I could hear hammering. Last time I'd watched Andy's home improvement show, he'd been refinishing a Craftsman cottage in Santa Monica, but they don't show episodes in order so I never know where they really are unless Mom tells me.

"Oh, dear," my mother said. "That sounds terribly … aggressive."

"Yeah, you think?"

"You know, I always thought Paul had a little bit of a crush on you, Suzie. But you never had eyes for anyone but Jesse. You didn't even apply to a single out-of-state college, which I still think was a mistake. Not that there's anything wrong with Jesse; you know Andy and I adore him, but when I was your age—"

"Mom," I said, in a tired voice. "Paul Slater is a dick hole."

"Oh, Suzie, really, must you use that kind of language? Sometimes it's hard to believe we sent you to private school. And I know you and Paul had your rough patches, but I always felt a bit sorry for him."

"Sorry? For *Paul*?"

"Yes. He was one of those kids who received plenty of money from his family, but no attention or love. He always seemed a bit lost."

"Lost? He seems to know exactly where he's going." And what he wants. Namely me.

"I think he wanted to be part of our family," Mom said. "Only not exactly your brother, if you know what I mean."

"Ew," I said. "Gross. And even if that's true, it doesn't explain why he thinks bulldozing our old house to build a *ten-thousand-square-foot* freaking McMansion over it would make us like him."

"No, you're right," my mother said with a sigh. "But I suppose to him, even negative attention from you is better than no attention at all."

"Huh," I said, thinking about this. "That could be true."

My mom was good to come to for advice. I couldn't tell her everything, of course, because she'd freak out. Things like tears in the fabric of the universe, ghosts, or ancient Egyptian curses were not her milieu.

But she understood people.

"Oh, dear," she said. "This is going to upset Andy and the boys so much."

"The boys? What about *me*? It's upsetting the hell out of me."

My mother sighed again in a weary way. "Suzie, really, do I have to keep telling you? If you expect to be taken seriously at your job, you have *got* to clean up your language—"

"Sweet crippling Christ, Mom," I said. "I'm not at work right now. And I keep telling *you*, it's not a job, it's an internship. They're not even paying me."

"Well, I'm sure there are a lot more paying jobs for school counselors here in LA than there are up there. Forget the house. Why don't you move down here? You can live with Andy and me. Jesse can join you when he's done with his residency, and if you two are really set on getting married, you could buy a nice little condo. It would be so much easier for me to visit my future grandbabies if they were right here in town than—"

It was going to be interesting to see what kind of grandbabies she'd have—if any—if I didn't meet Paul and he really did bull-doze 99 Pine Crest Road.

"Look, Mom," I interrupted her. "We can talk about all that later. I have to go now."

"All right, Suzie. I'm sorry about the house. But honestly, we had to sell. Andy and I were never there, and neither were any of you. And that place was too big to maintain as a vacation home. And so drafty. You're going to laugh, but you know, sometimes I could have sworn it was haunted."

This almost made me choke on my own saliva.

I never thought I'd be thankful for an interruption from CeeCee's crazy aunt Pru. "Suze? Is that you?"

"Oh, hi, Pru," I said to the long-haired woman dressed all in purple who'd wafted up. "Yes, it's me."

"Is that CeeCee's aunt?" my mother asked in my ear, sounding nostalgic. "Please tell her hello from me."

"Uh, my mom says hi, Prudence," I said, lamely waving the cell phone in CeeCee's aunt's direction so she'd understand my mother was on the phone.

"Wonderful. Do tell your mother how much I enjoyed the latest episode of Andy's show," Pru said. As usual, she had on an enormous floppy hat, as well as long silk gloves, in order to protect her skin from damaging UV rays, even though the sun had long since slipped behind the trees. Like CeeCee, Pru suffered from albinism. Unlike Cee, Pru fancied herself in touch with the psychic world. "He's really doing wonders with that new house."

"Yeah," I said. "I'll tell her." CeeCee's aunt was endlessly kind, but a bit of a whack job. True to form, she had a prediction for me.

"Oh, Suze," she called from the doorway of the coffee shop.

"Yes?"

"The child," she said.

I glanced around the outside of the shop, which was as whimsically decorated as the inside, festooned with twinkling fairy lights and wrought-iron café tables and potted shrubs.

"What child?" I asked her. There were no children in sight. It was twilight, and getting a little chilly. Only an extremely bad parent would allow their kids to run around outside the Happy Medium in the semidarkness. "There's no child here, Prudence."

"No, not here," Pru said. "The one you know from school."

What the hell was she talking about?

"That child is lost, and very frightened, and in so much pain," she went on. "And lost children in pain can sometimes be very cruel. Like wild animals, you know? They lash out and hurt others, sometimes without meaning to. But sometimes on purpose, too."

Then she smiled her happy, dazed smile and went inside the shop.

I stared after her, remembering too late that occasionally Aunt Pru's predictions actually came true.

"What was *that* all about?" my mother asked.

"Nothing."

I hoped.

ocho

It had grown fully dark by the time I got home, but I told myself I wasn't worried about Aunt Pru's warning. Despite the impressive amount of psychic power Lucia had shown back at the mission, she'd seemed primarily concerned with focusing it on Becca, not me.

"Lost children in pain can sometimes be very cruel." That could easily sum up Paul, and the way he was lashing out at Jesse . . . and at me.

My mother had also used the word *lost* to refer to him. He was no child, though.

Still, even if Lucia *had* chosen to attack me again, the Carmel Valley Mountain View Apartment Complex—as the management company of the building in which I lived had somewhat misleadingly named it—would have made an unlikely place to do so. The so-called "mountain view" was actually only of the winery-dotted foothills of what eventually turned into the Santa Lucia mountain range, the breathtaking peaks against which the massive waves of the Pacific crashed at Big Sur, much farther down the coastal highway.

How coincidental was it that the place where I lived looked out over the Santa Lucias, and the ghost I was currently trying to mediate was called Lucia? It wasn't that common of a name.

Feigning a lightheartedness I was far from feeling, I waved to my fellow tenants as I joined them in what had become a daily routine: the after-work trudge from our cars to our apartment doors, which we'd all unlock at the same time to get to our refrigerators and TVs and futons.

Still, I like my place. It's nothing fancy, just a one bedroom in a thirty-unit building off the G16. Kelly Prescott Walters would probably sneer at the idea of living here instead of some two-bedroom condo over in Pebble Beach with a sea view and a private hot tub (though now she probably lives in a $20 million mansion with her billionaire husband).

But in good traffic my place was a less-than fifteen-minute drive from Carmel Beach (and my classes and place of work). Plus the other tenants—mostly young newlyweds with small children and singles like myself, either divorced or not yet married—were friendly. It was always good to be home, the one place I never had to worry about being attacked by the souls of the dead, because, "Evil spirits cannot enter an inhabited house unless invited."

That's what Sir Walter Scott—who'd written *Ivanhoe* and a bunch of other books Father Dominic tried very hard to make me read—said, and it's (mostly) true. There are tons of ways unwelcome guests (of both the paranormal and human variety) can enter a home.

But there are also tons of precautions you can take to keep them out. I'm not just talking about hanging crucifixes or mezuzahs on the walls or doorways, either (though trust me, I have both. I'll take all the protection I can get).

Before I'd moved in, I hired my own security experts to replace the unit's dead bolts (in case any previous tenants—or their exes—had "forgotten" to return their keys).

Then I'd installed metal braces to jam the sliding glass doors to the balcony, even though they were located on the second floor. True, it was unlikely a burglar was going to scale the balcony of the unit below to break in.

But it wasn't burglars I was worried about.

Then I'd sprinkled a mixture of sea salt and boric acid (the powdered kind you can get in a box at the hardware store) across all the outside doorways and windowsills, as well as the seams in the kitchen counters. The salt was to keep out Non-Compliant Deceased Persons. The boric acid was to keep away roaches. I figured why not kill two unwanted pests in one? Like Paul had said, I'm a modern kind of girl.

Of course, none of that stopped Father Dominic from coming over and doing a house blessing, dousing the place in holy water (which got me worried about the boric acid congealing, but it ended up being fine).

I didn't mention to him that CeeCee's aunt Pru had already been over and done a Wiccan cleansing, smudging the place with sage, or that Jesse had lain a shining copper penny, head up, in each outer corner of the unit, sheepishly admitting it was something one of his sisters used to do (of course, back then it had been halfpennies, and they'd been made of solid copper. Today's pennies are mostly made of zinc), and he didn't really believe in it, but why not?

Why not indeed? We all have our superstitions. I wasn't going to begrudge anyone theirs. I have plenty of my own.

As soon as I'd locked the door behind me, I kicked off my wedges, undid my bra, and fed Romeo, the lab rat I'd stolen from my Operant Conditioning class after successfully training him to run a maze, then press a lever to feed himself.

The professor had warned us in advance not to grow too attached to our rats. It doesn't pay for clinical researchers to become emotionally attached to their lab animals, any more than it does for therapists or physicians to become emotionally attached to their patients. In order for the professional to best serve their client, they need to remain detached.

And virtually every achievement in medical history owes its lifesaving advancements to animal testing. Eventually most lab rats end up getting dissected.

But I only took the class because it was a requirement. I no more planned on going into clinical research than I planned on becoming emotionally attached to my rat (this was becoming an upsetting pattern: as a mediator, I also hadn't planned on becoming emotionally attached to any of the ghosts I'd attempted to mediate, but look what happened).

As soon as the final was over, I swapped out Romeo for a look-alike I'd found in a pet store.

Rats are a lot cleaner and smarter than people give them credit for. Romeo and I have grown to share a genuine and totally unique personal bond. He's paper trained, and likes to sleep on my shoulder while I watch TV. No way would I have left my little buddy in that lab for some PhD candidate to experiment on—possibly even kill—over the summer.

Paul was right: I'm probably going to be world's crappiest counselor.

But since his opinion isn't one that matters too much to me, I'm not worried.

While Romeo sat in his cage, contentedly chewing his dinner

of baby carrots and unsalted nuts, I sprawled out on the couch (also known as Gina's bed), and dialed Father Dominic's cell and home numbers. Of course he picked up on neither. I left a message I hoped had the right tone of professionalism and yet urgency.

"Hey, Father D, it's me. Sister E probably already talked to you about the alleged earthquake we had today in the office . . . yeah, not so much. But don't worry, I totally have it under control. Well, mostly. Anyway, something else kind of unusual came up . . . nothing serious. I'm just wondering if you've ever heard of an old curse from the *Book of the Dead* . . . something about resurrection and what happens when you destroy the resting place of a ghost?"

I couldn't say *exactly* what it was about, of course, because I knew the minute I did, Father Dominic would realize I was referring to Jesse. Then the old man would freak out and call him, as well. That kind of headache I did not need.

"So, anyway, just call me back as soon as you get this," I went on. "I'd really appreciate it. Hope you're having fun with all the other principals at your little conference. Bye!"

I hung up, pretty sure I wouldn't be getting a return call anytime soon. Father Dominic was nearly as bad as Jesse at dealing with phones, although at least Jesse liked to text. Father D's phone didn't even have texting capabilities. It was one of those mobiles for elderly people who can't see very well, with extremely large buttons. I'd gotten it for him out of frustration when he'd failed to return any messages at all for a week because he couldn't figure out how to retrieve his voice mail on his last phone. At least this new one had an enormous button that flashed MESSAGE when someone left one. I hoped he'd notice, and press it.

Checking my own phone, I saw I'd gotten several messages during my drive home. There was nothing yet from Shahbaz Effendi, the Egyptology student, but I told myself that didn't mean he was blowing me off. He could be sleeping. He could be off on an archeological dig. He could be in a different time zone, halfway around the world. He didn't necessarily think I was some lying weirdo.

At least CeeCee had gotten back to me. She'd been busy since I'd last seen her, only a short time ago:

> **CeeCee** Do you have any idea how many women/girls/babies with the first name Lucia have died in the state of California in the past ten years? It's one of the most common female names in the US (it means "light").

> Unless you can give me some narrower search parameters (city/county/year/cause of death), it's going to take me days to sort through these.
> Nov 16 5:45 PM

I was definitely going to have to upgrade that gift card.

One thing for sure, I wasn't going to tell her that Adam Mac-Tavish may have been ignoring *her* calls and texts, but he'd replied right away to an e-mail I'd sent him:

To: suzesimon@missionacademy.edu
Fr: adam.mactavish@michiganstate.edu
Re: Your House
Date: November 16 8:33:07 PM EST

Hey, Suze! Great to hear from you. Glad things are going so well . . . or not so well, I guess, given the news about your old house. Sorry about that.

Thanks for the congrats, CeeCee's right, I did make Law Review. It's not as big a deal as people think. Although I'll admit I've been partying pretty hard since I found out ;-)

But you managed to catch me in a sober moment.

I looked at the attachment you sent me, and though real estate/construction law is not my specialty, as far as I can tell, your old house was purchased (along with the others around it) by Slater Industries, which is a private company, through private sales. So they aren't in violation of the rule of eminent domain.

The houses are also situated just outside the historic preservation zone of Carmel-by-the-Sea, in the Carmel Hills.

You can get the place retroactively declared a historic landmark, but that will take at least sixty days. Only then will you be able to secure an injunction to stop the demolition. However, the work is scheduled to begin next week.

In other words, Suze, I'm sorry to tell you: you're screwed.

I'll be home next week for Thanksgiving break. Let's get together with CeeCee for a cup at the Clutch like old times!*

Adam

*I keep forgetting her aunt changed the name! I mean the Happy Medium.

Well, that was discouraging, but not as bad as I'd thought. At least there was something I could do. It was better than what I'd been picturing, which was standing outside my old house facing down Paul's bulldozers with a baseball bat.

I wasn't giving up hope . . . not yet, anyway.

I rolled over on the couch so I could get a better look out my balcony's open sliding glass door at the pool below. From where I lay, I could see that the exterior landscaping lights had come on, including the pool's. The unnaturally blue water beckoned to me. I knew it was full of chlorine and chemicals and probably the pee of my neighbors' children, but I didn't care. It was kept heated in cold weather and doing laps in it was heavenly compared to forty minutes on the elliptical in the gym.

It also helped me think. I had a lot of thinking to do.

Because while in addition to hearing from CeeCee and Adam, I'd received a few pleasant texts from classmates at school asking if I was going to join them for happy hour (bless their boozy little hearts), as well as an invitation from my stepbrother, Jake, to join him at his place for "brews and za" (but only if I brought along Gina after she got off work. Jake was so transparent—he'd been crushing on Gina for years), I'd also been left a few concerning voice mails.

The first was from Sister Ernestine, wanting to know how— *how on earth!*—I could have left the office looking the way I had, and just *what* I proposed we do about the triplets, my stepnieces.

The next one was from the triplets' mother, my stepbrother Brad's wife, Debbie, demanding to know who Sister Ernestine thought she was, suggesting that her daughters might have ADHD, when in fact they were only naturally high-spirited and creative little girls.

This was followed by a voice mail from Brad, asking if I could please get "that old windbag Sister Ernestine" off his back, as she was ruining his marriage. Then he wanted to know if I was joining Jake for "brews and za," and if so, could he tag along—anything to get away from Debbie, who was driving him crazy.

Great. Just great.

This was in direct contrast to his youngest brother, David (known to me privately as Doc, since he was also the most intelligent of my stepsiblings), who texted me a photo of himself in his dorm room at Harvard, wearing—for reasons he did not explain—a woman's bustier and full makeup.

I wasn't certain if he was coming out of the closet or purposefully challenging gender stereotypes for some class assignment. Knowing David, it could be either, both, or none of the above.

But I responded to his message immediately—as opposed to the ones from his older brothers, which I ignored—with a thumbs-up sign.

Last—but never least—there was a text from Jesse:

> **Jesse** Quieres jugar a médicos?
> Nov 16 5:47 PM

Medico meant doctor. I was pretty sure *jugar* meant play, as in *jugar al tenis*.

Was he teasing? Was he actually asking if I wanted to play doctor?

I was busy replying:

> Mucho gusto!
> Nov 16 6:15 PM

when my cell buzzed, indicating I was receiving another text. I eagerly clicked on the screen, hoping it might be Father Dominic (or the Egyptology student) calling with the answer to all my problems (or, even better, Jesse on a break from his rounds at the hospital, simul-texting me), when my smile froze on my face.

It wasn't Jesse.

> **El Diablo** Go ahead, don't text back. I know I'm going to see you on Friday @8.

> Don't make me do something we'll both regret, Suze. Well, that YOU'll regret.
> Nov 16 6:42 PM

El Diablo was the nickname I'd assigned to Paul in my phone. It seemed appropriate, given that I was pretty sure he was Satan.

After that I felt a little sick and knew I couldn't stay in my apartment a second longer, no matter how homey it felt with my pet lab rat chewing on his carrot stick and my boyfriend playfully propositioning me in Spanish.

My boyfriend who might cease to exist in a few days.

I needed to let off steam. I needed to clear my head. I needed to shake off the feeling that I'd been touched by something slimy.

Suppertime is the best time to hit my building's pool. Everyone else is using the gym or heating up their microwave dinners, huddled around their Ikea dining tables, watching *Jeopardy* or the nightly news or Netflix.

I'm not an exercise freak, but I have to stay in shape, not only so I can fit into my clothes, but so I can kick the butts of all the dead people (and sextortionists) in my life who keep pestering me.

I left my apartment, went down the stairs to the pool area,

kicked off my flip-flops, and peeled off my T-shirt and yoga pants, leaving them on a chaise longue with my towel. Then I slid into the brightly lit, heated water, dunking my head under (even though my hairdresser, Christophe, begs me to wear a swim cap. He says I'm ruining the highlights for which I pay him a small fortune).

But swim caps are ugly, and squeeze my head so I can't think. I do my best thinking when I'm doing my laps.

Under the water, I couldn't hear the sound of the light traffic over the G16, or the crickets chirping in the decorative plantings the apartment management company had put all around the pool. I couldn't hear the tinkling of silverware in unit 2-B (they keep their balcony door open at dinnertime, just like I do).

Soon all I could hear was the sound of water splashing and my own breathing as I began to swim.

After my laps were finished, I decided I'd dry off and drive to the hardware store—there was a Home Depot open until ten in Monterey—and buy every bag of rock salt they had in stock (they'd probably think I was a lunatic. It snowed so rarely in Carmel it was considered an apocalyptic event).

Then I'd sow every inch of 99 Pine Crest Road with it, and the soil around it, too. I'd even salt the yards of the neighboring houses.

I had no proof this would work, but what other choice did I have? My apartment was salted to keep troublesome spirits out. Wouldn't salting the ground of a place where dark acts had been committed keep that evil in?

That probably wouldn't stop a demon for long, but if I also got Father D over there to perform another one of his house blessings—and maybe, while he was at it, bless Jesse, too—it could help.

Not that I believed for one minute that Jesse was going to sit still for a blessing—at least not without an explanation. He went to mass every Sunday, and on holy days of obligation, as well. If there was a demon living inside him, it was going to take one hell of a blessing to drive it out. I was probably going to have to come up with an imam, a rabbi, and a Wiccan high priestess in addition to Father Dom to get rid of this curse.

If only I'd kicked Paul in the throat instead of the groin on graduation night. If I'd broken his hyoid bone and killed him, I probably would have gotten off on self-defense. If I offed him now that he was so well known—thanks to *Los Angeles* magazine and his own parents suing him—the case might garner a lot of publicity, and if convicted, I'd probably get some jail time . . . though still way less than Jesse, seeing as how I'm white, and a woman.

But any jail time is too much for a girl who can only sleep with three down-filled pillows on 100 percent cotton sheets.

Oh, what was I saying? I could never kill another human being . . . at least not one that I knew.

Or could I? In order to protect everything—and everyone— that I loved?

When did everything become so complicated? If it wasn't some jerk from your past showing up to blackmail you into having sex with him, it was a baby homicidal spirit wrecking your office. Non-compliant persons, both living and deceased, seemed always to be popping up from out of nowhere, ruining my life. Was I *never* going to be able to kick back and enjoy myself for a change?

It's unconscionable—to use one of Sister Ernestine's favorite terms—that I was thinking this exact thought when an NCDP appeared in the water beside me.

But I was so absorbed in my dark thoughts about Paul, listening to my own breathing and heartbeat, watching the shadow my own body made on the floor of the pool as I did my laps, that I didn't notice, despite Pru's warning not an hour earlier.

I didn't notice until its clawlike hands were wrapped around my neck, and it was shoving me under the bright blue water.

And suddenly, *I* was the one about to die.

nueve

I flailed in the water, swallowing deep gulps of it, while clutching at the sharp little fingers digging into my throat.

"Don't you hurt Becca," an all-too-familiar voice hissed into my ear when I managed to surface for one all-too-brief gasp of glorious air. "Don't you come near her again!"

There was nothing I could say in response. Even if there had been, I couldn't speak. Her grip on my throat was so tight I couldn't utter a sound, nor could I dig my fingers beneath hers to loosen her grip. Besides, she'd plunged us both to the bottom of the pool, her body—which should have been weightless—suddenly heavy as a refrigerator.

And I was the stray dog someone had decided to cruelly chain to that refrigerator for kicks before shoving both into the bottom of the lake.

All I could do was fight my way back to the surface against the weight inexorably bearing me down. But when I finally did reach the glorious air, instead of taking it in, I could only cough out the burning chlorinated water I'd swallowed.

And she continued to cling to my neck like a thousand-pound weight. How was that possible, when she was only the size of a doll, and a ghost besides? For someone whose name meant "light," she was anything but.

Once, in my quest to find the most effective cardio I could do in the shortest amount of time, I'd read that treading water vertically while bearing a heavy weight was the way to go. It's an integral part of U.S. Navy SEAL training: they tread water while holding a dive pack above their heads.

That had sounded way too brutal to me, but now I realized it was exactly what I should have been doing all along. Who knew U.S. Navy SEALs and school counseling interns had so much in common?

The next thing I knew, the kid had me strung up in midair like a salmon on a fishing line. I dangled there by my neck, still struggling to unloose her fingers, gasping for air, wondering in the distant part of my brain that could still register thought what I would look like to any of my fellow tenants who might happen to glance down at the pool from their balconies. They wouldn't be able to see the NCDP that was holding me by the neck above the water level. Would they think I was performing some kind of odd water ballet? Suze Simon, amateur mermaid. Perhaps they'd applaud, and compliment me later . . . if I lived until later.

Then she plunged me back into the deep end, and I wondered how I could have been so smug—and stupid—to think that she hadn't followed me home.

She'd not only followed me home, she'd watched me get out of my car, wave good night to my neighbors, then go inside to check my messages.

Sure, my apartment was ghost proof.

But it had never occurred to me to sprinkle a protective layer of salt around the pool. It wasn't even one of those environmentally safe saltwater pools that Andy goes around recommending on At Home with Andy. It was filled with human-harmful—and extremely foul-tasting—chlorine and other chemicals that were currently burning my throat.

"Lucia," I croaked when I'd finally managed to sip enough air to allow speech. "I don't think you understand. I'm on your side."

"No, *you* don't understand," she hissed in my ear, her long fingernails scraping at the skin of my cheek in an almost loverlike caress. This wasn't at all creepy. "Becca's mine. *My* friend. No one will ever hurt her again."

Okay, okay, I wanted to say. *I got it already.*

But I couldn't say anything more, because it hurt too much. My lungs were too full of water and my hair was plastered over my face (why hadn't I listened to Christophe about that swim cap?) and she still had hold of my throat. She'd pulled me well away from the sides of the pool, so I couldn't grab anything— except handfuls of water—to hit her with or find anything to push against. Where were my boots when I needed them? Oh, right, with Maximillian28.

There was only one thing I could think of to do, and that was to grab *her*. I needed to get her to loosen the iron grip that was cutting off my oxygen and causing the lights around the pool to slowly dim.

But my arms were feeling strangely heavy. Lifting them felt like lifting the two-hundred-pound weights Brad kept in his garage and was always challenging everyone to try to bench. I'd sapped too much vital energy fighting to stay afloat to be able to land a good punch, even if I'd felt okay punching a dead kid in the face, and I was really starting to, considering this particular dead kid was being such a pain in my ass.

But I could still grab. I thrust my arms up over my head until my fingers closed around something wet and stringy. At first, in my state of near unconsciousness, I thought it was seaweed. But why would there be seaweed in my apartment complex's swimming pool?

Then I realized I'd managed to grab twin chunks of her blond curls.

Hair pulling is dirty business—it's what toddlers and drunk girls on reality shows always resort to. But this was different. It was her or me, and it sure as hell wasn't going to be me. I had a wedding scheduled to Dr. Hector "Jesse" de Silva for next year in the basilica at the Carmel Mission. I had no intention of missing it if I could possibly help it.

I pulled with all my might, and to my utter relief, the claw-like fingers disappeared from my throat. Lucia's tiny, tenaciously strong body flipped over my head and shoulders and went splashing down into the water in front of me.

She landed on her back, so I could see her face. Her expression was priceless, one of utter surprise, like, *How did I get* here?

I would have laughed if I hadn't been so busy trying not to die.

For a moment we simply floated in the deep end of the pool, me busy choking up pool water, the dead girl appearing stunned by her defeat, even though it was only temporary. A spirit with that much power would quickly regather her energy—while I had none left. I had vastly underestimated the depths of her rage and determination to keep anyone from interfering with Becca. I had no idea what was going on with her and her human host, but whatever it was, Lucia wasn't going to let anyone part them.

Still, in those few seconds, her long blond hair circling us like a golden halo (oh, the irony), I couldn't help being struck by how incredibly sweet and vulnerable she looked. She was still clutching the stuffed horse she'd been carrying earlier that day, still dressed in her riding jodhpurs and boots, looking every bit like a pony-loving cherub who'd happened to trip and fall into the pool.

Then tried to drown me.

That was it. I was out of there.

I turned and began swimming away from her with everything I had left of my strength. If I could only reach the gleaming chrome ladder I saw a few strokes ahead of me, then pull myself up, I knew I'd be all right.

Of course I was only fooling myself. But I had to believe in *something*.

I kicked hard for the ladder, beginning to think I was going to make it—though my heart was pounding as if it were about to burst—when an icy cold, sharp-clawed hand clamped down around my ankle and attempted to yank me back into the crystal depths.

No.

Then at almost the exact same moment, a similarly steel-gripped, but also similarly familiar *warm* hand wrapped around my wrist and began pulling me toward the side of the pool. What was happening? Was someone trying to rescue me?

Oh, dear God, no. Not one of my do-gooding fellow tenants from the Carmel Valley Mountain View Apartment Complex, thinking I'd gotten a muscle cramp. Lucia would pull him into the water, too, and then the pool guy would find *both* of us facedown at the deep end tomorrow morning.

Could this day get any worse? I couldn't save myself and a civilian, too. I didn't have the strength left.

"Stop," I begged, pulling on my wrist, preferring to be

drowned by Lucia than allow her to take out an innocent by-stander as well. "I'm fine. Please go away."

But the grip on my wrist only tightened. I floundered as I tried to stay above the surface, pulled in two different directions by two entirely different but equally determined—and seemingly preternaturally strong—forces.

"You're not fine, *querida*," I heard a deep voice rasp.

My heart began to pound in a different way than before. *Jesse.*

I saw him kneeling by the side of the pool, his hands grasped tightly around my wrist. His expression was hard to read since his back was to the bright security lights, but I was sure he must be furious. The shirt and tie he was required to wear to work were both soaked.

"And sorry to disappoint you," he said, "but I'll never go away."

diez

I began to think I might actually have a chance of getting out of this thing alive.

The same thought seemed to occur to Lucia, since the cold, tentacle-like fingers wrapped around my ankle loosened. I heard her let out a last, furious hiss, and then, with a final burst of bubbles, as if the entire pool had suddenly turned into a churning cauldron of witch's brew, she was gone.

Then the crystal blue pool water turned as still as it had been before I'd slid into it. Except for the lapping of the water filter, the sound of the crickets, and my own heavy breathing, it was completely silent in the Carmel Valley Mountain View Apartment Complex pool.

Until Ryan, my neighbor in unit 2-B, called from his balcony, "Hey! You guys okay down there?"

Jesse was still holding me by the wrist, keeping me suspended half in, half out of the water.

"She's fine," he shouted up to Ryan. "Just a cramp."

"Tell her that's why she's supposed to wait half an hour after eating before going for a swim," Ryan said in a teasing voice before turning back to the television show he was watching inside.

Jesse didn't wait another moment before pulling me out of the water, soaking his shirt and tie even further, then carrying me to the closest chaise longue.

"Susannah, it's all right," he said, his expression an adorable mix of anger and anxiety. "She's gone."

"I know she's gone," I said. My teeth had involuntarily begun to chatter. "Stop being so dramatic. You're getting your work clothes all wet."

"Damn my clothes," he said. It was unusual for him to swear, at least in English. I'm the gutter mouth in our relationship.

He'd grabbed my towel from where I'd lain it on top of my clothes, and was bundling me in it. The chaise longue groaned a bit under our combined weight. The building management hadn't exactly forked out the big bucks for their poolside decor.

"You're shaking," he said. "Did she hurt you?"

"No. She's just a kid."

"A kid?" He laughed, but there was no humor in the sound. "A kid who nearly killed you. We're going to find out who she is and then we're going to—" Now he was swearing, fluidly, in Spanish.

"Jesse, stop it. What's the matter with you? Your specialty's pediatrics. You're supposed to suffer the little children."

"Not this one. This one has no chance of getting into the kingdom of heaven. She's getting exorcised by me straight back to hell, where she came from."

"She isn't from hell. She's frightened, and in pain."

"I think you're getting her confused with yourself, *querida*."

"No, I'm not. CeeCee's aunt Pru said so. She tried to warn me about it tonight outside the café, but I didn't pay attention."

Jesse uttered a few highly descriptive oaths about Aunt Pru. Even though he spoke in Spanish, I caught the gist.

"She was only trying to help," I said, in Pru's defense. "And you know she's right. Why are you doing that?" He was rubbing my skin through the terry cloth of the towel.

"You're in shock," he said. "You're cold, and you're wet, and you're shaking. I'm attempting to restore warmth and circulation to your extremities. Don't argue with me, I'm a doctor."

"I'm not in shock," I said. "I'm all right. I swallowed a lot of water, but I'm still in one piece. At least this one didn't ruin my boots."

"Your what?"

"My . . . never mind. What are you doing now?"

"Helping you to avoid going hypothermic by sharing my body heat." He'd pulled me onto his lap. "Do you disapprove?"

"Oh, no, I approve." I slipped my arms around his neck, burying my face in his shoulder, enjoying the warmth of his strong body and the faintly antiseptic smell that seemed permanently to cling to him, thanks to the many times a day he had to wash his hands. I suppose I didn't smell much better after the chlorine waterboarding I'd received at Lucia's hands. "How did you know that I was in trouble?"

"I always know." He tightened his arms around me, his lips intriguingly close to my right earlobe. "I *felt* her, all the way back at the hospital. Or I felt something, anyway. And then when I tried calling, and you wouldn't pick up your phone—"

"I went for a swim. My phone's back in the apartment."

"I knew there was trouble when I asked if you wanted to play doctor later," he said, "and you never replied."

"That's not true." I turned my head so that his lips, instead of being close to my ear, were next to my mouth. "I said *mucho gusto.*"

"I never got that text. How can your Spanish still be so terrible after studying all these years?"

His hands slipped beneath the towel to singe my bare flesh. I sucked in my breath. "Is that something you do to all your patients you treat for shock?"

"No." He pulled me closer to him. "Only you. You get special treatment."

His lips came down over mine.

I could feel our hearts thumping hard, separated only by the thin damp microfiber of my swimsuit and the white dress shirt he'd worn to work. He pressed my body back against the chaise longue, his tongue hot inside my mouth, his hand just as hot against my bare skin, while yet another kind of heat radiated from the front of his straight-fits.

Those straight-fits. They were always causing me problems. When it wasn't my gaze I had trouble keeping off them, it was my hands. Like now, for instance, especially since I could feel what was pushing so urgently through the front of them, practically branding the rivets of his fly into my thigh.

But I knew if I reached down and undid those buttons, then wrapped my fingers around all that masculine glory, the only thing I'd receive for my troubles was a groan, then a polite request that I stop what I was doing. I knew because it had happened a million times before. Jesse's commitment to staying on the righteous path was admirable, but it was also frustrating.

So I knew he wasn't going to strip off my bathing suit and do me on the chaise longue in the middle of the pool area at my apartment building. For one thing, that would be gross. Anyone, including Ryan from upstairs, could wander out onto their balcony and see us. And for another, that wasn't how either of us had envisioned making love for the first time.

Though I had to admit that at that moment, I didn't particularly care. I wished we were anywhere than the stupid pool deck. My bedroom upstairs, for instance, or his bedroom back over at Jake's. Except that even in those places he always managed to keep from ripping my clothes off, whereas I seemed to have a real problem not pawing at his. Maybe the curse was wrong, and *I* was the one with the demon inside me—

"Susannah," Jesse breathed into my ear after a while.

"I know." I removed my hand.

He pulled away from me, the chaise longue groaning in protest, and sat up, his back to me. It was hard to tell without being able to see his face, but he seemed like he was in pain.

I was familiar with the feeling.

"It doesn't have to be this way," I volunteered after a few moments of no sound but chirping crickets.

"Yes, it does," he said to the concrete. "The wedding's not until next year."

"Screw the wedding."

"Your parents would be delighted to hear that since they've already put down the deposit for the basilica and the reception."

"You know what I mean. I get that I'm not as religious as you are, but I really don't think God will mind."

"*I* mind."

"But most people these days don't wait until the wedding—"

"Most people aren't as indebted as I am to the bride and her family."

"Oh, for God's sake. No one cares about that."

"*I* care. What's worse is that I came here to rescue you, not ravage you."

"I believe there was mutual ravaging, and what little of it there was I thoroughly enjoyed."

"Still, you deserve better."

"I'm pretty sure I'm the best judge of that. And I decided I deserve the honor of being the wife of Dr. Jesse de Silva a long time ago. There's no greater honor, in my opinion."

The crooked smile he shot me hadn't the slightest bit of humor in it. "Thank you for the kind words, but what have I got to offer a wife? No family, no money, nothing but debt—over $200,000 of it. You know that as a resident, my salary averages out to about twelve dollars an hour, and that's for an eighty-hour workweek. That's less than what the orderlies earn."

I reached out to smooth some dark hair from his forehead. "I know what you're going to say, because you've said it so many times before, but I'd like to remind you once again that the income from my investments is enough to pay off your monthly student loans. If you'd just—"

He seized my hand so abruptly that for a moment I caught a glimpse of the darkness Paul had mentioned, and that Jesse usually kept so well controlled. A second later, however, it was gone, and he was pressing my fingers gently to his lips.

"Thank you again, but you and your family have given me quite enough."

"You're forgetting how much you've given *me*. Like tonight, for instance."

His dark eyebrows knit in confusion. "Tonight?"

"My *life*, Jesse. You gave me my life tonight. Like you've done a million times before, remember? A million and one, if you count this evening."

His eyebrows relaxed, and this time when he smiled there was both warmth and humor in it. "Oh, that. Well, it was the least I could do. You've returned the favor, occasionally."

"Occasionally. So you might want to cut the self-pitying bullshit about how you have nothing but debt to offer a wife. You've got plenty to offer. Not in the way of material things yet, maybe, but you're pretty good looking, in my opinion, and you've got the lifesaving thing down pat. And then of course there's what's in your pants. That's pretty impressive, too."

The smile turned self-deprecating. "How charming, Susannah. It's a pity my mother is dead, she'd be so proud."

"She should be." I reached out to straighten his tie—he was required to wear one to work, and looked extremely dashing in it—and ended up fingering the collar of his shirt. "Uh-oh. You really are soaked, aren't you? You can't go back to your shift in wet clothes. You'll catch a cold. You should probably take your shirt off and come upstairs with me and let me dry it for you."

"You don't have a drying machine in your apartment," he pointed out. "Are you trying to get me naked, Miss Simon?"

"It's called a dryer, not a drying machine, and yes, Dr. de Silva, I am."

"Are we ever going to talk about what happened here tonight, Susannah?"

"Well," I said. "When a man and a woman like each other very much, they start kissing, and then they get a funny feeling in their tummies. And in a normal relationship the man goes with the woman to her apartment, and they get naked and relieve each other of the funny feeling. Unless the man insists on waiting until we're married, and then the woman has a nervous breakdown—"

"Not that," he interrupted. "Though that was a very comical speech, and I quite enjoyed it. I meant the devil child."

"Oh, her. She's the very protective ghost of that girl at the mission I was telling you about—who happens to be Kelly Prescott's stepdaughter, by the way. I didn't think she'd follow me all the way out here from school. It was my fault, really. I should have been more watchful."

"Your fault? None of this was your fault." Jesse's normally warm brown eyes no longer looked particularly warm, and it was easy to tell there might be a gap in his résumé where *Spent a cen-*

tury and a half haunting a home as a spectral presence ought to have been. "Why is it that whenever Kelly Prescott's name comes up, trouble seems to follow?"

"Because she's a total bitch?"

The corner of Jesse's lips twitched upward. The darkness was gone as quickly as it had appeared. He stood, then held out a hand to me.

"I can see you're feeling better. Which is just as well, since I need to go back. I told them I was running out to buy cigarettes, and I've been gone way too long."

"Cigarettes?" I slipped my hand into his and allowed him to pull me to my feet. "Jesse, you don't smoke."

"No, but a lot of the nurses do. I needed them to cover for me, so my plan was to bribe them with cigarettes. But now I'm going to be even longer if I need to wait for you to get your things together, then follow you out to Snail Crossing."

"Snail Crossing? Why would you follow me out to Snail Crossing?"

I was confused. Snail Crossing was the name of the ranch house Jake had bought in Carmel Valley, then convinced Jesse to move into with him after Jesse got his fellowship at St. Francis (thank God, because I'm not sure how much longer even someone as religious as Jesse is could have taken living with Father Dominic, who'd supported him—with the help of the church—in the first year Jesse had found himself suddenly alive, before getting accepted to medical school).

Dubbed Snail Crossing because the front yard was so deeply tree shaded that snails crept across the pavers at all hours of the day and night, Jake's house had become our primary social hangout, the sight of many an epic barbecue, pool party, and deep intellectual conversation around the backyard fire pit.

But that didn't mean I had any intention of going there tonight. I'd ignored Jake's text about "brews and za" and his current crush, Gina, for a reason.

"You need to go there for your own safety, Susannah," Jesse said. "I know you've taken every precaution with your place, and it's probably one hundred percent secure against paranormal attack. But Jake's is even more secure right now, because that little hellion hasn't figured out where it is. And you know the kind of security system Jake has."

Did I ever. As soon as medical marijuana had become legal in the state of California, Jake—whom I'd always referred to in my head as Sleepy, because he'd seemed so out of it—stunned us all by revealing he'd parlayed his pizza-delivery earnings into the purchase of a plot of land in Salinas and modest storefront in Carmel Valley.

The result—Pot-Ential—does amazing numbers. A national newspaper recently named Jake one of the top business owners in the Monterey Bay area.

But just because marijuana was legal at the state level didn't mean banks were allowed to accept transactions involving the drug. This caused Jake to have, at any given time, hundreds of thousands dollars of cash sitting around in the safe at his house, because he didn't want to risk the lives of his employees by keeping it at the shop. He'd been forced to install a state-of-the-art security system—and purchase a large number of firearms—in order to fend off individuals who might mistakenly think that a hippy-dippy dispensary owner didn't know how to protect himself and his cash.

So in addition to having a large swimming pool, fire pit, and terrestrial mollusks, Snail Crossing was almost as impregnable as Fort Knox.

"It's better for you and Gina to stay there," Jesse said, "until we get this thing sorted."

I dropped his hand. "*What?*"

"I know you don't like it, but—"

"Don't like it? Jesse, I thought we agreed you were going to cut out the overprotective nineteenth-century macho man bullshit."

"That was before I saw that devil child coming after you tonight. Don't try to pretend that what happened didn't frighten you, Susannah. If I hadn't come along when I did—"

"Fine, she frightened me," I interrupted, shrugging loose from the arm he'd lain across my shoulders. This was not a good development. How was I going to get to Home Depot before closing to buy salt if I had to pack up and go to the Crossing? Especially with Jesse following me. "But not enough to drive me from my own home. For God's sake, Jesse, she knows where I work, too. What am I supposed to do, not show up to school tomorrow?"

"Tomorrow Father Dominic will be there," Jesse said. "He'll know how to handle her."

I let out a bitter laugh. "Oh, right! Jesse, no offense, but Father Dominic is the one who failed to notice her in the first place, and allowed all this to happen."

"Please." He laid both hands on my shoulders. "Susannah. How am I supposed to be able to work knowing you're here alone with that *thing* looking to harm you? And I know you would never allow Gina to risk her life for you. At least at the Crossing, there's Max."

"*Max?*"

Now fairly ancient, the Ackerman family dog lived with Jake and Jesse, padding around the house in search of bits of stray food to eat and sunny spots in which to fall asleep.

"Yes, *Max*," Jesse said. "You know he's always had a preternatural ability to sense when spirits are around. Look how he avoided your bedroom when you were in high school."

"Because *you* were there."

Funny how now that Jesse's soul was back in his body, Max was quite affectionate toward him. The dog certainly didn't seem to sense any kind of evil in him. Let Jesse's cat, Spike, walk into the room, however, and all hell broke loose.

"You know the safest thing to do right now is what I ask," Jesse went on, ignoring me. "If not for me, for the children."

"Children?" I echoed, bemused. "What children? Our future children? Let me tell you something, Jesse, those are getting harder and harder to imagine since you won't even—"

"The children whose parents might bring them to the emergency room tonight at St. Francis Medical Center," he interrupted, looking down at me with those big dark eyes. "How will I be able to concentrate on them when I'll be so busy worrying about you?"

I have to admit, for a minute I fell for it, lost in those gleaming eyes. I melted. Should I tell him? I thought. It wasn't fair of me not to. He deserved to know what Paul was doing. Look at him, so clean cut in his tie, so professional, so angelic. There wasn't an ounce of malevolence in him. He was so gentle, he cared so much about children. He'd never lay a finger on Paul . . .

Then I remembered the time he'd tried to drown Paul in the hot tub at 99 Pine Crest, and realized how easily he'd manipulated me.

I pushed him away.

"Oh, my God, you jerk. Fine. I'll do it, but for the children. Not for *you*."

"Good." He leaned down with a grin to scoop up my clothes and toss them to me. "Hurry. She used up a lot of energy in her attack on you, but now she'll have had time to regroup. I'll text Gina to ask what she needs from the apartment while you pack up Romeo and the rest of your things."

"Great." I rolled my eyes as he unlatched the childproof gate leading to the stairs back to my apartment, then held the gate open for me with one hand while he texted Gina with the other. "My dream come true. I finally get to sleep in your bed, and you won't even be there."

This caused him to glance up from his phone, one dark eyebrow raised. It was the one with the scar through it, a perfect crescent moon of skin where dark hair should have been. "Perhaps that's for the best," he said. "If I were in that bed with you, and you were dressed like that, you'd get no sleep at all."

"Promises." I accidentally-on-purpose grazed him with my breasts as I went through the gate in front of him. "Promises, promises. That's all I ever hear from you—"

He snaked an arm around my waist and pulled me hard against him, so quickly, and with such force, it momentarily knocked the breath from me. I dropped my clothes.

"What's the matter?" I glanced around in alarm, thinking that Lucia had reappeared, and he was snatching me from eminent danger.

But I realized the danger I was sensing was of an entirely different kind when he pressed me even closer against him, so close that I could feel the sharp definition of the buttons of his shirt— and the hardness of him through the rivets of his fly.

"I always keep my promises," he said in a voice that was deeper than usual.

Then he leaned down to kiss me, and I felt the danger—and his promise—through every nerve in my body. It coursed from my lips all the way down to my toes, and reawakened other parts that had only recently calmed down again after being overexcited by the chaise longue.

"Y-yes," I said, clinging to him a little unsteadily when he finally let me up for air. "You do keep your promises. I'll give you that."

"Hey, you two," I heard my neighbor Ryan shout from his balcony. "Get a room!"

Jesse pulled reluctantly away from me, shooting a hostile glance in Ryan's direction. "I'm really starting to dislike him."

"Yeah, me, too." I kept an arm around Jesse's waist, since I needed the support. I still felt a little shaky. "Let's get out of here."

once

I had classes Tuesday and Thursday mornings until eleven, which was rough for me even when I wasn't up late the night before recovering from an attack from a Non-Compliant Deceased Person.

But it was particularly rough that Thursday morning. Jake had been super excited about his unexpected overnight guests—well, one of them, anyway. He kept me and Gina up talking for hours, covering any and every topic he could think of, including but not limited to: what Jake would do if he got his hands on the "creeper" who was stalking us (the excuse Jesse gave him—and Gina—for why we'd suddenly had to crash at their house for the night); the tastiness of thin-crust pizza; what constituted a perfect wave, and why Jake was so good at riding them; and the unfairness of his not being made best man at my forthcoming wedding.

To avoid ill feeling, Jesse had appointed all three of my step-brothers groomsmen, just as I had three bridesmaids: CeeCee, Gina, and Brad's wife, Debbie. None of us were thrilled with the last choice, but it had been a necessary evil, since my stepnieces were our flower girls, and we needed both their parents close by to help keep control of them in the basilica during the ceremony.

Neither of us had appointed a best man or maid of honor. It seemed unwise to play favorites.

Jake had many things to say about all of this, and it was nice to see Gina laughing at his jokes (especially given how depressed she'd been lately over her stalled career).

But I had a hard time paying attention to the conversation. I still hadn't heard back from Shahbaz or Father Dominic, and even though I'd showered as soon as I got to the Crossing, I could still smell the chlorine in my hair from the pool back at my apartment, and the scratches on my neck from Lucia's attack stung (I'd hidden them beneath a high-collared sweater I'd brought along, so I could avoid having to answer any awkward questions).

Maybe that's why, when Gina and I finally stumbled into Jesse's bed together—it was king-sized, and I didn't feel it was fair for either of us to have to sleep on the couch, especially with a homicidal baby ghost potentially on the prowl—I still couldn't sleep, even though it was after three in the morning.

Then again, this is a problem I have most nights. No matter how soothing I try to make my sleep environment (based on advice from magazines and my therapist), I end up lying there staring at the back of my eyelids, trying not to think about my problems.

Since most of my problems are NCDP related, however, and NCDPs love showing up for nocturnal visitations—especially bedside—this was probably the root of my chronic insomnia.

But of course I couldn't tell Dr. Jo, my shrink, that. Or about the discussion I'd had with her deceased husband in the faculty parking lot, next to her Mercedes sedan, after my very first appointment with her. No accredited counseling program is going to graduate a student who believes she can communicate with the dead. That doesn't exactly look good in their alumni brochures.

Instead, I'd told her I couldn't sleep due to stress—school-related stress. Dr. Jo was in her late sixties, silver-haired but still spry, a lot like Father Dominic. Unlike Father Dominic, she wore a lot of bright colors, including bright red lipstick, even though she'd recently been widowed. Her husband—the NCDP who liked to hang around the school faculty parking lot—told me this was because she wanted to look cheerful for her patients.

She'd written me a prescription for a sleep aid—thirty pills only, nonrefillable—warning me that the pills were strong, and a better way to manage insomnia was through exercise. Had I thought about taking a yoga class? The college offered several.

I'd filled the prescription, but never taken a single pill—nor did I sign up for yoga. I could barely sit still through an entire episode of *The Bachelor* (Gina's favorite show). No way was I going to be able to downward dog away my problems.

For some reason on this night when sleep wouldn't come, instead of patiently counting souls of the dead I've helped move on, like I normally do, I did something even more insane than yoga. Something that was guaranteed to be my next really bad mistake.

But of course I did it anyway.

The moon had come out and cast Jesse's room—Spike, his yellow tomcat, watching over Romeo through the bars of his cage with elaborate disinterest; Gina, breathing deeply and contentedly beside me—in a blue glow. It seemed hard to believe that Egyptian curses, evil real estate developers, or demons existed.

But they did. I had the marks around my neck to prove it. And next time, my fiancé might not be around to save me, because my fiancé might be the one putting the marks there.

Maybe that thought was what made me lean over the side of

the bed to snatch my cell phone off the stack of ancient poetry and medical textbooks Jesse used as a bedside table, then text Paul:

> Fine. See you Friday at Mariner's @ 8.
> Nov 17 3:32 AM

No wonder I paid not the slightest bit of attention in statistics the next morning (required core, four units), spending the entire class looking for other mentions of the Curse of the Dead on the Web (there were plenty, but only in reference to movies with mummies in them), then was such a mess when I finally rolled into the mission.

What had I done?

My horror at myself is probably why it took me a few moments to notice the huge vase of white roses waiting for me on my desk. That, and the fact that the custodial staff had obviously been in to clean since I'd left the night before. The blinds had been screwed back into place—though as usual, they'd been pulled open to let in the sun that had burned off the morning marine layer—and Sister Ernestine must have had some student helpers come in to give a hand with the filing.

That's how I finally noticed the roses. There had to be at least two dozen of them, along with some white lilies and a few other blooms so exotic I had no idea what they were, sitting in an enormous—and undoubtedly expensive—crystal vase on my desk.

No one else was around—no tourists to be seen outside the windows overlooking the courtyard, no student aides, everyone's office doors shut, meaning they'd already left for lunch (I was running even more late than usual, due to having stopped by the hardware store after class to purchase salt. They hadn't had very much. I was going to have to hit up the grocery stores, as well).

Stunned, I leaned forward to inhale the flowers' fragrant scent, something I definitely wouldn't have done at work if anyone was looking. I didn't want people thinking I was a big softie who went around sniffing flowers.

I couldn't believe Jesse had done something so unbelievably sweet and extravagant, especially after I'd told him last night I didn't need material things.

But sending me roses the morning after an attack on my life?

That was exactly the kind of thing he would do. No wonder I was marrying him. How could anyone think there was an evil bone in his body?

There was a card tucked inside the waxen petals. I plucked it out and peeled open the stiff, expensive envelope, eager to read whatever amazing, romantic message Jesse had written.

But when I saw the message on the card, I realized it wasn't amazing, much less romantic. The flowers weren't even from Jesse. All my excitement drained away, and I was filled with cold, hard dread instead.

> *Counting the hours until tomorrow night.*
> *Thanks for saying yes.*
> *You won't regret it.*
>
> *Paul*

I dropped the card as if it had burst into flames in my fingers. "What the hell?"

I didn't realize I'd spoken aloud until the door to Father Dominic's office was thrown open and he came hurrying out.

"Susannah, is that you? Oh, good, you're here at last. I thought I heard your voice."

I jumped nearly out of my skin.

"Oh, hi, Father D." I scrambled to find the card I'd dropped where it had fallen upon the floor. "I didn't realize you were here."

"Yes, of course. I wanted to wait to leave for lunch until after I'd spoken to you. Oh, I see you got the flowers."

"Yes, I did." I swallowed. "When did these arrive?"

"First thing this morning," Father Dominic said. "They caused quite a stir. I assured everyone that they were most likely from your fiancé, and not a grateful parent. People around here get jealous so easily."

A muscle in my face must have twitched, since Father Dominic raised a snowy eyebrow and asked, "They *are* from Jesse, are they not, Susannah?"

"Yes, of course, they are." I crumpled the card into a ball, then threw the ball into the trash can beneath my desk. "Wasn't that sweet of him? He shouldn't have."

"After what happened last night? Of course he should have." Father Dominic must have noticed my dumbfounded expression, since he said, "I just hung up the phone with him. He told me what happened at your apartment. What a frightening experience. Thank goodness you're all right."

"Yeah, thank goodness." Thanks, Jesse. "Did you, uh, mention the flowers to him?"

"No, why would I? You know I dislike involving myself in your personal affairs, Susannah."

When I couldn't resist a snort at this, he added, "Any more than I already am, of course. Susannah, what on earth are you wearing?"

I looked down at myself. "What, this? It's a skirt."

"The length is very immodest."

"Are you kidding me? This length is not immodest. And these are leggings I've got on underneath. You might be familiar with them, they've been around since you were born, also known as medieval times."

"Nevertheless, you're probably going to have to change. Sister Ernestine isn't going to like it one bit."

"Change? Into what, Father D? I barely made it out of my apartment alive last night as it is. I don't have anything to change into. Plus, when Jesse sees me in this, there's a chance he might change his mind about that whole abstinence-until-marriage thing of his."

Father Dominic rolled his eyes. "Why can't you stop bedeviling that poor boy, Susannah? He's suffered enough for one lifetime, let alone the two he's been granted."

Me, bedeviling *him*? Yeah, right.

"So that's why you skipped lunch today, Father D, so you could *not* get involved in my personal affairs?" I headed over to the chair behind my desk so I could sit down and hide my too-revealing skirt. "You're doing a heck of a job of it already."

"You know perfectly well why I skipped lunch today. We need to talk about this spirit that attacked you."

"Yeah," I said. "Well, first things first. Did you get my message about the—"

"Susannah, I want to apologize to you."

That got my attention.

"Apologize? What for?" I couldn't remember the last time Father Dominic had apologized to me. Possibly never. "About not returning my message?"

"About what happened last night." Father Dominic lowered himself into the same mission-style chair across from my desk in which Becca had sat the day before, while I'd bandaged her arm. He had to lean at an odd tilt to see me behind the enormous bouquet. "Jesse gave me quite the earful about it, and I can't say I blame him. Sister Ernestine gave me her version, too, earlier this morning, but as you know, Sister Ernestine doesn't know the full story. I simply don't know how I could have missed it. I gave a welcome speech a few months ago to the entire student population. I stood in front of each grade and addressed them personally. How I could not have seen that Becca Walters was being victimized by a—"

I interrupted before he could go on further. "She's a lurker, Father. A real little pilot fish of a ghost. She hides until she decides Becca's in trouble, and then she attacks. I barely noticed her at first myself, and I was in this office alone with the kid. I had no idea how powerful she was until she got me alone, at home, in my own pool."

Father Dominic shook his head "But who is she? What could so young a child possibly have to be so angry about?"

"I don't know, Father. Only that her name is Lucia. CeeCee Webb is working on the rest. The key to all of it, I think, is Becca. Did you know Kelly Prescott is married to Becca's dad?"

"Of course. I was the officiant at their wedding last summer, which makes my blunder even less forgivable. Don't you read the alumni newsletters, Susannah? Your friend CeeCee writes them, I believe."

I picked up one of the stacks of files the student workers had left behind and, in order to avoid making eye contact with him, began to sort it. "Uh, I must have missed that one."

I didn't think it was worth going into the fact that I'd been invited to the wedding and bailed. That was my own business.

What was more concerning was that he'd officiated at their wedding, and *still* not seen the ghost kid? I wasn't going to say so out loud, but it seemed like Jesse might be right, and Father D was slipping. I'd only been trying to make the priest feel better when I'd assured him Lucia was hard to miss. But a ghost, at *a* wedding?

Hard to miss. *Really* hard to miss.

Maybe he wasn't the best person to consult about the Curse of the Dead after all . . .

For a man of his advancing years, Father Dominic would still physically be considered quite a catch on the senior circuit (if it wasn't for the vow of chastity he'd taken shortly after losing the love of his life, a young woman who, like Jesse, had been dead at the time. Unlike Jesse, however, she'd remained so). His snow-white hair was neatly trimmed without a hint of a bald spot, and at six feet tall, he didn't stoop or need a cane, thanks to good, clean living (except for his not-so-secret cigarette habit).

But he was hopeless when it came to electronics (and current Top 40 hits) and any joke remotely smacking of sexual innuendo embarrassed him.

And now it appeared that he wasn't quite as in touch with the spirit world as he used to be.

I wasn't sure how to handle this. They haven't yet isolated the genetic chromosome to tell if you're a carrier for mediatorism, though anecdotal evidence seemed to indicate it was an inherited trait. Scientists aren't eager to admit there's such a thing as ghosts, so it's not like any of them are rushing to formulate a test they can administer to someone to tell if they have my "gift." You either see dead people or you don't, kind of like how you're either gluten-sensitive, or you're not.

Father Dom used to see them. Now, apparently, he doesn't. At least, not when I need him to.

"Um, anyway," I said, deciding it was best to drop the subject, "I think I really established a rapport with Becca yesterday, so . . ."

"Oh, that's evident," Father Dominic said drily. "Especially by the look of this place when I got in this morning."

I glared at him. "What year was it you graduated from college? And how many counseling accreditations did they require for the job back then?"

He ignored this jab at his complete lack of formal counseling training. "How do you propose we handle this situation then, Susannah? I will admit that though your methodology has sometimes differed from mine, you've usually been on the mark. Jesse, on the other hand, seems to have what I'd call a less-than-helpful view on things—"

"Oh, I'm sure he does," I said, remembering the look on my boyfriend's face when he'd dragged me from the pool. "I was thinking of pulling Becca out of her fourth-period class and bringing her back here to the office for a friendly little one-on-one. Nothing threatening, though. I don't want to alarm Lucia."

"That would be an excellent plan if it weren't for the fact that Becca isn't in school today."

"Wait . . . what?"

He tapped the file he'd been holding tucked beneath one arm.

"Kelly Prescott—er, Walters—called early this morning to say that her stepdaughter wasn't feeling well and wouldn't be in school today."

This was deflating. "Oh."

"Sister Ernestine left this on my desk this morning." Father Dominic removed the file from beneath his arm and waved it at me. "Becca Walters's transcript. I'm not quite certain how the sister found it in all that mess, but she managed. I don't suppose you had a chance to review it."

"I must have missed it while I was busy applying much-needed first aid to Becca's arm and also keeping her friend from trying to murder me."

I knew there wasn't any point in telling Father D that even if I'd had a chance to read Becca's file, I wouldn't have put much stock into what it said. I have a ton of respect for teachers, who are some of the hardest working (yet worst compensated) people in the world.

But one of the reasons I was attracted to the counseling field in the first place is that it would allow me to help kids like the one I'd been—kids who have gifts that can't be measured on an aptitude test, or scored with a letter grade.

Another reason is that the more people I can help resolve their issues *now*, while they're still alive, the less work I'll have to do for them later, when they're dead.

It also made sense from a financial point of view. As a therapist, I'll get paid for the work I do—by *living* clients, who have things like insurance and credit cards. Taking money from the deceased is something I'm opposed to (though Paul's never suffered from this moral dilemma).

"Four different schools in the area in ten years," Father Dominic was saying as he slipped a pair of wire-rimmed glasses from his shirt pocket onto his nose, then flipped through Becca's file. "The latest being this one. She gets good grades, and is quite bright—that's why we accepted her, of course."

"Her father's sizable donation probably didn't hurt much, either, I'd guess."

He glanced at me over the rims of his spectacles. "I don't appreciate the sarcasm, Susannah. We treat all of our students the same, as you know, regardless of whether they're on scholarship or pay full tuition. But it does appear that Becca's had emotional problems. It looks as if there might have been some bullying at her former schools. "

"It's not hard to guess why."

"More sarcasm? The other children can't see that the poor girl is haunted."

"Of course not. But she tried to carve the word *stupid* in her own arm with a compass in the middle of class. They may not be able to see Lucia, but they can definitely tell there's something wrong with Becca. The less enlightened among them are naturally going to tease the crap out of her for it."

Father Dominic sighed. "If you talk like this about our students in front of Sister Ernestine, it's going to be extremely difficult for me to convince her to hire you full time, with pay. You do realize this, don't you, Susannah?"

I let out a sigh of my own. "Especially if I dress immodestly. Fine, Father, I get it. I'll ratchet up the sensitive psychobabble in front of the nun, okay? But in the meantime we've got to find out who Lucia is, and who or what it is she thinks she's protecting Becca from, before she protects Becca to death. Does it say anything in that file about horses?"

"Horses?" Father Dominic looked perplexed. "No. Why?"

"Lucia is dressed in riding clothes and carries a stuffed horse. You know the dead usually appear in the clothing they were wearing right before they bit the dust." He gave me a disapproving look. "Um, in which they felt most alive. Becca wears a horse pendant. She twists it when she's feeling nervous. Horses are the only clue I can find that links the two of them."

"Horses," Father Dominic murmured, flipping through the file. "Horseback riding. There's nothing in here about—" Suddenly, he froze as if he'd seen something in the file. "Oh, dear."

"What? What is it?"

"It's funny you should mention horseback riding, Susannah. Because I believe I do remember now a girl who—"

His blue eyes got a far away look in them as he stared out one of the office windows at a group of middle-aged tourists who'd just pulled up on a bus outside the mission, and were now milling around the courtyard, taking photos and admiring the flowers and statues and fountains. It was strange to go to school at a place that was also a tourist destination, and even stranger to work at one, especially considering all the money those tourists were spending in the gift shop (and the school still couldn't scrape together a salary for me).

But Father Dominic didn't appear to really be seeing these visitors from the Midwest.

"You know, I think I do recall a riding accident involving a child. It was in the newspaper—the one your friend Miss Webb works for—some time ago. It could very well have been around the time that Becca's troubles started."

Father Dominic glanced through the girl's file until he saw something. Then he stopped flipping and tapped a page, speaking in a more excited voice.

"Yes. Yes, exactly. Here it is. I remember now. It says here that Becca attended the Academy of the Sacred Trinity for first and second grades. That would have been around the same time that it happened."

"That *what* happened?" I love him like he was my own grandfather, but like my own grandfather, he drove me nuts sometimes. I had a feeling I knew what he'd say if I brought up Paul: *Well, what have you been doing, Susannah, to lead that boy on?*

"The accident," he said. "There's no mention of it in Becca's file, oddly enough. But I do think Becca *must* have known the girl. They would have been in the same grade . . . possibly even in the same riding class. Otherwise there's nothing else to explain their intense connection—"

"Wait," I said. "You think *Lucia* was the girl in the riding accident?"

"It would explain quite a lot. Becca would have been traumatized by such a tragedy."

"What tragedy?" I asked. "Not to say a riding accident doesn't sound terrible, and it's always awful when a child dies, but—"

"Not an accident like this," Father Dominic said. "This one was ghastly, which is why I remember it, even after all these years. The girl in question—who was quite young—was out riding with her instructor when her horse was spooked by something. It took off, but the little girl managed to stay atop it."

"Astride. I think they say astride, not atop . . . she wasn't thrown off?"

"Not right away. I remember the article saying she was quite a skilled rider, for her age. That's how she managed to stay astride for so long, and why it took so long for them to find her. And then when they did . . ."

"Yes?"

"It was too late."

doce

"I think I remember that the coroner ruled that her death was caused by asphyxiation," Father Dominic said.

"Asphyxiation?" I was confused. "Who strangled her, the horse?"

"Susannah, you watch entirely too much television."

This is untrue. I don't watch enough television. I don't have time, due to my studies, budding career, romantic life, and, of course, busy NCDP-busting schedule.

"When she fell from the horse," Father Dominic went on, before I could argue, "I believe her spinal cord was severed, cutting off her breathing. I suppose she might have been saved if her body had been found soon enough, but she wasn't . . . in any case, she died from lack of oxygen, which is what medical examiners call asphyxiation."

"Ew." I gave an involuntary shudder, thinking of Lucia's face, which, though usually twisted in anger when I'd seen it, had still been cherubically round. She had a mouth that, unlike my stepnieces, was shaped exactly like the rosebuds in the bouquet Paul had sent me, only smaller and pink, not white.

"That's a horrible way to die," I said.

"I agree. But I doubt the girl suffered long, if at all. An injury like that would have instantly paralyzed her." He heaved a little shudder himself. "And the girl's soul never revealed herself to me, asking for help . . . or for justice. Apparently she's chosen to reveal herself to you, now, though, hasn't she, Susannah?"

"She tried to kill me. That's the opposite of asking for help, Father D."

"Spirits aren't always aware that we have the ability to help them," Father Dominic said. "And even then, they're often sometimes too frightened—or stubborn—to accept our guidance. Jesse, you'll recall, wouldn't have dreamt of accepting your aid while he was in spirit form. He was the one rushing to *your* defense. And yet, in the end, it was you who—"

"Jesse wouldn't accept help if he were bleeding on the side of the road. It kills him that he had to accept scholarship money and student loans to pay for him to go school." Which was another reason I couldn't tell him anything about what was going on with Paul. He'd want to handle the whole situation himself, which would, of course, end in disaster.

"And if the girl you're talking about and the one I met yesterday are one in the same," I went on, "she'd rather choke me to death than let me help her."

"Still," Father Dominic said, after a beat. "You know we have a duty to—"

"Help Kelly's stepdaughter," I said. "I know. And help Lucia, too." I'd already switched on my computer and typed the words *Lucia*, *asphyxiation*, and *horse* into the search engine of my computer. "Oh, great," I said when I saw the results. "Porn. Why is it always porn? Thank you, World Wide Web."

The priest winced. "Susannah, please."

"No, look, Father, if your dead girl and mine are the same, I don't blame her for being pissed." I began to fish my phone from my bag, intending to compose a text to CeeCee. Her investigative skills were superior to mine. "Can you tell me anything more about her death? Anything else at all?"

"It was a long time ago, Susannah. Before you moved to Carmel. I suppose I could ask Father Francisco . . . he's still the headmaster at Sacred Trinity. I believe the funeral was held at the chapel there. I wish I could remember her last name. I believe I heard from Father Francisco that the family moved away afterward. Well, that would be understandable. Who would want to stay in the area after a thing like that?"

"Oh, no, who would?" I wasn't even trying to mask my sarcasm. "Did they shoot the horse, too? Because I'm sure everyone blamed the horse. They always do."

Hey C.C., here's more 411 on Lucia. Went to Sacred Trinity approx. 9-10 yrs ago. Died in horseback riding accident. Coroner listed cause of death as asphyxiation.

PS Is everyone insane? Not counting you, of course. And Jesse.
Nov 17 12:45 PM

"Was Becca there when it happened?" I asked Father Dom.

"It says right here in her file that she attended the Academy of the Sacred Trinity all-girls Catholic school in Pebble Beach for first and second grade. As I said, that would have been around the time of the tragedy. She then switched to Stevenson School the following year. One has to assume there's a good reason for her to have made such an abrupt transfer—"

"Becca did mention an accident," I said, thinking back to our conversation the day before. "She said her mom left 'after the accident.'"

The poor child." Father Dominic shook his head. "So much sadness in her life, and in such a short time."

"I think Lucia's the one who got the real short end of the stick there, Father."

"True. A year after, Becca transferred from Stevenson to a charter school, but that appears to have been a failure as well, because now, of course, she's here."

My mind was whirling. This was a lot of information. A lot of information about which there was nothing on the Internet.

Well, that made sense. Sacred Trinity wouldn't want to be associated with something so sad, and they had the money to make sure any reference to it stayed off Google.

"Do you remember where the riding accident occurred?" I asked. "Was it on Sacred Trinity grounds?"

"I honestly can't recall," Father Dominic said. "I suppose it would make sense that it was Sacred Trinity. They have facilities there for students to stable their own horses."

"They should have facilities there for their students to stable their own space shuttles with what they charge for tuition."

Sacred Trinity was one of the many private schools in the Carmel area with which the Mission Academy was in competition. But with Trinity's chic location on Pebble Beach's exclusive 17-Mile Drive, their Olympic-sized pool, tennis courts, lacrosse and soccer fields, and, of course, horse stables and riding trails, the Mission Academy was barely in the same league. All we had to offer these days as far as extracurriculars was basketball, Mathletics, and the spring musical. It wasn't any wonder Sister Ernestine didn't want to piss off Lance Arthur Walters. The daughters of royalty and celebrities attended Sacred Trinity.

The granddaughters of Andy Ackerman, the host of At Home with Andy, attended Mission Academy.

"But Sacred Trinity is located within the community of Pebble Beach, and the resort there has an equestrian center, too," Father Dominic said, loyally coming to the defense of a fellow Catholic school. "The accident could easily have happened along one of its riding trails, not Trinity's. Horseback riding is such a popular sport these days, especially among the wealthy, everyone seems to be doing it, even though it can be so very dangerous. And I don't believe there are any equestrian safety helmet laws in California."

I eyed him with affectionate skepticism. "Oh, okay, Father D. I'm sure that's the reason Lucia's been sticking around so long, trying to protect Becca, because she's upset about California's equestrian safety helmet laws."

"There's no need for more sarcasm, Susannah. Sacred Trinity is one of the premier girls' schools in the country. And Pebble Beach is a five-star resort. Surely what happened to the poor girl could only have been a tragic accident, not . . . whatever you're thinking."

"You know one of the things I love most about you, Father D, is that you always see the best in people." Smiling, I patted him on the shoulder. "Even in premier girls' schools and five-star resorts."

"And one of the things that troubles me most about you, Susannah, is that you're always prepared to see the worst in everyone. Didn't you work at the Pebble Beach Resort one summer when you were in high school?"

"I did," I said. "That's how I know they aren't perfect."

"False modesty is not a very attractive quality, Susannah."

"Fine. Yes, they hired me to work as a babysitter at the resort."

Father Dominic brightened. "Oh, yes, of course. That's how you met Paul Slater's little brother. How is Jack? What's he up to these days?"

I smile with a nonchalance I was far from feeling at the mention of Paul's name. "Jack? Last time I heard from him, he seemed to be fine. Much happier now that he's not living with his parents."

"And does he—well, communicate very often with the deceased?"

"I don't think so. In fact, I think he still tries to avoid it whenever possible. He's gotten into writing—screenplays, I think."

"Oh, that's a shame," Father Dominic said.

"A shame? Why?"

"Well, he had such promise as a mediator. But perhaps he was a bit too sensitive for the work. He might be better suited to the arts. Not like his brother . . . how is Paul? The two of you had your differences, but got to be on rather good terms again, toward graduation, as I recall. Have you heard from him at all lately?"

Now, of course, was the perfect opportunity to tell Father Dominic the truth about why I'd called him last night. That my interest in the Curse of the Dead wasn't merely intellectual, but had to do with Paul Slater, who was basically trying to blackmail me into sleeping with him.

"I don't know," I said flatly. "I haven't heard from Paul in years."

"Really? I'm surprised. He always seemed so fond of you. I realize those feelings weren't returned, but—"

"No offense, Father, but let's stick to the subject at hand, okay? What are we going to do about Kelly Walters's stepdaughter?"

Father Dominic blinked. "Of course. I'm sorry. I didn't mean to seem intrusive—"

"No worries. We just need to decide how we're going to

handle this. I know Jesse probably told you over the phone that he wants to exorcise the kid—"

"He did, but it's only because he's so upset about what happened to you. Obviously it's out of the question. She's a young soul in torment."

"Who's been tormenting another young soul for what appears to be years, and who also tried to drown me last night. As much as I enjoy sleeping in my fiancé's bed, I'd rather not be doing it with Gina."

"No," Father Dominic said drily. "Nor can I imagine sleeping with you is a particularly enjoyable experience for Gina."

"Wow, thanks. You know, this is all your fault. If it weren't for the debt he feels toward you and my family and the stupid church," I pointed out, "Jesse and I would be the ones sharing that bed, like a normal twenty-first-century couple. Any chance you could casually let him know that our souls are not *actually* going to be sent to eternal damnation if we make love before we're married, Father D?"

The priest looked amused. "I'm not the pope, Susannah. I don't have the power to change what's been official church doctrine for thousands of years."

"Well, you've always performed same-sex marriages off church grounds, so you don't seem to mind bending the rules of *some* church doctrine—"

I was surprised when Father Dominic's expression changed, and he interrupted, in an animated voice, "Susannah, you're absolutely right."

"Wait . . . I am?" I could hardly believe my good fortune. "You'll tell Jesse it's okay for us to have sex?"

"No, of course not." He looked horrified. "Don't be ridiculous. I mean you're right it's my fault about Kelly's stepdaughter. And it's high time I did something about it."

"What? No." I stared at him as he rose to his feet and began to rush about the office. "How is it your fault?"

"Susannah, I officiated at her parents' wedding and did not notice the poor, tortured soul clinging to her then, nor did I notice her at any time this semester since Becca started attending this school. So you see, it's my fault, and my responsibility."

A feeling of dread closed over me. It was far different than the feeling of dread I'd felt when I'd seen Paul's e-mail, or that the flowers on my desk were from him and not Jesse. But it was still there.

"Father D, I agree we need to do something, but don't you think we should probably wait until we have more information?"

"Nonsense. Find out what homework Becca is missing in her classes today and I'll drive to her house with the assignments personally. That way I'll be able to speak with her as well as her parents, as I ought properly to have done several months ago before their wedding, or at least when they first enrolled her here."

"Father Dominic, I get where you're coming from. I really do. And I appreciate that once again, you're trying to do the right thing. But I don't think you have anything to feel guilty about. At their wedding you had no idea there was anything like this going on. You didn't even see Lucia. Like you said, she revealed herself to me, not to you. So I really think I'm the one who—"

"Susannah, I'm not feeling guilty. I'm simply trying to do my job."

"Right, I know. But remember what happened last time?"

He glanced at me, confused. "Last time?"

"The last time the ghost of a very angry girl tore up this school."

He continued to look confused for a moment, then remembered. "The girl who desecrated Father Serra's statue? What on earth reminded you of her?"

"You said *she* was the most violent spirit you'd ever seen." And, uh, there was a rumor going around the school that *I'd* severed Father Serra's head. "And look what happened when you tangled with her."

"That was an entirely different situation, Susannah, as you well know."

"Maybe. But I still think it's a mistake to go out there. What makes you think you'll even see Lucia today? You didn't before."

"Really, Susannah, you don't seem to think very highly of my skills, as either an educator or a mediator."

"That isn't true."

Except of course that lately, it was.

"I assure you, Susannah, I've been dealing with troubled children far longer than you have. May I point out that you were one of them once?"

Before I could protest that I was never "troubled," only disruptive, he went on to say, "And you ended up far exceeding my expectations for you. Except for your somewhat colorful vocabulary—and your occasionally regrettable wardrobe, of course—you've grown into a wonderfully mature, accomplished young woman I'd be proud to call my own daughter. Well, granddaughter perhaps would be more apt."

I hesitated. "Well, thank you, Father. That's very nice. But shouldn't you still let me—"

"Let you what?" He was putting on his black jacket, checking in the mirror to make sure his clerical collar was straight. "Let you come with me? Then who will do your job? Sister Ernestine will certainly discover Ms. Diaz and Mr. Gillarte's affair if you are not here to make excuses for them. No, Susannah—" He turned from the mirror to look at me, not seeming to notice my astonished expression. I'd had no idea he knew about the Diaz-Gillarte imbroglio. "It's my responsibility, not yours."

"But." I had to try one more time. "Supposing she does reveal herself to you. She's not normal. Even you admit she's insanely strong. So if you piss her off, you could get more than drowned, or the head of a statue thrown at you—"

"Susannah, I've been doing this quite a bit longer than you. I do think I know my way around a mediation by now. Besides," he added with a grin, "believe it or not, children like me. It's entirely possible that Becca, and even her spirit companion, will listen calmly to what I have to say. Most people do, you know."

I tried my hardest to stop him. In retrospect, I should have tried harder. I should have called Jesse—even though he was back at the Crossing, catching up on the sleep he'd missed over the last forty-eight hours.

In retrospect, I should have made Gina or Jake wake Jesse up and drive after Father Dominic to stop him. Or I should have gone with him myself, especially after Aunt Pru's warning.

But he was so confident about it, so adamant that he could fix everything. And I was tired from my own lack of sleep, and preoccupied, I'll admit, about what was going on with my boyfriend.

And really, maybe it was insensitive of me to try to stand in the way of this, Father Dominic's last mediation (or attempt at one, anyway). Ageist, even. I didn't want to be accused of discriminating against someone because of their advancing years.

So I said, "Okay, Father D. If you're sure. I guess I could stay here and see what I can find out about the riding accident."

He nodded and said, "Good thinking."

It wasn't, though. It turned out to be terrible thinking.

Only I didn't know it until I heard Sister Ernestine pick up the phone in her office a few hours later, then cry, "*What?*"

That's when I knew how wrong I'd been.

trece

"That's how old people die. They fracture their hip, get pneumonia, then die."

That's what my stepniece Mopsy assured me of as we stood in front of the main reception desk at the hospital later that evening.

"Shut up, Emily," I said.

"But it's true. And you're not supposed to say shut up. You're supposed to sing the listening song. That's what Sister Monica taught us in school."

"I'm not going to sing the goddamn listening song, Emily."

"You're not supposed to swear, Aunt Suze. You're not supposed to swear *or* say shut up."

I took a deep breath, fighting for patience. The only reason my stepnieces were with me was because a fight had erupted between their parents over Sister Ernestine's request to discuss the possibility of their daughters having ADHD.

Even though we hadn't always (okay, ever) gotten along, I considered Debbie a loving and hands-on mom, especially given the fact that she'd had all three of her babies at the same time, without the aid of fertility drugs. Multiples ran in Debbie's family. She had an older cousin who'd had *two* sets of triplets, also naturally.

One might think this would have served as a warning to Debbie to use protection, but the opposite was true. Debbie was completely opposed to all forms of pharmaceutical products, including birth control—to Brad's everlasting chagrin—and vaccinations, despite Jesse pointing out that because of people like her, preventable (and potentially deadly) diseases like measles, mumps, and whooping cough were on the rise again in the state of California.

Debbie didn't care. She was convinced that keeping Flopsy, Mopsy, and Cotton-tail (my nicknames for my admittedly adorable but somewhat high-spirited stepnieces) drug and vaccine free was the right thing to do.

Although I didn't agree with her (and wasn't sure how long any school, even the Mission Academy, would keep accepting her bogus "health exemptions" from her quack doctor), in a weird way I admired her fiercely protective—if misdirected—maternal instinct.

Except that this latest tiff between her and my stepbrother over the subject had resulted in a communications gap so vast that neither of them had remembered to retrieve the girls after school. That's how I'd been forced to corral them into the backseat of my embarrassingly dilapidated Land Rover, then take them with me to the hospital when I'd heard the news about Father Dom.

Hospitals are the last place you're supposed to take children—especially ones who haven't had their vaccinations.

But what other choice did I have? I had to see Father Dominic as soon as he got out of recovery. They'd decided it was best to operate on his hip right away, as the "accident" he'd allegedly suffered at the Walterses's home had completely shattered it.

So it was to St. Francis that the four of us went.

I'd realized belatedly what a horrible idea this was not only when Mopsy opened her mouth to ask, "Why is your car so *old*, Aunt Suze?" (it had been in the family for ages until I'd inherited it, and there was no point in my buying a nicer car, since it was only going to be abused by my terrible driving, the triplets, and, of course, mediation-resistant spirits), but when she'd followed that up by declaring, in the hospital lobby, that Father Dom was going to die.

Even worse, the redhead at the hospital's main reception desk turned out to be someone new, who didn't recognize me as either Jesse's fiancée—I'd been to the hospital many times to visit him during his breaks—*or* a member of the clergy and therefore "family" of Father D's, and so wouldn't tell me the exact extent of his injuries, how he was doing, or which floor he'd been taken to.

"Look," I said to the redhead, pointedly ignoring Mopsy, the most outspoken of Brad and Debbie's daughters, "I get that you can't give me any information about what room Father Dominic is in for privacy reasons. But can you at least tell me his status? He was supposed to have been out of surgery an hour ago."

"I really couldn't say. It's against hospital policy."

The redhead—her name tag said to call her Peggy—didn't even glance at me. All her attention was focused on my stepnieces, who look like total angels to strangers, especially when wearing their school uniforms. In their matching navy blue plaid skirts, white short-sleeved blouses and knee socks, and French braids Debbie insisted on twisting their hair into every morning (which, by the end of day, like now, were always destroyed, looking like dark, wavy mushrooms around their cherubic faces), they resembled mini-Madonnas.

What they actually were was little hellions.

"Oh, my gosh, are you girls triplets?" Peggy said to them from her imitation mahogany tower. "You could not be any cuter!"

The girls ignored her, as they did everyone who asked if they were triplets, then commented on how cute they were. Flopsy poked Mopsy.

"Old people don't die of fractures."

"Yes, they do. Mommy's grandma died that way."

"Grandma's not dead. We saw her on the first day of school, remember? She gave us stickers."

"Not Grandma. Mommy's grandma. Mommy's grandma is dead from a hip fracture. Remember? She told us."

Mopsy kicked Flopsy. "Shut up!"

Mopsy kicked Flopsy back. "*You* shut up!"

Flopsy screamed at the top of her lungs, causing everyone in the waiting room to look at us.

"If you both don't shut up," I said, "I'll make you go sit in the car."

"You can't do that, Aunt Suze." Cotton-tail was the practical trip. "Mommy says it's against the law and if you do it again, she's going to tell the police on you."

Peggy overheard this, and stared at me in horror.

"It was an emergency," I explained. Though there was no way I could explain to her that the emergency had involved an NCDP who'd unexpectedly shown up at the park while I was babysitting them, and that they'd been safer in the car, as he'd been trying to resist mediation by way of pelting me with a municipal trash can. "And I left the windows cracked."

"It was so *exciting*," Mopsy said. "Especially when you threw that garbage can against the windshield, and it *exploded*!"

I most definitely could not explain that the NCDP had by that point been inside the garbage can.

To the girls I said, "Could you *please* cut Aunt Suze some slack? I'm trying to talk to the nice lady."

Behind me, I heard the sliding doors to the hospital's main

entrance whoosh open, and I whipped my head around, half hoping to see Brad coming to rescue me from the girls, but mostly hoping it would be Jesse.

My heart sank when it was neither, just some young guy with a goatee carrying balloons for a patient he'd come to visit.

I couldn't understand it. I knew Jesse had worked two back-to-back shifts straight through (which is technically illegal, but most residents do it, not out of choice so much as out of necessity), so I wasn't surprised he'd slept through the ringer on both his cell and the house phone when I called to let him know what had happened to Father Dom.

But he usually *felt* it when I was upset about something, even in his sleep, and came running.

So where was he? Why hadn't he called me back?

"Why do we need to cut you some slack, Aunt Suze?" Flopsy wanted to know.

"Because she's worried about Father Dominic, and you should be, too, stupid," Mopsy informed her. "He's probably going to die."

"I'm not stupid, you are."

"I'm not stupid, *you* are."

"Aunt Suze, she called me stupid."

"Hey, kids," I said brightly, reaching for my wallet. "Are you thirsty? Why don't you go get a soda? I see some machines over there."

Shrieking with joy at the prospect of sugar, which they were not allowed at home, the girls snatched singles from my hand and tore from the reception area at top speed, nearly crashing into several people who were waiting to see the triage nurse.

"Be sure to get lots of candy bars, too," I called after them. "The kind that rot your teeth. And don't talk to strangers. *Look*." I turned back to Peggy, leaning in very close and lowering my voice so that only she could hear me. "I am not in the mood for this right now. You're going to tell me where they've taken that priest, or I'm going to let those three unholy terrors you think are so cute get all hopped up on sugar, then turn them loose in your ER. I'm going to let them touch *everything*, and you do not want that, because guess what? They haven't had any of their shots. Who knows what kind of weird diseases they're carrying without even showing symptoms? Mumps. Polio. Whooping cough. Measles. Did you know that measles is still one of the leading causes of death in children worldwide? That because it's so infectious, nine out of ten people who haven't been vaccinated against it who come into contact with someone who has it will catch it. Is that really what you want? All those vulnerable, unvaccinated babies in your maternity ward to come down with measles in a matter of hours?"

Peggy's eyes widened to their limits, and she scooted her wheeled chair away from me. "I'm . . . I'm . . . I'm . . . I'm going to go get my supervisor."

"You do that," I said. "But remember, the longer you make me wait, the more contagions are festering on those little girls' hands. I hope you have a vat load of antibacterial lotion nearby."

While she was gone, I pulled out my cell phone to try Jesse again.

Four missed calls from him, and three texts!

For once, the texts weren't in Spanish, which indicated how dire he considered the situation. He spoke in English only when he was feeling calm, texted in it only when he was not.

> **Jesse** Got your messages. I've been trying to call you, but you aren't picking up.
> Nov 17 4:20 PM

What? I studied my phone more closely. Of course. The ringer had been switched off. Not only that, the screen saver had been changed from a photo of my pet rat, Romeo, adorably asleep on my fiancé's shoulder as Jesse read one of his medical textbooks, to one of all three of my stepnieces in the backseat of the Land Rover, leering into the camera.

I glanced at the vending area, where Flopsy and Mopsy were now fighting over a bag of Skittles. A favorite trick of the triplets was to sneak electronic devices out of the bag or pocket of whatever adult was nearby, then completely reset them and slip them back without the person ever suspecting.

When they were older they were going to end up either in prison or working for the NSA.

I sighed and scrolled to the next text.

> **Jesse** Don't worry, querida. Everything is going to be all right. I'll take care of this.
> I swear.
> Nov 17 4:25 PM

"I'll take care of this."

What was he talking about? What was there that he could take care of that I didn't have under control?

His next text was only slightly more illuminating.

> **Jesse** No one's at your office. You must be at the hospital. I will see you there.
> I stopped by the church to pick up a few of the father's things.

> **Te amo, querida.**
> Nov 17 5:05 PM

An ordinary person reading that text would have thought, "Oh, how sweet! Her boyfriend stopped to pick up the old man's toothbrush, a change of underwear, and maybe some pajamas and slippers and the priest's latest copy of *Catholic News*."

No. No way. Knowing my boyfriend, I suspect the things Jesse probably stopped to retrieve were the good father's Bible, crucifix, rosary, Virgin Mary medal, and holy water and sacramental wafers pilfered from the tabernacle on the altar inside the church.

Because those are the things you needed to perform a good, old-fashioned exorcism.

Great. Just great. While I completely agreed that no spirit should be allowed to attack a sweet, innocent old man like Father Dominic, who'd only meant to help her, that didn't mean I thought her soul should be cast into eternal damnation, especially now that I'd learned some of the details about Lucia's death from Father Dominic—and even more from her obituary, which CeeCee had managed to find and send to me earlier that afternoon.

I was wondering what to text back—*I can't believe you'd steal holy bread and wine from a church, but you won't have sex with me* didn't seem right somehow—when suddenly a new message popped up on my screen. I was assuming it was from Jesse until I clicked on it.

> **El Diablo** What did you think of the flowers?
> Nov 17 5:15 PM

Really? Was he kidding me? He really *was* the devil.

I was stabbing at my phone to delete all trace of him when something awful occurred to me, something that chilled me even more than Paul's text or the thought of my fiancé exorcising a baby banshee:

Jesse had been by my office to look for me. That meant he'd seen the flowers on my desk.

Damn!

And what had I done with the card Paul had written to me? With everything that had happened, I couldn't remember.

I was so screwed.

"Susannah?"

I started at the sound of the voice coming from behind me. Peggy had returned with a nurse I recognized from the many times Jake and I had dropped by to visit Jesse when he was working in the ER. The nurse recognized me, too, but fortunately not as the stepsister of the long-haired dude who liked to prank the hospital's volunteers by asking them gravely to please page, "Dr. Butt. Dr. Chafe Butt" (it was shocking how often they fell for this).

"Susannah, I thought that was you," Sherry said with a smile. "Peggy told me there was a crazy woman out here who was threatening to infect the maternity ward with measles. But then I saw who it was."

"Hi, Sherry." I almost melted with relief. "Yes, it's me. Sorry about the theatrics. They brought my boss in here a little while ago, Father Dominic from the Junípero Serra Mission Academy?"

She stopped smiling, which was never a good sign. "Yes, of course."

"Um, he's okay, right? I really need to get upstairs to see him, the sooner the better."

"Of course." Sherry used that soothing tone that nurses employ to make you feel better, even though you suspect they don't really believe a word you've said. *You don't drink more than three alcoholic beverages a week? Riiiight.* "Peggy, this is Susannah Simon, she's engaged to Dr. de Silva."

I saw Peggy give me a quick look, as if she was appraising me in a whole new light.

"Oh," Peggy said. "Really?"

It was evident from her flat tone that she disapproved.

I wasn't surprised. Jesse was extremely popular with the mostly female nursing staff (and some of the males, as well) because he was not only easy on the eyes, but also charming, good-humored, and occasionally brought cookies for everyone in the staff room.

Cookies *I'd* made, thinking it wouldn't hurt for him to get into the good graces of the staff.

I thought about grabbing Peggy by her copious red hair and smashing her face into her computer screen, but only briefly. I'd never have done it. Probably.

Instead I said, "It's really nice to meet you, Peggy. Sorry if I seemed, um, abrupt before. I'm just really concerned about my boss."

"No worries," Peggy said. "It's nice to meet you, too. Everyone here really likes Dr. de Silva, even our older patients. They always start out complaining he's too young to be a doctor, but then they look into his eyes. After that, they shut up about it." She laughed. "They say he has an 'old soul,' whatever that means."

I flashed her a brittle smile. "Yeah, I've heard that one before about him. So can I go see Father Dominic now, Sherry?"

"Of course, but I'm afraid he won't be very talkative. Dr. Patel is keeping him heavily sedated to help make him more comfortable."

"Wait." I gaped at the nurse. "Is he . . . is Father Dominic going to die?"

catorce

It felt like the bottom was dropping out of my world. Why hadn't I hugged Father Dominic good-bye when he'd left? Why had I let him leave in the first place?

The nurse smiled and put a reassuring hand on my arm.

"Susannah, don't worry. Dr. Patel, who performed his surgery, is the best in the area. And he says the father is doing very well for a man his age who took a fall down a flight of stairs. He's listed in serious, but not critical, condition."

"Oh," I said faintly. Serious, but not critical, condition? Was that supposed to be good?

And a fall down the stairs? That's what the Walterses thought happened? Lucia had them living in total and complete denial, especially given what I now knew about the first—and second—Mrs. Walters.

"If you wait a minute," Sherry went on, "you can go up with your fiancé. I overheard Dr. Patel filling him in on the case over the phone a few minutes ago."

I stared at her, only half conscious that Peggy, the redhead, had whipped her purse out from under the reception desk and was dabbing on some lip gloss. Peggy evidently had a thing for old souls . . . or at least hot Latino residents.

"Wait. What?"

Sherry smiled. "Yes. I heard Dr. Patel say that Dr. de Silva was just pulling into the parking lot."

"Oh," I said. "That's great." I wondered if my smile looked as frozen as it felt. "I'll just run outside then and see if I can find Jesse—er, Dr. de Silva. Those three little girls over there by the candy machines—they're my nieces. Their father is coming soon to pick them up. In the meantime, can you tell them where I went?"

"I'll keep an eye on them for you," Peggy volunteered. She was now checking her eyeliner in her compact mirror. "Dr. de Silva must be looking forward to becoming an uncle. He's so great with kids."

"He really is." When he wasn't trying to send their souls to hell. "I'll be right back."

I thanked them and turned to leave, heading like a robot through the sliding doors to the parking lot.

This was a disaster. Not only that Father Dominic was so severely injured, but that I hadn't had a chance to talk to him before seeing Jesse.

Even though his chosen profession now was healing the little children, Jesse had been raised on a sprawling ranch in the hard-scrabble California of the 1800s. He hadn't spent his youth, as Paul and my stepbrothers had, skateboarding, surfing, and playing video games. Jesse had grown up chopping wood, putting up fences, and killing things—and I'm not talking about chickens. As warm and loving as Jesse was, there was a part of him—a part that had nothing to do with the time he'd spent trapped in the spirit world—that was coldly practical when it came to putting suffering things that couldn't otherwise be saved out of their misery.

Another good reason never to tell him what had happened between Paul and me that night at graduation . . . or what was going on between us now.

Then suddenly there he was, striding across the parking lot, his head down, his fists stuffed into the pockets of his suede jacket, unaware of my presence.

At first.

A second later I saw that ink-dark head lift slowly, as if we had some sort of telepathic bond—which I prayed we did not, or he'd know the dirty thoughts I was having about the way he looked in those tight-fitting, strategically faded jeans. Our gazes instantly locked.

And then somehow I was across the few dozen yards of pavement that had separated us and in his strong embrace.

"*Querida*," he whispered in my hair as he held me. "It's going to be all right. Father Dominic is going to be fine."

"You don't know that."

"I don't, but he's strong. So much running around, chasing after students and spirits, has kept him healthy all these years."

"Until now."

He slipped a finger beneath my chin to tilt my face toward his. "Susannah, are you *crying*?"

I released him and stepped quickly, though reluctantly, away. His embrace was my favorite place to be, besides his bed, which smelled deliciously of him.

"Of course I'm not crying," I said, brushing a quick hand against my cheek. "I never cry. It's allergies. They're terrible this time of year."

Jesse gave me one of his lopsided grins, which they should trademark and sell on TV as a female sexual enhancement supplement. They'd make millions.

"It would be all right if you cried," he said. "I like it when you do. It gives me an excuse to play that overprotective nineteenth-century macho man you're always talking about."

"Like you ever need an excuse to do that. I heard you spoke to Dr. Patel. What did he say?"

"He says the father faces a long recovery, but if he can make it through the next twenty-four hours without infection, he should pull through."

I had to turn away to look very closely at the statue of St. Francis that stood beside the hospital's entrance, because I sensed a leak from the corner of one eye. Fortunately it was an old-fashioned statue in the same vein as the statue of Junípero Serra in the courtyard outside my office at the school (only the head had never been severed by an irate NCDP), so there was a lot to look at. Gathered at the feet of St. Francis were bronze sculptures of grateful animals he'd saved, instead of the Native Americans Father Junípero had enslaved.

"Susannah," Jesse said, reaching out to stroke my hair. I don't think my trick of staring at the statue was fooling him.

"So in other words," I said, trying to keep my voice steady, "he really could die. Emily said so."

"Emily? Emily's only five, and not a trained medical professional." Jesse put his arm around me and pulled me close again. His warmth was comforting, especially as the sun had begun to go down, and the air had become cooler. "He's very badly hurt. But he's also very stubborn, as you know."

I shuddered and buried my head against his chest the way Jesse's cat, Spike, sometimes did on the odd occasions when he was feeling affectionate.

"Jesse, it's my fault." My fingers tightened on the soft brown suede of his jacket. It was a coat I'd bought him for Christmas last year, one he'd chastised me gently for spending too much money on, but I'd refused to exchange it for "something more sensible." "I should never have let him go over there alone. I don't know what I was thinking. He said he could handle it, that Lucia was angry with me, not him, and so wouldn't hurt him, and that it was his responsibility because he should have seen her when he married Kelly and Becca's dad. But I should have known something like this was going to happen. He's so old, so far from the top of his game, and she's so strong, I should have—"

"You should have what? Tied him to his chair? You know Father Dominic better than anyone, Susannah. Once he has an idea in his head, no one can stop him. He has to have things his way."

"I know. But if he dies . . . if he dies . . ."

I couldn't even form the words out loud. If Father Dominic died, I would have lost the best mentor I'd ever had, and, absurdly enough, one of the best friends I'd ever had, as well. If someone had told me that the first day I'd walked into his office so many years ago, I'd never have believed it. What could an agnostic girl from Brooklyn and an elderly Catholic priest from California possibly have in common?

The ability to help wayward spirits find their way home, it turned out . . . even if, as Father Dom had pointed out, we hadn't always agreed on our methodology.

Without Father Dominic, I'd never have learned it was better to ask questions first, and save my punches for later. I'd never have found out who Jesse really was—the love of my life—or had the courage to bring him back into the land of the living. I certainly wouldn't be spending the rest of my life with him . . . I hoped.

Even though I said none of these things out loud, Jesse, as usual, knew what I was thinking.

"If he dies, we'll have lost the only person who ever believed in us," he said. "And who'll marry us? It won't be the same to be married by anyone else, Susannah. I won't have it."

"Jesse." I lifted my head from his chest. I felt his arms tense, and knew what he was about to say next. "Don't—"

"Don't tell me *don't*, Susannah." He dropped his arms. "You know why I came here."

I did, but for some reason I felt like if I didn't say it out loud, it wouldn't be true. My boyfriend didn't want to exorcise anyone. He couldn't. "To see Father Dominic, of course."

The darkness in his gaze had nothing to do with the color of his irises. I won't lie. It frightened me. "No. There's nothing I can do for him. He's in good hands. The best. I came to see you, to find out what you've learned. I need to know where she's buried, Susannah."

I squared my jaw. "What good will that do?"

"You know what. So I can send her back to hell, where she belongs."

quince

"Jesse, *no*."

I dragged him beneath the atrium that covered the circular drive where families pulled up to drop off nonemergency patients. There was a little gazebo not far from the St. Francis statue. The shelter was probably intended, with seating inside and mounted ashtrays nearby, for smokers who needed to step outside the waiting room to take a break, but we were the only two occupying it at the moment.

The sound of the bubbling water in the fountain would hopefully keep our voices from being overheard, and the bright pink and purple flowers on the bougainvillea vines crawling up the gazebo's walls would mask us from prying gazes.

"Jesse, you can't exorcise her." I pushed him onto a concrete bench inside the gazebo, then sat down next to him. I was glad for my leggings, since Father Dominic had been right: my skirt really was too short, and even through the cotton/Lycra blend, the stone was freezing against the back of my legs. "You don't know what happened to her to make her the way she is."

"I don't care what happened to her," he said evenly. "I care about what she did. She caused that man, the best friend we ever had, a concussion, three fractured ribs, and a shattered hip bone."

"But you don't know how Lucia died."

"I don't care how she died. All I care about is making sure she can't hurt the living, especially you or anyone else I care about. And I have everything I need to do that in my car right now."

"Oh, that's just great, Jesse. And did anyone at the mission try to stop you when you broke into the tabernacle?"

He raised one of those dark eyebrows. "I didn't have to break in. Father Dominic gave me a key years ago."

That stung. Father Dominic had never trusted *me* with a key, and he'd known me longer than he'd known Jesse.

"Besides," Jesse went on, "everyone who might have noticed is upstairs in the ICU, waiting to see how the father recovers."

"Which you should be doing, instead of running off to the cemetery to exorcise the soul of a frightened little girl."

"That 'frightened little girl' as you call her nearly murdered my future wife."

I had to suppress a smile at the word *wife*—I couldn't help it. I was still annoyed with him, though. "CeeCee found the article about the alleged accident that killed her. Will you read it first before you go tearing off to cast out Satan?"

His jaw tightened. He was annoyed with me, too. "Only if it says where she's buried."

"Jesse, that's harsh. What if I'd exorcised you when we first met?"

"You *did*."

"Not on purpose. And I felt terrible about it later, when I found out you weren't so bad."

"Bad *looking*."

"That isn't fair, and you know it. I fell in love with *you*, not your looks. How could I not, when you've saved my life so many times?" I reached out to squeeze one of his biceps—impressively large, especially for a physician—through a suede sleeve. "Of course your looks don't hurt."

I must be losing my touch, because he was unmoved. "This girl is trying to destroy lives, Susannah, not save them."

"Agreed. But there could be mitigating circumstances." I tugged my phone from my bag. "Read the article. It does say where she's buried."

He held out his hand. "Then I'll read it."

I pulled up the article CeeCee had sent me, then passed the phone to him. "I doubt you'll still think she's evil after you read this. More scared, like Aunt Pru says."

He lowered his eyebrows with disapproval as he took the phone. "CeeCee's aunt Prudence suffers from delusions."

"Right," I muttered. "Doctors. Everyone's got a disorder."

"Counselors," he shot back. "Everyone needs therapy."

I rolled my eyes, then put my hands into the pockets of my leather jacket to keep them warm as he read, glancing from his face toward the triplets, whom I could view past the bougainvillea, through the windows of the waiting room. They'd run out of money for snacks, and were now ricocheting around the triage area, jacked up on all the forbidden sugar they'd consumed. Peggy, the receptionist, had risen from her post behind the reception desk, looking stricken, begging them to stop. The girls were ignoring her.

Good luck, Peggy.

I'd read the article CeeCee had sent so many times I knew it practically by heart, along with her text.

CeeCee Hey here's the info you wanted. Lucia Martinez, 7 yrs old, died 9 yrs ago. I think I remember when this happened. Sad.

You owe me dinner and a movie.

PS He called!
Nov 17 2:15 PM

She meant Adam had called. He'd called because I'd reminded him that he should, but of course she didn't need to know this.

I was happy he'd called her. The article, however, hadn't left me feeling nearly as good.

SACRED TRINITY STUDENT KILLED IN
HORSEBACK-RIDING ACCIDENT

Carmel, CA—A student who attended the Academy of the Scared Trinity all-girls school in Pebble Beach died Saturday afternoon from an injury sustained after falling from a horse.

The Monterey County Sheriff's Office confirmed the identity of the student as Lucia Martinez. Martinez was 7 years old.

The accident took place in Del Monte Forest along one of the many riding paths maintained by the

Academy of the Sacred Trinity Equestrian Center, at which Martinez was taking riding lessons.

According to witnesses, Martinez lost control of the animal after it became startled during a routine trail ride.

"Both horse and rider disappeared into the woods," said Jennifer Dunleavy, spokeswoman for Sacred Trinity. "One of our instructors went after her, searching and calling, but couldn't find either of them. There are more than thirty miles of trail that run deep into the forest. The school sent out additional riders to help with the search, and notified police, as well, who sent reinforcements. Even if they'd found her sooner . . . but they didn't."

Martinez was reported missing at approximately 10:30 a.m. Saturday, said Deputy Eric Robertson, a sheriff's spokesman. She wasn't found until approximately 5:30 p.m., seven miles from where she was last seen.

Authorities believe Martinez became dislodged from her horse after it attempted to jump a small ravine, and fell, striking her head. She was wearing a helmet, but suffered a broken neck.

"Lucia was an exemplary rider for her age," said Martin Shorecraft, director of athletics at Sacred Heart. "But we still took every precaution for her health and safety. Sometimes accidents like this simply happen."

Martinez, who lived in Pacific Grove, was declared dead at 8:30 p.m. on Saturday at St. Francis Medical Center in Monterey. The medical examiner ruled the cause of death as asphyxiation.

A spokesperson for Sacred Trinity who asked not

to be identified said that the horse that the child was riding has been put down.

Martinez's death elicited immediate and mournful responses from the community.

"Lucia will live on forever in the hearts and minds of all those she touched here at Sacred Trinity," said Father Francisco Rivera, the headmaster at Sacred Trinity. "We are deeply saddened to hear of her passing."

"Lucia was a sweet and happy girl who lived life to the fullest," said Anna Martinez, the victim's grandmother. "She always wanted a horse, and to learn to ride. Both those wishes came true. She died at the happiest moment of her life."

Lucia's funeral will be held at 1 p.m. a week from Saturday at the Sacred Trinity Chapel. She will be laid to rest at the San Carlos Cemetery in Monterey, California.

There was a photo that accompanied the article. In it, a solemn, round-faced little girl with long blond bangs and curls down to her shoulders gazed into the camera, her chubby hands folded neatly on a table before her. It was a school photo—she was in her Trinity uniform—so smiling wasn't strictly encouraged, but her large brown eyes weren't smiling, either.

Maybe Lucia was just a kid who'd always been unhappy, despite her grandmother's assertion.

Or maybe she'd sensed her tragic fate to come.

When Jesse lowered my phone, I asked, "Well? Do you still want to kill her?"

"She's already dead," he said calmly. "I can't kill her. But I can keep her from killing someone else."

"You know what I mean, Jesse. Look at her photo. That girl

was scared to death of something. And I don't believe she died from falling off a horse."

"I don't see how you got that from reading this article."

Jesse was nothing if not stubborn. Well, you sort of had to be if you were going to survive what he had and come out of it with your sanity intact.

"I got it from having common sense, Jesse. If Lucia died at the happiest moment of her life, like old granny Martinez says, why hasn't she moved on to her next life, or gone up to heaven to eat cotton candy and play the harp all day, or whatever it is that happens to people who really do die without having left behind any loose ends? Instead she's down here on earth, guarding her friend Becca to within an inch of her life. Something went on in those woods, something no one at Sacred Trinity is talking about because they either don't know, or are covering it up. But Lucia knows. That could be why she was killed, to keep her quiet."

"Is that why they killed the horse, too, Susannah? To keep it from giving evidence of what it knew?"

I blinked up at him, not certain if he was being serious or sarcastic. With Jesse, it was sometimes hard to tell, especially at moments like this, when his expression was so completely impassive.

Almost completely impassive. Even though it had grown dark enough outside to trigger the landscape lighting, and the cars pulling into the parking lot had their headlights switched on, I was able to see that his brown eyes had cleared of the shadows that had been hovering there before.

"I knew that part would get to you." I couldn't help grinning at him. "You have a soft spot for horses."

"I have a soft spot for *children*," he corrected me. "Especially children who've been neglected or treated cruelly."

"Which Lucia obviously was—"

"I wouldn't say *obviously*. We don't have evidence of that . . .

yet," he added when I inhaled to protest. "But I'll admit it's worth investigating, if we can do so without ending up here, like Father Dominic."

"Fine." I snatched my phone from his hand. "We can start with the investigating I did online after I got the article from CeeCee."

"My favorite kind." His tone was wry. "No one is likely to be put in mortal danger while doing online investigations. What did you find out?"

I gave him a sour look. "The Martinezes did move away after the alleged accident like Father Dominic said, but they didn't go far, only up to Marin County. They own a few vineyards. She's got two older brothers. There are no reports on file of anything ever happening to them. And after her death, the family was so heartbroken they adopted two more little girls from the foster care system. Special needs." I showed him the photos I'd found earlier in the day on the Martinez family's Facebook page. "See? Cute, right? They have llamas on their farm, too. Who doesn't love a llama?"

Jesse glanced at the photos and nodded, though he refused to utter the words *cute* or *llama* out loud. He was too manly. "That puts the Martinez family in the clear for abuse, then. For the adoption to go through, social services would have had to thoroughly investigate them, and visit often. Obviously, they passed."

"Which is probably why Lucia isn't following *them* around. She's not worried about them. She's worried about her friend Becca."

"Clearly," he said. "But why?"

"That's what I can't figure out. Whoever was able to get close enough to Lucia to kill her must still have access somehow to Becca . . . whether Becca knows it or not. That's the only explanation I can think of for why Lucia is so protective of her."

"Someone from the riding class?"

"I thought about that. But Becca says she doesn't like horses, despite the pendant she wears, which is shaped like one. I checked Google Earth, and there aren't any stables on the Walters property, nor is Becca enrolled in riding classes anymore. I wouldn't be, either, if I were her, after what happened to her friend."

"At the hospital in cases of child abuse, it's almost always someone in the home. If it wasn't someone in Lucia's home . . ." Jesse let his voice trail off suggestively.

"You mean Lance Arthur Walters? He's the obvious suspect. He'd have had access to Lucia, if the two girls really were friends growing up. He'd be my number-one suspect, except for one small problem."

"What's that?"

"If Lance Arthur Walters killed Lucia, why hasn't she pushed *him* down the stairs, the way she did Father Dom? But I checked, and Becca's dad has never been admitted to the ER here, not even for so much as a bee sting."

Jesse frowned with disapproval. "Susannah, how could you possibly get that information? Hospital records are supposed to be private."

"Oh, please. Nothing's private when you're a billionaire. Every move that guy and his family make is in the news. That's how I found out about Becca's mom."

"What happened to her mother?"

"When Becca was talking about her mother, she mentioned an accident. I thought she meant Lucia's accident, but she didn't. The first Mrs. Walters used to host a yearly society luncheon at their house to raise money for breast cancer research. The year Lucia died, she canceled it—not because of what happened to Lucia, but because Mrs. Walters broke her ankle in a fall. The following year, the luncheon was held by someone else because

Becca's mom no longer lived in Pebble Beach. She'd divorced Becca's dad and moved to Manhattan."

Jesse looked skeptical. "You think the poor woman was driven from her own home—and child—by a spirit she couldn't see?"

"I do. And if what happened to Mrs. Walters was anything like what happened to me at the pool last night, I don't blame her. Keep in mind she couldn't see her attacker. It must have been terrifying to her."

"But you don't think the woman killed the girl, do you?"

"No, I don't. Because a couple of years after that, there was a new Mrs. Walters—not Kelly, a different one. And she, too, suffered a fall. She was no longer able to host the Carmel-by-the-Sea Go Red for Women luncheon to raise money for heart disease research due to a broken wrist—"

"They really report these things?" Jesse interrupted, disgusted. "Why is this news?"

"Because," I said. I often had to explain to Jesse why things like what certain celebrities were wearing—or who they were dating, or divorcing—was news. He still had trouble believing why anyone would be interested. Of course, he also had trouble understanding why it took so long for the U.S. to get involved in World War II. "These fund-raisers are where all the socialites go to show off their new designer shoes and handbags. And of course they do some good for charity, too. And for people like me, who are trying to uncover clues to solve a crime. That's how I found out the second Mrs. Walters left Becca's dad, too, probably because she was being haunted by an unseen, menacing force—"

Jesse could take it no longer. He burst out, "If I had these women come into my ER as patients, two wives in a row with fractured limbs, I'd suspect the husband of abuse, Susannah, not an unseen, menacing force."

"Of course you would," I said. "Because you're a doctor, and a good one. And if we didn't know for a fact that there's the tortured soul of a murdered child living in that man's house, I'd say you were right. But we do know that. Combine that fact with the fact that Becca's dad is constantly in the news for traveling somewhere to give a speech about something, or to open a new branch of his company, or donate a giant check to some hospital in some foreign country—"

"I don't see how that makes him innocent of abusing his former wives, Susannah."

"The guy is never home! I'm guessing he barely even saw his former wives, let alone his daughter. So how could he be the one abusing them? It doesn't add up. What does add up is this: the people Lucia attacked so far—me, Father Dominic, and the two previous Mrs. Walters—all have one thing in common. *Becca.* I was attacked when Lucia misinterpreted my putting disinfectant on Becca's wound as 'hurting her.' We know Father Dominic ended up in the emergency room for trying to help Becca, and I'm guessing that's what sent the two Mrs. Walters there, too. *That's* what sets Lucia off. Like Aunt Pru said, she's frightened, and she's in pain. She may not even be able to tell the difference between helping and hurting."

Jesse continued to look skeptical. "And Mr. Walters?"

"Maybe he's a monster, but only to his daughter's friends. Or maybe he's completely innocent, and doesn't know how to show affection, and keeps getting serially remarried out of the hope that his new wife will take care of the problem of his maladjusted kid. It's no wonder Becca's so depressed, and has had to transfer schools so many times. She can't ever get close to anyone, because whenever she tries, Lucia pushes them away—literally."

The skepticism in Jesse's dark eyes turned to thoughtful concern. "But now your friend Kelly is living there—"

"Do you think I haven't thought of that? Kelly's in real danger.

Then again, based on the behavior I've seen her exhibit around Becca so far, she might be the last person we have to worry about Lucia hurting."

He winced. "Susannah."

"I know, that's harsh. But, Jesse, you didn't see Kelly yesterday in the office. I did. Trust me, if it's true Lucia's coming after anyone who gets too close to Becca, then Becca's dad picked the perfect new wife. Not to speak ill of a former classmate."

"Didn't Kelly used to go out with Paul Slater?"

"Oh, yeah, a long time ago." I managed a derisive laugh. "That's ancient history. God, Jesse, don't you read the online Mission Academy alumni newsletter? Get with the times."

He shook his head, then slipped an arm around my shoulders, bringing me close for a hug. "How can someone so young and so beautiful be so jaded and cynical?"

"Too much time hanging around with dead people?"

He released me from the hug, but kept the arm around my shoulders. "I wouldn't doubt it. All right, I suppose it does make sense that Lucia is protecting Becca from whoever it was that hurt her. And it's a good bet it wasn't a horse."

I snuggled against him. "I knew the horse thing was what was going to change your mind about exorcising her."

"It wasn't the horse. It was you, as you know perfectly well."

"Sure. You may have everyone else fooled with your pursuit of a medical degree, Dr. de Silva, but I know the truth. You're really a vaquero at heart. Admit it."

"I've told you repeatedly that I never herded cattle in my life. Sometimes I think you're the one who needs to have the demons exorcised out of her."

"You're probably right," I said, enjoying the close-up view I was getting down the vee of his shirt, and the rock-hard feel of those solidly carved chest and shoulder muscles. "Maybe we should head to your car. Since you've already got all the necessary equipment, you could start driving the devil out of me right now."

The lopsided grin I loved so much appeared. "I think for you it would take more than a few vials of holy water."

"That wasn't the kind of equipment I was talking about." I slid my lips along his neck while my hand crept playfully toward his belt buckle.

"Susannah." His fingers locked around my wrist in an iron grip. "Need I remind you that this is my place of work?"

"No one can see us in here."

"Uncle Jesse!"

Suddenly three small, plaid-skirted projectiles came sailing through the entrance to the gazebo to launch themselves against my fiancé. Their timing was, as always, terrible.

"*Oof*," said Jesse, wincing painfully as Mopsy kneed him in the exact spot I'd been about to place my hand.

"Do you have any gum for us, Uncle Jesse?" the girls cried, patting down the pockets of his brown suede jacket.

Jesse had long been a favorite of my stepnieces due to his habit of carrying bubble gum with him. He was the one who'd taught them how to blow bubbles. It was a skill I'd shown him one day while waiting in an endless line at the Department of Motor Vehicles. While he'd declared gum chewing a disgusting habit in adults (bubble gum had not yet been invented the first time he'd been around), he now found it beneficial in entertaining his younger patients while they were receiving painful medical procedures.

"I don't know," Jesse said, pretending to extract a stick from behind Flopsy's ear. "Do I?"

The girls shrieked with appreciation. The insides of their mouths had been stained red from whatever they'd extracted from the vending machines.

"Hey." Their father strolled up behind them, looking sheepish. "The nurse said you guys were out here. Sorry it took me so long. Thanks for looking after them, especially after what happened. Is Father D going to be all right?"

I rose from the bench and crossed to Brad's side so we could speak without the girls overhearing.

"We don't know," I said. "Jesse said if he makes it through the next twenty-four hours, he should be okay. Where *were* you?"

"Oh, you know." Brad looked down at the sidewalk, his hands in the trouser pockets of his ill-fitting suit. He kicked a fallen bud of bright pink bougainvillea into the grass. "Debbie's dad wouldn't let me leave, even though I told him about the kids. He made me inventory all the new SUVs we got in at the lot today. It was his way of getting back at me, I guess, for fighting with Deb. But of course all it did was make *your* life hell. I'm really sorry. Debbie couldn't come pick them up because she and Kelly have Pilates or yoga or some goddamn thing on Thursday nights."

I winced. It didn't help that the only job Brad had ever been able to keep was with his father-in-law, Debbie Mancuso's dad, the Mercedes King of Carmel. Trying to keep up with the mortgage payments on the overpriced home on the golf course Debbie insisted they *had* to have in Carmel Valley Ranch (because that's where all her friends who couldn't afford houses in Pebble Beach lived), plus pay the fees for the girls' private school education wasn't easy. My mom and Andy helped out where they could, and both Jake and I had given Brad a few loans, too.

But I didn't know how long the two of them were going to be able to keep it together, especially since Debbie insisted on being a stay-at-home mom, even with the girls gone all day (the mission believed a full-day kindergarten program improved cognitive development. It also improved the mission's tuition coffers).

Debbie said she needed the "me" time to be the best mom

she could be. A lot of her "me" time seemed to be spent working out at the gym with a personal trainer, buying clothes, and going to lunch with the likes of Kelly Prescott Walters.

Of course, Brad took a lot of "me" time for himself, playing golf and partying at Snail Crossing.

I totally understood their need for so much "me" time, since being the parents of rambunctious triplets (and the spouses of one another) had to be really exhausting.

"Brad, you've got to find a new job. One where you aren't dependent on your father-in-law for your income."

"I know." He kicked at another dried bougainvillea bud. "But who'd want to hire me? I don't have a college degree. I barely managed to graduate high school. I know I screwed up. At least I have them." His gaze rested tenderly on his three daughters, who were now having a contest to see who could stretch their gum into the longest strand.

My own gaze rested on Brad—not exactly tenderly, but with more affection than in the past. He'd driven me crazy the entire time we'd been forced by our parents to live together—so much so that I'd given him the private nickname Dopey, and often wished for his premature death.

But his love for his daughters—and the fact that I rarely, if ever, had to watch him drink directly from a milk carton anymore—mostly made up for that.

"Hey!" he yelled at the girls, startling me. "What have I told you before? Gum stays in your mouth!"

That's when I noticed something sitting beside Jesse on the bench, something I hadn't seen earlier because it hadn't been there earlier. It was white and fuzzy, with brown spots on it. It was shaped like a stuffed horse.

Lucia's stuffed horse.

Jesse noticed the direction of my stare. He'd never seen Lucia's horse, and had no way of knowing it belonged to her. But he knew it didn't belong to the girls, because it was gleaming with the faint otherworldly glow all paranormal objects give off when they've recently made the journey from their dimension to ours.

That was why Jesse reached out instinctively to knock it from the bench, even though it could not hurt the girls. Not being mediators, they couldn't see it. Still, his hypervigilance was not something he could turn on and off like a switch.

It turned out not to matter, however.

"*That's mine,*" Mopsy said, and snatched the horse from beneath his fingers, then hugged it to her heart.

dieciseis

"I don't think this is a good idea," Jesse said.

"Your objection's duly noted. And you're obviously not the only one. Debbie doesn't seem too happy about it, either."

It was much later. Jesse and I were seated in uncomfortable lawn chairs beside the fire pit in the backyard of Brad and Debbie's three-bedroom house in Carmel Valley Ranch.

Brad's fire pit paled in comparison to the one his older brother had constructed at Snail Crossing. Jake's was made of limestone and was sunk into the ground and surrounded by luxurious built-in couches in a wooded area of the Crossing's backyard, not far from the redwood hot tub (which comfortably fit ten).

Brad's fire pit was an overturned metal drum that he'd placed not far from the girls' swing set, engendering the wrath of his wife, who felt this was unsafe.

This wasn't all that had engendered Debbie's wrath.

"You don't have to stay," I whispered to Jesse, for what had to have been the fiftieth time since we'd pulled through the gated entrance to the golf resort community in which my stepbrother and his wife lived.

"Of course I have to stay. I'm not going to leave my future wife alone in a house that's being haunted by a murderous demon child."

"We don't know that she's haunting it. And I thought we established that she probably isn't murderous, just overprotective. A lot like someone else I know ..." I let my voice trail off suggestively.

He ignored me. "Then why, precisely, are we here?"

"To make sure the girls are okay."

We had to keep our voices low because Brad and Debbie were inside the house having what they called "a discussion," but what I thought might better be described as a domestic dispute. Debbie hadn't been too happy when she'd come home from Pilates to find that she had houseguests.

I could understand it. I probably wouldn't be too thrilled, either, to come home from my exercise class to find that my stepsister-in-law and her boyfriend had shown up at my house with their overnight bags.

Still, it was for a good cause. Too bad we couldn't explain what it was.

Every once in a while we could hear Brad's and Debbie's voices through the thin walls and vinyl siding of their bi/split level. Their home was lovely, but it hadn't been made of the soundest construction material. I wondered if Slater Properties had had something to do with it.

"Why did you have to pick tonight, of all nights, to invite them over?" I could hear Debbie demanding with perfect clarity from inside their kitchen (all stainless-steel appliances, but the dishwasher and trash compactor were often broken, usually at the same time).

"I told you. They invited *themselves* over, Debbie." Brad sounded tired. "Something about a class Suze is taking. She needs to observe kids in their home environment overnight."

"Great. So she chooses tonight to do it? With no advance warning?"

"She's my sister. What was I supposed to do?"

"She's your *step*sister. And you could have said no. God, you are such a pushover, Brad. You let everyone walk all over you. Did you lose your balls as well as your brains when you got that concussion playing football in high school?"

"Hey," Brad said. "Could you keep it down? They can probably hear you. And it was wrestling, not football."

"Ask me how much I care, Brad."

"You know, I really don't understand it," I said to Jesse, taking a sip of the wine we'd brought, along with a couple of pizzas. "How do you think it happened?"

"Father Dominic was probably taken off guard," Jesse said. He reached out to squeeze my hand reassuringly. "But like I said, he's strong. His vitals were looking much better before we left."

I remembered the father's pale and battered face as I'd last seen it underneath the fluorescent lights of his hospital room, how sunken his eyes had looked beneath those paper-thin lids, the frailness of his hands resting on the blue blanket, the tangle of IV tubes flowing from them.

If that was "much better," I'd hate to know what "worse" looked like.

"And we made good use of those items I 'borrowed' from the church," Jesse went on. "That Medal of Mary we hung over his bed should keep him safe tonight, along with all the holy water."

"That isn't what I meant," I said. "I meant the girls. How could *that* have happened? How could they be *mediators*?"

"Oh, that," Jesse said. "Well, as you so astutely explained to me only last night, Susannah, when a man and a woman like each other very much, they make love, and when they do, if they don't use protection—like your stepbrother and sister-in-law— sometimes the man's sperm can fertilize the woman's egg, and if either of them is carrying the genetic chromosome for com- municating with the dead, then there's a chance their baby could turn out to be—"

I punched him in the shoulder, causing him to slosh some of the wine in his glass. But it was okay, since Max—whom we'd stopped off at the Crossing to bring along, as he's such an excel- lent ghost detector—jumped up immediately, eager for the possi- bility that some food might have been spilled. Disappointed that it was only wine, however, he lay back down at our feet with a sigh.

"Ow," Jesse said, rubbing his shoulder where I'd punched him.

"I didn't hit you that hard. And that's exactly what I mean. I don't think either the Ackerman family or the Mancusos are carrying the mediator gene. I didn't meet a single person at Brad and Debbie's wedding who seemed remotely intuitive. Did you?"

"No." Jesse poured more wine into his glass. "And sometimes I think you don't know your own strength. But I've always felt that your stepbrother David is very perceptive. Occasionally I was able to communicate with him back when I was . . ."

"—dead," I finished for him when he hesitated to say the word.

"Yes. Thank you."

"No problem."

I took a sip from my glass and looked up at the stars—what I could see of them through the many electric wires intersect- ing the sky across the yard from Brad and Debbie's neighbors' houses—and wondered how I was ever going to get over to Car- mel Hills to salt the old house now. It seemed that fate, in the form of Lucia Martinez, was conspiring against me.

"I agree, David's a really insightful kid," I said. I was speaking quietly so neither the girls, who had upon occasion opened their bedroom window to spy on us after being put to bed, nor Debbie or Brad would overhear me. "But David's not those girls' dad. Brad is. And Debbie's their mom. Brad is much less intuitive than good old Max here, and Debbie thinks vaccines *cause* diseases. So how can their kids see ghosts? And how are we ever going to explain that to their parents?"

"We're not going to," Jesse said. "Any more than I explained to them that in a previous lifetime I watched entire families die from smallpox. If Debbie doesn't believe the substantial scientific proof that vaccines will protect her children from disease, how likely do you think she is to believe that they—and you and I—can see and speak to ghosts?"

"Uh, very? Especially now, since that toy the girls had belongs to the ghost of a child who died before they were born—a child who tried to murder their school principal this afternoon. The girls shouldn't have been able to see it, let alone have possession of it, unless they're mediators, which they can't be, because no one on either side of their parents' families has ever been a mediator—"

"That we know of."

"Fine, that we know of. And yet, they could see that toy. And Lucia, too, apparently."

Jesse couldn't deny it was true. When I'd snatched the toy away from the triplets and asked them where it had come from, Cotton-tail had volunteered, "He belongs to our friend Lucy. But she lets us borrow him sometimes."

"Yeah," Mopsy had said. "Whenever we want, basically."

A chill had passed over me even though I'd been wearing my black leather jacket. It had gotten worse when their father had laughed and asked, "You've never met Lucy, Suze? What's wrong with you? Lucy's their favorite new friend. They play with Lucy all the time at school, don't you, guys?"

"Sometimes," Flopsy had corrected him. "Sometimes she comes to school, sometimes she doesn't. She wasn't in school today."

"But she's here now, isn't she?" Brad had asked. "Lucy's standing over there, right, Emma?"

He'd pointed at one of the bougainvillea vines to the left of Mopsy.

The girls had glanced in the direction their father was pointing, then looked scornfully away.

"No, Daddy," Flopsy had said in a pitying voice. "Lucy isn't here right now. Lucy went home."

Brad had given me another sheepish grin and shrugged. "Oops, sorry. Lucy isn't here right now. I guess she left her toy behind." He'd said the word *toy* like it had quotation marks around it.

I'd looked from the girls to their father, my feeling of horror turning to one of incredulity.

"Wait a minute," I'd said to my stepbrother. "Can you see this?" I'd held up the stuffed horse.

"Sure," Brad had said. "Of course I can see it." Then he'd given me a broad wink.

I still hadn't been able to tell if Brad could see the toy or was only play-acting for the girls.

"If you see it," I'd said to him, "tell me what it is."

"An elephant, of course," Brad had said.

The girls had fallen over themselves with laughter that their tall, invincible father had gotten the answer wrong.

So Debbie and Brad's daughters were mediators. How could I not have recognized the signs until a very dangerous—and very angry—ghost had decided to use them to deliver a message to me? I couldn't fathom it.

But that's what Lucia's giving them her toy at the hospital, right under my nose, had to be. A message.

But about what? To say what? That she could get to the people I loved—the most vulnerable and innocent of all—anytime she wanted?

Hadn't she already delivered this message by nearly killing Father Dominic?

So many things had begun to fall into place. Like this great-grandmother the girls were always talking about, the one who'd broken her hip, then died of pneumonia. When they mentioned things she'd said, they weren't things she'd said to them before she'd died, but *after*.

And their extraordinarily high energy level, and frequent outbursts, including the one the day before, when they had sensed all the way in the kindergarten classroom Lucia's attack on me in the office, and Sister Ernestine had been summoned to calm them down.

All of these were signs not that they had ADHD, as Sister Ernestine suggested, but that they could—and often did—communicate with the dead.

This gift—as Father Dominic chose to call it—affected different people in different ways. It had caused Paul's younger brother Jack to withdraw into himself, giving him night terrors and eventually agoraphobia. I'm sure my therapist, Dr. Jo, probably would have said he lacked the "inner resiliency" to handle so much psychic energy coming at him all at once, until I'd shown him how to process it.

Other people, however—like Paul, and my stepnieces—found this psychic energy stimulating rather than draining, and enjoyed having twice as many playmates as their friends (even if no one but them could see them) . . . or making twice as much money because of it.

I was already feeling a lot of guilt for not having picked up sooner rather than later on all the clues about the triplets, and for many of the things I'd done to NCDPs in front of them.

The question now was, how much of it had they understood? And just what, precisely, was their relationship with Lucia? Were their lives really in danger from the little girl? Or was she, as the girls insisted, a playmate? It seemed hard to believe that creature who'd tried to drown me in the pool and nearly killed Father Dominic and seemed slowly to be draining the life from Becca Walters was on friendly terms with anyone.

I wished, for the hundredth time that evening, that Father Dom were not lying unconscious on the third floor of St. Francis Medical Center. He would have known exactly what to do—not only about the triplets, but about Lucia.

Then again, his conviction that he'd known what to do about Lucia was how he'd ended up in the ICU in the first place.

We were on our own with this one.

We'd had no luck questioning the girls back at the hospital, nor later when we'd arrived bearing pizza. Brad had been anxious to get them bathed and fed before Mommy got home, and the girls had been too excited about having Uncle Jesse and Aunt Suze over to rationally answer any of my questions about their new friend Lucy.

Then Mommy had returned. Debbie had been none too happy to find us there, even though in addition to pizza, we'd brought her favorite wine—the good kind, from a vineyard in the area that sold their bottles to expensive restaurants in New York City for three times what they cost locally. Debbie had drunk a whole bottle on her own and was working on a second one.

"I just don't get it," I said to Jesse as he poured me some of the very good wine from an extra bottle we'd hidden in the car. "Brad used to tease me that he knew I had a boy in my room, back in high school, because he said he heard us talking. But I think he only overheard *my* end of the conversation. He never actually saw you. And Debbie never did, either. So how can their children be mediators?"

"Neither of your parents saw spirits. Obviously it can skip a generation. Maybe even two or more." Jesse poured a splash of pinot noir into his own glass. "And we don't know that the girls are full-fledged mediators, necessarily. Children tend to be more sensitive in general to paranormal phenomena than adults. They're more imaginative, and more open-minded."

"*Sensitive?* Did you see those girls fighting over that horse, Jesse? They each grabbed a leg and pulled. If I hadn't stopped them, they'd have ripped it apart, then killed each other. I wouldn't exactly call the Ackerman girls sensitive."

"Well ... a better description might be high-spirited, like their aunt."

"I'm not even related to them by blood, remember? None of that is from me."

I shivered in the cool night air. The fire from Brad's pit wasn't doing much to cut the chill, though the pungent smell of the smoke was pleasant, as was the crackling sound of the wood as it burned.

"What I don't get is how this could have happened right under our noses, without us ever noticing. I had no clue. Did you?"

"The girls had that private language," he reminded me. "They spoke it among themselves until last year."

I straightened. "That's right! How could I forget? You even wrote that paper on it—cryptophasia. Debbie was so worried the mission was going to put them into special education."

"But it's not unusual for multiples. There've been many incidents of siblings—mainly twins, but occasionally triplets and quads—developing their own language. And, like your nieces, they usually grow out of it by the time they get to school."

"That's why it took so long for us to catch on." I relaxed a little. "And all of us thinking it was so cute probably only encouraged them to use it more, and be *more* secretive. Well, all of us except Debbie. She didn't think it was cute. And she was right! Jesse, they must have been talking to each other about the ghosts they were seeing. Could we have been bigger idiots?"

"I think you're being a little hard on yourself," Jesse said mildly.

"Do you really think Lucia plays with them, like they said, or is she only setting them up to push them down the stairs, too, when they least suspect it?"

"You're the one who keeps insisting she's an innocent child in pain."

"She is," I said hastily. "I'm sure."

"You'd better hope so. Otherwise, if she murders Brad and Debbie in their sleep tonight, we'll end up with custody of your nieces, since we're their appointed legal guardians."

"Why do you think we're here? Brad and Debbie don't have life insurance. We can't let them croak. We'll have to put off having our own kids in order to be able to afford to raise theirs."

He glanced around the balding, toy-strewn lawn and muttered something rapidly in Spanish. I didn't understand what he said, but I understood the tone.

"Oh, my God, Jesse, I was kidding! Would you stop worrying so much about money? I told you, I have plenty. And we can get on the having children of our own thing tonight, if you want." I laid a hand upon his knee. "I'm pretty sure their guest room door has a lock on it."

The look he gave me was crushing. "Really, Susannah? That's where you'd like for us to make love for the first time, in your brother Brad's guest room, where he keeps his wrestling trophies?"

"Stepbrother. God." I removed my hand. "Way to ruin the moment. When are you going to—"

Max leapt suddenly to his feet. But this time it wasn't because either of us had dropped food, or even spilled our wine. Max had sensed something he didn't like in the darkest corner of the yard, over by the girls' pink and white fairy playhouse, big enough only for three very small girls (and one sheepish step-aunt) to squeeze into.

"What—?" I began, but Jesse shushed me.

All the fur on Max's back had risen, and he began to growl, deep in his throat. For an elderly dog of such a mild, friendly temperament, Max had reverted with startling abruptness to his lupine ancestry. His lips were curled to reveal yellowed fangs I was certain I'd never seen before.

Now Jesse placed a hand on *my* knee, but unfortunately it was only to keep me in my seat, since my instinctive reaction had been to rise and head toward the fairy playhouse sitting so benignly in the blackness.

"Stay where you are," Jesse whispered, his own gaze never leaving the innocuous plastic structure. He'd risen and begun following Max, who'd sunk down to his haunches and was creeping toward the dark corner of the yard like a wolf stalking prey.

"I'm sure it's only a raccoon," I said, not believing for an instant that it was only a raccoon.

Jesse confirmed this suspicion when he said, "Max has never growled like that at a raccoon." He'd reached into the pocket of his coat and extracted a small shiny object that he pointed in the direction of the playhouse.

My heart skipped a beat. I don't know if I was more frightened or impressed. "Is that a *gun*?"

"Of course it's not a gun, Susannah. It's a cordless lamp." Jesse noticed I hadn't obeyed his command to stay where I was and was creeping along behind him. "What are you doing? Get back to the house."

"Don't be stupid. What's a cordless lamp? Oh, you mean a flashlight. Oh, *Jesus.*"

Jesse had switched on his flashlight and trained the bright blue beam at the playhouse. As soon as he did, it seemed to startle whatever was inside.

What happened next came in quick succession. Max snarled, then lunged at what came bursting through one of the playhouse's windows.

At first, because it made a flapping sound, I assumed it was a bird.

But since it was also very large and glowing with the intensity of a pair of car headlights, right into my eyes, and let out a scream as piercing and shrill as a kettle left too long on a hot burner, I knew it was no bird. It was something otherworldly.

And it was very unhappy to have been disturbed.

diecisiete

I threw my hands over my head, unable to stifle a shriek of my own. I heard Jesse shout beside me, and Max barking as he turned into a vicious guard dog from a prison movie.

When the shrill banshee shriek finally faded from my ears, I lowered my arms and opened my eyes to find that the light had gone. The yard was once again in darkness, except for the light cast by the thin sliver of moon that had just begun to rise, the warm red glow from the fire pit, and the yellow patches of light cast from the windows of Brad and Debbie's house. In their reflection I could see Max running around the yard, sniffing frantically to locate the quarry he'd flushed from the playhouse.

On either side of Brad and Debbie's house, I saw neighbors parting the curtains and looking through their own windows, wondering what could possibly be going on next door. Nothing at all happened inside Brad and Debbie's, which was odd. How could they not have heard something that had roused the rest of the block?

"What," I whispered to Jesse, knowing we were being watched, "was that?"

The beam from Jesse's cordless lamp was still trained against what now looked like a perfectly ordinary pink and white fairy castle . . . with one exception.

"I think we both know." He'd sunk down to one knee in front of the three-foot door to the fairy castle. He pointed to something in the grass. "She left something behind."

"What is it?" My ears were still ringing from the shrillness of the scream. I wasn't sure if it was Lucia's or my own. "It better not be a bloody horse head, or I will lose my shit."

Jesse prodded it. "A horse head? Oh, you mean *The Godfather*." This was one of the many movies I'd made Jesse watch in order catch up with modern American culture. "No. It's quite small. I think it's a flower."

"A *flower*?" I knelt down in the grass beside him. "Are you sure? That sounds awfully tame for Lucia."

"Yes." He lifted a small purple thing from the grass. It was no larger than a tube of my lip gloss. "A flower. Bougainvillea, I think."

Bougainvillea? Why did that seem familiar?

An uneasy feeling—I'd been having way too many of those lately—came over me. I tapped him on the shoulder. "Give me the cordless lamp. I want to see something."

He passed me the flashlight, and I leaned over to shine the beam inside the playhouse.

Then I froze, my blood suddenly going as cool as the evening air around us. "Crap."

"What is it?" Jesse joined me in peering inside the fairy castle, but when he saw what I'd seen, his curse was in Spanish, not English, so it sounded a little classier.

Flowers. That was all. No bloody body parts, no Satanic symbols scrawled on the wall, no bizarre ritualistic runes made of sticks. Only flowers. Not just a few, either, scattered across the floor the way the triplets had been practicing for when they were in our wedding, but *hundreds* of dead flowers dumped as if someone had been getting rid of their yard waste, using the girls' fairy castle as a trash receptacle.

Except that I knew who that someone was, and the yard waste had been carefully selected. It was *all* bougainvillea, all pink and purple flowers, like the ones that had been growing on the vines on the gazebo outside the hospital, beneath which Jesse and I had sat talking earlier that evening about Lucia Martinez's murder.

As if that wasn't creepy enough, four dolls sat around the table inside the playhouse (the very table at which I'd had pretend tea with the girls last week), their eyes staring unblinkingly at us through the dead bougainvillea blossoms that had been poured over their heads. The dolls were dressed in what I knew to be their "fanciest" outfits—because I'd been the one badgered into buying them—gowns that were now stained brown and yellow by the decomposing flowers.

I'd seen some pretty upsetting stuff done by the souls of the dead in the past, and even worse done by the living.

But the blank-eyed gazes of those dolls staring out at me from the darkness, amid that sea of flower corpses, was something I knew was going to haunt me forever.

I dropped the flashlight in order to press a hand to my mouth, then staggered away from the playhouse.

Jesse was at my side in an instant.

"What is it?" he asked, putting his arms around me protectively. "The dolls?"

I shook my head. "The smell." Rotting bougainvillea stinks, especially in great quantities.

But I was lying. I was ashamed to admit how much the dolls had unnerved me. It wasn't only their dead-eyed stare, but the fact that they looked just like my nieces—or how my nieces thought they looked. The girls had picked out the dolls themselves last Christmas from a catalog that advertised a line of "create your own dolls," so each girl had selected a doll she felt represented herself. Flopsy and Cotton-tail had chosen mini-me's, with blue eyes, long brown hair, and fair skin.

But Mopsy, ever the iconoclast, had scandalized her ultra-conservative maternal grandparents by choosing a doll with brown skin and even darker brown hair and eyes, a fact that had flattered and amused Jesse so much that I'd had to whisper to him during Christmas brunch to settle down, in case Grandpa Mancuso overheard him crowing, "She picked a doll that looks like me! I always told you, Emily's the smart one. She wants to follow in my footsteps."

I certainly hoped he was right, since if Paul got his way, Mopsy was the closest thing to a daughter Jesse was likely to get.

The fourth doll at the table had been a hand-me-down from one of the girls' Ackerman cousins. She had blond hair that had been roughly hacked in front to give her the appearance of bangs.

Her resemblance to Lucia was close enough to cause my stomach to clench.

"What do you think she's trying to do?" I asked. "Send us another message?"

"Yes." Jesse had retrieved the flashlight from where I'd dropped it. He switched it off, then put it back into his pocket. "I think so."

"But what? What's she trying to say?" I couldn't believe how creeped out I was. They were only dolls, not severed limbs. "If it's 'Don't go in the playhouse,' I got it, loud and clear."

He put an arm around my shoulders and pulled me to him.

"I don't think that's what she's saying. I don't think she meant to frighten you."

"Frighten me?" I had my face buried in the soft suede of his coat. It smelled good, a combination of suede and vanilla and smoke from the wood burning in the fire pit and antibacterial soap from the hospital. In other words, it smelled of Jesse. "Who said I'm frightened? I'm not frightened." I was scared to death. "Grossed out, maybe. The ad says 'Say it with flowers,' not 'Say it with dead, decomposing flowers.' That is one weird way to express yourself, even for a child."

"Not for a dead child," Jesse said, stroking my hair. I don't think he believed me about not being frightened. "Think about it. It makes sense."

"What does?"

"Dead flowers from a dead child. What else does she have to give? When you're dead, you don't have many options. You've heard of pennies from heaven?"

I lifted my head to look at him. "Of course I have. People who find pennies in weird places and think that the ghost of a loved one has left them there on purpose for them to find. But Jesse, that's not a real thing."

"Of course it's a real thing." He tightened his grip on me, his dark-eyed gaze intensifying on mine. "I get that it's hard for you to understand. Communication has always come easily for you. You've never had a problem talking to anyone, alive or—what do you call them? Oh, right. Even the non-compliant deceased persons. And you've certainly never been dead. But supposing there came a day when you tried to reach out to someone you loved, and that person could no longer see or hear you. That's what's it like to be dead, but unable to cross over. Can you imagine the kind of living hell that would be?"

Yes. Like walking through the valley of the shadow of death.

I could hear it in his voice, and feel it in the way he'd sunk his fingers so deeply into the flesh of my upper arms. My heart twisted for him.

"Of course, Jesse." I reached up to lay a hand along his cheek, but he flinched, ducking his head away.

He wasn't rejecting my caress. I'm not even sure he noticed what he'd done. He simply wanted to finish what he was saying.

But they were back. The shadows in his eyes. I could see them, even in the dim lighting of the yard.

You can take the boy out of the darkness.

He continued in a low, rapid voice, "Of course you'd do whatever you could to signal to that person you're still there, whether it's leave a penny, or dead flowers, or shake the house down. You're so hopeless, you wouldn't notice what you're doing is terrifying them. You just want them to know you're not really gone. You understand that, Susannah, don't you?"

But you can't take the darkness out of the boy.

"Yes," I said. "I understand that, Jesse."

I realized how far Jesse had come, in one evening, from wanting to exorcise Lucia to identifying with her, and possibly even sympathizing with her.

I also realized that he was finally talking about what being dead had been like for him.

I wondered if he realized it, too. But I didn't want to push him too far by asking. Instead, I asked, "So what do *you* think Lucia was trying to say with those flowers?"

He glanced at the playhouse. "That she's sorry."

"Sorry?" My jaw dropped. "She's *sorry*?"

"Why not? They're the same flowers from the bougainvillea tree outside the hospital. It's likely she saw you there with your nieces."

"You were there, too. You're the one who gave them all the gum."

Jesse grinned. Every time he grinned, it was like sunshine after a week of overcast days. Or maybe coming home after spending way too long in the valley of the shadow of death.

"That's what I'm saying. I think she saw us with the girls and realized we're friends, not foes. The flowers are her way of trying to make up for what she did."

"In that case, she delivered them to the wrong place. They should be in Father Dom's room in the ICU."

"I'd have enjoyed seeing that," Jesse said, a wistful look in his eyes.

"Me, too."

I tried to match his light tone, but inside, I didn't feel nearly as playful. Maybe because I knew he was right . . . Lucia had left the flowers for me, her first attempt to reach out to an adult she thought she could trust, and how had we repaid her? By allowing—even encouraging—Max to chase her off from my stepnieces' yard, probably the only place in the world where she'd felt free to be the child she'd once been, frightening her half out of her wits (if that piercing scream had been any indication).

Worse, Jesse's heartfelt admission about the loneliness he'd suffered when he was dead—how he'd longed to reach out to those he'd loved, but had been unable to—had reminded me of someone else from my past, someone who definitely did not have anywhere near the issues of Jesse or Lucia, but who was almost as messed up, in his own way.

What was it my mother had said on the phone about Paul? Oh, right: *He was one of those kids who always received plenty of money from his family, but no love or attention.*

How different was that from being a ghost, by Jesse's definition, someone who kept reaching out to people and having those people not be able to see or hear him?

I had way too many ghosts in my life right now, clamoring for my attention. For the first time, I wasn't sure I could handle them all on my own. One of the things that had become clear in my sessions with Dr. Jo was that I "compartmentalized" too much and "wasn't open" about whatever "trauma" it was I'd experienced in my past. This, she felt, was holding me back, and was probably causing my insomnia.

Of course, I had good reason not to reveal my past to Dr. Jo.

But if Jesse was going to open up to me about his past, maybe I needed to be more honest with him about mine. Not just my past, but about the danger he was in . . . that we were both in, if Paul succeeded in his plan.

"Jesse," I said, reaching for his hand. "I have something I think I need to tell you."

He looked concerned. "What is it, *querida*?"

"I was going to tell you before, but I was worried you'd get mad."

"I could never get mad at you."

I laughed. "That's actually a good one."

Naturally, he got mad. "Susannah, *you* never make me angry. Sometimes the things you *do* make me angry—well, annoyed—because you don't always seem to think things through before you—"

"See, this is exactly what I'm talking about. I haven't even told you what it is, and you're already mad."

Jesse's dark eyebrows came rushing together. "I didn't say I was mad. I said I was annoyed. You're *annoying* me by telling me how I'm going to feel. You're a very perceptive woman, Susannah, but you don't live inside my head, so you can't tell me what I'm going to feel."

I didn't like how this was going. I especially didn't like the little muscle I saw begin to leap in his jaw, visible even in the darkness of the yard.

"Let's just drop it, okay?"

"Susannah, you can't just—"

I heard the scrape of a screen door.

"Suze? Jesse?" Debbie's voice called out to us from the back porch. She was struggling to pull her shirt back on. So now I knew why it had taken her and Brad so long to check on us: they'd made up from their fight, probably all over the kitchen floor. "What are you guys doing out here? What was Max barking at before?"

I pulled my hand from Jesse's, a surge of relief flooding through me. I don't think I'd ever been so grateful to see Debbie before in my life.

Screw Dr. Jo. Screw Paul. Screw ancient Egyptian curses and bloggers who wouldn't call me back. I'd handle this one on my own. Some secrets were better off staying secret.

"Nothing's wrong, Debbie," I called to her. "There was just a . . . a raccoon in the playhouse. Max scared him off."

"A raccoon?" Brad joined his wife on the back porch, sounding excited. "Which way did he go? Hold on, let me get my rifle."

Oh, God.

"Susannah," Jesse said, catching my arm as I began striding back toward the house. "What is it? What were you going to tell me?"

"Seriously, forget it. It was nothing."

"It didn't sound like nothing."

"Well, it was."

Fortunately a childish voice called from the open window upstairs. "Mommy? What's going on?"

"Oh, great." Debbie sounded irritated. "Now the kids are up. Nothing, sweetie. Just a raccoon. Max chased it away. Go back to sleep."

"Mommy." Mopsy sounded drowsy, but upset. "It wasn't a raccoon. It was Lucy. Max scared her. Don't let Daddy shoot her."

Looking up, I saw three small, dark silhouettes crowding one of the upstairs windows. I could dimly make out the girls' faces as they stared down at us, their expressions concerned in the moonlight.

"Girls." Debbie came down into the yard until she stood beneath the girls' window. She'd done an amazing job of whipping her body back into shape after their delivery with both Pilates and a tummy tuck (paid for by her father, the Mercedes King), and she knew it. She liked to show off her great figure by wearing a lot of Spandex. She stood craning her neck to look up at the girls, a glass of barely touched wine in her hand. "You know perfectly well Lucy isn't real. I've asked you repeatedly to quit making up stories about her. Now get back in bed, all of you."

Mopsy ignored her mother, and shifted her appeal to me. "Aunt Suze, don't let Max get Lucy. She's our friend."

I glanced at Jesse. I didn't have to say anything out loud. He nodded and said, "I'll get the dog." He started after Max, who'd found his way back to the playhouse and was digging through the bougainvillea, where he'd apparently picked up the odor of something edible. Jesse hauled him out by his collar, though Max put up a struggle. "That's enough for tonight, Max," I heard Jesse saying to the dog. "Good boy."

"Don't worry, girls," I said, crossing the yard until I stood beside their mother. I looked up at the three worried little faces, barely discernible in the moonlight. "Max can't hurt Lucy, and neither can your dad. Lucy's a ghost, and dogs and guns can't hurt ghosts. Now do as your mother says, and go back to bed."

"Okay, Aunt Suze," the girls said in tones of bitter disappointment—not about their ghost friend, but about having to go back to bed. One by one, their little heads disappeared from the window.

When I turned back toward their mother, I found her staring at me in disbelief.

"What?" I asked.

"Suze," Debbie said. "Lucy's their invisible friend."

"So?"

"She's a figment of their imagination. You just called her a ghost. I know how popular that stupid video game *Ghost Mediator* is, and I'm fairly certain some of the parents in the girls' class let their children play it, even though it's age inappropriate and much too violent. But Brad and I are actively trying to discourage the girls from believing in the supernatural."

I stared back at her. "Oh . . . kay."

"Deborah." Jesse came by, dragging Max by the collar behind him. "You send the girls to Catholic school. Part of their religious education involves instruction in the Holy Trinity, which includes the Holy Spirit."

"Oh, that's different," Debbie said, using the simpering tone she always adopted whenever addressing my fiancé. It was like Jesse gave off pheromones that some women couldn't help reacting to. Obviously I was one of those women, but at least I tried not to show it . . . in public, anyway. "We obviously want them to have strong *moral* beliefs. But with the exception of the Holy Ghost, ghosts aren't real."

I'd had enough. "How do you know they aren't real?" I walked around her, back toward my lawn chair, in order to retrieve my glass of wine. "They could be."

"Oh, really?" Debbie dropped the simpering tone since she was addressing me. "Could they, Suze? The same way you told Emma wine is filled with vitamins when she asked why you drink so much of it? Is that real? Thanks a lot for that, Suze, by the way, because she asked if she could have wine with her breakfast tomorrow morning."

"Yeah, well, there *are* vitamins in wine, Debbie." I lifted the bottle of wine we'd brought with us, and topped off both Debbie's glass and my own. "But for your information, I also told her the health benefits only work for people who are over twenty-one. And there's a lot of crap you believe in that isn't real, either, Debbie, but we go along with it just to keep the peace. So I suggest you do the same, as far as Lucy is concerned. Cheers." I clinked her glass.

Debbie stared at me in astonishment just as Brad came bursting out of the back door, his rifle pumped and loaded. "Which way did it go?"

"Not tonight, amigo," Jesse said, gently removing the rifle from his hands. "Not tonight."

dieciocho

I had more trouble than ever falling asleep that night.

It was only partly because Debbie had gotten rid of the bed in the guest room—along with all of Brad's wrestling awards, which she'd relegated to the garage—so she could convert it into her "crafting center."

So I had to share a bed down the hall with Mopsy, while Jesse was banished to the hard, lumpy couch in the living room (which didn't have a door, with or without a lock for privacy).

We could probably have gone back to our own beds to sleep, mine at my apartment, and Jesse's at Snail Crossing, since it appeared there was no longer any danger to the girls. But I still had the "study" for my class to complete.

Even if we had, I still wouldn't have avoided what Jesse asked me as we were walking back into the house after putting all the wine bottles into Brad and Debbie's recycling bins:

"Susannah, what was it you were going to say to me before

in the yard? Something you were worried was going to make me angry?"

I'd laughed. "Oh, I told you, it was nothing. An idea I had for the wedding, that's all, but I changed my mind. You don't want karaoke at the reception, right?"

"Karaoke?"

"See? I knew it. Fortunately the deposit's refundable."

"Fine. I don't believe you, but fine. By the way, who sent those flowers that I saw on your desk when I stopped by your office this afternoon?"

"Oh, no one," I'd said. "Just a grateful parent."

I don't know how I'd managed the airy tone, especially when it was clear he'd been reading my mind again.

He knew. He knew perfectly well who the flowers were from, and maybe even what I'd been about to tell him in the yard. Perhaps I'd planted the image in his head, worrying so much about Paul, stirred by the blossoms Lucia had strewn across the floor of her new playmates' playhouse, the faces of their dolls.

Dead flowers from a dead girl. Live flowers from a live man . . . who wouldn't stop haunting me over a former ghost.

He didn't say anything more about it, however, and his kiss good night when we parted ways for bed, me for the second floor, him for the first, was as warm as ever.

That wasn't what kept me awake.

I don't think it was the text message Jake sent me, either, saying that he was going to "escort" Gina back to the Crossing from her shift at the Happy Medium. He said he was worried that the "creeper" back at my apartment building might have figured out where she worked. He wanted to make sure she got home safely.

Or the text I got from Gina letting me know that she and Jake had decided to go out to eat after her shift and she hoped I didn't think this was going to "make things weird" between us.

Also, she knew there wasn't a "creeper," it was just another of my "ghost things" (a carnival psychic had spilled the beans in front of Gina about my "gift" when we'd been kids). She wasn't going to mention this to Jake, though, she added with a winking smiley face.

Great, just what I needed—my best friend going out with one of my stepbrothers. Like it wasn't bad enough a former high school nemesis had married one of the other ones.

That was enough to send me downstairs to Brad and Debbie's kitchen for a glass of milk (even though this had never helped "trigger soothing waves of slumber" for me in the past, as experts claimed it would, I kept hoping for a first time).

What I'd actually been hoping for was a chance to slip out of the house and over to 99 Pine Crest Road, to scatter what little rock salt I'd managed to acquire.

But glancing into the living room as I passed it, I knew this was going to be impossible. The sound of my putting the glass of milk I'd just emptied into the dishwasher caused Jesse to roll over on the sofa—which was both too short *and* too narrow for his comparatively enormous frame—and mutter something unintelligible. One bare arm dangling to the floor, the other flung uncomfortably over his head, he looked about as comfortable as poor Max, still locked up in the garage.

Jesse wasn't wearing a shirt, and the blanket Debbie had given him had tangled down around his legs as he'd tossed in his sleep, exposing his chest and most of his boxer briefs, including the dark mat of hair between his pecs that then thinned into a tempting highway leading to the waistband of his shorts, where I could plainly see the bulge I felt nearly every day but was (mostly) forbidden to touch until our wedding day.

That's when I realized all the milk in the world was never going to put me to sleep.

The house was completely quiet. Debbie and Brad had gone (bickering again) to bed hours ago, and the girls had been quietly slumbering when I'd left them.

What would happen, I wondered, if I knelt beside the couch, kissed Jesse awake, then slipped my hand beneath that waistband?

Now who was the one with a dark side? Me. It was me!

And there wasn't enough rock salt in all the Home Depots in the world to contain it.

Jesse must have felt it, too, since as I stood there staring, he lowered his upflung arm and rolled over, nearly falling off the couch. Startled, I rocketed up the stairs, not wanting him to catch me standing there staring at him while he slept.

I was racing by Debbie's "craft center" on my way back to the girls' room when I saw it—the thing that kept me awake for the rest of the night (like the memory of what was beneath that waistband wasn't enough).

At first it was only a flash, something I wasn't even sure I'd seen. I walked right by the open door, intent on my own filthy thoughts, before it registered.

Then I froze in my tracks, a chill that had nothing to do with the cold night air going down my back.

Lucia.

I backed up two steps, then peeked through the open doorway.

She was there all right, standing solemnly in the center of the room, her round, cherubic face full of its usual gloom.

"Lucia." I pressed a hand to my pounding heart. "You shouldn't sneak up on people like that. You seriously scared the crap out of me."

She said nothing. She merely stood there in her riding clothes, her heels together, her bangs curling into her large, dark eyes, her mouth a tiny, reproachful pink rosebud.

"Look," I said, coming into the room and closing the door behind me so we wouldn't be overheard. "I'm sorry about the dog. He's shut up in the garage so he won't bother you anymore. And thank you for the flowers. But you shouldn't have done what you did to Father Dominic. He's a good man, and he wasn't there to hurt Becca. No one wants to hurt you, either, Lucia. We all want to—"

She lifted one arm. I flinched instinctively and took a stumbling step backward, toward the door. Normally I'm not such a coward, but I remembered only too well the strength in those pudgy little arms.

She wasn't trying to hurt me, however. She was pointing at something on the wall.

I looked in the direction she was pointing. It was Debbie's "inspiration board."

Debbie had shown it to me earlier, though I hadn't paid too much attention. It was one of her crafts. She'd had each of the girls make one, too. Theirs had been more amusing. Cotton-tail, it turned out, was heavily inspired by the theatrical work of Jiminy Cricket.

"What?" I asked Lucia, stepping toward Debbie's inspiration board. "Is there something here about what happened to you?"

Lucia looked angry, which I'd come to realize was her go-to expression.

But before I had a chance to duck for cover, she disappeared, which was admittedly a relief. I had to hand it to the kid: she was learning to handle her emotions. Now instead of lashing out, she was going to her happy place, wherever that was. I didn't care, as long as it was far away from me.

I switched on a desk lamp so I could examine Debbie's board

a little more closely, looking for what Lucia had been trying to show me. It was an elaborately decorative thing, corkboard covered over with ivory wrapping paper, then bound with gold ribbon and strands of imitation pearls. She'd pressed photos of supermodels onto it with thumbtacks shaped like crowns, and here and there were also photos of the girls, a few as babies, but most of them were more recent, many of them from events I recognized. There were no photos at all of Brad, or of me. I tried not to take it personally.

At first I couldn't see what Lucia could possibly have been pointing at. There was nothing at all on it to do with her, nothing about horses, or Sacred Trinity, or Becca, or even Kelly Prescott Walters, Becca's stepmom and Debbie's best friend.

Then I realized Lucia hadn't been pointing at something connected to her. It was something Lucia wanted me to see because she thought it was connected to me. Maybe it was another way of her saying she was sorry? She must have sensed the bougainvillea blossoms hadn't been a hit, but this, *this* would really help me out.

It was CeeCee's alumni newsletter, printed out from Brad and Debbie's home computer, and turned to a page with a photo of Paul Slater, looking dark-haired and blue-eyed and tanned and relaxed as he leaned against a sports car, his muscular arms folded across his chest, a self-satisfied smirk on his handsome face. The car was a Porsche (of course it was. He'd always driven expensive sports cars.).

The caption beneath the photo read, *Business Is Booming for One Mission Academy Alum*. The article beneath it read, *Paul Slater Becomes Overnight Success*.

Ouch. Really, CeeCee? I was going to have to have a word with her about her hyperbolic headlines.

Hanging next to the photo was the tassel from Debbie's high school graduation cap. I recognized it because I had one just like it.

Or I'd had one, anyway. It had disappeared the night Paul had shoved me up against that wall and I'd kneed him in the groin, then run right past Debbie, who'd been so delighted to find him there, since her own boyfriend, Brad, had been busy throwing up on Kelly Prescott's Louboutins.

How had Paul put it?

Oh, right. I'd left him to Debbie's not-so-tender ministrations. "She straddled me like she thought I was a damned gigolo," Paul had complained.

Well, so what if Paul and Debbie had had their fun graduation night? Brad's the one who married her. Seven months later, Debbie had given birth to triplets.

Triplets born prematurely and with the gift of mediation, which neither of their parents or grandparents possessed.

And then, like a bolt from the sky, I knew what Lucia was trying to tell me—why she thought this would help.

It didn't help, though. It kept me awake for the rest of the night.

It was probably going to keep me awake forever.

diecinueve

I drove the girls to school the next morning, while Jesse drove to the Crossing to drop off Max, then to the hospital to check on Father Dom.

I didn't mention anything to him—or anyone—about my suspicions concerning my stepnieces. What was I going to say, exactly? "Guess what? Okay, you'll never guess, so I'll just tell you: I'm pretty sure my stepbrother's kids aren't really his."

No. Just no.

And even if in her quest to get me to open up more during our therapy sessions Dr. Jo is always telling me how keeping secrets leads to elevated levels of cortisol, the stress hormone, how do I know what Lucia suggested is true? So she pointed to a photo of Paul hanging from my sister-in-law's bulletin board. That doesn't prove anything.

Still, as they argued with one another in the backseat of my car over which one of them was going to get to tell the story for show-and-tell of how their aunt Suze and uncle Jesse had spent the night at their house, I checked out the girls' reflections in my rearview mirror, and couldn't help noticing how closely they resembled a certain mediator I happen to know.

They had the coloring—dark hair and blue eyes—and slim, tennis player build of both Jack and Paul Slater, instead of the sturdy, Nordic structure of the Ackermans (who, with the exception of redheaded David, were all blond).

Once I noticed this, I couldn't *un*notice it, no matter how much I wanted to. I could only wonder how I'd never seen it before.

Brad, I was certain, didn't know. Did Debbie? She was shallow, and had occasionally followed her best friend Kelly's lead in school and been nasty, even spiteful.

But I'd never seen her perform an act of outright cruelty—at least not so cruel as to force a man to unknowingly raise another man's child . . . or children, as in this case.

Why then had she hung that photograph of Paul on her inspiration board? And why had Lucia pointed at it with a look of such solemn accusation on her face? She couldn't have been accusing Paul of murder. Paul hadn't even lived in Carmel at the time of her death.

And while I knew better than anyone how willing Paul was to commit murder—if you could call unleashing a demon curse murder—what interest would he have in killing a child?

None. That wasn't his style.

I was halfway to the school when my phone rang. Normally I don't even look at my phone when I'm driving—especially if the girls are in the car or I'm driving through early morning marine layer, like now.

But what if it was Jesse calling from the hospital because Father Dom had taken a turn for the worse? What if it was Shahbaz, the blogger, calling to tell me he knew how to break the curse?

What if it was Paul, calling to say he'd come to his senses and that he was sorry?

It wasn't. It was my youngest stepbrother, David.

Something was wrong. David and I only talked on Sundays. I jabbed at the speakerphone.

"David? What is it? What's happened?"

"Uncle David!" the girls screamed excitedly from the backseat. "Hi, Uncle David!"

"Uh, hi. Oh, great. The girls are with you." Although he was fond of his nieces, there was a notable lack of enthusiasm in David's voice. "Am I on speakerphone? I was hoping we could talk in private, Suze."

"I stayed at Brad and Debbie's last night, so I'm taking the girls to school with me. What's wrong? Why are you calling? Today's not Sunday."

"I'm aware that today is not Sunday, Suze." Doc's tone suggested he suspected I might have been lobotomized since he'd last seen me. "I'm calling because I heard what happened to Father Dominic. Is he okay?"

I relaxed my grip on the wheel. "Oh. Yeah. Jesse's on his way to see him now. He already talked to his doctor this morning, and Dr. Patel said Father Dom did well overnight, so everything should be—"

"What happened to him?"

"He fell. It happens." I was conscious that the girls were listening, so I chose my words with care. "Old people fall down sometimes."

"And break their hips and get pneumonia," Mopsy added helpfully.

"Simmer down back there and watch your video," I commanded, meaning the tablet I'd purchased for them to use in the car (as a means to keep them from pulling out one another's hair, and me pulling out my own in frustration). "Or I'll make you get out and walk to school."

The girls laughed. I had to admit the threat had probably lost some of its punch since I used it every single time I drove them somewhere, but had yet actually to follow through.

"Well, what's this weird thing your mom was talking about when I called her last night, about our old house getting bought by that Paul Slater guy?" David asked. "And does it have anything to do with that e-mail you sent to Shahbaz Effendi about some Egyptian curse?"

I nearly slammed on the brakes, and not just because the pickup in front of me, carrying crates full of freshly harvested pomegranates, had swerved suddenly to avoid hitting a cyclist.

"How the hell did you find out about that?"

"Because Shahbaz goes to my school, Suze," David said in a patient voice as the triplets hooted in the backseat because I'd used a curse word. "He's a grad student in NELC—that's the Near Eastern Languages and Civilizations Department here. After he got your e-mail, he looked you up on the Web to find out who you are. But of course you don't have any social media accounts, so all he could find was some celebrity website that lists you as Andy Ackerman's stepdaughter, and me as one of his sons. It also mentioned that I go here, so he got in touch with me through the school directory to ask if you're really as mentally unstable as you sounded in your message to him—"

"Mentally unstable?" I interrupted, offended. "Where does he get off, accusing *me* of being mentally unstable? I'm not the one who sits around translating curses written in hieratic script all day so I can post them on the Internet where anyone can find them and—"

"And what, Suze?"

Well, okay. Maybe I might have sounded a little mentally unstable to someone who goes to an Ivy League school and isn't entirely familiar with my side job.

A nervous glance in the rearview mirror showed me that the triplets' dark heads were bent over the tablet. I wasn't fooled, however. I knew them. They were completely eavesdropping.

I took David off speaker and lifted the phone to my ear, risking a penalty if I got caught talking on a non-hands-free mobile device while driving. But I decided the risk of allowing the girls to overhear David's side of this conversation would be worse.

"Look, David, it's nothing. I contacted Shahbaz for a client I'm working with."

"Suze, don't even try. I went to Shahbaz's blog and looked up that curse you asked him about."

Crap.

"It specifically references the darkness that will be unleashed upon anyone who dares to resurrect a departed soul, and what can happen if the dwelling place of that soul is destroyed. Your 'client' is obviously you and Jesse is the soul you resurrected and this has something to do with Paul tearing down our old house. So don't tell me not to be silly. I'm not a child anymore. And I want to help."

Wow. I was starting to think that the photo David had sent of himself wearing women's clothing hadn't been for fun—or a class on gender studies—after all. David was no longer the awkward nerdy kid I'd privately nicknamed Doc. He was all grown up now, and he wanted to let me know it.

"Okay, fine," I said. "But, David, there's nothing you can do. I have it all under control."

"Oh, do you? Then why did you spend last night at Brad and Debbie's? You can't stand Debbie. Last time we had dinner together, you called her a self-centered harpy and said you hope she gets nail fungus under her gel manicure."

Yikes. I really needed to cool it on the wine. "Okay, well, I might have been having a moment of—"

"Clearly you think the girls are in some kind of danger."

"They were," I admitted. "But not anymore. And that had nothing to do with—"

"Does Jesse know Paul bought the house?"

Wow. David was good. Too good. "No, but only because Jesse's got a lot on his plate right now. He's still waiting to hear about that grant. I really don't want to stress him out or bother him right now with inane little—"

"Okay, that's it," David said firmly. "I'm changing my ticket and coming home tomorrow instead of next week."

"What?" I nearly hit the back of the pomegranate truck. "David, no! That's a terrible idea. It's totally unnecessary."

"Unnecessary? Father Dominic *is in the hospital*."

"Yes, and being well taken care of. So please don't—"

"It's okay. I already turned in all my papers for this semester. I can tell my instructors I have a family emergency."

Of course he'd already turned in all his papers. He may be a grown-up now, but he hadn't changed *that* much.

"David, there's no emergency. Father Dominic is going to be fine. What happened to him had nothing to do with that, uh, other thing." I glanced at the girls. Still watching their video, except for Mopsy. I caught her gaze in the rearview mirror as she looked up, realized I was watching her, then glanced away again, ever so quickly. The little faker. "And there's nothing we can do about that other thing, unless your friend Shahbaz mentioned something?"

"No, Suze, Shahbaz says he's never heard of a way to break the Curse of the Dead because curses aren't *real*." David sounded exasperated. "They were written to scare away grave robbers, not because high priests in ancient religions actually had the ability to put curses on people."

"Sure," I said mildly. "Just like ghosts aren't real. Just like people who can see ghosts aren't real. Just like all those people who found King Tut's tomb didn't die of random mosquito bites and suicides and murders a year later—"

"Listen, Suze, I know. But what did you want me to say to him? I couldn't exactly go, 'Look, I know curses aren't real—except that my stepsister communicates with the dead, has proven that multiple universe principle is, in fact, a reality, and occasionally travels to a parallel dimension somewhere between life and death that no one else has proven exists.' I didn't want him to think *I'm* nuts."

I rolled my eyes. It was way too early in the morning to be talking to a sensitive genius.

"Okay, David," I said. "Thanks for trying, anyway. Look, I gotta go; like I said, I'm driving—"

He wasn't giving up that easily, though. "Listen, Suze, I thought of another way you can handle this thing. Something a lot easier than breaking some mummy's curse."

"Oh, yeah? What's that?"

"Just go back through time and buy the house yourself."

I was so startled I almost missed the turn to the school. I had to stomp on the brakes and swerve at the last minute, which caused the girls to sway dangerously in the back, even though they had their seat belts on.

Fortunately they weren't prone to motion sickness, and also enjoyed carnival rides, so they cheered instead of vomited.

David, unaware of the traffic drama, went on excitedly. "Look, you already created this alternate universe in which we're all living, the one in which Jesse never died—which makes no sense to me, since according to the Novikov self-consistency principle, that means we shouldn't be able to remember that time Dad and Brad found his skeleton in the backyard. But we all do. So it makes sense that you should be able to do it again. Only this time, make it so *you're* the one who buys the house from Mom and Dad, not Paul. Then everything will be fine. At least I think it should. Right?"

I'd managed to recover control of the car and, despite some irate honks from a few other motorists, get into my correct lane.

"David," I said when I found my voice again. "That's a great plan. Honestly. But it isn't going to fly. Mediators can't go popping back and forth through time without having to pay the consequences in the form of major loss of brain cells and cosmic tears in the universe." Quoting Paul left a bad taste in my mouth. "That's how this whole mess got started in the first place."

"Oh." David sounded let down. "I hadn't considered that."

"Yeah. And really, if time travel were that easy, don't you think I'd be doing it all the time, trying to prevent plane crashes and Hitler and stuff?"

Now he sounded shocked. "Of course not. That would be a complete violation of the grandfather paradox—"

"And even if I wanted to, I couldn't have bought our old house. My dad didn't leave me *that* much money. And Jesse would never in a million years want to live there."

David's voice went up several octaves. "Why *not*?"

"Because our old house is where Jesse got M-U-R-D-E-R-E-D, remember?"

The girls immediately began murmuring the letters of the word I'd just spelled, but fortunately got nowhere as it was too advanced for the kindergarten set. Plus reading at the academy was being taught by sight or "whole language" rather than phonetically, which meant most students were reading well below their grade level (an opinion I'd been told by Father Dom to please keep to myself).

"Well, where *are* you two going to live, then, after you get married?" David demanded testily. "Some gated community, like Brad and Debbie? Oh, yeah, I can really see *that* working out. Hey, maybe Jesse could start playing golf with all the other doctors, while you shop with their wives."

I really did not want to continue this conversation, not only because we'd reached the school parking lot, but because all of a sudden I could hear my mother's voice in my head, suggesting that Jesse and I move to Los Angeles. *It would be so much easier for me to visit my future grandbabies if they were right here in town . . .*

"Look, David," I said. "I appreciate the help with Shahbaz, and also your advice, but honestly, the best thing you can do right now is stay exactly where you are and not mention a word of this to anyone. Especially Jesse. Okay?"

"Um, okay." He didn't sound convincing. "Tell everyone hi from me, and that I love them. I'll see you soon."

"David. Are you listening to me? *Please* don't—"

But he'd hung up.

"Aunt Suze," Mopsy asked from the backseat. "What's a mediator?"

veinte

The first thing I did when I got to my desk was to throw Paul's flowers into the trash, vase and all. The second thing I did was look up Becca Walters's class schedule. She had geometry first period. Excellent.

Now all I had to do was hope she showed up to school.

"That's a waste," Sister Ernestine remarked as she bustled past my trash can on the way into her office.

I glanced at the flowers. The nun had a point. Every petal was still snow white and perfect.

"The smell's giving me a headache," I said, though of course my headache had predated the flowers and this didn't explain why they were in the garbage, one foot from my desk.

"If you didn't want them, you could have given them to poor Father Dominic at the hospital."

"I think we can do better for Father D than used flowers."

"They're still perfectly good. Maybe you could put them in the basilica for the worshippers to enjoy."

I closed my eyes and said a quick prayer for strength to the nondenominational god of single girls and mediators.

"You're so right, Sister." I leaned over and picked the vase out of the trash can. Fortunately the glass was still intact, so it wasn't leaking. "Are you going to lead Morning Assembly today in Father Dominic's absence?"

"I am." The nun was straightening her wimple in the same mirror Father Dom had straightened his clerical jacket the day before. "I've been named acting principal by the archdiocese until Father Dominic recovers enough to return to work, which will hopefully be soon."

It wouldn't be soon. It would be weeks, possibly months. I'd never get hired as a paid staff member unless I adjusted either my attitude, or how much I was needed around the Mission Academy.

Which is why I artfully arranged Paul's flowers on the windowsill in Sister Ernestine's office while she was giving the Morning Assembly message—which included a request for the entire student body to bow their heads in a moment of prayer for Father Dominic's speedy recovery.

As soon as Assembly was over, I pulled Flopsy, Mopsy, and Cotton-tail out of their line back to class.

"Family emergency," I told Sister Monica, who responded by looking relieved.

"What's the matter, Aunt Suze?" Flopsy asked as I hurried them along the open-air corridor, past all the other classroom doors, until we got to where Becca's geometry class was being held. "What's the emergency?"

"The kind where I need you guys to go out into the courtyard and play quietly with your friend Lucy for a bit while I talk to her friend Becca. If you do that, without bothering us, I'll buy you whatever you want for lunch."

The girls exchanged excited glances. They couldn't express

their joy the way they wanted to, because shouting in the breeze-way was forbidden, but their body language—they looked as if they were about to scream and do backflips—said it all. Chicken fingers and fries were infinitely preferable to the healthy lunch—turkey wraps and carrot sticks—their poor, long-suffering mother had made them.

There's no getting around it: I might have helped a lot of people get into heaven, but I'm seriously starting to doubt my chances of ever getting there myself.

"Can we," Mopsy whispered to me intensely, "play in the fountain?"

The ancient decorative fountain in the center of the mission's courtyard, near which the students were expressly forbidden from going, was my stepnieces' favorite place in all of creation. I'd like to have said this was due to their exquisite aesthetic taste, but I feared a different explanation.

"You may play *near* it," I said. "Not *in* it."

When all three girls began to pout, I gritted my teeth. "Listen, we are *not* going through this again. The people who put coins in that fountain made wishes as they threw them. If you fish them out and steal them, it's like stealing people's wishes, and that's as wrong as stealing their money—which is against the law, by the way, as we have discussed repeatedly in the past."

The three of them had been dragged into the office so many times for stealing coins from the fountain that they were known around the teacher's lounge as the Three-K Banditos.

Mopsy opened her mouth to protest, but I cut her off, asking, "What did Jiminy Cricket say about wishes?"

Cotton-tail promptly replied, "They come true when you wish upon a *star*."

"There's nothing in that song about *fountains*." Mopsy always had an angle.

Realizing that I was never going to get them to play nicely unless I sweetened the bribe—fries were losing their currency—I said, "Look, just this one time you can fish for coins from the fountain, but *only* if you promise to put them back when you're done." Their faces fell, and I added, through gritted teeth, "Fine. I'll reimburse you after school from my own wallet, you little swindlers."

Their faces lit up once more. The idea of scooping slimy quarters and dimes from the bottom of an old fountain brought them such happiness (because it was *free money*), I now knew beyond a shadow of a doubt that they were Paul Slater's daughters. He loved money more than anyone I'd ever met.

"All right, be quiet and let me concentrate."

I turned and rapped loudly on the door to Becca's first-period classroom. No one had phoned in to say that she was staying home sick for the day, which surprised me. If the beloved principal of my school had nearly died at my house the day before, no way would I show up to class the morning after, if only to avoid nasty questions from the student body. This kid either had no common sense whatsoever, or a stepmother who wanted her out of the house. I suspected the latter.

Without waiting for anyone to answer my knock, I opened the door and entered the classroom.

"I'm Susannah Simon," I said to the harassed-looking teacher, Ms. Temple. She wasn't one I knew from my own days as a student at the Mission Academy. "I'm from the administrative office. Becca Walters is needed there. Now."

As was typical when anyone was called to the office, the entire class began to catcall and hoot. All except for Becca, who was seated in the second-to-last row, near the windows, which looked out over the achingly blue sea. She seemed to be continuing her campaign to appear as inconspicuous as possible. She still had not brushed (or seemingly washed) her hair, her uniform was as ill-fitting as ever, and she wore the same bandage I'd affixed to her wrist two days earlier. It was now gray and frayed around the edges.

Lucia stood at her side, solemn-faced as always. Unlike Becca, Lucia did not seem surprised to see me, nor did her face turn bright red as she met my gaze.

"All right, students, simmer down," Ms. Temple said, in a bored voice. "Becca, take your things in case you aren't back by next period."

Becca stood up, gathering her books with fingers that shook so nervously it was inevitable she'd drop one of them. This caused the hooting not only to increase, but for some of the boys to call out even ruder remarks than before, and the girls to smirk and whisper among themselves.

Ms. Temple, who appeared to be only a little older than I was, did nothing about any of this. Instead she took the interruption as an opportunity to pick up her cell phone and check her messages.

The only person in the room who looked the least bit concerned for Becca—besides me and her little ghost companion, who was one step behind her—was Sean Park, the tenth-grade computer whiz who'd saved my office desktop. He was sitting in the front row, gazing back at Becca with a look of compassion, while occasionally throwing his peers glances of disgust.

I shared his feelings.

After making sure Becca and her invisible bodyguard had safely exited the room into the hallway, I turned to look back at the class. The students were still buzzing among themselves, while Ms. Temple continued to check her phone. To my surprise, I saw that she was texting someone.

I understand that teachers work very long hours for too little pay. So do I.

But honestly.

"Hey," I said. Possibly I said it a little too loudly, since the teacher wasn't the only one who looked over. My outburst got the attention of the students, as well. All gazes fell upon me, so I decided to use the opportunity to make a little announcement.

"In case any of you are wondering," I said, with a pleasant smile, "I'm the same Suze Simon who knocked the head off the Father Serra statue a few years back. And if I hear of a single one of you giving Becca Walters shit ever again, I'll do the same to you. Have a nice morning."

I slammed the door on their stunned expressions.

Out in the corridor, Becca was looking up at me, wide-eyed.

"Wh-what did you say to them?" she asked.

"Nothing." I continued to smile as I wrapped an arm around her shoulders. "Come on. We need to have a little chat."

Becca resisted my perfectly friendly overtures.

"That wasn't nothing," she said. "I heard you say—did you say something to them about *me*?"

"No. You worry too much." I noticed that Lucia had begun to glow with spectral rage, and added, "Oh, calm down, Casper. I'm only going to talk to her. Go hang out with your three amigos over there."

Becca looked around, oblivious as always to her ghostly companion. "Who are you talking to?"

"That's what we're going to chat about." I waved at my stepnieces. "Girls, could you help me out here?"

They didn't need any further coaching. Mopsy raced up to Lucia, gripped her by the arm, then whispered loudly, "My aunt Suze said we could take coins from the fountain!"

"But we have to put them back," Cotton-tail warned. "It's wrong to steal wishes."

"And money," Flopsy added. "But Aunt Suze says she's going

214

to pay us back, whatever we take, from her own wallet. We're going to be *rich*."

Becca stared at me as if I were a whack job while the three girls—four, really, but she couldn't see Lucia—raced off into the courtyard, where the bright morning sun had already begun to burn off the thick fog I'd been driving through. It significantly dimmed Lucia's aura . . . though she continued to throw me solemn looks, not quite trusting me with her precious Becca . . . yet.

As soon as they reached the wide stone fountain—which this early in the morning had yet to attract any adult visitors—the three living girls peeled off their shoes and socks and jumped in (exactly as I'd told them not to). Even Lucia looked tempted to follow suit. It was hard to believe she was the same spirit who, the night before last, had tried to drown me.

"Who are they?" Becca asked, her gaze following the triplets.

"They're my stepnieces," I said. "I brought them so we could talk. Last time we got interrupted, and it wasn't by any earthquake. Those three are here to keep it from happening again."

Becca looked more bewildered than ever. "I don't know what you're talking about. I do know about *you*, though. My stepmother told me—"

"Yes, I'm sure Kelly had plenty to say about me." I steered her by the arm through one of the stone archways. "Well, I've got a lot to say to you. But not about her."

Becca immediately put on the brakes, refusing to budge from beneath the chilly shade of the breezeway. "We aren't allowed to go out here," she balked, staring at the warm, sunny courtyard like it was the pit of a lava-filled volcano, and she was the hapless missionary I was about to sacrifice to the native gods.

"You are if you're escorted by a staff member. And lucky you, I just happen to be a staff member."

I pulled her off the smooth flagstone and onto the pebbled

pathway that meandered through the courtyard's many garden plots. She came blinking into the sunlight as cautiously as a mole person.

It might have been November, but in Carmel, that's one of the most beautiful months of the year—which was why Jesse and I wanted to be married in November, only a year from now. An explosion of brightly colored flowers—milkweed, bougainvillea, azaleas, wisteria, and rhododendrons—lined the paths and even the rooftops of the breezeways and buildings surrounding the courtyard. The milkweed had attracted monarch butterflies, which flew in lazy circles around the yard like low-flying, drunk hang gliders.

Though the stucco walls were three feet thick, and the birds flitting across the clear blue sky overhead were calling noisily to one another, it was still possible to hear the organ music being played at morning mass over in the basilica.

"Sit," I commanded Becca when we came to an ancient stone bench in a mossy alcove, not far from the fountain the girls were marauding. The bench, coincidentally, was beneath the feet of the Father Serra statue I'd so wrongfully been accused of decapitating.

Maybe this was why Becca looked more nervous than ever as she sat down. "I didn't mean it about my stepmother. All she said was—"

"I don't care what Kelly said about me." I sat down beside her. "I want to know what really happened to Father Dominic. But first, I want to know what really happened to your friend Lucia Martinez."

Becca stared at me as round-eyed as if I'd slapped her. "L-Lucia Martinez? Wh-who's that?"

"Come on, Becca, don't bullshit me." I'd had about as much as I could take from this girl. "You know exactly who Lucia is. You like the game *Ghost Mediator*? Well, your old friend Lucia's ghost has been following you around for years. You want to know how I know that? Because I'm a real-life mediator, and it's my job to send her to the next level."

Becca stared at me expressionlessly for several seconds from behind the lenses of her glasses.

Then she burst into tears.

veintiuno

Great. Just great. You would think after all these years I'd have figured out how to deliver this kind of news without causing young girls to burst into tears.

But no.

It was a good thing Jesse wasn't around. He was infinitely more tender and patient than I was, and would probably have given this particular mediation one out of five stars based on my swearing alone.

I pulled a minipack of tissues from my messenger bag and passed it to Becca. A mediator needs to be prepared for any emergency.

"Becca," I said, glad for the soothing sounds of the worshippers singing hymns over in the basilica, since they would hopefully keep my voice—and Becca's sobs—from carrying over to the girls. "I'm sorry. I didn't mean to be quite so . . . blunt. I know this is probably very new to you. But Lucia's ghost really has been following you around for years, probably since the day she died."

Becca took a tissue and dabbed at her streaming eyes with trembling fingers. Her breath came in short, hiccupy sobs.

"How . . . how can that even be possible?" she asked. "Lucia? Here?" She glanced furtively around the courtyard, as if expecting a ghoul to leap out from behind a nearby rhododendron. "I don't believe you. This is some kind of trick."

"It's not a trick, and she's not there. She's over by the fountain, playing with my nieces. You can't see her. But trust me, she's there. She's dressed in riding clothes and carrying a stuffed horse."

Becca inhaled sharply. Something I'd said had struck a chord. I wasn't sure what, but she was squinting toward the fountain. "How come you can see her but I can't?"

"It's a genetic thing. But trust me, she's there. She's the one who tore up the office the other day."

Becca was so startled she stopped crying. "Wh-what?"

"You heard me. That was no earthquake. Lucia didn't like it when I tried to touch you, even though I was only trying to help." Becca's eyes, behind the lenses of her glasses, had gone as bright and shiny as the coins the girls were fishing from the fountain and holding toward the sun. "What can you tell me about how Lucia died? She hasn't exactly been illuminating on the subject. She seems to be mostly concerned about you."

For the first time since I'd met her, Becca smiled—really smiled, with her whole face. It transformed her, turning her from an average-looking girl to a very much above-average, almost startlingly attractive girl.

"I can't believe she's worrying about *me*. I don't understand why, since she's the one—" Becca broke off. The smile hadn't lasted long.

"Yes, I know, Becca," I said, gently. "She's the one who died. But the dead aren't always known for their logical reasoning skills.

If they were, I'd be out of a job. Why is Lucia so worried about you, especially now, so many years after her death?"

"I don't know," Becca said, her eyes filling once more with tears. She reached up to clutch her horse pendant. "Or . . . or maybe I do. What happened to her was my fault."

"Your fault? How was it your fault? I know you went to school together, but you were little when—"

"She died because of me," Becca said, the sides of her mouth trembling. "That's why I wear this necklace. To remind me that it's my fault she's dead, and that I . . . that I have to live life for the both of us. She was my best friend."

"Okay," I said skeptically. "But you told me the other day that you hate yourself. If you really want to live life for Lucia, you might want to start by living it for yourself."

Her fuzzy eyebrows furrowed. "I *am* living life for myself."

"I don't think so, Becca. You don't treat yourself very kindly. Did you get your stepmom to take you to see a doctor for that cut? I know you didn't, since you're still wearing that nasty old bandage." She attempted to hide her wrist in embarrassment, but there wasn't really anyplace she could put it, except folded under her opposite arm. "That thing is going to get infected if you don't keep it clean, you know. And what is with these glasses? They're filthy." I plucked them off her face before she could stop me, then peered through the lenses, getting a surprise after I did so. "Becca, these aren't even prescription! What are they, a disguise?"

She snatched them back. "No. Why are you saying all these mean things? I thought you were supposed to be helping me. These glasses make me feel more comfortable."

"As what? The girl no one will ever notice? Look, Becca, I get it. Your dad married a woman who's barely ten years older than you and looks like a supermodel. I'd feel insecure, too. But don't expect me to believe this bullshit about you living life for Lucia when you barely live at all. Now how exactly did Lucia die because of you—which, by the way, I highly doubt?"

Fuming, Becca threw her glasses into some nearby milkweed, disturbing a pair of butterflies, which took off into the air in indignation. "Why don't you ask her, if you really can communicate with ghosts . . . which, by the way, *I* highly doubt?"

"I already told you, the dead aren't known for their logical reasoning skills. Lucia will barely speak to me. And I'm pretty sure when Father Dominic tried, she tossed him down a flight of stairs.'"

Becca blanched. "Oh, my God. Wait, he—"

"Yes. Father Dominic is also one of us—and it almost got him killed. See why being a mediator isn't all it's cracked up to be? Lucia's dangerous, Becca—not because she's evil, but because she's afraid. Afraid for you. Now you've got to tell me why, so I can keep her from hurting anyone else."

Becca shook her head hard enough to cause her hair to whip her cheeks.

"I can't. Don't you see? I told Lucia about him, and she *died*."

"Him?" I was confused. "Him who?"

"*Him*," she whispered. Her eyes weren't only tear filled anymore. They were fear filled. "He killed her, just because she was going to tell them what he did to me. If I'd done what he said and not told anyone, she'd still be alive today. That's why it's all my fault."

And then I did understand. Of course. *Him*.

Wasn't there always a *him*? I had a *him*. Why wouldn't Becca, as well?

Only Paul Slater was just a manipulative creep, not a child killer.

"Becca, it's okay." I laid a hand on her non-injured arm. "You didn't do anything wrong. Tell me who it is. He can't hurt you any—"

"What are you talking about?" She wrenched her arm away. "Of course he can. He made what happened to Lucia look like an accident. He could do the same to you or me just as easily." Her voice was ragged from tears and desperation. "Do you think I haven't been hearing it my whole life, practically? 'Accidents happen.' But what happened to Lucia was no accident. I can't prove it, but I know."

"Then tell me. Tell me so I can fix it."

"You *can't*."

"I can, Becca."

I heard a bell ring, and beneath the breezeway, students began to file from their classrooms, switching from first period to second. I hoped Becca didn't notice.

"I can't bring Lucia back to life, Becca," I whispered urgently. "But I can maybe bring her some peace, and help you live the life you deserve. But only if you help me. *Please*."

She wasn't looking at me. She was staring off at the fountain, fingering the horse pendant around her neck.

"He had to have spooked that horse on purpose, then rode after Lucia and killed her when she was far enough away from the group that they couldn't see." Becca's tears spilled down her cheeks and onto her white uniform blouse. She made no move to wipe them. "She was a good rider, the best of us, but her horse was scared of snakes—all horses are, but hers especially—and if someone left something across the trail that looked like a snake—" She shuddered. "That's how I think he did it. Then all he had to do was follow her ... and ..."

"Why, Becca?" I asked. "Why would he do that to Lucia?"

She nodded, aware of the tears now. She'd lifted a tissue from the pack I'd given her to dab at her eyes and blow her nose. "That's why it's my fault. It was so stupid. It just slipped out. She saw that I had a candy bar, and she wanted to know where I'd gotten it, because we weren't supposed to have candy in school, and like an idiot I said *he'd* given it to me. And then she said she wanted candy, too, and that she was going to ask him for some. And then I realized what I'd done, because of course he'd told me horrible things would happen if I told anyone. So I got scared, because I didn't want him to do to her what he'd done to me, even if afterwards he did give me candy. So I told her that she couldn't say anything to anyone about it, not even him, and she wanted to know why, and so—"

"You told her."

"Y-yes."

I should have been used to it by now. It was so tragically ubiquitous, you'd think it would fail to surprise me.

But even now, sitting in one of the warmest, sunniest, most peaceful places on earth, touted all over the Internet for its beauty and highly meditative benefits, as I listened to the laughter of my stepnieces and the sound of hymns playing inside the basilica, I felt suddenly cold.

This must have been what it was like for Jesse, living in the valley of the shadow of death. Cold, dark, and no sunlight ever to warm him. I fought an urge to reach for my cell phone and call him, just to hear his voice. I couldn't do that in front of Becca. She had no one to call.

"So Lucia said she was going to tell on him?"

"Yes," Becca said, looking as wretched as it was possible for a human being to look. "She was like that, you know. She always took charge of things. Not really bossy, but . . . well, kind of."

I thought of how Lucia's hands had felt around my throat. Bossy was one word for it.

Becca's eyes were overflowing. "I was so stupid. I remember feeling relieved. I remember thinking, 'Well, Lucia will tell, and then everything will be all right.' But instead—" She broke off.

She didn't need to go on. I knew what had happened instead.

I reached out to lay a hand on her fingers, which were nervously shredding the tissue in her lap. "What was his name, Becca?"

She shook herself, seeming to come out of whatever dark shadow that she'd temporarily slipped into. "Wh-what?"

"His name. The man who . . . gave you the candy."

"Oh." She had to think about it. She thought for a long time, watching a couple of butterflies flit by. "Jimmy, I think. That's what everyone called him. Jimmy." She said the name apologetically, like it was a vulgarity she felt sorry for having been forced to utter in front of me.

"Do you remember his last name?"

"I'm sorry. I don't . . . I can't . . . He was tall. I remember that. But I can barely remember anything else about him."

She did, but she wouldn't allow herself to. She'd have blocked it out, along with his name, the way we all try to block out our worst childhood memories.

"That's all right, Becca. Did you tell anyone—anyone besides Lucia—about him?"

Her eyes widened. "No, of course not. Not after . . . not after what happened to Lucia. I didn't . . . I couldn't . . ."

"I understand." She didn't want to be his next murder victim.

"I'd quit riding after that, so I wouldn't see him anymore," she said quickly. "He worked in the stables. I think he was some kind of handyman or something. He did other odd jobs, too, around the school."

He. She wouldn't say his name.

"I tried to avoid the stables as much as I could. But then one day after . . . it happened, Sister Regina Claire made our whole class go down there to lay a wreath for Lucia. And *he* was there. He came up and asked if he could speak to me and I had to say yes, you know, because it would have looked weird for me to say no. But I knew he couldn't do anything, because they were watching. Anyway, he whispered that it was a shame what had happened to Lucia, and to her horse, and it would be an even bigger shame if I ever told anyone else about . . . about what we'd done, because then the same thing that happened to Lucia might happen to my parents, or Shasta—my horse."

I felt a spurt of rage when she mentioned the horse, even though this wasn't the first time I'd heard such a thing. Abusers often threatened to injure family members and pets in order to control a victim. They know that children worry more about loved ones than they do their own personal safety, and that pets are often as beloved as any human family member.

"What else did he say?" I asked, having a hard time keeping my voice steady.

Becca shrugged, picking at the bandage I'd affixed to her wound, attempting to peel it up from one side where the adhesive had come loose. "Just that he knew where I lived. He said it would be a shame if one day when my dad was driving to work, or my mom to the store, and their brakes didn't work, and one of them had a terrible accident—"

I reached out and laid a hand across her fingers, stilling them before she could tear the bandage off completely, revealing the gouge marks she'd created earlier in the week.

"It's all right, Becca," I said, as gently as I could. "I completely understand why you didn't tell anyone."

"I should have." Her voice was small. "If I had, Lucia would still be alive today."

"Maybe," I said, holding her hands more tightly. "Or maybe you'd both be dead."

"That might be better," she said matter-of-factly, looking down at the bandage. "That might be better than this."

"No." I held firmly to her hands, thinking of the shadows in Jesse's eyes. "It wouldn't. Trust me."

"I'm a coward." The tears fell again, hot and fast, dropping onto our clasped hands. "A stupid, weak coward. I made my parents sell Shasta. I told them I didn't like horses anymore, which isn't even true. I love them. I just . . . I thought Shasta would be safer living somewhere else. I even . . . this is going to sound crazy, but I still think I see *him* sometimes downtown, you know? I barely remember what he looks like, but I still think I see him, everywhere I go. And you know what I do when I think I see him? I hide. Even if it's just behind a wall or a parked car. I'm so stupid!"

She tried to laugh at herself, but there was a sob in her voice. My heart wrenched for her as I remembered the word she'd carved in her arm.

"You're not stupid, Becca," I said. "You were a little kid who was traumatized and then did your best, given your limited resources, to protect yourself and the people you love." I gently squeezed both her hands until, finding them finally still, I released them. "What I don't understand, Becca, is if you kept thinking you saw him, why did you stay? Why didn't you move away to New York with your mother, where you'd be safe?"

She blinked up at me as if astonished that anyone could ask such a silly question. "But what about my dad? He can't leave because his company is here. So I have to stay here to make sure *he's* okay."

Of course. Indisputable kid logic. Becca could barely take care of herself, but she still considered it her job to protect her father from the man who'd killed her friend.

"Okay, Becca," I said. "I get it. And I understand now why

you feel as if you have to punish yourself by cutting your arm. But no more, all right? Jimmy will never be able to hurt you or anyone else ever again."

She raised her tear-filled gaze to my face. "Really? Why not?"

"Because," I said. "You've told me. And I'm a mediator."

veintidos

In promising Becca that I was going to stop Lucia's killer from ever hurting anyone else again, I may have been *slightly* over-reaching.

I know that Becca had said she thought she'd seen him around town, and there was always a slim chance she had.

But I considered it more likely that this was a symptom of post-traumatic stress, her fight-or-flight response—and Lucia, clinging to her as always like a limpet—triggering a false alarm. Becca had probably seen someone who resembled Jimmy, and, unable to distinguish if the threat was real or perceived, her body had automatically reacted, heart rate, breathing, and stress levels rising as she'd tried to avoid him.

Enough of these kind of encounters, false or not, and anyone would start to lose it.

It was likely Jimmy had put as much distance between himself and the crime scene as possible in the nine years since Lucia's death. There was approximately zero chance he was still in the area, and a less than zero chance that I was going to be able to track down where he'd gone . . . not without his last name, and a whole lot of luck.

And I don't believe in luck.

It was right as I was thinking this that Becca looked up from the pile of tissues she'd massacred and squinted across the sun-bathed courtyard. "Is that Sister Ernestine?"

I followed her gaze. The nun was standing beneath the nearest breezeway with her arms folded across her ample chest, peering at us disapprovingly . . . or more specifically, peering at the triplets, who were still busy scooping coins from the fountain, their small bodies visibly more inside it than out of it.

Busted.

"Oh, yes," I said breezily, giving Sister Ernestine a casual wave. "No worries."

Wrong. Worries. Big, big worries.

Becca evidently sensed my unease, since she drew her hands from mine and asked, "You aren't going to tell her anything about this, are you?"

"Not if you don't want me to. But I do think you ought to tell your parents, Becca. You've been through something really terrible, and in some ways you've handled it really well, especially for someone so young—" I saw her puff up a little at the praise, like a flower soaking in the sun. The poor girl's self-confidence was in ruins, and no wonder. She'd been living in terror for years. "But you really ought to be talking to a professional mental health counselor—"

She gave me a horrified look. "I *have* talked to one! You."

"I'm not a professional, Becca. I'm still in graduate school. I'm just an intern here at—"

"But you're a mediator!"

I glanced at Sister Ernestine. "Not so loud, okay? That's supposed to be just between you and me. And I mediate for the undead. You're alive, Becca."

"I can't." She shook her head. "I can't tell anyone else. I did once before, and it . . . it turned out to be a disaster."

"Wait a second." Sister Ernestine had decided my wave was a little too casual for her taste, and had begun to stride across the courtyard toward us. I wasn't sure whom she was going to yell at first, the triplets or me. If it was the triplets, and the sister startled Lucia, she was going to be in for a big—and possibly painful—surprise. I needed to head her off at the pass before that happened, but I also needed to hear what Becca was about to say, because it sounded like vital information.

Fortunately Sister E wasn't in the best of shape, and waddled more than she walked. It took her approximately forever to get anywhere.

"When I asked if you'd told anyone else about this, Becca, you said you hadn't—"

"I didn't. I swore I wouldn't. But in second grade at Sacred Trinity they had us do our first Rite of Reconciliation . . . you know, confession, in the booth, and everything? And I figured since it was anonymous, and the priest couldn't see me, I could tell *him* what had happened."

I blinked at her. "Wait. You told a *priest* at Sacred Trinity about Jimmy?"

She nodded. "I thought—well, I guess I thought confessing to a priest wouldn't be the same as telling. They aren't allowed to report what they hear in confession to the police, right?"

"Right," I said, still in shock. "The seal of the confessional is absolute." I knew this from two years of Catholic school and eight years of hanging around a priest who happened to be my boyfriend's confessor, and wouldn't tell me a word they'd discussed, no matter how hard I'd wheedled. "You told this priest *everything*?"

"Yes. But nothing happened the way they said it would in religion class. You know how when you're in there, you can see the priest's face through the little screen, but the priest isn't supposed to be able to see you, unless you want him to?"

I'd never been to confession, not being Catholic, but I'd seen this on TV. "Sure."

"Well, after I started telling him everything, he pulled away the partition, so he could see my face. And then he asked my name. They aren't supposed to do that, are they?"

Suddenly I didn't notice Sister Ernestine's progress anymore. All of my attention was focused on Becca. "No, they aren't. What happened next?"

"Well, then, the priest told me that I was going to burn in hell for having told so many lies, and that the only way I'd be spared was if I came to his office after school so he could personally give me lessons in faith—"

I let out a curse word so blistering Becca wasn't the only one I shocked.

"Miss Simon!" Sister Ernestine was just a few yards away, her wimple fluttering behind her in the breeze. "May I please have a word with you?"

"In a minute, Sister." To Becca, I said, "I need the name of that priest."

"Not in a minute, Miss Simon. *Now.* Mass will be letting out momentarily and I will not condone—"

"Becca. *What was his name?*"

"Oh, why?" Becca held both fists to her mouth, looking consternated. "What does it matter? I never went to the stupid faith lessons. I was too afraid. I went home from school that day and told my parents that I hated Sacred Trinity and I'd never go back because the girls there were mean, and my parents let me transfer to—"

Thank God. Her poor, clueless parents had done one thing right, at least. "I need the name of that priest *right now*, Becca."

"Why? Am I in trouble? Are you going to go talk to him?"

"No, you're not in trouble. If I talk to him, I'll keep your name out of it. Now *what was his name?*"

"Father Francisco," Becca whispered, staring down at her lap. It was covered in the strips of tissue that she'd nervously shredded. "It was Father Francisco."

"Thanks." Before I stood up, I carefully plucked Becca's glasses from the milkweed into which she'd thrown them. In a louder tone, I said, "Well, I think that's enough for one day, don't you, Becca? Becca and I were just discussing *The Scarlet Letter*, Sister Ernestine, which she's currently reading for English class."

"Were you?" Sister Ernestine asked, panting as she reached us at last. "I was unaware that we were now holding tutoring sessions in the courtyard."

"I think it's a refreshing change. Studies show that exposure to nature helps people feel more energized, which heightens their sense of well-being and causes them to retain more information."

"That may well be true." Sister Ernestine stared at Becca with the same laserlike intensity I'd often seen Romeo focus on a piece of fruit I was holding in front of him. "But it won't be good for Miss Walters's well-being if she falls behind on her studies, and the bell for second period has rung, so I think she'd better return to class."

"Oh, yes, of course. It was nice talking to you, Becca. Remember everything I said. You really should think about having a chat with your dad. And maybe your stepmom, too. She's not so bad." I wasn't sure about that last part, of course, but it seemed like a therapeutic thing to say.

Becca eyed me skeptically as she gathered up her things. "Okay. Maybe I will. Thanks, Ms. Simon."

"Don't forget these." I held out her glasses.

"That's okay," she said. "I don't need them." She didn't add the word *anymore*, but it hung in the air like one of the many gold-and-black-winged monarch butterflies, tantalizingly close.

She turned and walked away. I'm sure it was only my imagination that she seemed to be standing a little taller than before.

If so, it was probably only temporary. She'd been through so much. She'd never "get over it," an expression some patients liked to cling to like a life raft. *When am I going to* get over *this crippling sense of guilt I have that I'm responsible for my best friend's murder, Doctor?* There would be no *getting over* what Becca had been through. "Moving on" was what Dr. Jo like to call it.

Which was funny because it's what we mediators called it, too.

"What," Sister Ernestine said, speaking out of the corner of her mouth so that if Becca looked back at us, we wouldn't appear to speaking about her, "was *that* about?"

"You wouldn't believe me if I told you." This, at least, was the truth. "If I could tell you, which I can't. She thinks of me as her guidance counselor. So I have a professional obligation to keep everything she told me confidential."

"Hmmm," Sister Ernestine said as she continued to observe Becca's progress across the courtyard. "Are you aware of your professional obligation to keep from cursing at and threatening our students and faculty, Miss Simon? Because Ms. Temple has filed a formal complaint against you for doing so. Apparently you terrified her first-period geometry class earlier today."

I swallowed. "I'm also aware there's an exception to the rule of student–guidance counselor confidentiality: when the counselor becomes aware of a situation that might put other students at risk."

Sister Ernestine's pale gray eyebrows rose. "Other students? What other students? Please tell me this doesn't involve Sean Park. I know he and Becca Walters are lab partners in chemistry class. That boy is far too intelligent for his own good. I *knew* he was up to something. Miss Simon, we can't afford this kind of thing, not now with what happened yesterday to Father Dominic at that girl's house. Her father is a major donor."

"No, Sister. It doesn't involve Sean Park, or this school, at all. How well do you know Father Francisco over at Sacred Trinity?"

I had no idea what Sister Ernestine did in her personal time, but I hoped it wasn't playing cards, because she had the worst poker face I'd ever seen. The second I said the name, her mouth twisted as if she'd just bit into the foulest tasting thing she'd ever had the misfortune to eat.

I should have known. Even Sister Ernestine had a *him*. Maybe every single woman in the world has a *him*. Men, too. I'd had the misfortune of meeting Jesse's *him* once.

"Wow," I said. "That bad, huh?"

She immediately assumed a more neutral expression. "So you weren't out here discussing books with Miss Walters after all."

"No. So, Father Francisco? What have you heard?"

Sister Ernestine looked prim. "I will not discuss my personal feelings regarding a fellow educator with an intern. Especially when three of my own students are knee-deep in the waters of a fountain that's been preserved since the 1700s—"

I glanced at the girls. "They're having the time of their life."

"It's the *fountain* I'm worried about, Miss Simon, not your nieces."

"Look, Sister, I'm sorry about that," I said, trotting to keep up with her as she began striding toward the fountain. When she wanted to, the sister could really motor. "But Becca's having a really difficult time right now. She's never told anyone, including her parents, what she just told me. I'm hoping she's going to choose to come forward with the story herself. But in case she doesn't, I'm going to need time to gather information before I can file a report."

"Report?" The nun glanced at me sharply. "Against Father Francisco?"

"Well, he's definitely involved. I was thinking I should go poke around over at Sacred Trinity to get more information . . . but please don't worry," I added hastily. "I won't say I'm affiliated in any way with the Mission Academy. I'll probably need the rest of the afternoon off, though."

To my surprise, Sister Ernestine said, "Of course," as casually as if I'd asked to borrow a pen.

I was so shocked I was rendered momentarily speechless. The nun used the opportunity to continue briskly, "But kindly remember that failure to report a known act of child abuse within thirty-six hours after you've become aware of it can result in a fine, six months in jail, or both. That's California State Penal Code. So if that girl *did* say something about Father Francisco—or whoever—you're obligated to report it. Just because the man's good looking—and a priest—doesn't mean we'll be doing any covering up for him. I'm in charge now that Father Dominic is in the hospital, and what I say goes."

And with that extremely startling statement, she turned to shout, with impressive force, "You, there! Emily, Emma, and Elizabeth Ackerman! Get out of that fountain right this instant."

The girls scrambled immediately from the fountain. I didn't blame them. I knew what it was like to be on the receiving end of the sister's whiplike commands.

What I wasn't so familiar with was what it was like to be her ally. But that's what I was, suddenly. And I had no idea why.

But I liked it.

"Sister," I said. "Thank you. And you don't have to worry about me. I'll take care of this thing with Father Francisco, whatever it—"

"Yes, you will. If I come back out here in five minutes and see any of you in this courtyard," Sister Ernestine bellowed as she stalked away, "there will be no recess for any of you for the rest of the day. Is that understood?"

Wow. Nuns are tough. But maybe they have to be.

The girls, terrified, were scrambling to put on their shoes and socks. Lucia, who hadn't bothered to remove her riding boots, glanced around for Becca. Not seeing her, she began to look upset . . . until she saw me, and also that Sister Ernestine was moving away, back toward the building in which the classrooms were held. Lucia raced toward me.

"Are you and Becca done talking?" she asked when she'd reached me.

"Um," I said, looking after Sister Ernestine. "We are. It was a good chat. Becca told me how you died."

I waited to see what kind of reaction it would have on her, but aside from a slight tightening of the already small mouth, there was none. I felt it was all right to go on.

"I'm going to try to find the man who hurt you, Lucia. I know you don't want him to hurt Becca or anyone else. Do you have any idea where he is?"

Lucia thought about it. Finally she said, "In the woods. He threw me down into that creek. I hurt my head." She blinked accusatorily at me. "He's probably still in the woods if someone would just go look."

If someone would just go look. Ghosts—especially if they were young when they died—often became confused about time, believing everything came to a standstill after their deaths. To Lucia, Becca would always be seven, and her killer was still at the place where she'd died, murdering her over and over again.

This was no way to exist.

But this was what Paul thought Jesse should be condemned to, for no other crime than that Jesse was keeping Paul from getting what he wanted—me.

"Okay, Lucia," I said. "Thanks. I'm going to go find Jimmy, and see that he never bothers Becca again. Okay?"

I had no way of knowing this was true. I only hoped it was.

Lucia seemed to accept my assurance. She nodded solemnly. Her only focus, after all, was Becca. And, for whatever reason, the parentage of my stepnieces.

"Here." Mopsy deposited a large handful of sopping-wet coins into my hands, which I'd stupidly held out when she said *here*. "I'd say that's about forty-five dollars."

"It's not. One of you please take these away from me, they're really disgusting."

"Two hundred dollars?" Flopsy asked, cupping her hands so that I could transfer the coins to them.

"No," I said. "Not even close."

"Three hundred million dollars!" yelled Cotton-tail.

"No. Please stop shouting."

"It's seven dollars and sixty-five cents," said Lucia. "I counted already."

"Fine. Now go put them back. Later I'll give you seven dollars and sixty-five cents—if you can figure out how to divide it up among yourselves, which I sincerely doubt."

The sisters groaned, but I overheard them grudgingly agree it was the right thing to do as Lucia steered them back toward the fountain. "Because," the little ghost reminded them sternly, "it's a sin to steal people's wishes."

It was a sin to steal their lives, too. And I was determined to make sure that whoever had stolen hers paid for it.

veintitres

"I don't see why you won't allow me to beat a confession out of the priest," Jesse said. We were in his car waiting in line at the visitor entrance to 17-Mile Drive. "It would be faster."

"Uh." I pulled down the sun visor in order to check my lip gloss in the vanity mirror. "Because this is twenty-first-century America and I don't want us to go to jail?"

I couldn't read Jesse's expression, since his eyes were shaded by dark sunglasses. The afternoon sun was blazing down on us. Jesse's car was a BMW roadster convertible, a loaner from Jake, who'd decided he needed something roomier so he could simultaneously transport his surfboard, Max, and any girl he might be dating. He'd upgraded to a Mercedes Benz G-Class SUV, so Brad could get the commission.

Then again, I didn't need to read the expression in Jesse's eyes. I could hear his disapproval in his voice.

"I don't see how you think anyone will be able to find you

to put you in jail," he said. "No one will recognize you after you take off that costume."

"Costume?" I looked down at myself. I was wearing a black skirt and jacket combo set I'd purchased months earlier at a Saks in San Francisco, along with a prim white blouse. "This isn't a costume. I bought this outfit months ago to wear to job interviews." And funerals.

I only hoped the next one I attended wouldn't be Jesse's.

By inviting him along on my trip out to Sacred Trinity, I was hoping to keep him busy enough to avoid hearing that Paul Slater was back in town, and why.

I'd driven by 99 Pine Crest Road on my way home from work only to find it crawling with inspectors in hard hats. There was no chance I'd be able to sneak onto the property to salt anything before my dinner at Mariner's later that evening.

A large sign had been plastered across the front door, readable from the street:

WARNING: NO TRESPASSING

—PROPOSED DEMOLITION—

IF INTERESTED IN SALVAGE CONTACT:

SLATER PROPERTIES

There was a phone number listed in marker underneath.

The sign—and the men in hard hats—meant it was real. Paul hadn't been bluffing. Not that I'd ever suspected he had, but—

"And the glasses?" Jesse asked, intruding on my thoughts.

I glanced at my reflection in the vanity mirror. I'd swapped my sunglasses for the nonprescription eyeglasses Becca had abandoned in the courtyard.

"Oh, these. I'm supposed to look like a mom. Don't you think they make me seem older?"

"Your mother doesn't wear glasses. Neither does your sister-in-law. They don't wear their hair that way, either."

I lifted a hand to my head, having forgotten the heavily hair-sprayed updo I'd given myself when I'd gone back to my apartment to change.

"We're supposed to look rich enough to be able to afford to send our child to one of the most expensive private schools in the country, Jesse," I explained. "That's how we're going to get into Sacred Trinity to ask about this Jimmy person. They don't let just anyone come strolling onto school grounds these days, you know."

Jesse smiled. "Rich mothers wear their hair like that? And glasses they don't need?"

"No one will know I don't need them," I said. "More importantly, no one from the school district will recognize me in these hideous things."

"So that's why we're using my car, and not yours. I'd wondered."

"Exactly. No parent who could afford Sacred Trinity would be caught dead in my car. Do you remember our names?"

I could tell by the tilt of his head that he'd rolled his eyes. "Dr. and Mrs. Baracus. Am I supposed to be Greek?"

"B. A. Baracus isn't Greek. He's a character from *The A-Team*, a television show, played by a man named Mr. T." At Jesse's disapproving expression, I said quickly, "Don't worry, it's a very old TV show, no one will remember it. Well, there was a movie, but I had to think of something fast. I didn't expect to get an appointment for a private tour on such short notice. But who cares? It worked, didn't it?"

"What if they decide to look up Dr. Baracus on the Internet?"

"All they'll find is that the word *baracus* means bad attitude. There's a kind of poetic justice in that, don't you think?"

"Yes, considering I have in the trunk all the equipment I need to beat a confession out of the priest," he said, his gaze on the vanity plate of the Lexus in front of us: CARMEL1. "Everything Jake had in the house to subdue an intruder—"

I swiveled toward him, shocked.

"Jesse, no! No one is beating a confession out of anybody. We're on a fact-finding mission *only*."

He adjusted his grip on the steering wheel, his broad shoulders hunching under the jacket of his dark suit. "I think we could discover more facts more quickly if we handcuffed the priest to a radiator, then doused him with water, then shocked him several times with your stepbrother's taser."

You can't take the darkness out of the boy.

"I hate child killers, too, Jesse, but how about going for a more subtle approach that won't get either of us charged with assault?"

"Your attitude," Jesse said, "really isn't as bad as our name implies, Mrs. Baracus."

"I'm only asking that you think of our darling daughter, dear, sweet little Penelope."

He shook his head. "No imaginary daughter of mine will be called Penelope."

I bit my lip to keep myself from blurting that imaginary children might be all we ever had. What was the point? If Jesse was willing to chain a priest to a radiator, I could only imagine what he'd be willing to do to Paul.

"You didn't really put all that stuff in the trunk, did you?" I asked.

"Of course. Along with Brad's .22 Hornet."

At my disbelieving glance, he shrugged. "What was I supposed to do with it? He wanted to go raccoon hunting last night, remember? I had to hide it from him somewhere."

"So you brought it along today? Great. Just great, Jesse." I eyed the armed guard who was checking each car before collecting their toll and then waving them through the gate. 17-Mile Drive, the only route to the Academy of the Sacred Trinity, was a coastal road, running through Pebble Beach along the Pacific coastline. It was as possible to see sea lions and sea otters sunning themselves on the beach along the drive as it was to see $20 million mansions.

Of course, if you weren't a resident, you had to pay for the privilege of using the road—the current rate was ten dollars, unless you had a guest pass, which, as parents of a prospective student at Sacred Trinity, we did.

"Do I have to remind you that you are *not* actually Dr. Baracus," I asked Jesse, "but a medical student and former ghost, and one with forged identity papers?"

"Actually," he said, lowering his sunglasses and glancing at me, "I'm a medical resident, not a student. And why are you so suddenly concerned about my identity papers, Mrs. Baracus?"

"I'm just wondering if driving with a rifle, handcuffs, and tasers in the trunk of a BMW that doesn't even technically belong to you is such a good idea."

"Are you afraid I'll be racially profiled on 17-Mile Drive? *Nombre de Dios*, Susannah." Jesse clicked his tongue at me. "Have you so little faith in your fellow man?"

I snorted. "Nothing I've heard lately about my fellow man has done much to restore it."

He grinned and slipped his glasses back into place. "I'll have to work on that later. And anyway, I'm not Jesse de Silva, medical resident, anymore, but Dr. Baracus, wealthy plastic surgeon, father of Penelope, remember? They'd never check *his* trunk for implements of torture."

"Very funny." None of this was striking me as particularly amusing. "So you're on duty at the hospital all night tonight?"

"Starting at five," he said. "Perhaps, if we finish torturing the priest early, we can have dinner together beforehand, and I can begin restoring your faith in mankind?"

"Of course." No way was I going to mention that I already had dinner plans. "But we're not torturing the priest. God, could this line be any longer?"

"Why are you so tense, Susannah? It's a beautiful Friday afternoon in Carmel-by-the-Sea. Everyone has come down for the weekend to take advantage of the weather and have a nice scenic drive along the coast. You should be enjoying the fact that you live here and can take this drive with your husband-to-be anytime you want."

I gave him the side-eye. Had David already called him? Was he trying to make me feel guilty on purpose?

No. If David had told him what was going on, he wouldn't be sitting here in line to get onto 17-Mile Drive. He'd already have found Paul and tased him to death.

And Jesse had always been more sanguine than me about waiting in lines—and interviewing possible murder suspects— probably from having spent such a long time stuck between the worlds of the living and the dead.

God, I was the worst girlfriend in the world.

"Um, no reason," I said quickly.

But of course it was because I'd already received a text from Paul a little while earlier.

El Diablo Can't wait until 8. Meet for a predinner cocktail, hotel bar, 5PM.

Wear something sexy.
Nov 18 1:20 PM

"So, five o'clock, huh? I'm sure we'll be done with all this by then. I can drop you off at the hospital. How is Father Dominic, anyway?" I asked, hoping to change the subject.

"He's doing better. They moved him out of the ICU. He's regained consciousness, and is perfectly lucid. He asked about you."

"Really?" This was nice to hear. "What did he say?"

Jesse's grin was crooked. "He told me to tell you not to exorcise Lucia for throwing him down a flight of stairs."

I couldn't help laughing. It was good to know Father Dominic was feeling better.

He glanced at me. "You know, in those glasses, with your hair like that, you look like a teacher. My first teacher, actually."

"Like from when you were a little kid? In the one-room schoolhouse?"

"Yes. Miss Boyd. The town paid for her to travel all the way from Boston to take the job of educating the few children whose parents could spare them from their farms and ranches."

I frowned. "I don't know if I want to look like some lady from the 1800s."

He glared at me. At least, I thought it was a glare. Then I realized I'd misinterpreted the heat in his glance. It definitely wasn't disapproval.

"You should," he said. "She was a very intelligent, beautiful lady, like you. She didn't swear as much, though. In fact, she never uttered a single curse word in my presence."

"Really?" I crossed my legs with elaborate casualness, making sure the slit in my skirt revealed a lot of thigh. This was no easy feat in a roadster. "Did Miss Boyd ever make you stand in the corner for being naughty in her classroom?"

"I would never have dreamt of being naughty in Miss Boyd's classroom," Jesse said, his gaze glued to the slit. "I felt privileged every time I was in her presence, receiving any education at all. There were many days my father couldn't spare me from the ranch."

"That must have been so hard for you," I said sympathetically, leaning toward him.

"It was hard." His gaze moved from my thighs to my chest. Leaning forward had caused my seat belt—which I always strap beneath my breasts to keep them from getting squished—to give them a boost. Score.

"But look how much you've accomplished since then. Miss Boyd would be so proud."

I couldn't believe this. After all the parading around I'd done in front of him in swimsuits and miniskirts, what ended up turning him on was a pair of glasses and my hair in a French twist.

Of course I would make this discovery in a tiny car in line to go find out the identity of a murderer, and on the day Paul Slater was in town, threatening to trigger a demonic curse and blow up my house. If I didn't have bad luck, I'd have no luck at all.

"Jesse," I said, reaching up to undo one button of my prim white blouse.

"Yes?"

"Are you telling me you were hot for Teacher?"

A car honked, long and loud, behind us.

"Oh, darn," I said, rebuttoning my blouse. "It's our turn in line."

Jesse looked annoyed as he shifted. "Hot for Teacher. No, I was *not* hot for Teacher. What does that even mean, hot for Teacher? That's disrespectful of teachers, Susannah."

"You'd better let me do the talking," I said, patting him on the hand. "You seem out of sorts." I leaned over him to gush at the security guard as Jesse pulled up to the tollgate. "Hi. Dr. and Mrs. Baracus, here to see Father Francisco at the Academy of the Sacred Trinity. We should be on the list."

The guard glanced at her clipboard while Jesse gazed impassively at the road through his dark sunglasses. *Hot for Teacher*, I heard him mutter scornfully under his breath.

"Oh, yes. Here you are!" The guard smiled and handed Jesse a pass, along with a map with directions to the school printed on it. "Enjoy your visit, Dr. and Mrs. Baracus."

Jesse returned her smile, his so dazzling, with his white teeth and gorgeously kissable lips, I don't know how she didn't faint at the sight of it. "I'm sure we will."

The school turned out to be on grounds four times as big as those of the Mission Academy, though Sacred Trinity housed half as many students, being for girls only. The main building resembled a country manor estate, something straight out of one of those historical movies where the people all sit around getting served tea. It came complete with a long, impressive driveway (lined by Italian cypress trees) that passed gently sloping lawns before stopping in front of a wide, ornately carved stone staircase, leading to an even wider, more ornately carved double doorway.

"One good earthquake," I said to Jesse, "and this whole place will come tumbling down. Who do they think they're trying to impress?"

"Dr. Bad Attitude."

We parked in a lot that looked as if it had been designed for a world-class modern art museum, not a school, it was so well landscaped, and were greeted at the main entrance by Sister Mary Margaret, director of admissions. She'd no doubt been alerted to our arrival by the security guard at the gate—not the gate to 17-Mile Drive, but to the school. On the website, it had said that daughters of foreign princes attended school there. Security was clearly a priority.

Just not when it came to local girls with the last name of Martinez.

"Dr. Baracus," the nun said, glowing with enthusiasm as she stepped forward to shake our hands. "Mrs. Baracus. I'm so delighted to meet you. Welcome to the Academy of the Sacred Trinity."

I shot Jesse a triumphant look. They totally hadn't looked up *baracus* on the Internet. Or, if they had, they were hedging their bets that Jesse—or I, not to be sexist—was so rich we'd carefully kept ourselves off the Web, like the families of many of their students. The wealthiest people in the world don't share photos of their private jets and Rolexes on Instagram, as they do not care to have their children kidnapped and held for ransom as a result of advertising that wealth.

Sister Mary Margaret was Sister Ernestine's opposite in every way. Young where Sister Ernestine was old, lean where Sister Ernestine was plump, Sister Mary Margaret fed us a well-rehearsed but sweetly enthusiastic speech about the benefits of educating our adorable daughter Penelope—Jesse frowned every time her name was mentioned—at Sacred Trinity.

The percentage of Sacred Trinity girls who went on to college, we were told—was the highest in the tri-county area— 100 percent!—and the percentage who went on to Ivy League colleges—well, Sister Mary Margaret didn't want to brag, but it was high.

If they weren't murdered, of course, before they finished first grade, I thought, but didn't say out loud.

Jesse looked annoyed during much of Sister Mary Margaret's spiel, for which I didn't blame him. He was playing the role of the brilliantly wealthy plastic surgeon—the medical specialty that pulls in the most money these days—incredibly well, but I could tell that having to hear the words *thanks to Father Francisco* so often was wearing on his last nerve. It was wearing on mine, too.

"Thanks to Father Francisco," Sacred Trinity was no longer

on the brink of financial disaster due to mismanagement by the previous headmaster. Father Francisco had swooped in a decade ago and saved the day with his fiscal know-how.

"Thanks to Father Francisco," the Sacred Trinity girls' choir had gone from being nearly disbanded to being number one in the state. They had even recorded an album. Did we want a copy of their CD for Penelope? Of course we did. Penelope would love it.

"Thanks to Father Francisco," the Sacred Trinity school library's floors had been stripped of the exotic wood the father's predecessor had laid there. Father Francisco had replaced the floor with a more sensible wood, donating the difference in cost to a literacy charity. Wasn't he the most wonderful man?

"Did Father Francisco do the labor himself?" Jesse asked Sister Mary Margaret.

She looked momentarily confused. "Er . . . no. He hired a contractor."

Jesse was unimpressed. "Then he probably didn't save that much money."

I had to stifle a laugh. Sister Mary Margaret didn't know what she was up against. Every time he was on call, Jesse saw children suffering from maladies caused by improper diet. Their parents simply couldn't afford to feed them properly.

Yet here, in the same community, was a school that had paid $150 per square foot for flooring, and charged for tuition for its kindergarten what Jesse had paid per semester for medical school . . . though of course it did offer, even though in Carmel the temperature rarely fell below fifty degrees, heated stalls for the horses their students wished to board there. We found this out as we were given a tour of the grounds.

By then Sister Mary Margaret had neatly passed us off to a "student tour guide," a slender, dark-eyed junior, Sidney.

I was well acquainted with the psychology behind student tour guides, since we had them at the Mission Academy, as well. It was more effective for school administrations to have socially garrulous, nonthreateningly attractive students give tours to parents of prospective students than for them to be given by people like Sister Mary Margaret. In the students, parents saw what their own children could grow to be if they attended such a fine institution.

And student tour guides were better at fielding the pricklier questions, like Jesse's tense: "When can we meet this famous Father Francisco we've heard so much about?"

"Oh, sorry," Sidney said, batting her long, dark eyelashes (she wore extensions and a good deal of dark eyeliner, but I'm sure it fooled a lot of the parents). "He's in San Luis Obispo today at a conference."

I knew the conference Father Francisco was allegedly attending—the same one Father Dominic had gone to—had ended Wednesday night. He'd either extended his trip so it could include a few nights of gambling in Vegas, or he didn't want to waste his valuable time chitchatting with a couple of prospective parents.

I'd put my money on the former. Most private schools no longer considered themselves educational institutions, but small profit-making corporations, and couldn't afford to blow off potential investors.

Sidney had charmingly explained to us that giving tours was one of her favorite things to do because "it gets me out of calculus" and "will look good on my college applications." Her dream was to go to Yale and become the "greatest actress since Meryl Streep."

Sidney had nothing to worry about. She was well on her way.

"How long have you attended Sacred Trinity?" I asked Sidney as we made our way toward the heated stables. I'd asked to see them as "Penelope" had a pony.

"Since kindergarten," Sidney said. "I love it here so much. My parents live in San Francisco. I see them on weekends. But I'd much rather be here than in the city. Too crowded."

Sell it, Sidney.

"So you would have been here when that girl died," I said casually as the barn and stables, plus riding ring, came into view, the stables large but tidy, painted white with green trim, the barn done in traditional cliché—but attractive—red barn paint. "What was her name, darling?" I squeezed Jesse's arm. I was leaning on it because it was difficult to walk on the school's gravel paths in my high-heeled pumps. "That poor girl who died? Lucy something?"

"Lucia," Jesse said, right on cue. He appeared immune to Sidney's charms.

"Oh, God." Sidney's red plaid uniform skirt swayed sassily ahead of us on the path. "Yes. Lucia Martinez. I'll never forget it. What a nightmare. I was a year ahead of her. But they still made us all take, like, bereavement classes to make sure we weren't going to go mental or whatever."

Then she seemed to remember to whom she was speaking and flashed a quick embarrassed smile over her shoulder. "Not, you know, that it wasn't completely terrible, what happened to her. Horseback-riding accident. But nothing like that would ever happen to your daughter. It was a completely freak accident. It could never happen again."

"Yes," I said, remembering what Becca had said she was tired of hearing everyone say: "'Accidents happen.' I'm sure."

By that time we were at the stables. As fortune had it, a lesson was going on. A strong-looking older woman in jodhpurs was standing in the middle of a grassy ring, directing six or seven girls on extremely healthy-looking mounts.

"Ms. Dunleavy." Sidney called to her from the white wooden fence. "I have some nice people here who'd like to meet you."

Jennifer Dunleavy—I recognized the name from the newspaper article CeeCee had sent me about Lucia's death—walked over to the side of the fence where Jesse and I leaned, inhaling the not unpleasant smells of horse and fresh-cut grass and hay. She removed a glove to shake our hands as Sidney expertly introduced us. Jennifer Dunleavy's grip was firm but not overwhelming.

"Dr. and Mrs. Baracus's little girl has a pony," Sidney explained. "If they decide to enroll her here, they'd be interested in boarding it."

"Great," Jennifer said with a big smile that looked sincere. "We definitely have the space. I've got a lesson right now, as you can see, but Mike can show you around. Mike!" She called to a hired hand who was holding a paint can, doing touch-ups. He smiled and began strolling over.

"Oh," I said quickly. "My friend's stepdaughter took riding lessons here for a time, and she said there was the most marvelous man who had the most amazing touch. What was his name again, darling?" I squeezed Jesse's arm again.

"Jimmy," Jesse said woodenly. I could tell he was ready to hit someone, though not anyone present at the current moment.

"That's right," I cried. "Jimmy! Is Jimmy still here? I'd love to meet Jimmy, if I could, and for him to show us around."

Jennifer's face clouded over. For a moment I thought it was because the name disturbed her. Then I realized her clouded expression might only have been because she couldn't place the name right away.

"Oh, *Jimmy,*" she said at last. "You must mean Jim Delgado."

And just like that, I had a last name for Becca's tormentor and

Lucia's murderer. I tried not to squeeze Jesse's arm too hard in my excitement.

"Oh, that's right," I said. "Delgado. Jimmy Delgado."

"But good grief," Jennifer went on. "He hasn't worked here in nearly a decade."

I didn't bother hiding my disappointment. I figured a rich lady like Mrs. Baracus wouldn't hide her feelings. She'd definitely pout if a store didn't have her favorite brand, or a rich private school no longer employed her favorite child killer.

"Oh," I said. "What a shame. Mrs. Walters said so many good things about him, too."

Jennifer's eyebrows went up questioningly at the name.

"Mrs. Walters?"

"Yes. That's my friend. Lance Arthur Walters's wife, Kelly Walters, of Wal-Con Aeronautics. Surely you remember. Her stepdaughter went here for a time . . . Becca Walters?"

I saw Sidney make a slight moue of distaste at Becca's name. Well, Becca had never been a very popular girl.

But then, none of them were aware that Becca had had good reason to make herself as inconspicuous as possible: Jimmy Delgado.

"Such a lovely couple," I went on. "We met on a committee to raise money for breast cancer research. Kelly just couldn't stop raving about this school and of course Jimmy's horse-handling skills. What a shame. I don't suppose you know where Jimmy Delgado went?"

I felt Jesse gently squeeze my elbow. He knew I was lying about Kelly, and also laying it on too thick.

But what Jesse doesn't know—because he has too much integrity, which is one of the reasons I love him so much—is that there's no such thing as laying it on too thick when it comes to people who are only interested in you for your money.

"Well," Jennifer said, looking truly regretful. "I do know where he is, but I'm afraid it won't do you any good, Mrs. Baracus. Jim Delgado doesn't work with horses anymore."

"You know where he is?" Jesse couldn't hide his surprise.

"Sure," she said with a laugh. "Jimmy's still right here in town. I see him all the time. But good luck trying to get him back into horse handling. He came into some money awhile ago, and now he owns his own business. Delgado Photography Studio. He specializes in children's portraits."

veinticuatro

If anyone at the school noticed that the wife of wealthy plastic surgeon Dr. Baracus looked a little tight-lipped as her husband hurried her back to their BMW, they didn't mention it. They probably thought I was nauseous from having another bun in the oven.

To them, this must have been good news: Penelope Baracus was getting a potential baby sister! This meant more tuition money for them later down the line. *Ka-ching!*

But once we'd gotten safely in the parking lot and could no longer be overheard, I let loose. With word vomit, not actual vomit, since by then I'd found some chewable antacids in my bag—along with the various other items I'd shoved in there back at my apartment—and was concentrating on chomping them down, one by one. The chalky coating on my tongue kept me from tasting the bile that kept rising in the back of my throat.

"What the hell?" I didn't say *hell*, though. If the tip jar from the office had been nearby, I'd have owed it five dollars. Well, more like fifty after my tirade. "He's still in town. He didn't go anywhere. He's still *right here in town*."

"Take it easy, Susannah," Jesse said in his smooth, deep voice. "This is good news. It will only make it easier for the police to arrest him after Becca tells them what she knows."

"The police?" I was shocked at his naïveté, though I suppose I shouldn't have been. The police routinely got involved in his abuse cases at the hospital. As a medical practitioner, he was required to notify them, and they were required to respond. "Jesse, Becca could barely tell *me* what happened, and I'm hardly an authority figure. She found it easier to articulate that the guy had given her candy—*candy*—than that he'd molested her, which is completely normal for a survivor of abuse, but I honestly don't see her being able to go to the cops about any of this soon. And even if she were to, there's not a shred of evidence to connect Jimmy Delgado to Lucia's murder. Becca didn't actually *see* him kill her. And it's not like Lucia can testify."

"But Delgado threatened to kill Becca's parents if she told anyone what he did to her."

"Sure, he threatened to. He threatened to do a lot of things, but he never did any of them, except what he did to Lucia, which we can't prove. Even the things he did to Becca are her word against his, and she's a kid who, thanks to me, now thinks the ghost of her best friend's been following her around for the past decade. If she opens up her mouth about that, no one's going to believe *anything* else she says. I definitely screwed the pooch on that one."

We'd gotten into the car, where I began pulling off my uncomfortable pumps, one by one, and hurling them to the floor. Jesse watched me with one eyebrow raised in amusement. "Screwed the pooch?"

"Yeah. It means messed up. It's more polite than saying—well, you can figure it out."

Now one corner of his mouth went up. "I think you're being too hard on yourself."

"Am I? If we're to believe what that Dunleavy woman says, Delgado's a respectable business owner. He's got the money to hire a good defense attorney, one who'd rip Becca to shreds in five minutes on the stand, given her current state of mind. And what are the chances Becca's parents are going to allow that to happen? Zip."

Jesse's half smile vanished. "But a photographer of *children*? You know what that means, Susannah."

"Yeah. About that." I pulled my phone from my bag and scrolled to the article about Lucia's death. "Becca said he used to do lots of things for the school, not just work in the stables. Take another look at that photo of Lucia."

Jesse took the phone from me and stared at the photo. "What am I supposed to be seeing?"

"The photo credit. The print's really tiny, but as soon as I heard it, I knew the name sounded familiar."

" '*Photo by James Delgado*,' " he read aloud, then glanced at me. "*Nombre de Dios*."

"Right? They probably thought they could save a few bucks by having their friendly amateur photographer-slash-handyman, Jimmy Delgado, do the school photos that year. All they'd have to pay was printing costs. It was right after Father Francisco started and the school was in all that financial trouble, as we know from our little tour."

"No wonder Lucia looks so solemn," Jesse said softly. "She knew Becca's secret. And his."

"Of course it doesn't prove anything, either, but if he did murder her, wouldn't the coroner have—?"

"You told me that Becca said Jimmy's tall. A broken neck would look the same to a coroner who didn't know to suspect foul play, whether she'd suffered a violent fall from a horse or been thrown to the ground by a tall man who wanted her dead."

"That's what Lucia says happened."

A muscle leaped in Jesse's jaw. "So exhuming the body would be useless. Any DNA evidence he might have left would be destroyed by now by the embalming process and by time. But what about the money?"

"What money?"

"Delgado got the money from somewhere to suddenly quit his job at the stables and open his own business. The timing is right. While I'm guessing there wasn't enough money from the sale of that library flooring to open a photography studio, I think Father Francisco got the money from somewhere to bribe Delgado to leave Sacred Trinity and keep his mouth shut about what he did to Lucia."

"Yes," I said, after thinking about it. "You're right. Father Francisco only pretended not to believe Becca's confession. He must have gone straight from the chapel to Delgado and told him he'd have to leave. Sacred Trinity was already in bad financial straits. They couldn't afford another scandal."

"And Delgado demanded money in exchange for leaving without a fuss." Jesse switched on the ignition and backed the car from the parking lot. "And once again, thanks to Father Francisco, Sacred Trinity was saved."

"Amazing Father Francisco." I stared grimly at the neat rows of Italian cypress trees as we headed down the school's driveway back toward 17-Mile Drive. "Is there no miracle he can't perform?"

"Yes. One. He can't hide the money trail from him to Delgado. Somewhere there has got to be a record of it—the priest withdrawing it, and Delgado depositing it."

"A lot of donations made to churches are in cash, as you well know. You've seen the collection plate as it goes around." As Jesse's bride-to-be, I occasionally tagged along when he went to church to give a good impression to the local bishop, since we needed his permission to marry in the mission basilica (I must have done a good job since we got it—though a fat lot of good it was going to do us now).

"And even if Father Francisco did write Delgado a check," I went on, determined to keep my mind on the matter at hand, "it doesn't connect either of them to Lucia's death. It's still Becca's word against theirs. There's no *evidence*, Jesse."

"No." He eased the BMW out into the traffic on 17-Mile Drive. "That leaves us with only one option."

"Yeah," I said. "Look up where Delgado Photography Studio is, then tell Lucia. Then she can do to Jimmy what she did to me in the pool the other night. Let's bring lawn chairs and a six-pack so we can watch. It'll be more fun than the fireworks on Fourth of July."

"No." Now more than one muscle was leaping in Jesse's jaw. "Don't tell Lucia. I'll take care of Delgado."

"*You?*" I whipped off Becca's glasses, squinting at him in the late-afternoon sunlight. "I was kidding about sending Lucia after Jimmy."

"Well, I'm not." Jesse gripped the wheel more tightly, and not because people were driving like maniacs, although they were, it being a Friday afternoon in Northern California. "This isn't a job for a child."

"Well, it isn't a job for you, either."

"Why not? I killed a man once. I'd be more than happy to do so again, in this case. Or two men, actually."

"You killed a man once, Jesse, because he was about to kill you, and me, too. This isn't the same."

"How?"

"Because that was self-defense. This is vigilantism."

"Well, in some cases a little vigilantism is necessary. Delgado needs to be stopped, and so does the priest."

I was more thankful than ever I hadn't told him about Paul.

"That may be true, but not this way, and certainly not by you. You swore an oath to do no harm, remember?"

"If destroying a monster prevents it from doing harm to others, and preserving the quality of life of the rest of my patients, I'm upholding that oath. That's how physicians who administer lethal injections to prisoners on death row justify their actions."

Whoa. I'd thought last night that he was making progress when he'd told me how it felt to be dead, unable to reach out to the people he'd loved.

But this wasn't progress. This was premeditation . . . something with which I was not unfamiliar, but that still didn't make it all right.

"Okay," I said, hanging on to the passenger door. He was taking the hairpin curves along the sea at an impressive clip now that the traffic was thinning out. "Well, I guess that's what you'd better do, then. Go ahead and take out Jimmy and the priest. I'll enjoy CeeCee's headline: "'Young Physician Wastes Promising Future with Sizzling Hot Wife by Murdering Scumbags.'"

Jesse didn't laugh. "Someone has to do it, Susannah."

"Yeah, but like I said, that someone doesn't have to be you. Your job is to save lives, not take them."

"Like *I* said, sometimes by taking one, you can save others. And if I don't do it, who will? You?"

"Why not me? It's not like . . ."

"Like what?"

I clamped my mouth shut, realizing what I'd been about to cavalierly admit to Jesse: that I'd been contemplating killing Paul ever since I'd received that e-mail from him. The only reason I'd agreed to have dinner with him was because afterward, when we retired to his hotel room for "dessert," I planned to mediate him, permanently.

But this was another thing a girl should keep secret, right? There's no reason for her intended to know *everything* about her.

"Never mind," I murmured, looking out over the sea. It had been burnished amber by the sun, slowly sinking toward the west. The sky, the beaches, the water—the whole area, as far as the eye could see, was glowing with the same golden sheen as Lucia's hair . . .

Saint Lucia is the one they always show wearing a crown of lit candles around her head, usually at Christmastime. She'd supposedly worn the candles around her head in order to be hands-free while leading hundreds of Christians to freedom through the darkness of the catacombs beneath Rome, a job not unlike my own, leading the souls of the dead to the light of the afterlife.

"What did you say?" Jesse asked. The wind rushing past us from behind the windshield was noisy, making it hard to hear.

"Nothing. Look, how long is your shift this weekend?"

"I'm on call starting at five tonight. I'm not off again until tomorrow afternoon."

"Okay," I said, shouting to be heard above the wind. "Great. I'll get in touch with CeeCee and see what she can find out about where Jimmy Delgado lives." I made a big show of pulling my phone from my purse. "Then maybe we can hit him—and Father Francisco, assuming he's back from his alleged conference—tomorrow night."

By tomorrow night, if things worked out the way I was planning, the Delgado Photography Studio and possibly even Sacred Trinity would be in ashes.

The only thing still standing would be 99 Pine Crest Road. I hoped.

"We?" Jesse threw me a suspicious glance as we headed through the gate that said THANK FOR YOU VISITING 17-MILE DRIVE. PLEASE COME AGAIN. "Not *we.*"

"Yes, *we,*" I said. "I'm your fiancée. I understand you're not entirely up on twenty-first-century social mores, Jesse, but it's considered rude these days not to invite your fiancée to your vigilante party."

His lips twisted into a cynical smile. "Not this time, Susannah."

"What do you mean, not this time? What kind of sexist bullsh—?"

"I'm well acquainted with your feelings about my nineteenth-century macho-man ways, Susannah, and I'll be the first to admit many of those ways were wrong. But some of them aren't. Some of them work better than your twenty-first-century ways, which seem to allow child murderers to go unpunished and"—he held up a hand to silence me when I began to protest—"young girls to needlessly suffer. So perhaps just this once you'll allow me to do things *my* way."

"Oh," I said. "Oh, okay, Sheriff de Silva. I'll just go decorate some bonnets while you execute a few criminals without due process."

His smile became even more infuriatingly cynical. "You don't even know how to sew."

"Yeah, well, I do know how to shoot a gun. I've been taking target lessons with Jake over at the range in Monterey. But if you don't want me around, fine. I'll just sit quietly at home like a good little bride-to-be while you're out fighting the bad guys."

His lifted his gaze from the road to glance at me.

"I do want you around, Susannah," he said. "That's why I want you at home. I've lost too many people—all the people—I love. I can't lose you, too. Do you understand? That's why you have to let me take Delgado myself, alone. I want you around forever."

"Oh." Now I felt like a jerk for having called him a macho man so many times. Not, of course, that it made a difference. If anything, his admission only strengthened my resolve not to change a single thing I was planning to do. "Well, when you put it *that* way. Okay. Okay, sure."

Even through the dark lenses of his sunglasses, I could see that his gaze hadn't strayed from mine. "Why do I get the feeling that you're hiding something from me, *querida*?"

"*Me?*" I asked in an innocent voice as I texted rapidly. "I would never hide anything from you."

> **Drinks sound good. See you at 5. Can't wait.**
> Nov 18 4:15 PM

veinticinco

"Simon, you came. I have to admit, I didn't think you—" Paul jerked back, apparently regretting his decision to kiss me hello. "When did you start wearing *glasses*?"

"Hello, Paul. You haven't changed a bit. Still rude as ever."

"No, really, what's with the glasses? And why is your hair up like that?" He looked slightly horrified. "I instantly recognized your amazing ass, of course, as soon as I came in, but then when you turned around—" He heaved a mock shudder. "Ever heard of contacts?"

"They're not prescription. And you're late. You said five. This place turns into a meat market after five thirty. You're lucky I didn't run off with one of these other nice gentlemen who don't mind my glasses at all."

Paul may not have found my glasses alluring, but plenty of other patrons at the Carmel Inn hotel bar had found them no deterrent to asking if they could buy me a drink. The diamond on my left finger didn't seem to bother them, either. Finally I'd put my bag on the seat beside me and said it was occupied: I was saving it for my husband, B. A. Baracus.

Only one guy got the joke. He'd bought me a vodka tonic in appreciation.

"Poor baby," Paul said as he handed me my bag and slid onto the stool, giving my new friend the evil eye. "I feel sorry for any guy who tried to hit on you. Did you knee him in the balls?"

"That's an extra special move that I reserve for extra special guys like you. Where were you? Buying the Vatican so you can knock it down to put in a strip mall?"

"I'm glad you got your sense of humor back. I was worried you were going to be pissy about all this." He made eye contact with the busy bartender. "What she's having." Then he eyed my drink. "That better not be something nonalcoholic, like club soda. I want your defenses down tonight for when I take full and total advantage of you."

"Wow, you really are still just as in love with yourself as you were in high school, aren't you?" I made a slashing motion beneath my chin to the bartender. "He won't be having anything, sorry. We have to go."

"What do you mean?" Paul's face fell. "I just got here. Look, I apologize for being late, I had a conference call about the properties—you can't believe how nasty people are being about my tearing down that house of yours. I thought *you* were a bitch about it, but that damned historical society, *shit*. And I'm sorry I made the crack about your glasses. I thought I left instructions to dress sexy, but with your hair like that, and the glasses, you look more like a schoolmarm than a sex kitten."

"Schoolmarm?" I laughed. "I'll take that as a compliment. You don't know what that means to me, truly." I took him by the arm, then almost dropped it in surprise. He'd been working out, maybe even more than I had. I could feel his bicep through the expensive

Italian wool of his suit. It wasn't as big as Jesse's, but it was rock solid, which was a little daunting, considering what I had planned. "But we have an appointment elsewhere."

"Appointment? What kind of appointment? Oooh, is it here in the hotel, for a couples' massage? I hear they have outstanding sea-salt scrubs, really rough, the way I like it." His dark eyebrows furrowed. "Suze, I like the initiative, but you're making this too easy. It's way more fun when you play hard to get."

"Then you're in for the time of your life tonight." I dropped the keys to the BMW in his hand. "Here, you're driving."

He stared down at the keys. "Where are we going?"

"Not far. A photography studio over on Ocean."

A slow grin spread over face. "Wait. Are we picking up naughty portraits you had made of yourself for me?"

I couldn't believe it. Then again, I could. Maybe he *was* the child in Aunt Pru's prediction after all—so lost, all he could think of were ways to hurt me for not loving him.

Well, tonight he was going to get what he wanted: my full and uninterrupted attention.

"Yeah, Paul. That's exactly what we're doing. Picking up naughty portraits I had made of myself for you. Now come on, we have to hurry, since you were so late. He closes up shop at six."

Paul was so excited he practically skipped through the bar. I couldn't help noticing how much female attention he attracted (and not because he was practically skipping). He was even taller than I remembered, his neatly trimmed dark hair curling crisply against the back of his tanned neck. Either the shoulders of the suit jacket were padded, or he'd bulked up there, too, in the muscle department.

Well, I suppose being a multimillionaire, he could afford a couple of personal trainers, along with a chef and a nutritionist. He certainly seemed to have found a good stylist. His pale blue tie perfectly matched his pale blue pocket square, which in turn matched his pale blue eyes.

"Your attitude toward all this has certainly improved," he remarked as we headed out the revolving lobby doors to stand beneath the porte cochere, waiting with the other guests for the valets to bring their cars. "What happened to change your mind from the other day? I mean, aside from the obvious—that I hold your boyfriend's life . . . or rather, afterlife—in my hands."

"Well." I affected the bored demeanor of Mrs. Baracus, tired of her jet-set life. "We did have some good times, I suppose, you and I."

He grinned. "We did, didn't we? Remember when we shifted back to the Old West and that lady kicked you out of your own house because she thought you were a whore? That was the *best*."

I kept a smile plastered on my face, even though I noticed an older couple standing near us, also waiting for their car, the wife pretending to be concentrating on reapplying her lipstick, but clearly eavesdropping.

"I do remember that. Then you stuck a gag in my mouth and left me tied up in a barn while you tried to kill Jesse. Even then, you had a one-track mind."

The wife smeared her lipstick, then elbowed her husband, hard, in the ribs.

Fortunately the valet roared up in Jake's car, which I'd convinced Jesse I should use for the weekend, as he didn't need to be parking a BMW with a trunk full of weapons in the hospital parking lot.

"What if it gets broken into?" I'd asked him. "Some lunatic could find Brad's rifle and next thing you know, he'll come running into the ER, shooting up the place. Do you want that on your conscience?"

Jesse had admitted that no, he did not want that on his conscience, but mentioned that I watch too much television and have a tendency to catastrophize things. If only he knew.

"Nice ride," Paul said as he slid behind the wheel of the convertible. He adjusted the seat to accommodate his longer legs. "I guess people with graduate degrees in counseling make more scratch than I've been led to believe."

I buckled my seat belt. "Just drive."

He did as I asked, taking us up Ocean Avenue, downtown Carmel's main drag, at a breakneck speed. Even though there was still a little less than a week to Thanksgiving, the town council had decided it was never too early to start decorating for Christmas, so tasteful white fairy lights wrapped the trunks of the palm trees up and down the street.

"Ah, Suze." Paul sighed happily. "Being back in your company is like having a refreshing breeze in my hair. Or maybe that's the actual breeze. I forgot how freaking cold it gets around here when the sun goes down. Where are we going again?"

I told him the address and pointed. "It's that way."

"I'm aware of that, Suze. I used to live here, remember? And once principal construction begins on the new development— well, it's probably better not to bring that up. You sure you're not still pissed at me, Suze?"

"Not now that I've become more accustomed to the idea," I lied.

"Well, I just want you to know that you don't have to worry. If things don't go the way I'm hoping tonight—but I'm feeling very optimistic that they will—I will do everything in my power to protect you from that boyfriend of yours once he goes all savage beast on you. There's a safe room on my new jet, you know."

It was extremely hard to summon up a smile, but I managed. "That's so sweet of you, Paul. Pull over. We're here."

We were lucky to find a parking space. The art galleries and shops tended to stay open late, especially on weekends and holidays, when there were more tourists in town. The owners hoped the window displays would catch the eye of couples strolling down the street after dinner, and that they'd enter the store and buy a coffee table shaped like a couple of leaping gray whales for a mere $40,000.

Delgado Photography Studio was a picturesque little place tucked between a jewelry store and a shop that sold handcrafted women's clothing made of all-natural materials that even Aunt Pru wouldn't be caught dead in, if she could afford it, which she couldn't because the cheapest thing was a scarf for $200.

Delgado's had a black-and-white theme. All brick, it was painted black to look more avant-garde, with some blown-up black-and-white photos in the window of the sweeping cliffs of Big Sur and crashing surf of Monterey Bay, surrounded by smaller black-and-white headshots of children—mostly girls—staring with intense energy into the camera, their hair windswept or stuck to their round cheeks from sea spray.

I felt the bile rise once again in my throat. Fortunately I still had plenty of antacids in my purse. Among other things.

"This is the place?" Paul asked, looking at the photos in the display window. "These don't look very sexy. They're all of kids." There was a noticeable lack of enthusiasm in his voice.

"Just wait. May I have the keys?"

"Sure." Paul surrendered the car keys, then watched as I went to the back of the convertible.

"What's in there?" he asked, pointing at the large sports bag I drew from the trunk.

I winked at him. "Supplies."

Paul grinned. "Whoa. I get it. So this whole thing"—he waved a hand over my outfit—"with the glasses and the suit is a getup for the photo session, and you're going to change once you get in there? Go from schoolmarm to sex kitten?"

"Something like that," I said, walking to the studio door.

"Kinky," Paul said appreciatively. "You know, I like how into this you're getting, Simon. You're making me feel kind of bad for what's going to happen to Jesse when we—" He made a slashing motion under his neck, the same one I'd made to the bartender to cancel Paul's drink order. Only Paul made it to show how casually he planned to cancel Jesse's life plans. "Especially since I heard what happened to Father Dominic. I know I said I don't read the Alumni Newsletter, but I glanced at today's update, and saw he had a fall."

"He did." I joined him at the door, standing only a half foot away from him, my high heels making me tall enough to lift my chin and look him in the eye.

"I'm sorry about that," Paul said, his face only inches from mine. "I know how much you like that old man. I sent him some flowers, and a donation to the school, since I figured that's what a decent person would do, and that's what he'd really like—you, too. And God knows, I can spare the money."

"That was sweet of you, Paul." My gaze dropped to his lips. "Thank you."

"I'm not all bad, you know, Suze," he whispered. His gaze was on my lips, too. "I mean, I am, of course, but not really. I'm not *dark*. Not like that boyfriend of yours. I like you, and that has to count for something, right?"

"Does it, Paul?" I asked. "I'm not sure it's enough, exactly. But you know what I *do* know?"

"What?" he asked, his hands going to my hips.

"You're not the only one."

His lips had begun dipping down toward mine, but now he pulled away slightly, looking confused. "What do you mean?"

"Who's bad. I'm bad, too. Much worse than you."

"Oh, yeah?"

He grinned, liking the sound of that, leaning forward so that he was pressing me into the doorway. I could feel every inch of him through the Italian wool of his suit. It wasn't lined. That must be itchy, I thought, in the distant part of my brain that wasn't extremely alarmed at feeling another man's private parts against me. Was he even wearing underwear? It didn't feel like it. Trust Paul to go commando. Quicker access.

"You don't know how long I've been waiting for you to admit that, Simon." His breath was warm on my cheek. "But now that you have, we can finally—"

I reached up to lay a finger over his lips. "Not that kind of bad, Paul," I said. "I mean your-worst-nightmare bad. You thought tearing down my house was going to release the darkness inside of Jesse? Wait until you see the darkness it's released in me. Come here. I'll show you."

I grabbed his tie, opened the door to the photography studio, and pulled him inside after me.

veintiseis

"You must be Mr. and Mrs. Maitland," the man behind the desk said, beaming, as we walked in. "I'd almost given up hope."

"Sorry we're so late." I smiled at him. "My husband had a business meeting. Do you mind if I set this down over here?" I indicated the sports bag over my shoulder. "It's heavy."

"Oh, please, allow me." The man—taller than I'd expected, even though Becca had warned me—hurried out from behind the shiny black lacquer desk to relieve me of the bag. He set it where I'd been meaning to, next to a black plaster statue of a young female ballerina, standing in third position. Her tutu was of real black tulle.

"You must work out," the man said to me, laughingly, because the bag weighed so much.

"I do. Are you Mr. Delgado?"

"I am." He extended his right hand. He had short-cropped graying hair that looked as if it had probably been dirty blond at one time, and a sizeable gut. "James Delgado. It's a pleasure to meet you, Mrs. Maitland."

I tried not to let my nausea show as I slipped my fingers into his. "Same here." His hand felt like any other hand, even though it had killed Lucia Martinez, one horse, and for all I knew, many other innocent creatures as well.

He wore wire-rimmed glasses and had the large, raw-knuckled hands of someone who'd worked, at least for a while, outdoors—or possibly in a stable. He looked a bit like Santa Claus, as the beard, glasses, and belly had prematurely aged him. According to the small business owner's license CeeCee had found for him online—after much complaining—James Delgado was thirty-five years old.

Looking at him, it would be impossible to guess he was a child killer.

Paul, it was clear, had no idea.

"*This* guy's the photographer?" he asked in a loud whisper, directly in my ear. Even though I'd let go of his tie as soon as we'd walked in, he was still sticking to me like glue. He seemed confused, probably because of the bit just before we'd come in, where I said he'd released something in me. He still didn't understand that what he'd released in me wasn't anything flattering.

I shot him the kind of annoyed glance a rich wife would give her hapless husband.

"Yes, dear. Remember? We talked about this."

"We did?" Paul was much slower than Jesse to pick up on my cues. He stood looking around the gallery, which, like the wall outside, was painted black. This made the photographs on the wall stand out more starkly. Even the floors and ceiling were black.

How daring, I'm sure a young Jimmy Delgado had thought when he'd come up with the concept.

I gave him an apologetic smile. "Sorry, Mr. Delgado. My husband, Victor, was in meetings all day. I didn't really get a chance to discuss this with him."

"I understand." Delgado gave Paul a sympathetic smile. "Such a shame you're only here for the weekend, Mr. Maitland. And for a conference, too! Carmel is simply beautiful this time of year. But don't worry, I've assured your wife I can squeeze in your girls. I happen to have had a cancellation tomorrow—the birthday girl has the flu—so it's fine if you want to drop your adorable daughters off for some headshots. You and your wife don't even need to stay if you want some private time. My assistant and I are used to wrangling rambunctious multiples."

After that speech, I had to dive into my bag for the antacids, so I didn't get to see Paul's expression as he echoed, "Multiples?"

"That's right, darling." I dug my phone from my purse, too, as well as the antacid tablets, then scrolled to the photo the triplets had taken of themselves and set as my screensaver the day before. "I've set up an appointment for Mr. Delgado to do some headshots of your daughters."

Paul only looked more confused than ever.

"I e-mailed Mr. Delgado some photos of them earlier," I went on, "and he wrote back right away. He thinks they've got real modeling potential. I think so, too. Don't you?"

I showed Paul the photo of Flopsy, Mopsy, and Cotton-tail. He took my phone and stared at the photo without a single flicker of recognition.

"Uh, sure, honey," he said. "Whatever you say."

It was obvious from his expression that he'd not only never seen a photo of the triplets before in his life, but that he was hurt—hurt that the only reason we were in the studio was to con Delgado, *not* for me to take off my clothes and give Paul a professional eight-by-ten glossy print of myself in my naked glory, perhaps posing with a tastefully positioned feathered fan.

If Paul was reading CeeCee's newsletter, he was skipping any entries about Debbie, because they *always* included a photo of the triplets.

But seeing their likeness so close to him, I was more convinced than ever that they were related. They could have been clones, except for the fact that the girls all had braids and freckles.

Passing my phone back to me, Paul whispered, "Is this about some goddamned ghost?"

"You're just figuring that out now?" I whispered back.

"I swear to God, Simon, if this makes us late to dinner—"

"No one said anything about being late to dinner."

His jaw hardened. The blue-eyed gaze narrowed at me. "The deal was that we were going to—"

"—have dinner at eight o'clock. With *dessert* afterward. Don't worry, we won't be late." I pressed a button on my phone and said in a much louder voice, "Victor says tomorrow will work fine, Mr. Delgado."

"Wonderful, wonderful!" Delgado was clapping his hands, circling back toward his desk. "I hope you won't find this presumptuous, but if you wouldn't mind, I printed out a brief contract, and it would be lovely if you could sign it so we can get everything squared away for tomorrow, and be ready to go when you drop off the girls. It's really nothing too complicated, I think you'll agree, just a cancellation agreement, instructions about reproduction rights, that sort of thing. Boilerplate, really."

"Oh, Victor will be happy to sign," I said, patting Paul on the shoulder. "Won't you, Victor?"

I couldn't believe there were parents in the world who'd be

stupid enough to fall for this guy's spiel. Would anyone actually leave their kids, unaccompanied, with this creep?

"Sure," Paul said with a sigh, moving toward the desk. "I'll sign it."

Well, that answered my question.

While Delgado went over the "brief contract" with Paul, I walked around the studio, pretending to admire his hideous photos. Some of them weren't portraits of kids, but landscapes or extreme close-ups of the weathered faces of homeless people that Delgado had blown up to five times life-size. I suppose he thought this made him extremely sensitive and artistic.

A lot of the criminals I'd mediated had thought of themselves this way: outsiders who no one in this world could understand. Society simply wasn't sensitive enough to comprehend their suffering. This is why—in their opinions—they hadn't really been breaking the law: the law did not apply to them, because they were so special.

I kid you not. I'd heard it a thousand times.

There was another room off the main gallery. This appeared to be Delgado's office. In keeping with the black-and-white theme, everything in it was white. It contained another desk, this one with a laptop computer on it. No one was sitting at the desk. There was another door from this office. When I tried it, I found that it led to a very spare, very tidy windowless bathroom, also in white.

There were no other doors.

"So your assistant isn't here right now, Mr. Delgado?" I asked as I came back into the main gallery.

"No," he said with a rueful smile. "I let him go home early today. It's Friday, and with the beautiful weather we've been having lately, he wanted to go to the beach. How could I say no?"

"How could you?" I looked out the display window, past the gigantic portraits hanging there, at the few people walking by. It was dinnertime, and getting cold. Everyone sane had headed indoors. "We were your last appointment?"

"Yes, but well worth the wait. I'm glad I met with Mr. Maitland's approval." He beamed at Paul. "It's not every day I get to photograph triplets."

I reached out and grabbed the cord to the blinds in the display window. I snapped it so that the metal blinds closed with a loud crash.

"Oops," I said. "How clumsy of me."

"Oh." Delgado was seated at his desk. His smile disappeared, but he didn't look alarmed. "That's all right, Mrs. Maitland. That happens, er, all the time."

"Does it?" I asked. "How about this?" I stepped to the front door and locked it.

Now he began to look alarmed. He glanced at Paul, as if for reassurance. Paul's expression seemed to make him feel better, since Paul was staring at me. Paul didn't look alarmed, however. He looked exasperated.

"Suze," he said. "Come on. I thought we were here for—"

"For what, Paul?" I reached down and unzipped the sports bag. "To get kinky? Oh, don't worry. We are. Just not in the way you thought."

"I thought your name was Victor." Delgado glanced at Paul in confusion.

"Did you?" Paul glared at him. "Victor Maitland? The villain from the old eighties movie *Beverly Hills Cop*? Then you're an even bigger chump than I am, because you could have looked up the name when she first called to make the appointment, you idiot, but you didn't. I got it right away, but I still didn't walk out the door, like I should have. Now she's got both of us." Paul turned to face me, then sighed when he saw what I'd retrieved from the sports bag. "Oh, great. There's no bunny outfit in there, is there?"

"Sadly for you, no." I leveled the .22 Hornet at them. "Jimmy, get your hands away from that phone, or I'll put a bullet in your chest."

"You do and they'll hear the shot next door and call the cops."

Delgado didn't sound like a fawning photographer anymore. He sounded more like a man who might once have killed a terrified little girl. Because she didn't understand his own suffering, of course. I was sure now that must be how he rationalized it to himself.

"I don't care," I said, taking careful aim. He had a black T-shirt on—to go with the theme of the place—with a yellow smiley face in the middle. It was easy to center the target. "It will be worth going to jail to kill you."

"Suze," Paul said. He, like Delgado, had his hands in the air. "Think about this. They have the death penalty here in California. Do you really want to go to the chair for murdering a guy whose only crime is taking really bad pictures?"

"Hey," Delgado said, sounding offended. "I've won a lot of awards."

"Seriously, dude?" Paul looked disgusted. "From who, your mom?"

"Paul." I kicked the bag. "Stop it. There are some cuffs in here. Get them out and put them on him."

Paul lowered his hands, looking relieved. "Oh, shit. I thought you were mad at me, too."

"Oh, I'm mad at you, Paul," I said, keeping the rifle level at them both. "But I need your help right now. So get out those handcuffs."

"Fine." Paul bent to dig through the sports bag with ill grace. "But if you think this is how it's going to be when we're married, Suze, with me helping you out with your crazy ghost do-gooding missions, you're high."

I rolled my eyes.

"Paul," I said. "I still might shoot you, considering the mood I'm in, and I can't promise it will be only to maim. So try to stay on my good side, okay?"

He dug more energetically through the sports bag. "I get it. You're mad about the thing with Jesse. Maybe I went too far. I can call off the demo. It'll cost me, but I can do it. But guns, Suze? And"—he pulled a taser from the sports bag and blanched—"these things? *Really?*"

Delgado, meanwhile, had his own worries.

"Who sent you?" he barked at me gruffly. "If it's about the money, you can tell Ricky I got it."

"It wasn't Ricky. I don't know any Ricky. It was Lucia Martinez." I kept the rifle trained at the center of his smiley face T-shirt. "Remember her, Jimmy? She went to Sacred Trinity."

Delgado actually looked a little relieved. Whoever Ricky was, he was more scared of him than he was of the memory of what he'd done to Lucia. He lowered his hands slightly.

"But that was an accident. Everyone knows that was only an accident."

I gritted my teeth. "If I hear the word *accident* one more time . . . there's a witness that says otherwise."

Delgado looked confused. "Witness? What witness?"

"A witness who told me exactly how you killed her. How you purposefully spooked Lucia's horse, then chased after her through the Del Monte Forest and how, when you caught up with her, you pulled her down from her horse and tossed her headfirst into a creek."

"No." Delgado's color had risen in the bright studio lights. His face was now the color of his work-reddened knuckles. "None of that is true."

"It's all true," I said. "I told you, there's a witness."

"There isn't!" he roared, leaping from his chair just as Paul was coming toward him with the handcuffs. "There wasn't any witness! No one else was there!"

I grinned at him smugly. "Except you, right? That's how you're so sure."

Delgado, realizing he'd just confessed to murder, launched himself from behind the desk. I'd known he was going to make a move—trapped rats always do, eventually. Even tame ones, like Romeo, will attack if they feel threatened enough.

But Delgado's mistake was that he went for Paul, not for me. Leaping out from behind the desk, he threw a brawny arm around the younger man's throat and cried, "Stay back! Stay back, or I swear to God I'll snap his neck."

Paul was pretty unhappy about this turn of events. "Um, Suze?" he croaked. "I think he means it."

"Hold still, Paul." I strode calmly toward them, the rifle raised.

"Wh-what are you doing?" Delgado cried. "I said stay back!"

"Yeah," Paul said. "He said stay back, Suze."

"Duck, Paul," I said, and when I'd closed the distance between us to about a yard, I swung the gun around like a baseball bat, hitting Delgado in the side of the head. He staggered, then slowly went down, though it took a couple more blows to convince him to stay there.

"Goddammit, Suze," Paul cried as Delgado slumped on top of him, eventually pinning him to the floor beneath his greater weight. "Get him off me. Get him off!"

"I'm trying. Stop being such a baby." The larger man weighed a ton. Fortunately, he wasn't dead. I hadn't wanted to kill him, of course. That's why I'd tried to avoid striking him in the temple. Jesse had explained to me once that he'd seen more severe brain injuries caused by punches in bar fights than he had by gunshots in the St. Francis ER. A well-placed punch could kill just as surely as a bullet.

"Thank God," Paul said, scrambling to his feet and adjusting his suit when I'd finally succeeded in rolling Delgado off him. "And who are you calling a baby? I think I've got a right to complain. What I am is accessory to kidnapping and attempted murder. Did this guy really kill a girl?"

I nodded. "She was in the first grade at the time."

"Ew." He made a face. "And I thought it was only his hideous art that was a crime. Oh, no." He noticed a stain on his sleeve. "Suze, this is a six-thousand-dollar suit. Who's going to pay for this?"

"You're the multimillionaire. Deal with it. Come on, let's cuff him before he wakes up. I want to look at his computer and see if there's anything on there I can use to connect him to the murder or any other criminal activities. Do you still carry a gag?"

"Oh, Suze." He waved his pocket square. "Always."

"Make use of it. I do not want Mr. Delgado's screams disturbing the good citizens strolling the downtown Carmel shopping district."

Paul did as he was told, while I went to work erasing all the footage on the gallery's security system (which consisted of a set of video cameras—Delgado was obviously a fan of the At Home with Andy show, and his do-it-yourself methods—in two corners of the studio), then searching his computer for incriminating evidence. The desktop wasn't password protected, leading me to believe there'd be nothing interesting on it.

But after opening a locked drawer at the bottom of the black lacquer desk—easily done with one of the keys I found on a chain inside Delgado's pocket—I discovered the *real* computer—a laptop that was not only password protected, but sitting beneath a .44 Magnum handgun. Loaded.

Wow. Lucky for me the drawer had been locked. Not so lucky for Jimmy.

Resting beneath the laptop was a locked cashbox. None of the keys from Delgado's keychain fit the lock, so Paul and I took turns smashing the cashbox against the cement floor until the thin metal lid finally broke open.

Cashboxes, I've found, generally aren't that well made. Or it could be that the people who construct them never anticipated someone throwing them against a cement floor a bunch of times. Amateurs.

Inside was a surprisingly large amount of money—$50,000 in cash, banded, mostly hundreds and twenties—along with Delgado's passport, the passport of a man I assumed was his assistant, and a dozen thumb drives. I made the mistake of plugging the thumb drives into the desktop to see what was on them.

I instantly wished I hadn't.

"Well?" Paul asked. He'd found some bottled beer in a small minifridge in the back office—after first mentioning that it was no wonder Delgado was so overweight: he kept a "buttload" of candy in the cupboards—and was walking around, drinking it, restless as Romeo on his wheel after too many grapes. "What's old Jimmy been up to in his spare time?"

"Pretty much what I expected." I switched off the screen, but unfortunately not before Paul happened to stroll behind me and get a good look.

"What the—"

Paul dropped the bottle. It broke, smashing into a hundred pieces. The glass looked like amber, floating in a quickly spreading puddle the color of Lucia's hair across the ink black floor, toward the body of the man who'd killed her.

veintisiete

Paul didn't have much to say on the ride back to the hotel. I was driving. I didn't trust him to do so, not only because of how completely freaked out he was by what had just happened, but because he'd also finished off all the beers in the minifridge and was currently working on a fifth of whiskey he'd found hidden in a back drawer of Delgado's desk.

The last thing we needed now was to get pulled over by the Carmel PD. If the officer asked where we'd been, Paul was likely to blurt the truth. Then it would be straight to jail for both of us.

"Cheer up," I finally said to him, because he looked so miserable, slumped in the passenger seat, staring unseeingly through the windshield. "You actually did something good tonight, for once in your life. There's one less child killer on the streets."

Paul only grunted and continued to stare out the window.

"It's what you're *supposed* to be doing with your God-given talents." Oh, the irony! If only Father Dom could hear me now. "And it's not like we didn't give him a choice."

Paul snorted. "Some choice."

"Hey. It's more than he gave Lucia."

Paul grunted in disgust.

I shook my head. It had been a mistake to leave Paul in charge of the handcuffs. While I'd been sifting through the data on the thumb drives, Delgado had regained consciousness, wriggled free, then gone for his gun that one of us (Paul) had foolishly left on the black lacquer desk.

Fortunately I'd had the rifle close by.

"Bad idea, Jimmy," I'd said, aiming the mouth of the Hornet at the center of the smiley face on his chest.

That smiley face. I'd never be able to look at one again without thinking of . . . well, very unpleasant things.

You'd have thought the blows I'd given him would have convinced him otherwise, but Jimmy still woke up with escape on his mind. I saw his gaze go from me to the cashbox—smashed open on his black concrete floor—to the thumb drives scattered across the desk in front of me.

"That's right, Jimmy," I'd said, holding the rifle steady. "We found everything. I've already called the cops. They'll be here any minute." Ha! Oh, well. You can pull off just about any performance if you believe in it enough. "So even if you shoot us both and make a run for it—which I doubt you're going to be able to do, because I'm pretty good with this thing—they still have all the evidence they need to prosecute. So what's it gonna be, Jimmy?"

I saw his beady little eyes darting around as he thought about it good and hard, weighing his options. Make a break for it and hope for the best? Stick around and let himself get arrested?

I don't know why I never considered option three. If I had, I might have been able to prevent it.

Stop. Wait. Don't. That's what I should have said in the seconds before I saw him, as if in slow motion, lift the .44 Magnum toward his own head, then pull the trigger.

But there wasn't time.

I was careful not to look at the corpse as I snapped at Paul to help me pack up. I was concerned someone might have heard the gunshot and called the cops—for real this time.

But no one had. Outside, the lights on the trunks of the palm trees along the meridian still twinkled, and somewhere Christmas music was playing over a loudspeaker. "Silent Night."

Paul snaked the whiskey bottle out from beneath the dashboard and took a swig. Fortunately we were the only car on the boulevard, and all of the shops along Ocean Avenue were closed.

"Look," I said to Paul. "Child killers—and especially child sexual predators—don't do very well in California state prisons. They have a high gang member population. Gangs have their own code of ethics, and taking out a pedophile can earn a member as much—or more—respect as killing a snitch, or a rival gang member."

Paul snorted. "Did you learn that in your little counseling school?"

"No." I refused to let him get under my skin. "Jake told me. And Delgado knew it, too. That's why he made the choice that he did. He knew he was going to die anyway."

"That's just great, Suze," Paul said. "And if he comes back tonight in spirit form, looking for revenge, what are you going to do?"

I gave him a disbelieving look. "That guy? Revenge? He shot himself in the head because he was too much of a coward to face the consequences of his own actions. Trust me, wherever he is now, he's staying. Hopefully reincarnated as a cockroach."

"Fine. But if you think I'm letting you out of our agreement just because of that little stunt back there, you're crazy." Paul announced this just as I was pulling the car into the hotel's circular drive. "We're still having dinner together at Mariner's. I'm not losing the reservation I made for two for the chef's tasting menu. It's supposed to be one of the top ten restaurants in the country. And by God, Simon, you're going to sit across from me and pretend to enjoy it like the goddamn lady I know you can be when you put your mind to it. But first I'm going up to my room to take a shower and burn this suit." He sniffed his sleeve, then made a face. "Ugh. Eau de perv."

"Are you serious?" I stared at him. "After all that? You still actually expect me to . . ."

"Fulfill your side of our bargain, Simon? Of course. Even though what you put me through tonight *more* than made up for anything I might have done to you on graduation night."

"I'm not talking about what you did to me on graduation night. I'm talking about—give us a moment, will you?"

I said the last part to the valet who'd come up to my side of the car to open the door for me. We'd pulled in beneath the porte cochere, which was much more crowded than it had been when we'd left. There were now a dozen handsomely dressed older people waiting for their cars, some of the men in tuxedos, and some of the women wearing fur coats against the brisk November chill—all sixty degrees of it.

Friday nights were dead in downtown Carmel because Friday night was cocktail party night in northern California, when the rich trotted out their best clothing to see and be seen in all the best hotel ballrooms and private mansions (on the pretense of raising money for charities).

"Paul," I said, feeling a rising tide of panic growing within me. "You can't be serious. If you think for one minute I'm actually going to let you—"

"Yes, you are, Simon. Those things you did back there? You're right. You *are* bad. You can't help it. You have an evil streak in you a mile wide, just like me. And I love it. We belong together."

"No, we *don't*, Paul. My kind of bad helps people. Your way only hurts them."

"Hurts so good," Paul slurred drunkenly.

"Oh, my God." Everything was falling apart. "Look, Paul, you're obviously not feeling well. Let me take you to your room."

"*Excellent* plan," Paul said.

"I think it would be better if you handed over the keys," the valet said.

"I'm not staying long," I replied without even glancing at him.

"I think you *are* staying," said the valet firmly. "Don't you and Mr. Slater have a dinner reservation?"

That made me glance up. There was something oddly familiar about the valet's voice.

It wasn't until I looked into his face that I realized why. A chill passed over my entire body.

The man holding my door was no valet. It was Jesse de Silva.

veintiocho

"Monsieur," said the waiter, bowing as he laid a napkin over Jesse's lap.

"*Gracias.*"

Jesse didn't look at all bothered by the fact that he'd invited himself to dinner—and forced the waitstaff to add a third chair and place setting to what was obviously a table for two—even though everyone else in the restaurant was staring at us.

Things like that don't faze Jesse at all.

In fact, I think he was enjoying himself, especially when the sommelier brought over the bottle of Dom Pérignon that came paired with the first course on the tasting menu, chilled oysters on the half shell, topped with Beluga caviar.

"I brought my own bottle," Paul grumbled, and filled his champagne flute with the whiskey he'd brought from Delgado's studio.

The sommelier looked disapproving, but since Paul was a paying guest, there was nothing he could do.

"As you wish, sir," the sommelier murmured, and walked away.

Mariner's was the Carmel Inn's four-star restaurant, voted the top destination in the Bay Area by *Forbes Magazine*, and Paul had gone all out, reserving its best, most romantic table—known locally as "the Window Table" because it was tucked into a dark corner of the restaurant that happened to be paned on both sides by floor-to-ceiling glass, and jutted out a dozen yards above the crashing surf of the southern most edge of Carmel Bay, so that diners had the giddy sensation that they were eating on a cliff, a private aerie above the sea.

Only the aerie was not so private or romantic tonight, since the restaurant had been more than happy to add a third place setting and chair at the Window Table, per my fiancé's request.

"So," Jesse said. "What are we celebrating?" He lifted his champagne glass. "The fact that I'm a demon?"

Paul raised his own glass. "I'll drink to that if it means you'll finally go to hell, de Silva."

"Stop it," I snapped. "Both of you. Jesse, how did you—?"

"Your stepbrother David was trying to reach you," Jesse said with a shrug. "But you wouldn't pick up—as usual. So he called me to see if I knew where you were. He seemed to have something particularly urgent to tell you, so naturally I asked what it was. David being David, he was reluctant to betray your confidence, Susannah, but eventually I convinced him it was in his best interest. Imagine my surprise when I discovered *I* was the reason he was calling. Or rather, the fact that I seem to be under some sort of curse."

I felt as if someone had poured ice-cold champagne down my back instead of into my glass. "Jesse," I said. I was going to kill David. "Look. I can explain . . ."

"Oh, I'm sure you can," Jesse said, enjoying his food with a gusto I found surprising for someone who'd just discovered he was destined to lose his soul and become a mass murderer. "I look forward to hearing all about it. Yes, I will try the wine, thank you." He smiled up at the hovering waiter.

"But how did you know we'd be here?" I hadn't told David—or anyone—about my evening plans.

"Where else would Paul Slater stay when visiting Carmel?" Jesse set aside his fork to take a sip. "Only the best. Now, where shall we begin? With the bargain I heard the two of you mention, or whatever happened between you on graduation night?"

"Jesse," I said after I'd taken several gulps from my water glass. My mouth felt as if it were filled with sand. "It's not what you think."

"Oh, it's quite all right, *querida*." There was a dangerous glint in his dark eyes. "If a man is doomed to murder everyone he's ever loved, it's nice to know he has reason to do so."

"Jesse." I choked. "Stop it. You know that isn't true."

"Which part, precisely, Susannah?" Jesse drained his wineglass. "I told you that we may no longer have a mediator-ghost connection, but I can still tell when you're lying to me, and you've been lying to me all week. Those flowers on your desk at work? They weren't from a grateful parent. They were from *him*." He glared at Paul.

"Guilty as charged." Paul winked at him. "But isn't she worth it?"

I felt a spurt of rage at both of them.

"Oh, yes, that's right, Jesse," I said, before he could react to Paul's jab. "Ever since high school, Paul and I have been having a torrid affair behind your back. That's why I took him and not you to the murder tonight. Paul's much better at murder than you are."

Paul looked confused. "Wait. Are you being sarcastic?"

"Yes, you idiot," I said to him. "We almost got shot tonight because you don't even know how to fasten a pair of handcuffs."

"Then why did you take me?"

"Because I couldn't let *Jesse* do it. He's got too much to lose."

Paul sank back into his chair, looking stunned. "Shit. She used me."

"Oh, grow up, Paul. Jesse, listen, I—"

"I thought we'd talked about this." Jesse had folded his arms across his chest in such a manner that his biceps were bulging beneath the suit jacket he wore (jackets and ties were mandatory for male diners at Mariner's). Jesse's wasn't as expensive as Paul's, but he still looked very, very good in it. "I had to promise to work a half dozen shifts to get another resident to cover my shift in the ER tonight, and then, after waiting here for you for over an hour, I learn that you're late because you *killed Delgado*? How could you even think of doing something like that after what you and I discussed this afternoon, Susannah?"

"First of all, I never said I killed Delgado. He took his own life. Second of all, I'm sorry I lied. But I told you, I didn't want you risking your reputation for a sleazebag like—"

"And I told *you* I didn't want you risking your life."

"I'm sorry," I said again. I'd never seen him so angry. "But I said I wasn't going to sit around decorating bonnets. You should know by now I'm not that type of girl. And it turned out to be worth it. I have Delgado's client list. Not the clients who bought his regular photographs—he had a separate thumb drive of private clients who bought what he called his 'specialty photos' . . . photos you definitely don't want to see. Father Francisco's name is on that list."

Jesse made a face as if he'd tasted something bitter, but all he'd done was take another, slower sip from his champagne glass, which the waiter had come by to superciliously refill. "Ah. The good news never ends, does it?"

"It *is* good news, Jesse," I said urgently, gazing into his eyes, which were still dark with suppressed anger, and something else I couldn't entirely identify. "There was enough on that thumb drive to put Father Francisco—and a lot of other people—away, maybe even forever. I'm going to turn everything over to CeeCee tomorrow."

Jesse's lips twisted. "So the world is supposed to believe that Delgado had a crisis of conscience before he killed himself, and sent his list of private clients to the local press?"

"I think that's best. CeeCee will make sure Becca Walters's name stays out of it."

Jesse nodded thoughtfully. "And perhaps this will allow the spirit of Lucia to rest."

"Not to interrupt this touching moment, but can I just say one thing?" Paul held up one hand.

"No." Jesse stabbed an index finger in Paul's direction. "You should shut up, unless you want to end up like Delgado. And *you*"—his furious gaze snapped back toward me—"can hardly blame me for thinking the worst, especially after what David told me tonight. What *bargain* were you two arguing about when you pulled up? And what could possibly have happened graduation night? I was with you almost the entire time."

"Jesse," I said. "I wanted to tell you. I really did. But I was afraid of how you'd react—like *now*, for instance."

He looked indignant. "What am I doing wrong?"

"Everything! I had this situation completely under control until you came in here—"

"Oh, please." Paul groaned. "Much as I'm enjoying watching you squirm, Simon, I need to go shower, because I smell like a

Venezuelan flight attendant. So I'm calling it quits for the night. I can assure you, de Silva, nothing happened on graduation night except one little moment of indiscretion on my part, for which your girlfriend kneed me in the balls. And then tonight, as the coup de grace, she forced me to watch a degenerate blow his brains out. There. Are you happy now? Seriously, I give up. She's all yours."

Jesse made a lunge at Paul as he rose to leave the table, catching him by the lapels of his suit jacket and causing all of the dishware to rattle noisily, and some of the silver to slide to the floor.

"She was never yours to give, Slater," Jesse hissed, his face only inches from Paul's. "Nor is she mine. Women aren't horses, they don't belong to one man or another, though maybe you think they do, since you've evidently been working so hard to steal her away."

"I wouldn't call it work." Paul did not sound particularly troubled by the fact that there was six feet or so of fuming former ghost looming over him. "Not when you've made it so easy by failing to properly tend to her needs."

Fortunately the sommelier hurried over at that exact moment, and he and I both managed to pry Jesse away from Paul in time to keep him from physically assaulting him . . . but not in time to keep every head in the restaurant from swiveling toward us.

I felt all of Jesse's muscles tense beneath my fingers. He was itching to heave a punch in Paul's face, and truthfully, Paul deserved one.

But neither the sommelier nor I wanted a scene in Mariner's, especially at the Window Table. With our combined weight and a combination of pushing and pulling, we managed to get Jesse back into his seat before he did any damage.

"Jesse, please," I begged him as the sommelier fussed over him like a mother hen, folding his napkin back over his lap, since it had fallen to the floor, and brushing off his suit. "Paul's drunk. And, even if he completely messed it up, he did do you a favor tonight. You know you can't afford to be anywhere near people like Delgado."

Jesse turned his glare on me. I felt like one of the tiny cakes inside my stepnieces' vintage Easy-Bake Oven, burning under the bright white lightbulb.

"Did me a *favor*?" He looked incredulous. "Susannah, I don't need those kind of favors, from him or anyone, especially when they involve you. And," he added with a dark glance in Paul's direction, "he's a little *too* drunk, don't you think?"

"What? No." I hurried back to my own seat just as the second course, a gold-rimmed plate of Monterey Bay wild salmon with Meyer lemon, was being laid there by a team of servers so professional they gave the appearance of not having noticed there'd been a near knockout in their restaurant. "He seems fine to me. Wait, what are you—"

I broke off as Jesse reached down beneath my chair.

"Really, please, carry on, you two," Paul slurred drunkenly from the chair he'd sunk back into. To my amazement, he still hadn't left the restaurant. "Pretend like I'm not even here. I'm used to it."

Jesse pulled my bag from beneath the table and began to rifle through it. Suddenly I knew *exactly* what he was doing . . . and what he was looking for. My heart flew into my throat.

"Jesse, no," I cried, reaching for the leather straps to snatch the bag away. "I—"

But I heard the distinctive rattle, and knew his fingers had closed over the prescription pill bottle before I could stop him. He pulled it from the depths of the bag and squinted at the label in the dim candlelight on the restaurant table.

"What are those?" Paul asked interestedly. "Suze, did you bring party favors? My kind of girl."

"They're not the kind you'd like, Slater," Jesse said, quickly opening the bottle and dumping the contents into his hand. Counting swiftly, he asked, "How many have you given him?"

"Just a few. I put them in the whiskey bottle when he wasn't looking. I didn't want him to taste them."

Jesse swore. "You gave him sleeping pills *in* alcohol?"

At Jesse's appalled expression, I shrugged. "It is a big bottle. He'll be fine, just a little out of it for a while."

"Thank you for your medical diagnosis, Dr. Simon." Jesse had already pulled out his cell phone, ready to dial 911. "Why would you do such a thing?"

I bit my lip. I was going to have to tell him eventually. Look at everything that had happened because I hadn't told—because *Becca* hadn't told. Oh, wait. We were talking about me now.

But in the end, Paul was the one who spilled the beans.

"Sleeping pills? That's a new low, even for you, Simon." He reached into his jacket pocket for his own cell phone. "I should have known you never had any intention of holding up your end of the bargain. I'm texting Blumenthal to go ahead with the demo on Monday."

This caused Jesse to pause while making his call. "There that word is again. Bargain. What *bargain*?"

"Um," I said, my panic rising to new heights. "Nothing. Just—"

"Oh, ho." Paul grinned as he continued to tap into his phone. "*Awkward*. Sorry, Simon. But a deal is a deal. And by attempting to drug me into a stupor, you just voided ours."

Jesse's dark gaze burned into me. "Susannah. *What is he talking about?*"

Before I could say a word, Paul went on, "Oh, don't be too hard on her, de Silva. You should be impressed, as a matter of fact. It's hard to find women as loyal as this one these days—at least ones who aren't interested only in your money, which wouldn't be a problem for you, I know, but for me, I—"

"Okay, that is *enough*."

I stood up, throwing my balled up napkin to the side of my newly delivered bowl of black truffle risotto with Parmigiano-Reggiano, which at this point I had no interest even in trying.

"Come on, Jesse," I said. "We don't have to sit here and listen to this. Let's go."

But Jesse stayed where he was.

"No," he said. His eyes were as dark as Paul's were light—but even darker than usual, since I saw the now-familiar shadows creeping in. "I'm interested to hear about this bargain."

I began to feel afraid, despite the string quartet playing lightly in the background.

"Jesse, he doesn't know what he's talking about. He's . . . he's on drugs, remember?"

Paul took a deliberate swig from the whiskey bottle. "Sweetheart, I've got news for you. I pop pills like candy. How do you think I maintain my extremely unhealthy lifestyle while looking so good? A few sleeping pills mixed into my hooch aren't going to bother me in the least because I took four dexies before we left the bar. Anyway, what the two of you have together is really sweet, and I'm envious, especially since you both have to know by now it's going to end."

"And how is that?" Jesse asked.

"Well, there are no documented cases that *I* know of human and reanimated corpse copulation, but I think it's likely such a thing would fly in the face of all physical and natural law. If you ask me, *that's* what's probably going to unleash whatever demonic entities reside within the good doctor here. But what do I know? I'm no expert. I guess we'll find out Monday, won't we? Oh, that's the bargain we had, de Silva. Your girlfriend was going to let me bang her if I didn't tear down her old house. But now that deal is off. So good luck not slaughtering the bride."

veintinueve

"*Jesse.*"

He didn't respond. Instead he rose from his chair and swept wordlessly past me—but not, as I initially feared, to lift Paul Slater from his chair and hurl him through the nearby plateglass windows.

To my surprise, Jesse walked right past Paul—who'd shrunk in his seat, clearly expecting some kind of blow—then out of the restaurant, never once looking back, though I called his name again. The last I saw of him, he was disappearing out the front door, his broad-shouldered back stiff as a soldier's at attention.

"Ouch," Paul said, straightening in his chair. He reached for his whiskey bottle. "That must have smarted, Simon."

"Shut up, Paul." I lowered myself into the nearest seat. Even if I'd wanted to go running after Jesse—and I didn't see what that would accomplish—I wasn't sure my legs could support me. "I can't believe you just did that."

"Oh, please." Paul poured pinot noir from a new bottle into

one of the many glasses in front of my plate. "If you two really had such a great relationship, he'd have stuck around, no matter what I said."

I gave him a sour look. "He left to keep himself from killing you."

Paul laughed. "Probably. I bet he's waiting out in the parking lot for you, faithful dog that he is. Woof, woof."

"You're disgusting." But I hoped he was right.

"May I make a suggestion? Leave here with me on my jet. That guy is going to go full Satan's spawn on Monday, especially now, seeing how much you've pissed him off. And as much as you've annoyed me, too, Simon, with your behavior tonight, I really would hate to see you die. I dislike seeing beautiful things go to waste. Which reminds me, before we go, help me finish this wine. It's twelve hundred dollars a bottle."

That child is lost, and very frightened, and in so much pain, Aunt Pru had said. *And lost children in pain can sometimes be very cruel. They lash out and hurt others, sometimes without meaning to. But sometimes on purpose, too.*

Maybe she really had meant Paul, and not Lucia.

"Paul," I said, ignoring the wine and reaching into my bag. "Do you recognize this photo?"

Paul glanced briefly at the screen saver on my cell phone, then shrugged.

"Sure. You showed it to the dirtbag earlier. Why?"

"They're my stepnieces." I scrolled through the photos of the triplets on my phone, giving him a brief slide show. "Brad and Debbie Ackerman's triplets. Only you knew her as Debbie Mancuso, of course."

"That's fascinating, Suze. How come you're not trying the wine? You really shouldn't miss it. It's got some nice earthy undertones."

"Brad and Debbie's daughters are mediators, Paul," I said. "That's why I'm showing you their photos. Do you know how rare that is? That there should be so many mediators in the Monterey Bay area? Think about it. There's you, Paul. And your little brother, Jack. And Father Dom, of course. And now Jesse. And then Debbie Mancuso's triplets, which she conceived very shortly after graduation night."

Paul had taken a sip of the twelve-hundred-dollar wine he'd ordered. But when I said the words *graduation night,* he choked. He managed to get everything down except a little trickle that dribbled out of the side of his mouth. He wiped it away with his napkin, glancing down to make sure none had gotten on his precious suit.

"Really?" he asked. "Like I said, fascinating. But why are you telling me all this? I'm not a huge fan of kids. I'd rather talk about us."

"This has to do with us," I said, resting my elbow on the table and my chin in my hand as I regarded him closely. "You, me, and Jesse, and what's going to happen on Monday if you tear down my house. If that curse is real, and Jesse does start going after everyone he loves, that's going to include those kids. Those kids who see ghosts. How do you think Debbie Mancuso ended up with triplets who see ghosts? Especially since she's never shown any sign of being a mediator, and neither, as we all know, has my stepbrother Brad. I was hoping you could shed some light on the matter."

"*Me?*" Paul pointed at himself, his eyebrows raised as high as they would go. "What would *I* know about it? I don't know anything about kids."

"To my knowledge, lack of information about children has never medically impeded anyone from having them."

"Look, I know what you're getting at, Simon, but they can't be mine," Paul declared. "I don't care what Debbie's been telling you. I have never not used a condom in my life, and for very good reason. Do you have any idea how much I'm worth? Do you think I'm not fully aware that there are desperate women all over this country who'd love to trap me into fathering some snot-nosed brat so I'll be paying them gold ducats until the kid is eighteen? No, *thank you*."

"Paul, please," I said, looking around at all the diners who were now staring at him. "No one is trying to trap you into paying anything, particularly not Debbie. She's never said a word about this to me—"

"I should hope not!" He pointed at me. "I am a very, *very* careful guy."

"Paul, I don't like this any more than you do. I love those girls, and I would give anything for Brad to be their father. He is their *real* father, in my opinion. But not genetically. You yourself admitted to me that you weren't too careful graduation night. You said you barely remembered what happened. You used your drunkenness, in fact, as an excuse for what you did to me. But you weren't too drunk," I went on, "to remember that later on that evening, Debbie Mancuso, and I quote, straddled me like she thought I was a damned gigolo, unquote."

Paul dropped his head into his hands. "Oh, hell. Fine. *One time*. I may have forgotten to use a rubber *one time*. But how could she have gotten knocked up with *three kids* from *one time*?"

"Teens and women over the age of thirty-five are more likely to give birth to twins and triplets than women aged twenty to thirty-five." When he stared at me in disbelief, I shrugged. "It's called science. Look it up."

"Well, if you think you're getting a cheek swab out of me for a paternity test, you're—"

I leaned forward and lifted the wineglass from which Paul had been drinking. I poured its remaining contents into the floral centerpiece, then wrapped the glass loosely in my napkin and tucked both glass and napkin into my bag.

"They can lift DNA for paternity suits from all sorts of things these days, Paul," I explained. "It costs a bit more, and takes a bit longer, but they can do it."

Paul looked as if he was about to have a coronary. "You can't . . . I'll . . . My lawyers will . . ."

"No, they won't. Because the test's going to come back positive. Those girls are your daughters, and they're already starting to need special care. They can't tell the dead from the living."

"What do you want from me, Suze?" he asked, spreading his hands wide, palms up. "I think it's pretty clear I'm not going to be any help to them. I'm not mediator material."

"No, you aren't. Fortunately they have a doting aunt who'll help teach them those skills, now that I know that's what they are."

He looked relieved. "Fine. No problem. You did a great job with my kid brother, Jack. He doesn't even speak to me, but whatever. So what do they need, then? Money?"

"No. They already have parents—and grandparents—who love them and will provide all they need in that department . . . for now. But you still need to step up. I don't think it's ever occurred to Debbie that you're the father of her children, or if it has, she's never seriously considered pursuing it. But she may now that you've been going around buying up property all over Carmel. Things aren't going so well between Brad and Debbie. A chunk out of your wallet would probably go a long way toward helping her with some of the stress of raising rambunctious five-year-old triplets who see dead people. Then suddenly *you'll* be saddled with them. And with Debbie, of course. Maybe I should mention to her that—"

He blanched. "You're bluffing. Brad's only your stepbrother, and you know he's a chump, but you still love him. You'd never put him through something like that."

"Wouldn't I? I'm not so sure. Maybe he has a right to know. And I'm sure Debbie Mancuso's father, the Mercedes King of Carmel, would be delighted to find out his granddaughters are yours and not Brad Ackerman's—"

"Fine, Simon. I get it, okay? If you promise not to tell anyone about me possibly being the father of those kids, I won't tear down 99 Pine Crest Road."

"Oh," I said. "You're *definitely* not tearing down 99 Pine Crest Road. Do you want to know why? Because you're giving it to me."

treinta

Paul was right about one thing. Jesse was waiting for me outside the restaurant.

I almost walked right past him ... not because I wasn't expecting to see him. I was. Or at least, I'd *hoped* he'd be there ... but because when I noticed the dark figure standing in the shadows of the porte cochere, there was a red glow coming from its mouth.

"*Jesse*?" I nearly dropped my bag in astonishment. "Are you *smoking*?"

"Susannah." He leaned forward to stamp out the cigarette in one of the fairy-lit planters. "I wasn't expecting you so soon."

"We decided to skip dessert. Well, *I* decided to. Since when do you *smoke*?"

He shrugged, looking embarrassed. "I don't. Well, I do, obviously, sometimes. But not often. It sets a bad example for the patients."

"Now who's been keeping secrets?"

I studied him in the dim lighting. It was late, and so cold out the valets had gone inside to keep warm. We were alone in the cool night air. Now that he'd put out the cigarette, he had his hands shoved into his jacket pockets to keep warm, and was regarding me with a look I could only describe as wary.

"Well?" he asked, finally. "Where is he?"

"*He's* paying his four-thousand-dollar dinner bill," I said. "*We're* leaving. Here."

He looked down at the decorative plastic sack I held toward him as if it might contain explosives. "What is that?"

"It's a homemade banana nut muffin. Mariner's makes them for all its dinner guests. You're supposed to have it for breakfast tomorrow. You left without yours."

His mouth twisted into a grimace. "That's all right. You can have mine."

"What's the matter, Jesse?" I asked lightly, dropping the muffin into my bag. "Don't you care to remember your dining experience at Mariner's?"

"I do not."

"I don't particularly want to remember it, either." I held out my hand. "I'm sorry."

For a few agonizing heartbeats, we stood there beneath the porte cochere, my hand stretched toward him across the red carpet. There was no sound except for the waves crashing against the beach a few dozen yards below.

What was happening? Was he going to just let me stand there forever with my hand out? Did he have any idea how hard it was for someone like me to apologize?

He did. Finally he lifted one of those hands from his pockets and wrapped his strong fingers around mine.

"You have nothing to be sorry for, Susannah," he said, his voice as warmly reassuring as his hand. "None of this was your fault. It was *his*."

"Thanks, Jesse. You still should have had heard about it from me, though. I *wanted* to tell you, I was just—"

"Afraid I'd get angry," Jesse said. "Yes, I know. But I should have trusted you, as well. Let's just say we both made mistakes—not only tonight—and leave it at that." He'd begun steering me toward Jake's BMW, which I saw parked a dozen feet away. "Susannah, do you actually believe it?"

"What?"

"This curse. That—"

"Of course not," I interrupted. "I don't believe there's a murderous bone in your body . . . toward anyone but Paul, anyway. But even if it's true, we don't have to worry about it anymore."

"What?" He looked startled. "David said there was no way to break the curse. He said he'd been looking into it with some friend who—"

"It doesn't matter. Ninety-nine Pine Crest Road isn't getting torn down."

His voice didn't sound so warm anymore all of a sudden. "*Why?*"

"Because I own it."

We'd reached Jake's car, but Jesse didn't move to pull the keys from his pocket. He did drop my hand, however. "You *own* it? How do you own it?"

"Well, I don't own it quite yet," I explained. "There's still some paperwork I'll have to sign. And apparently there are going to be some tax issues. I suspect I'll get slammed pretty hard. But Paul's going to sign the house over to me in exchange for my never revealing that he's the triplets' real father, and for my giving them mediator lessons there when they're older."

Jesse stared down at me in silence for several beats. It was a little hard to see his face, since the lighting in the parking lot wasn't that great and the moon was playing hide-and-seek with the clouds. But I had the impression that he wasn't too happy.

This was confirmed when he let out a blistering curse (in Spanish, of course), and said, finally, "*You're* the one who is possessed."

"What?" I stared up at him. "What are you talking about?"

"Everyone is so worried that *I* have a dark side? *You're* the one I think we should be worrying about."

"Oh, come on, Jesse. You want us to be honest with each other? Then let's be honest. You had to have suspected."

"No, Susannah, the possibility of Paul Slater being your nieces' father never entered my mind, and I'm wondering how *you* knew."

"Because Lucia told me," I said, before I could think.

As soon as the words were out of my mouth, I saw in his eyes the betrayal I'd inflicted. But it was too late to undo the damage.

"Lucia *told* you?" Jesse looked as if he'd been slapped. "And you never said a word to me?"

I backpedaled at once.

"I wasn't going to say a word to anyone," I insisted. "It seemed like the kind of thing that ought to be kept a secret—"

"From *me*? We're supposed to be getting married!"

"What do you mean, *supposed to be*?" My heart twisted. "Jesse, I can understand you being angry with me, but don't you think it's a little extreme to get *this* angry—"

"I'm not angry with you, Susannah." He dragged a hand frustratedly through his thick dark hair. "I . . . I don't know what I am."

"Use your words." It was a phrase we'd employed frequently with the triplets.

"Fine." He glared at me. "I'm disappointed."

"Disappointed?"

I don't think he could have chosen a word that hurt more. Lord knew Jesse and I had argued in the past, but he'd never before trotted out that particular weapon from his arsenal. It pierced my heart like the blade of a stiletto, the pain causing in me a wild desire to hurt him back.

"Are you kidding me? Oh, excuse me, Dr. de Silva. I didn't mean to *disappoint* you. God knows I'll never be as elegant a lady as your precious Miss Boyd. I thought I was doing you a favor tonight—"

"I've told you before I don't want favors from you, Susannah," he snarled. "I've never expected any and I've never asked for any. All I've ever wanted from you is the *truth*."

"Which I've always given you, Jesse," I said. "I admit I may not always have told you things as promptly as I should have, but I've always told you eventually."

"Eventually? You mean years later, in the case of what happened between you and Slater on graduation night. And would I have even found out about your little plan for tonight if David hadn't called?"

"Which little plan?"

His lips twitched cynically. "So many you can't even keep track! The one involving the *bargain* you made with Slater."

Oh, *that* plan.

"I was never actually going to go through with that bargain, Jesse. I was going to use the handcuffs and taser on him that you put in the car for Father Francisco. But then—"

"*Nombre de Dios.*" He looked heavenward. "I suppose because I showed up here, you couldn't. And it's a good thing that I did. A man like Slater, who has no scruples about using force against a woman, would only have enjoyed—"

"No. I used those on Delgado. Paul would have figured out what I was up to if I'd brought that bag up to his hotel room. I used the sleeping pills on him instead."

Jesse shook his head incredulously. "And did you see how effective they were? He takes pills like those for recreation, Susannah!"

"I know." My shoulders sagged. "I guess noncompliant living persons aren't really my specialty."

"I wouldn't say that. Come here."

I'd been studying my shoes. Now I looked up, feeling a twinge of hope. "What?"

"I said come here. You're shivering."

I took a step toward him, and he peeled off his suit jacket and laid it over my shoulders.

He might have been angry with me—and part demon—but unlike Paul, who was all human, he was still a gentleman. The heat from his body quickly penetrated mine, warming me all over.

More than the warmth from his jacket, however, the fresh clean scent of him and the brush of his fingers against my skin reminded me how much I loved him.

"Oh, Jesse," I said. "Can we not fight? It's the *worst*."

He appeared unmoved. "No, Susannah. The *worst* is hearing that your future wife has volunteered to open a mediator school in her old home for the sole purpose of educating *Paul Slater's* daughters."

"Jesse, come on. You know that it isn't what I meant. Not a school. I was thinking of the clinic we've always talked about opening. You'll look after children's physical well-being, and I'll look after their mental health. You should see the promo design CeeCee came up with . . ."

"You can't open a medical clinic in a residential neighborhood, Susannah."

"Oh," I said. "Well, yeah, you're probably right. We'll just have to live there, then."

"In the house where I *died*?"

"In the house where *we* fell in love. A house I scored for free, in case you missed that part."

Any couple that had spent as much time as we had in a long-distance relationship (not only because we'd been away at different colleges, but because one of us had been undead for a part of the time we'd been together) was bound to fight—us maybe even more than other couples, given our peculiar situation . . .

But we'd never had a fight like this.

Resolving conflicts is what I do, however. There are lots of ways to resolve conflicts. Not all of them include weapons.

At least, not weapons that come in a sports bag.

And from the heat that I'd seen flare in Jesse's eyes, I was beginning to get a good idea what kind of weapon would be best used to resolve this conflict. Fortunately, it was one I had in my arsenal. I'd been trying to use it on him, to little avail, for a long, long time.

Thanks to Paul, I now had a good idea why. It was the last thing he'd set out to do, but Paul had, in trying to split Jesse and me apart, handed me the key to finally bringing us together.

"Come on." I reached out to seize him by the belt and was pleased when he allowed me to tug him a few inches toward me. "The best way to resolve this issue is to prove Paul wrong."

The eyebrow with the crescent-shaped scar lifted. "In what way?"

"I think if there's even the slightest doubt that there's something wicked still lurking inside you," I said, pulling him even closer, "we should work on unleashing it. It's basically my duty as a mediator, in fact."

He was now leaning against me, pressing me back against

Jake's car. I could feel the steady drum of his heartbeat through the material of his suit coat, along with the muscles of his thighs against mine. The heat he was giving off made it hard for me to believe there was any part of him at all that might possibly still be in the grave. But you never know.

His mouth twisted. "Susannah—"

"Shhh. I've been training for this for a long time." I was still holding on to his belt buckle. "I'm ready to take on this very important mission."

"Susannah." He had a hand on either side of the car, trapping me within his long, muscular arms. "I know you're joking, but this is serious. You wouldn't have gone through all this if you didn't at least partly believe—"

"I'm not joking, and it doesn't matter what *I* believe." I fiddled with his belt buckle. "What do *you* believe? If the real reason you've put off our making love for so long is fear that it might release something unholy, then I think we have an obligation to find out." I kept my gaze on his, my fingers locked on his belt buckle. "The truth is, Jesse, I ain't afraid of no ghost."

He looked down at me with dark eyes that were filled with something unreadable.

"Perhaps," he said, dropping his hands to my waist, "you're right."

My pulse gave an unsteady lurch.

"What I prescribe is that we both go back to the Crossing tonight," I said, my voice suddenly a little hoarse, "and split a bottle of wine, and discuss how disappointing I've been, in great detail, in your bedroom. For therapeutic purposes I think we should do this unclothed."

His response was the lopsided grin that I'd missed so much— no trace of cynicism in it this time.

"We could try that," he said, ducking his head to press a kiss along my throat. "Or we could discuss some of your less disappointing qualities."

I feigned shock. "Wait . . . I have some?"

"I can think of a few." One of his hands had risen from my waist to linger dangerously close to my left breast.

"Name one. Let's see what it unleashes."

"Hmmm. Strong-willed?"

"Not very flattering. Try again."

"Witty."

"Oh, good." The hand drifted closer to my breast as his lips traveled closer to my mouth. "How about another?"

"Beautiful."

"I like it. What else?"

He said something unintelligible. As he'd continued to kiss me—one kiss for each word—I'd felt something through the front of his suit trousers that proved at least one part of him was decidedly *not* disappointed in me.

"We could discuss those things, too," I said as both his hands now cupped my breasts, and his lips pressed hungrily against mine. "I'm open to winging it."

"Susannah, Susannah, Susannah," he whispered after a little while. "*Te amo.*"

"Me, too," I whispered back, slipping my arms around his neck. The best part of fighting was always the making up afterward. "Back at you."

He'd just given me one of those long, simmering kisses that, in my experience with him, generally led to even more long, simmering kisses, when the sound of someone clapping caused us both to start and turn around.

There was no telling how long he'd been standing there beneath the porte cochere, silently eavesdropping. The wind from the ocean was blowing the smoke from the cigar he was smoking in the opposite direction, which was why I hadn't noticed it. I'm usually more sensitive to those kinds of things.

"Brilliant," Paul said, still applauding, the cigar clenched between his teeth. "A stunning tour de force. I haven't seen a performance that entertaining since . . . well, the porn in my room upstairs."

I felt every one of Jesse's muscles tense. I grasped the shoulders of his jacket beneath my fingers, knowing exactly what was about to happen.

"Jesse, don't," I warned, fear clenching my stomach. "He's not worth—"

But it was too late.

He was on Paul in three strides. The sound of bone thudding against bone was sickening, almost the same sound the rifle butt had made as it connected with Delgado's skull.

It's odd what your consciousness focuses on in moments like that. Mine was seized by the cigar as it went flying from Paul's mouth into the night air—sending a shower of red sparks after it—only to land on the concrete at my high-heeled feet, followed, a few seconds later, by Paul's face, in a shower of equally red blood droplets.

"I warned you," Jesse said to Paul, breathing heavily as he stepped over his inert body to take me by the arm and steer me away from the carnage. "But you wouldn't listen."

Paul's only response was a groan as he struggled to sit up.

"Jesse." I was completely shocked by the violence of what I'd just witnessed, and I'd witnessed quite a lot of violence that evening. It wasn't hard for me to believe, in that moment, that Jesse did have a demon within him. He'd just unleashed it on the person he hated most, instead of those he loved. "You didn't have to—"

"Yes," he said in a voice that chilled me with its iciness. "I did."

Then he pressed something into my hand. When I looked

down to see what it was, I was surprised, in some dim part of my brain, to see the keys to the BMW.

"Go home." Jesse was holding on to my shoulders and giving me careful verbal instructions. "Your home. Hurry. It will be better if you leave now."

"Why?" I asked stupidly. "Where are you going?"

"Don't worry about me. I'll be all right. I'll call you when I can."

"Call me? I don't understand. Where are you going?"

But then I saw the valets come bursting out from the lobby, speaking rapidly and excitedly to Jesse in Spanish, and I heard the siren in the distance, and I saw the slow, evil smile on Paul's face through all the blood as he sat up.

Suddenly I understood exactly why Jesse had given me his keys, and knew precisely where he was going.

All I could do was get into his car and drive home.

treinta y uno

David wouldn't stop apologizing. He sounded like he was crying, practically, over the phone.

And I was making things worse by saying all the wrong things.

"Well, it's true Jesse probably never would have gotten arrested for assaulting Paul Slater if it weren't for you spilling the beans about the curse to him," I said. "Which just goes to show some things really are better kept secret."

"I'm so sorry, Suze! I was just really worried. When you didn't return any of my messages—"

"Oh, my God, David, I was kidding." I hadn't been kidding, actually, but after the day I'd had, I was too tired to think before I spoke.

I grabbed a beer and a carrot from the fridge, dropped the carrot into Romeo's cage, then went to sit by Gina on my futon couch. I'd found her watching television when I got home, though she'd muted the show, deciding my phone calls were more interesting than her recorded episodes of *The Bachelor*.

"He's only going to have to spend one night in jail," I assured David. There, that sounded better. "At least according to his lawyer."

This failed to reassure David, however.

Jake had already contacted one of his high-powered attorneys (when you're in a business like my oldest stepbrother's, you keep legal counsel on retainer. I tried not to feel nervous that Jake called his "DUI Guy") and sent him down to the jail to ensure that Dr. Hector de Silva received the finest possible treatment until his arraignment (which wasn't scheduled until early tomorrow morning).

The Monterey County Jail was actually supposed to be one of the better correctional facilities in the state—not that any of them were that great—so Jesse had lucked out in that regard. Like so many buildings in Northern California, it was on the National Registry of Historic Places. Cesar Chavez had been imprisoned there during the Salinas Valley lettuce boycott. Both Brad and Jake had spent time in what some referred to as "The Bay Area's Most Affordable B and B" for various small scuffles and infractions.

"Jake says the food leaves something to be desired," I told David over the phone. "But you get to meet a lot of interesting people."

"This isn't making me feel better, Suze," David said. "What about Jesse's job? Is he going to lose it?"

I tried not to allow the unease I felt about this show in my voice. "I'm sure he'll be able to keep his job. Everyone at the hospital loves Jesse. And this whole thing was just a misunderstanding that happened while Jesse was off-duty. The charges against him are being dropped." I swigged from my beer. "Everything's going to be fine. You'll see."

"How did you accomplish *that*?"

"Let's just say Paul was more than happy to cooperate."

Paul's actual response—or I should say, responses—to my text telling him that he'd better drop the charges, or I'd tell the Mercedes King the truth about him and Debbie, had been less gracious than that.

> **El Diablo** Fine. But I want you to know that animal cracked my jaw in two places.
> Nov 19 12:40 AM

> **El Diablo** And now you've seen it with your own eyes, Simon. He's not the saintly good doctor he pretends to be. There's a devil inside him.
> Nov 19 12:41 AM

> **El Diablo** When you need to be rescued from him, call me. I MIGHT come get you.
> Nov 19 12:42 AM

> **El Diablo** But probably I'll just let him crack YOUR jaw so you can see what this feels like.
> Nov 19 12:43 AM

Harsh. But very Paul-like. I thought it was interesting that he considered Jesse the devil when it was very clear to me, between the two of them, who was the real prince of darkness.

Of course I didn't share the details of Paul's texts with David, but what little I did say alarmed him anyway.

"Suze! Isn't that intimidating a victim? You could get in trouble."

I had a nice laugh at the idea of Paul being a victim, though truthfully I wasn't finding anything about the situation too funny.

"David, you have no idea of the stuff I've done this week alone that I could get in way worse trouble for."

"Well, what about the house? And the curse? I've been talking to Shahbaz—we've met a couple times, actually—and it really doesn't look like there's any way to break it. At least, not any way written about in ancient Near East culture. I've read about a few Wiccan curse removal practices that you could try, though. I know Father Dominic wouldn't approve, but—"

"David," I said, pausing with my beer midway to my lips. "You haven't told this Shahbaz guy anything about my gift, have you?"

"No," David said, in a voice that sounded so guilt-stricken I knew he was lying. "Well, not in so many words. But I think he'd understand if I did. He's actually very astute, and he's really concerned about our old house being torn down. He understands how unsettling it might be for someone to see their childhood home destroyed to make way for a subdivision, regardless of whether or not there's a curse involved."

"Aw," I said, touched by the wistful note in David's voice. "That's really sweet of him. But I think the house is going to be saved."

"Really? How?" David was so surprised his voice cracked.

No way was I going to tell David about Paul being the true father of his nieces—especially if he was that upset about the house—so I said only, "It looks like the demo plans have been delayed. So we've got time to work on some alternative strategies."

"How did you manage *that*, Suze?"

"David, it's really late here, so it must be even later there. Shouldn't you be asleep?"

"I told you before, Suze, I'm not a child anymore. I want to help!"

"I think you've helped enough," I said. "And I don't mean that in a bad way. Really, David, I don't know what I'd do without you. But I've got to go to bed. Good night." I hung up before he could say another word.

"God." Gina passed me the bowl of buttered popcorn that had been sitting on her lap. "It sounds like you've had a spectacularly shitty night."

"Tell me about it." I shoved a handful of popcorn into my mouth. It tasted like salty ash, but that was due to the day's events, not Gina's popping skills. "I just need to decompress for, like, an hour."

"Fine." She lifted the remote. "What do you want to watch?"

"Anything but *The Bachelor*. I've had enough of bachelors for one night."

"Your wish is my command." She aimed the remote at the screen and flicked through the channel guide. "Uh, looks like our only palatable choices are your favorite, *Ghost Mediator*, or one of those budget bridal gown shows."

"Good God. Budget bridal gowns, please."

She grinned. "I thought so. Budget bridal gowns it is."

We watched until we fell asleep—well, one of us, anyway. I got up quietly so as not to disturb her, then padded to my bed . . .

. . . but was still wide awake an hour later, unable to get one image out of my mind:

Stop. Wait. Don't.

There was a lot of blame to go around for the evening's events, but Jimmy Delgado's death was squarely on me. That was one soul I'd failed to save . . . not that it had been a soul worth saving.

Jesse, though. What was he doing now? Was he, too, lying

awake in his cell, thinking of me? Was he warm enough? What if he didn't have a blanket? Was he getting along with the other prisoners? What if Paul did not, in fact, drop the charges like he said he was going to? Could I really tell anyone the truth about the triplets?

These were the thoughts with which I was torturing myself when I realized I was not alone in my room.

I knew who it was before I opened my eyes.

I rose up on one elbow and stared at her. Even though I'd sensed her presence, my heart was still thumping.

"You can't keep doing this," I said. "You're going to give me a heart attack."

Lucia didn't reply. She just stood there at the side of the bed, a soft aura glowing all around her, looking at me with those huge dark eyes. She wore the same somber expression she always wore, her mouth the same pink rosebud of disapproval.

What had I done wrong now? Maybe she didn't like that I slept in the same room as a rat, or in an old black tank top and yoga shorts.

Or maybe she didn't like that I hadn't tried very hard to keep her murderer from offing himself. He was never going to get his day in court. At least, no court on planet Earth.

"How did you even get in here?" I looked around. She shouldn't have been able to enter my apartment, the place was so barricaded against evil spirits, between the salt and the house blessings and the crosses and the mezuzahs.

On the other hand, Lucia wasn't exactly evil.

"What can I do for you, Lucia?" I asked her. Talking to this kid was like talking to the stuffed animal she clutched in her hands, she was so unresponsive. "Is it about Jimmy? Er . . ."

I realized, belatedly, that only Becca had ever called Lucia's killer by his name, and even she didn't like to. Lucia herself had been too traumatized by what he'd done to her ever to mention him by anything other than "he."

"Is it about the, um, bad man?"

I sat up in bed, careful to move slowly so as not to alarm her. There was no sound in the room except my voice, and the gentle grunts of Romeo, who'd woken and immediately begun cleaning himself in his cage.

"Because he's gone, Lucia." This seemed a fitting euphemism for what had happened to Delgado. Gone. He was gone. "I found him and made sure that he'll never hurt you, or Becca, or anyone else ever again."

Lucia only continued to stare at me in silence, her eyes gleaming as luminously as the rest of her. I couldn't read her expression. Was she apprehensive, or reproachful?

"Tomorrow I plan on taking care of the priest who hurt Becca, too. Okay?" My voice broke a little. "Not in the same way as Jimmy, but ... he'll never be able to hurt anyone either. I'm sorry things got so messed up, and that they took such a long time to fix. Not that they'll ever really be fixed, but ... well, you know. This was a tough one, Lucia. This one was really hard."

I reached up to move some hair from my eyes and found, when my fingers came away wet, that I was crying. Me, who never cried.

All the signs were there. My cheeks were damp. My throat had closed up. My eyes stung.

This wasn't allergies. I was crying. Crying for Lucia.

For Lucia, or for Becca, or for me? Maybe for the triplets, too, and a little bit for Jesse. Crying for all of us.

Lucia only continued to stare at me owlishly.

I reached for my cell phone, which I kept on the nightstand, and scrolled through the photos I'd stored on there.

"Look, Lucia. I found your family. They've moved away from here, but not too far. They have a vineyard north of San Francisco. It looks really nice. They don't have horses, but they have llamas. See, here's a picture." I held the screen on my phone toward her so that she could see. The glow lit up her face even more brightly than her own spectral radiance. "There's your mother, and your father, and your brothers. And look, see here? After you died, they adopted two little girls." This caused her to lean in closer. I finally had her attention.

"I've been wondering about it," I went on. "Why did they adopt two girls? And I think the reason they had to adopt two is that one little girl wouldn't have been enough to replace the hole in their hearts that you left behind. That's how much they loved you."

Lucia glanced from me to the photo then back again, her eyes wider than ever.

But I still couldn't tell if she understood. I could hardly see anything myself, because of my tears.

How could I get through to her?

"Please, Lucia," I said. "You just have to be patient a little bit longer, and then everything will be all right, I swear. Well, maybe not all right. Nothing will ever be all right for you, I know that. But I swear I'll make things right for Becca. That's what you want, isn't it?"

She did something then that shocked me, and I've been working with the souls of the dead for a long time. I didn't know I could be shocked anymore.

But Lucia managed, by climbing onto the bed and crawling toward me, her arms stretched to reach around my neck.

Not to strangle me this time, though.

To hug me.

Even more shocking, I put down my phone and hugged her

back, a dead seven-year-old who shouldn't have even been in my room in the first place.

This was a violation of every ghost-mediator—and patient-therapist—protocol in the book. Lucia needed to cross over to the other side to be with the people she belonged to—the grandmother who'd claimed she'd been such a happy girl, and had since passed on herself, and was probably waiting impatiently for her granddaughter to hurry up and join her. Ensuring that this happened was my job.

But here I was, hugging her instead of letting her go, allowing her to lay her cheek—cold and smooth as marble—against mine, holding on to her as tightly as she was holding me. Her sadness, deep and dark as a grave, seeped into me . . .

Or maybe the only sorrow I felt was my own. Maybe it had been there all along, neatly boxed away. Maybe that's what had been keeping me awake at night for so many years, but I'd never allowed myself to feel it, until the touch of that cold cheek to mine caused the box to open, and all the emotions I'd packed so tidily away in there came rushing to the surface.

"It's okay, Lucia," I whispered, rocking her a little. "Everything's going to be okay. I promise."

She pulled away from me slightly, then laid a hand upon my own cheek, which, unlike hers, was not cold and smooth as marble, but hot and wet.

"I know," Lucia whispered back, gazing into my eyes. For the first time since I'd met her, she smiled. "That's what I came to tell *you*."

Then, in a burst of golden light that lit my room like a sun shower, she was gone.

treinta y dos

For the first time in a long time, I slept. I didn't wake until nearly nine in the morning, when my cell phone buzzed. It was my stepbrother Jake calling.

Jake. Jesse. *Jail.*

"Oh, my God, how is he?" I cried, snatching up my phone. "What's happening?"

"He's out." Sleepy sounded extremely pleased with himself.

"He is?" I sat bolt upright in bed. "Is he all right? Where is he? What happened? Can I speak to him?"

"All charges dismissed. See, it pays to have the very best criminal attorney on your side. Got a DUI? Call the DUI Guy. Not that that was applicable in your boy's case, but—"

I didn't want to burst Jake's bubble, since I knew it wasn't his high-powered attorney's skills, but my slick mediating that had gotten Jesse off the hook.

"Thanks so much, Jake," I interrupted. "I really appreciate it. I'm sure Jesse does, too. Where is he? Can I speak to him?"

"He's right here in the car with me. I'm driving him back to the Crossing because he says you have his car? Boy, that's good, because if Five-Oh looked inside the BMW and found all that, er, contraband, even the DUI Guy wouldn't have been able to get him off—"

"Jake, can I speak to Jesse?" Sometimes I wondered if all of my stepbrothers, with the exception of David, had been dropped repeatedly on the head as newborns.

"Uh . . ." I heard a slight murmuring, and then Jake came back on the line. "Sorry, Suze, maybe later, all right?"

I tried to keep the acid out of my tone because I knew none of it was Jake's fault. He'd been a really good friend to both of us. But I was angry. "*What?*"

"Listen, Suze, don't worry, nothing bad happened to him, he's just a little worse for wear. I mean, come on, Suze." Jake's tone dropped to a whisper. "The guy spent the night in jail. No one wants to talk to their fiancée first thing when they get out of jail."

"I would," I said. I swung my legs over of the side of the bed. "I would want to talk to my fiancé first thing when I got out of jail. In fact, I thought we were going to head over to the arraignment *together* and I was going to serve as a character witness and—"

"Well, Suze, you know what? Sometimes there's stuff men don't want their lady involved in, and this is one of those things."

"What *lady?* I'm not anyone's lady. What the hell are you even talking about? And how could Jesse possibly not want me involved? I'm already involved. What happened? Did he get beat up in jail? Is there something he's hiding? Put him on the phone right now, Jake, or I swear to God, I'll—"

"I think it would be better if I got him home first and rested and fed and showered up," Jake said in a more normal tone. "Then you can come over later and the two of you can talk. All righty, Suze?"

"All righty? Don't you *all righty* me. Who are you, his new life coach?"

"See?" Jake was whispering again. "This is *exactly* why I didn't want you down at the courthouse. You're too emotional."

"Emotional? *Me?* What about him? *He's* the one who—"

"Picking up the groom from the courthouse after he's spent the night in jail isn't the job of the bride. It's the job of the best man. Which is another reason why you guys should have appointed me as best man, and not groomsman. And I don't know what's up with this Paul guy, but do not, and I mean *do not*, ever bring up his name again around Jesse. Every time they mentioned it in court, this muscle in his face started twitching—"

"Don't worry, I have no intention of mentioning Paul, not now, or ever. But listen, you've got to tell me. Is it *me* Jesse's mad at, or just Paul? Because honest to God, Jake, if he calls off the wedding, I'm going to lose it. That dress has been hanging in my closet for so long I think it's got more cobwebs than my vagina."

"Uh-oh," Jake said. "I'm starting to lose you. I think I've just hit an area where there's no cell service."

"There aren't any of those on the way from Monterey, you moron."

"See you later this afternoon, Suze. Bye, Suze." Jake hung up.

I lowered my cell phone and then sat there, feeling like punching something. Lucia had said everything was going to be all right, but as far as I could tell, her prediction was about as accurate as the local weather forecaster's. It had called for sunshine, but as usual a thick marine layer hid the "mountain" view—and just about everything else, as well—outside my windows.

Gina was already up and out of the apartment—a text she'd

left on my phone said she'd gone to an audition (Carmel-by-the-Sea's outdoor theater was always putting on musicals), then to run errands.

This was fine with me. I had plenty of errands of my own.

"What's this?" CeeCee asked, looking at the laptop and cashbox I set down on the table between us at the Happy Medium an hour later, after I'd showered, dressed, and met her for a breakfast of grits (her) and pancakes with extra tofu bacon (me, and only because the Happy Medium is vegetarian).

"Oh," I said, swallowing a large gulp of coffee. "Just everything you need to break the story of the decade. Well, maybe not the decade, but the year, at least. Your editor is going to love you. You could probably get a job at the *San Francisco Chronicle* with a story this big."

"I don't want to work at the *Chronicle*." CeeCee opened the cashbox. It was easy to do so, since the lid was broken, and hanging sadly on its hinges. "I just want off the police beat. Geez, Suze! How much money's in here, anyway?"

"Fifty grand. Don't look at what's on the thumb drives around here, or in front of anyone under eighteen." I glanced around the café, which was bustling. It did some of its best business during the breakfast hour, which was why Gina was dying to snag the Saturday morning shift. CeeCee's aunt had assured her she'd get her chance, but only after she'd "paid her dues" with the less busy night shifts. "It's pretty gross."

"Oh, yeah?" CeeCee, unfazed, was already working on deciphering the password on the laptop. "What's up?"

"Pretty soon a guy is going to walk into the Delgado Photography Studio over on Pine and find his boss, James Delgado, dead from a self-inflicted gunshot wound. That stuff you have there was locked inside his desk. When you get a look at what's on it, you'll know why he chose to off himself. There are two client lists—one for his regular photos, and one for photos he was distributing illegally according to U.S. federal child exploitation laws."

CeeCee made a face. "How charming."

"Yeah. I think a good thing for you to say in the story you write about it—before you turn all this stuff over to the police—is that you found it in a padded envelope on your doorstep this morning. You have no idea who could have left it there, but you assume it was Jimmy himself, out of shame and remorse for all the terrible things he did. But that's for the police to determine, of course."

One of the many things I liked about CeeCee Webb was that she didn't waste time asking stupid questions. Her sense of morality was well honed, but highly flexible. And she was professional to the core.

She also knew a good thing when it walked up and was presented to her at the breakfast table.

"Great," she said, her gaze never leaving the screen in front of her, even as she occasionally reached over to consume a mouthful of grits. "No problem. One thing, though. What if they ask me for the envelope?"

"Sadly," I said, "you threw it away, and it already got taken to the dump. How could you know it contained something so incredibly important?"

"True. So I take it, since you're involved, this Delgado didn't really commit suicide?"

"Oh, no, he really did. Maybe you could mention in your story how there've been a number of studies suggesting people like him would rather die than face the social stigma of having their crimes exposed—or quit committing them."

"Nice line, thanks, I'll use it." She continued to type. "What was that other thing you mentioned you wanted to speak to me about?"

"Oh, yes. Well, considering I'm giving you this truly enormous story, I was wondering if you could stifle another one."

Now she did look up from the screen, her violet eyes playful. "Susannah Simon, are you trying to impede the freedom of the press?"

"Absolutely. Since you write the local police beat, could I ask you *not* to report in it that Jesse got arrested last night for assaulting Paul Slater?"

The look in the violet eyes went from playful to gleeful.

"He *did?* How delish! Were you there? Did you see it? Tell me everything. Was the carnage extensive? What did Paul say to get him so angry? What in God's name were you even doing with Paul in the first place? And why didn't you invite *me?*"

"If I promise to tell you everything," I said, "in excruciating detail, will you promise to do everything you can to make sure the whole thing stays off the Internet and out of the paper? I think it would mortify Jesse if his colleagues at the hospital found out."

"Cross my heart." She made a slash with her finger across the faded gray Mission Academy sweatshirt she wore. "And hope to die. Are you going to eat your tofu bacon?"

"No. It's disgusting. Why can't they serve turkey bacon here, at least?"

"Aunt Pru won't allow animal by-products in her establishment. That's soy milk you're putting in your coffee."

I uttered a four-letter word, nearly dropping the metal pitcher.

"Sorry. Now tell me everything. Where did it—"

"Hello, girls." Aunt Pru swooped down on our table, her many bangles jingling. "Did I hear my name?"

CeeCee slammed down the cover to Jimmy Delgado's computer. "Good morning, Aunt Pru."

"Busy working, I see." She kissed the top of her niece's head, which was turning pink beneath CeeCee's snow-colored hair. "She's so industrious, isn't she, Susannah?"

"Like a busy little bee," I said, standing up and gathering my messenger bag. "Which reminds me that I, too, have work to do, and must run."

"Oh, how sad." Pru looked regretful while CeeCee scowled, angry that I was escaping without having shared the tale of Jesse's arrest. "But it all turned out the way I said it would, didn't it?"

"What did, Prudence?" I was busy digging through my wallet for cash. I figured treating CeeCee to breakfast was the least I could do.

"With the little girl. She never meant to hurt anyone. She was only frightened, and in pain. But you helped her, didn't you?"

I froze, staring at her, then finally managed a smile. So "the lost child" had been Lucia all along. I ought to have known. Paul Slater had never been lost a day in his life. He'd always known the exact path he was taking.

Too bad it was the wrong one.

"I think so, Pru," I said. "Thank you. But I didn't do it alone. I had a lot of help from my friends."

treinta y tres

I don't know what I was expecting when I pulled up in front of the house where Becca Walters lived. I knew the Walterses were wealthy, of course.

But I didn't think the Walterses's domicile would be one of the $20 million mansions on 17-Mile Drive that Jesse and I had made fun of on our way to Sacred Trinity the day before, joking that it was the kind of place Dr. and Mrs. Baracus would live in.

With the Pacific as its "private" beach, stunning oceanfront swimming pool and spa, ten bedrooms and baths, and multiple "guest cottages," Becca's house looked more like nearby Pebble Beach Resort than a private home.

But that illusion was shattered when I had to speak into an intercom in front of a private gate in order to enter. Even then I was worried—because for once I'd used my real name—that I wouldn't be granted access, particularly since it was Kelly who answered.

"Suze Simon?" she echoed. It was hard to tell if she was more surprised or annoyed.

"Yes, hi, Kelly, it's me." I had to lean very far out the side of the car to reach the intercom, which was built into one of the colossal columns that flanked either side of the long driveway leading to the house.

Of course the Walterses had named their abode. All the really chic properties along 17-Mile Drive had names. A plaque on one of the columns outside Becca's house said it was called CASA DI WALTERS.

It could have been worse, I guess, although I couldn't think how.

"I'll only take up a few minutes of your time," I assured Kelly. "I want to talk to you and your husband about Becca."

After a long pause, a buzzer finally sounded, and the massive wrought-iron gates swung open electronically. I'd been granted access to Casa di Walters. I felt like a commoner being allowed a visitation with the queen. Queen Kelly.

I had to wander around the vast property for a while before I found them. There was no maid or even a housekeeper to greet me at the door (surprisingly), though I tried knocking and ringing the bell. I would have expected Kelly to have a maid, and also to have forced the maid to dress in one of those uniforms with a frilly white apron.

Possibly Kelly couldn't get Lance Arthur to go along with this plan. Or maybe they gave the maid weekends off. This seemed likelier to me than there being no maid.

Finally I heard the familiar *thwock-thwock* of tennis balls being struck with racquets, and realized the family was in the backyard. The forecaster had *not* turned out to be wrong about the weather. The sun had burned off the morning fog, and was now causing me to boil beneath the black cashmere cardigan I'd thrown over the tank top I'd paired with jeans. Since it seemed clear my fiancé and I were on the outs—or something—I'd dressed for comfort rather than unleashing sexy inner demons. I even had on my second-best—and only—pair of butt-kicking boots.

I found Kelly on the court enjoying an energetic game of doubles with her new husband. Up close, and dressed in tennis whites, Lance Arthur Walters looked better than he had in photos on the Internet. He actually looked sort of nice, for a bald, red-faced, middle-aged billionaire. When he noticed me, he halted the game—Kelly had seen me first, but made a point of pretending not to—and came rushing over, using a towel to wipe off some of his copious sweat.

"Hello," Lance Arthur beamed, his right hand outstretched. "You must be the teacher I've heard so much about recently from Becca."

Kelly trotted along behind him, her long blond ponytail swinging. She was not sweating at all. She wasn't even glowing.

"She's not a teacher," Kelly said sourly.

"Suze Simon." I shook Becca's father's hand. "I work in the administrative offices at the Mission Academy. Kelly and I were both in the same class there, actually."

Lance Arthur turned around to regard his young, pretty wife in surprise. "Were you? You never told me that, darling. Then you ought to have Susan over for Pilates, with your other friend. What's her name? Oh, yes, Debbie."

"Debbie is my sister-in-law," I said.

Lance Arthur nearly keeled over in shock. "Sister-in-law? No! You don't say! Kelly, why have I never met Susan before? Debbie's her sister-in-law! Why, this is such a coincidence. And Becca speaks so highly of Susan."

Kelly stared at me with daggers in her eyes. "I didn't know *Susan* was such a fan of Pilates."

"Oh," I said, beginning to enjoy myself. "I love Pilates. I do it every day."

"Every day!" Lance Arthur had steered us toward a matching outdoor chair and table set on the side of the court that was shaded by a bright yellow sunbrella, beneath which someone—the absent maid?—had set a pitcher of freshly made lemonade and several glasses. He poured a glass for me, then one for Kelly and himself. "How tremendous. You must come take a class in our private studio, Susan. It's really state-of-the-art, and we have a top-notch instructor, just top-notch. Debbie and Kelly simply adore Craig, don't you, Kelly?"

Kelly flopped down onto one of the yellow-cushioned sun loungers and said, "Oh, we do."

I bet Debbie and Kelly adored Craig. I bet Craig adored Kelly, too, especially during the long weeks at a stretch that Lance Arthur was out of town on business.

"I might do that," I said. "Thanks so much for the invitation." The lemonade tasted amazing, not too tart, and not too sweet. There were real strawberries floating in it, too. Nothing but class for Lance Arthur. "Listen, I didn't mean to interrupt your game. I really came here to check on Becca. I'm sure Kelly told you, Mr. Walters, that—"

"Oh, please call me Arthur! Any friend of Kelly's is a friend of mine, Susan."

"Right, Arthur. Well, as I'm sure Kelly's told you, Becca had a little problem at school the other day, and I just wanted to follow up after Father Dominic's unfortunate visit to see how she's doing."

"Wasn't that a terrible thing?" Walters pulled out one of the chairs and sat down at the table, looking concerned. But mostly I think he was resting from the trouncing Kelly had been giving him on the court. He was still sweating profusely, especially around the man-boob area. "When Kelly told me, I was just shocked. I hope he got the flowers we sent, and the check, too."

So he'd meant Father Dominic's "accident," not what had happened to Becca.

"Yes, it was terrible," I said. I didn't join him at the table. I wanted to spend as little time in Kelly's presence as possible. "But I was actually referring to Becca—"

"But what about Becca?" Lance looked from my face to Kelly's. Kelly's was unreadable, as she'd slipped on a pair of large designer sunglasses with gold frames and reflective lenses and picked up a fashion magazine from a nearby outdoor coffee table. To my amusement, she'd begun flipping through it, bored from the conversation. "I thought Becca was doing better. No one mentioned a word to me!"

"Becca *is* doing better," I assured him. I wanted to snatch the magazine from Kelly's hands and hit her with it, but settled for saying, "I only wanted to make you aware that it's come to my attention that Becca may have been more affected by the death of a childhood friend than she let on. I believe she and Becca used to take riding lessons at Sacred Trinity?"

Lance Arthur Walters, to his credit, knew exactly whom I was talking about.

"Yes, of course. Lucia Martinez. That's the little girl who fell off her horse and died." He looked at Kelly. "She was in Becca's first-grade class. What a tragic accident. I know you would have been quite young when it happened, but you might have read about it in the papers, Kelly."

Kelly lowered her magazine, and then her sunglasses. She looked confused. Obviously she never read anything that didn't include pictures of women wearing couture. "Oh?" she asked noncommittally.

"In the next few weeks, some news stories might be coming out concerning someone who worked at Sacred Trinity when Becca and Lucia were there," I said, opening my bag and digging through it. "You might want to have Becca speak to a professional about how that makes her feel. Only if she wants to; I wouldn't force her. This person is very good." I finally managed to locate one of Dr. Jo's business cards, and laid it on the table beside the lemonade pitcher. "I feel confident she can help. All of you." I stared directly at Kelly. "She does family counseling, as well."

Walters picked up the card. "Well, thank you, that's very kind. But I hardly think—"

"It's only a suggestion. Where is Becca, anyway? I have to go now, so I'd like to say good-bye to her on my way out."

"Over by the pool," Walters said, pointing in an offhanded way behind him as he studied Dr. Jo's card. "Family counseling. Do you really think—"

"Well, it's been nice meeting you. Call me about getting together for Pilates, Kelly. Honestly, I can't wait! It sounds super-duper fun."

"Oh, I'll be sure to, *Susan*," Kelly said acidly, and turned back to her magazine.

I found Becca around the corner, floating on a raft in a magnificent infinity pool that looked out across the Pacific.

Becca was completely oblivious to the gorgeous view, however, being deeply absorbed in something on her phone. She had on a red bikini and dark sunglasses, her long hair scooped into a ponytail that looked not unlike her stepmother's. In fact, if I hadn't been told to look for her by the pool, I would have walked right by her, she looked so un-Becca-like.

"I don't believe it." I plopped down onto a chaise longue.

"Can it really be Becca Walters I see before me? I barely recognized you out of your uniform."

She gave a start. She'd been so wrapped up in her phone she hadn't noticed my approach.

"Oh, my gosh," she said. "Ms. Simon! What are you doing here?"

Incredibly, she paddled over to the side of the pool, got out, and ran over to give me a shy, drippy hug.

I don't know what came over me, but I hugged her back, just as I had Lucia the night before, though I didn't hold Becca quite as tightly. And I didn't cry this time.

I could see why Becca liked hanging out by her family's amazing pool. The sound of the water trickling over the infinity edge into the catch basin was almost as relaxing as the pound of the surf on the beach a hundred yards away. There was a nice breeze. I peeled off my cardigan to feel the sunshine on my arms. A person could really escape their problems in a place like this.

Unless, of course, their problems haunted them no matter where they went.

"You look good," I remarked to Becca as she pulled a pair of khaki shorts and a T-shirt over her wet suit. "Did you do something to your hair?"

Becca reached instinctively for her hair, embarrassed. I saw that she was still wearing the horse pendant, but now it was outside her shirt, instead of hidden inside it.

"Um, yeah. Well, I washed it, and stuff. Some of the things you said to me the other day in the courtyard made sense, about living for Lucia by taking better care of myself."

I tried to hide my surprise. "Oh. That's good."

"Yeah. It's hard, though." She picked at the bandage on her arm. I noticed it was a new, waterproof bandage, not the one I'd put on her. "It doesn't make me feel any less guilty."

"Well, sometimes you have to take it day by day. Maybe even minute by minute."

"Yeah," she said. "I guess that makes sense."

Now that I could see so much more of her bare skin, I noticed that Becca's arms and shins bore many faint white scratch marks, scars from previous attempts to punish herself.

But those would fade with time and—with enough love and support from her family and friends—eventually maybe even go away forever.

"I don't know if this will help, Becca." I figured I might as well get it over with. "But I came to tell you in person that I checked on Jimmy Delgado—that's the full name of the man who hurt you and Lucia—and he's dead. He committed suicide."

Becca looked at me much as Lucia had done, without expression.

I felt encouraged to go on.

"There'll probably be some stuff about it in the local papers, and maybe even on the local news, since it happened kind of recently." Uh, like last night. "Later on, there might also be some stuff about Father Francisco getting arrested. But your name will never be connected to either of those stories, unless, of course, you want to come forward. But that's totally up to you. I told your dad just now that you were very close with Lucia Martinez, closer than he knew. I'm sorry, Becca," I added, since I sensed by her lowered eyebrows that this had upset her, "but I had to tell him. He loves you a lot, you know."

I clutched the mattress of the lounge chair I was sitting on, waiting to gauge her reaction. It was a long time before she replied.

"Okay," she said finally, reaching up to twist the horse pendant. "I'm glad, I guess." She was gazing out across the pool, toward the Pacific.

"Uh . . . glad? That your dad loves you? Of course he loves you, Becca."

She looked at me. "No. I mean I'm glad he's dead." Then she tensed up, biting her lip in dismay. "Wait . . . that's wrong, isn't it? It's wrong to be glad someone's dead."

I had to repress a smile. "I don't think so. Not if you're glad he'll never hurt anyone again. I'd sure be glad if I were you."

"Oh. Okay." Her shoulders relaxed. "Because I don't want to be a bad person. For a really long time, that's how I've thought of myself."

"Yeah," I said. "About that. I gave your dad the name of someone I think you should go talk to if you start wanting to hurt yourself again. Or maybe just in general. She's very good to go to for advice."

The look of relief was replaced with one of anxiety. "Why can't I just keep talking to you, like this?"

"I already told you, Becca, I'm not a licensed therapist."

"Oh, right. You're just a mediator. You only help ghosts."

"Right. But I'm happy to talk to you anytime you want . . . as a friend."

"Maybe you could give me some pointers." She indicated her phone, which she'd thrown on the chaise longue. "I was just playing your game."

It took me a couple of seconds to realize what she meant. "*Ghost Mediator?* I told you, that game is completely—"

"Stupid, I know." She rolled her eyes, smiling, but then the smile faded a little. "How's . . . how's Lucia doing? I haven't—is she around right now?" She glanced furtively over her shoulder. "I wanted to say . . . I wanted to ask if you could tell her I'm trying—*really* trying this time—to live for the both of us. I'm actually going to try to have fun."

There was something sweetly pathetic about a sixteen-year-old girl assuring me that she was going to try to have fun. I had to hide my smile behind my hand, pretending I was scratching my nose.

"Becca, I think that's a great idea."

Encouraged, she went on, "I got invited to a party tonight at Sean Park's house—it's not a *real* party, a bunch of us are going to have a *Ghost Mediator* ultimate showdown—but I said I'd go, and Kelly said she'd drive me. She's going to take me to the mall later this afternoon to buy a new outfit, and we're going to get our nails done."

This time I didn't bother hiding my reaction. "She *is*?"

"Yeah. She got really excited about it. She knows a lot about clothes and girlie stuff, and said anytime I need help, to just come to her."

I was stunned, even though I knew I shouldn't have been. Of course Kelly was finally bonding with Becca. For one thing, Becca had finally expressed an interest in something that interested Kelly, as well—fashion and beauty products. And for another, Becca was no longer haunted by her ghostly guardian whose presence Kelly might actually have been able to sense. Kelly wasn't stupid. She'd managed to snag Becca's father, after all.

"You know," Becca went on, thoughtfully, "it's really weird, but ever since I talked to you, and you told me ghosts are real and that Lucia has been watching over me, I don't feel . . . I guess I don't feel afraid anymore. Even before you told me he—Jimmy—was dead, I'd decided to go to Sean's party. Would you tell Lucia that, please, Ms. Simon? Not only that I'm going to have fun for the both of us, but that I don't feel afraid anymore?"

The sun poured down across the turquoise water in the pool, casting golden flickers of light across the travertine tiles of the pool deck and the undersides of the palm fronds above our heads. I couldn't see Lucia—I knew she'd moved on last night, and was happy wherever she was now.

But it *almost* felt as if she were there . . . enough so that I was inspired to take Becca's hand and do my best imitation—I'm ashamed to say—of the lady from the ghost mediator TV show.

"She knows, Becca. She already knows. And she says thank you. Oh, wait . . ." I gazed at a point just left of Becca's shoulder, near an outdoor kitchen that included a state-of-the-art grill and wet bar. "It's hard to hear because she's starting to fade. Lucia is . . . yes. It's true. She's stepping toward the light."

"Oh!" Becca pressed a hand to her mouth. "Is Nana Anna there with her? Lucia loved her grandmother so much."

"Um, yes. Nana Anna is calling to her. It's time for Lucia to go to Nana Anna."

"Is Taffy there, too?"

I hesitated. "Who's Taffy?"

"Her horse."

Crap. I'd forgotten about the horse. "Yes. Taffy, too. Lucia is surrounded by and filled with love, especially her love for you, a little of which will stay with you always."

Oh, God, this was so corny. How did the Ghost Mediator live with herself?

But then again, it wasn't *entirely* untrue. And it was clearly helping Becca. There were tears of happiness trembling at the corners of her eyes. Shows like *Ghost Mediator* brought people joy, which was a good thing (though the fact that the star charged for her services off camera still made me furious, since of course she was a total fake).

"Lucia will always be with you, in your—"

Suddenly the warm wind gave a particularly strong gust, rustling through the palm fronds overhead and causing the surface of the pool to ripple. It lifted Becca's ponytail and blinded me for a moment by sending a thick dark wave of my own hair across my eyes.

When I'd brushed it aside, I could see that all the flickers of light reflected from the surface of the pool had shifted, and instead of dancing on the pool deck or the undersides of the palm fronds, they'd centered on Becca, glimmering across her face and legs and arms, like dozens of golden butterflies coming to rest their wings on her . . .

Or hundreds of flickering candle flames, sweetly circling her head like Saint Lucia's crown.

But that was impossible. What was going on?

"Oh!" Becca cried, raising her arms to gaze at the dazzling light show. "It's Lucia! I see her. I can *feel* her! Ms. Simon, she's here!"

Becca was right. Someone was there.

But it couldn't have been Lucia, since Lucia had crossed over the night before. It was someone else—someone with paranormal powers every bit as strong as Lucia's—someone who wanted to give Becca the kind of celestial farewell that her friend would have, if she'd still been around.

Someone who smelled suspiciously of smoke from a wood fire, suede, vanilla, hospital soap, and just a tiniest hint of cigarettes.

Jesse.

treinta y cuatro

"Who's here?" Kelly appeared from around the corner of the outdoor kitchen, carrying a tray with the lemonade pitcher and her magazine on it. "It's only me. What's wrong with you two?"

The lights vanished just as suddenly as they'd appeared, the wind dying, the surface of the pool going still. Above our heads, the palm fronds ceased to rustle, and the only sound that could be heard was the rumble of the Pacific and the rattle of the ice in the pitcher as Kelly approached.

But I could tell from the joyous smile on Becca's face that that split second of warm, sunny contact had been enough. She would remember it for the rest of her life.

"Nothing's wrong," Becca said to Kelly, still smiling. "We were talking about a friend of mine. Weren't we, Ms. Simon?"

"Yes," I said, hastily gathering my bag and standing up. The distinctive Jesse scent vanished, and all I could smell was the ocean and the crisp sharp scent of the chlorine from the Walterses's pool.

Where was he? Nearby, obviously. "A good friend. Well, it's been nice visiting with you, Becca, but I have to go now."

"Do you really?" Becca asked, disappointed. "Can't you stay for lunch?"

"No, she can't," Kelly said. She set the tray of lemonade in the exact spot on the chaise longue where I'd been sitting so that she could ensure I wouldn't rejoin them, then lowered herself onto the chaise beside it. "Debbie's here. I'm sure you'll want to say good-bye to her on your way out."

"Debbie?" It took me a second to figure out who she meant.

"Yes, your *sister-in-law*?" Kelly gave me a dirty look. "Surely you remember her. She and I are taking Becca to the mall to get a new dress and a mani-pedi because she's got a party tonight. Don't you, Becca?"

Becca glanced at her stepmother. "Yeah, I do. I mean, I do have a party. I didn't know Mrs. Ackerman was coming over—"

"Well, she's here. We're having lunch first on the veranda. I'd invite Ms. Simon but Paolo didn't prepare a large enough salmon. I'm sure *Susan* will understand."

"Oh, I do." I was already turning to go, thankful for the heads-up. Debbie was the last person I wanted to run into, especially if Jesse was somewhere on the premises. "I'll see you guys later."

"Bye, Ms. Simon!" I heard Becca calling after me. "And thank you!"

I waved over my shoulder as I hurried down the side steps to the driveway, not even glancing back.

Debbie, I was certain, would enter through the house, not the yard. There was no chance I'd run into her and have to make awkward small talk. Fortunately I'd driven Jake's BMW, so she might not even have recognized it in the driveway—at least not as readily as she would the dilapidated Land Rover, about which she—and her father—constantly complained. Why wouldn't I allow the Mercedes King to sell me a nice E-Class sedan? Leases started at only $579 a month.

I peered over the security gate leading from the pool to the Walterses's sprawling front yard, which sloped all the way down to a thick stone wall to 17-Mile Drive and from there, the sea.

There was definitely a male figure leaning against a car by the beach, across the street from the stone columns leading to Casa di Walters.

I couldn't tell, at that distance, who it was, but the car I recognized by sight. It was a Land Rover. *My* Land Rover.

My heart somersaulted inside my chest.

The steps from the pool down to the driveway were quite steep and zigzagged a bit, and I was taking them at something of a clip so I didn't even see that there was someone coming up them until I nearly collided into him—or her, as it turned out.

"Jesus!" Debbie yelled. "Watch it! Oh, Suze. What are *you* doing here?"

"Oh, hi." Debbie was wearing a long yellow maxi dress and clutching a large turquoise beach bag and hat. She looked great, and, from the smug expression on her face, she knew it. "Sorry, I didn't see you. I was just . . . I came by to see Becca's dad about some issues she's been having at school."

"Wow." Debbie's tone was flat. "I guess the Mission Academy offers special services to *some* of their students, the ones with fathers who are huge donors. If my dad coughed up a hundred thousand donation, would my girls get special home visits, too?"

"I did pay your girls a home visit this week, Debbie, remember? No hundred thousand donation necessary."

"Right." She snorted. "That was for some class you're taking.

Don't pretend like it was because you or anyone else at that school cares about the girls."

I reached out and grabbed her arm before she could move past me on the stairs.

"Actually, Debbie, I do care about your girls."

I was anxious to get down to Jesse, but I knew I had to attend to this little matter first. It was another one of Paul's messes I felt obligated to clean up.

"That test I conducted at your house showed that your girls are gifted—really gifted, Debbie. And I was wondering if you'd be interested in enrolling them in this new program I heard about through the school I go to."

Debbie stopped trying to continue up the stairs and lowered her sunglasses so she could stare at me over their gold frames, intrigued. There was nothing most parents loved hearing more than the word *gifted*, especially when applied to their own child.

"It's really exclusive—and very expensive," I went on quickly. Debbie had to lean in to hear me above the pound of the surf. "But I think I can get the girls a scholarship, so it would be free."

Lord help me if she ever found out *I* was the program.

But Debbie's interest sharpened perceptibly at the other magic word. "*Free?* Are you sure?"

I nodded. "Positive."

"What test was it that showed that the girls are gifted? I mean, their father and I have always thought they're gifted, but Sister Monica and especially that cow Sister Ernestine seem to think the opposite."

"Their father? You mean Brad." I studied her reaction carefully.

"Of course I mean Brad, Suze." She whipped off her sunglasses to squint at me in the strong sunlight. "Who else would I mean? What is wrong with you? Have you been sampling Jake's wares? You know you should lay off that stuff, especially if you're going to be driving."

She wasn't bluffing. Debbie truly believed that Brad was the father of her children, and that I, as usual, was the one with the problem.

And who was I to disabuse her of that notion? Wasn't it better for everyone that she—and Brad—go on believing this? I thought so, at least for now. Baby steps. One secret at a time.

"It's a new test," I said with a shrug. "Sometimes highly creative and intelligent children can be a challenge, especially to educators who are already overburdened with so many other students. But I think this program could really help the girls. It's after school."

"Wow." She smiled, slipping her sunglasses back into place. Smiling, Debbie actually looked like a nice person. "That sounds really great, Suze. You know, I've been thinking for a while about going back to school myself. But it's been so hard with the girls and all."

"Well," I said with a smile. "Maybe now you'll have the time. There's only one small problem."

The smile disappeared. "What's that?"

"In order for the girls to qualify for the scholarship, you'll have to show proof that they've at least started their vaccinations. This program doesn't allow for medical *or* religious exemptions from immunizations. Something about wanting to stop the spread of disease to unvaccinated newborns and those with compromised immune systems?"

Debbie scowled. "Oh. *That.*"

"Yeah. That. I'm really sorry. It doesn't seem like such a huge compromise to me, though, since you're going to have to do it anyway—unless you plan on taking them out of the Mission Academy entirely and homeschooling them."

She'd been gazing out toward the sea until I dropped the H-bomb. Then she whipped her head toward me. "Homeschool? No. No, I don't think so. I'll have to talk to Brad." She fumbled in her tote for her cell phone. "But I think he'll agree. Keeping them at the academy and then enrolling them in this gifted thing would probably be best. Oh, no, look at the time. I gotta motor. Kelly's hired a personal chef, and he made salmon." She lifted the skirt of her maxi dress and began to run up the steps. "Thanks, Suze, for all the help. By the way, I think I saw Jesse waiting for you, down at the beach."

"Yes," I said with a smile. "You did."

treinta y cinco

I never in a million years thought I'd be so happy to see my nearly twenty-year-old Land Rover.

Of course, it was more the sight of the figure leaning against the utility vehicle that made my heart beat a little quicker. His fingers were tucked loosely into the front pockets of his formfitting jeans, his dark hair tossed a little by the strong wind from the beach. He was perfectly unconscious of my approach (the soles of my second-best butt-kicking boots were rubber). He seemed transfixed by the sight of the sea.

Or maybe he was napping behind the dark lenses of his sunglasses. He'd had a long night, after all.

"How on earth did you know I was here?" I asked after I'd pulled up beside him and was getting out of the BMW.

Jesse turned his head, then gave me one of those slow, drowsy smiles I'd come to love so much.

"An app," he said. "Jake installed tracking systems in all his cars in case they were ever stolen."

"Oh." I was slightly disappointed. "I thought you were following me via our fiercely strong mind–body–spiritual connection."

"Well, that, too."

I joined him against the side of the car. The view was impressive. The sea was a deep, azure blue, the sky as cloudless as the forecasters had promised it would be. Seagulls wheeled in circles overhead, their cries lost in the pound of the surf. An occasional car went by, sightseers ogling both the surf and the expensive homes along 17-Mile Drive.

"So that *was* you a little while ago, and not Lucia, stopping in to say good-bye to Becca?" I asked.

"I may have helped Lucia give Becca a proper good-bye." He hadn't removed his fingers from his pockets, but we were standing close enough, our backs pressed against the car, that it felt as if we were touching.

"Bullshit," I said. "That was all you. I'd recognize your romantic touch anywhere. Besides, the cigarette smoke gave you away."

"I don't smoke."

"Not anymore, you don't."

His grin caused something to shift inside me. "You're right, I don't."

For a long time I'd suspected there was an electric current passing between us. It had always been there, even when he'd been an NCDP, and hadn't wanted to admit he loved me, a living girl whose job it was to rid the world of people like him.

In the years since his heart had begun to beat again, that current had only grown stronger. When we were apart, it stretched. I wondered if there was anything that could truly break it. Even death, it seemed, hadn't been able to.

"So Paul wasn't completely wrong," I went on. "There *is*

something left over from the grave inside you. But I don't think it's darkness. In fact, I think it's light."

Jesse swore in a very unangelic manner and strode away from the side of the car to lift a rock and hurl it at the waves. "Why, even on a beautiful day like this, do we still have to talk about *him?*"

"Because if we don't talk about it I'll never understand it, Jesse. And I want to. I really, really want to."

"*Why?* Why is it important? Why can't it simply be?"

"Well, for one thing because you nearly killed him last night."

"I wish I had."

"If you had, you wouldn't be standing here on the beach with me right now, throwing rocks at the waves. You'd still be locked up somewhere."

"But I'm not, *querida.*"

"Right. You're not. Instead, you can give—and apparently receive—messages from the spirit world. Don't get me wrong, I get them, too, but not the way you do. I talk to ghosts, but not *all* the ghosts, *all* the time. And I can't do magic tricks like the one you performed back there. It's a little spooky that my boyfriend— the mild-mannered physician—can do light shows with his mind. But then again, you used to be a spook, so I suppose I shouldn't be surprised."

"Well, if it doesn't bother me, it shouldn't bother you," he said, coming back to lean beside me against the car. "It would be nice, however, if you'd trust me enough to let me in on *your* little secrets once in a while. And also check your cell phone."

"*Me?* What about you? You're the one who didn't want to see me after getting out of jail."

"Because there was something I wanted to surprise you with, something I didn't know until I got out and the police returned my phone. But I wanted to tell you properly, in person, after I'd showered off the not very romantic odor of prison from my body. So please check your phone."

"If you want to see my reaction, then why didn't you just—"

"Susannah, I love you, but you are the most frustrating woman in the world. For once in your life, don't argue. Just do it."

I opened my bag and pulled out my phone. I'd received several new texts, mostly from classmates wondering at my absence from happy hour the past few nights. There was one that particularly piqued my interest, however.

> **Jesse** Me dieron la beca.
> Nov 19 1:10 PM

"I have no clue what that means," I said.

He looked thoughtful. "Perhaps you have that mental block that prevents otherwise intelligent people from learning new languages," he suggested.

"No, because I can speak French. If this were in *French*—"

"It's all right, *querida*. You're good at many other things. And at least you have your looks."

"I'm seriously going to kill you. Just tell me what it says. What's the surprise?"

"If I told you, it wouldn't be a surprise." He was enjoying himself. I could tell, since he was smiling as he walked around to the passenger side of the Land Rover. This was his way of getting me back for not telling him about Paul. "I will admit, in addition to picking up your sad excuse for a vehicle, I made a stop at your place. These were waiting outside the door for you. Saturday delivery? They must be important." He pulled a couple of packages from the front seat.

"Seriously," I said, staring at the text. "Is *beca* bacon? If you're offering to take me out for breakfast, the answer is yes, even though it's already lunchtime, because I had a really disappointing breakfast today."

"Bacon is *beicon*," he said. "Here, open your packages."

"We should get out of here," I said. "Kelly wasn't exactly thrilled to see me, and neither was Debbie at first, though I think I won her over."

I glanced at the packages—both addressed to Ms. Susannah Simon. One of them was a large next-day air priority box, the other a legal-sized padded envelope, stamped "Deliver by Hand"; return address, "Slater Properties." It felt lumpy, as if there might be something small and jagged—such as keys—inside.

I looked up at Jesse in wonder. "No," I said, hardly daring to believe it. "So soon?"

He shrugged again. "One of us must be very persuasive."

"Or intimidating," I said, tearing open the envelope.

Sure enough, there was a set of keys inside, attached to a plastic key fob marked "99 Pine Crest Road." There were also a number of documents requesting my notarized signature. But one of them was a deed, with my name typed in as the owner.

Finally, there was an astonishingly brief note from Paul, scrawled in his execrable handwriting on Carmel Inn stationery.

Suze,

> *Here are the items you requested.*
> *No matter how much you might hate me—or who you*
> *marry—I will always be here for you. You know how to reach me*
> *if you need to.*
> *You're a worthy adversary, Simon.*

I suppose that's why I always have, and always will,
love you.

Paul

Jesse stood reading the note along with me over my shoulder. I'd seen no reason not to let him, since I'd had no idea it would contain anything like the sentiments it did.

As soon as I got to the last lines, I began to blush.

I reached out to crumple the note into a little ball, but Jesse stopped me, tugging it from my hand.

"No, why?" I asked, attempting to snatch it back. "He's such a—" The words I used to describe Paul were ones I doubted Miss Boyd had ever uttered, much less heard of, even during her undoubtedly rough and memorable ride from Boston out west.

Jesse, shaking his head, tucked the note into the back pocket of his jeans.

"It's good to hang on to things like this," he said matter-of-factly. "You never know when they might come in handy later."

"Oh, and you accused *me* of being possessed by the dark side?" I said. "And if this is the surprise, it wasn't a very good one. I already knew he was sending this stuff over."

"That wasn't the surprise. You still aren't thinking very hard. Shall we go?"

"Go where? Breakfast?"

"No. To inspect our new home."

My heart leapt. I put my arms around his neck. "*Our* new home? Are you serious, Jesse? You really don't mind living there?"

"I seem to be destined to do so. But one thing I will *not* do, Susannah, is sleep in the room in which I died."

My room. The best room in the house, with a huge bay window (complete with a window seat that my stepfather, Andy, had lovingly built for me) that on clear days had a view stretching straight down to Carmel Bay, with an attached full bath in which Jesse had once bandaged my feet. It was the first time he'd ever admitted he'd hoped to become a doctor, but his father needed him too much on the ranch ever to have allowed it.

Now all of Jesse's dreams were coming true.

Maybe mine were, too.

That's what I came to tell you, I couldn't help remembering Lucia had said when I'd assured her everything was going to be okay.

"Maybe we should wait until we see what the realty company did to the room while they were staging it to sell," I said noncommittally. "I highly doubt they kept the forget-me-not wallpaper, or those frilly curtains my mom picked out. Maybe they turned it into a craft center, like Debbie's."

Jesse dangled the keys to my car in front of me. "Let's go find out. Don't forget your other package."

I glanced at the next-day-air package. "Is that my surprise?"

He rolled his eyes behind the sunglasses. "No."

We swapped cars. It was good to be back in the Land Rover, though it turned out the drive to the Carmel Hills from Casa di Walters was not short, especially on the last sunny Saturday before Thanksgiving. Traffic was terrible, and though there were no stoplights, I had plenty of stops of other kinds—mainly tourist related—to examine the next-day-air package Jesse had left on my passenger seat.

I didn't recognize the name of the sender—a woman in Arizona—but I tore it open anyway.

I was shocked when I saw what was inside:

My boots. The black leather platform boots I'd lost in the

online auction the other day. My perfect non-compliant deceased person butt-kicking boots.

How was that even possible? I'd been timed out of the auction when Lucia had ransacked my office. I hadn't been able to submit my final bid, let alone type in my name or payment information. Maximillian28 had slipped in and stolen them out from under me.

There was a note tucked into the box, but I wasn't able to grab and read it (since I was trying to be a good driver) until I pulled up in front of my house—*our* house.

As soon as I did, I snatched up the note. It was computer generated, like a gift card from a store. The seller had sent the boots to me on behalf of the buyer. The buyer was Maximillian28, of Carmel Valley, California, which made no sense to me at all until I read the note.

Susannah,

>*Saw these and thought of you. They look just like the ones you lost. I hope they are.*
>
>Te amo.

Jesse

Jesse? *Jesse* was Maximillian28?

It was only then that I remembered the day I'd dragged him around the mall in Monterey, fruitlessly searching for these exact boots after my original pair had been destroyed, and how they'd been sold out everywhere in my size. He'd gamely tagged along, only occasionally pointing out that there were dozens of other black leather platform boots on the shelves. He'd never once rolled his eyes as I'd described how poorly designed and *not right* those other boots were. He'd *paid attention*, and turned out to be Maximillian28 (named for the Ackerman dog and Jesse's age—if one counted only the years during which his physical body had been alive).

Of course. He'd do anything to make me happy . . . anything within his power, which, not having inherited millions from his family—because they'd all died out over a century ago—was buy me the impossible-to-get boots I wanted.

And save my life, over and over.

I was still laughing—or something—when Jesse pulled up behind me in front of 99 Pine Crest Road.

"Oh," he said when he leaned in to see why I was still in the car. "You opened it. Are they the right ones?"

"Exactly right," I said.

"Are you *crying*?" He looked astonished.

"No. Allergies. God, I love you."

"You have a strange way of showing it sometimes." He opened my car door for me. "Come on, let's go see this place. I can't say it looks very promising from the outside. They've ruined your mother's landscaping."

It was true. The steep, sloping yard that led up to the rambling Victorian house was still dotted with the flowers my mom had planted there, but they'd been crushed beneath the careless boots of the construction workers I'd seen outside the house the day before.

That wasn't the only change to the place. The trunk of the pine tree I remembered so well—because it grew beside the porch roof I used to leap from when escaping my room, or various murderous spooks—was now growing dangerously close to the foundation.

"Slater wasted no time putting the other houses on the block back on the market, I see." Jesse pointed. There were two men in coveralls hammering signs into the front yards of our former neighbors. Now, instead of warning that the houses were slated for demolition, the signs said:

FOR SALE

SLATER PROPERTIES

CARMEL HILLS EXCLUSIVE

PRICED TO SELL

The only house on the street without a sign in front of it was mine.

"Oh, how nice," I said. "We'll have new neighbors." I didn't mention out loud my next thought, which was that I hoped I wouldn't have to mediate any of the non-compliant deceased relatives those new neighbors might bring along. This was always a problem. "Hang on, let me try these."

I pulled off my second-best pair of boots and tugged on the new ones. They fit perfectly, and of course looked great. The heel was sexily stacked and gave me a lot of height, while at the same time being easy to walk on. When I got out of the car and stood up, my eyes were almost level with Jesse's.

"Ah," he said with the lopsided grin. "Now I remember why you liked them so much."

"Right?" I didn't have to stand on tiptoe to kiss him on the lips, only tilt my head. His mouth tasted of fresh mint. Whatever he'd been doing since he'd been released from jail, he'd cleaned up nicely. I took him by the hand. "Thank you. Now let's go see where we're going to raise our own demon spawn."

treinta y seis

It smelled the same. A combination of old wood and the faint scent of something CeeCee had always referred to as "books."

"You're crazy," I'd told her the first time she'd said it. "We have books, but not *that* many."

"No," she'd insisted. "Your house smells great. Just like old books, in a library."

I hadn't wanted to tell her that the odor she was mistaking for books was actually old souls. There are always a few of them roaming the halls of older buildings, especially libraries. The supernatural don't have an unpleasant odor. If you can smell them at all—and you mostly can't, unless you're extremely perceptive, like CeeCee—it really is remarkably (and comfortingly, if you're a reader) like old books, or vanilla.

Instead I'd said to her, "I think the word you're looking for is mildew. The source of it can be traced to Brad's feet."

When I flung open the front door to 99 Pine Crest Road, I

was shocked to be hit in the face with the exact same odor—not of Brad, but of Jesse, before I returned his soul to his body.

I glanced back at him in surprise, speechless.

"What?" he asked. He couldn't smell it, of course. You can't smell yourself. Or the way you smelled back when you were a ghost, anyway.

"Nothing," I said.

It was irritating how right Paul had been. And also how bloodthirsty. Imagine if he'd achieved his goal, and torn the place down. What would have happened to Jesse? What would have happened to *me*? To the girls? To everyone I knew and loved?

I shuddered, shoving the thought resolutely away. It didn't matter. What mattered was that I'd won.

It was startling to see the walls looking so empty without the framed photos that had always hung there, of my mom and Andy on their wedding day, and my stepbrothers and me at various celebrations; the windows so naked without curtains or shades; the rooms so bare of furniture; the wooden floors so polished (they'd always been scuffed when we'd lived there, thanks to my stepbrothers' skateboards and Max's claws).

The realty company that had staged the home for my mom and Andy while they'd been trying to sell it had changed nothing structurally. It was a house that had been built in the mid-1800s, after all, back when they'd known how to make things that lasted. Life on the frontier had been fraught with very different perils than life in the twenty-first century.

"Look," I said, touching the single defect in the molding in one wall of the front parlor. "They didn't even fill in the bullet hole."

Jesse gave me a tolerant smile. "I thought you hated that bullet hole."

"Well," I said with a shrug, swinging on the newel—it needed tightening, I noted—as I headed up the stairs. "It started to grow on me over the years."

The midday light was shining through the stained-glass window at the top of the staircase, making a blue, red, and yellow pattern on the floor of the hallway outside my old bedroom. I stepped around it, noticing through the open doors to my stepbrothers' old rooms that they'd been left relatively unchanged, except that this was the cleanest I'd ever seen them.

The door to my old room—the room that sat above the front parlor, the only bedroom in the house with an ocean view, the room in which I'd first met Jesse, and changed my life forever—was open, as well.

I stepped across the threshold.

Everything was different. Gone was the cream-colored wallpaper dotted with blue forget-me-nots, as were the frilly curtains, caught up with ruffled tiebacks. The walls were painted a deep, dark blue. The white paint on the wainscoting had been stripped, the wood returned to its original deep mahogany color to match the rest of the paneling throughout the house, then covered in a high gloss.

Even the window seat Andy had installed—though still there, and still covered in the cushion my mother had custom fitted—was now paneled in a dark cherry wood. The cushion was deep blue, to match the walls.

"Now *this*," Jesse said as he came up behind me, "is a bedroom."

I slammed my messenger bag onto the highly polished wood floor. "Shut up."

"Susannah, you used to complain about how much you hated the way your mother decorated this room, though you loved her too much ever to tell her so." He crossed the room to test the cushion on the window seat by sitting on it. "You said it in no way reflected your personality. Now it does."

"Since when does navy blue match my personality? Have you ever seen me in navy blue? This room looks like an L.L. Bean catalog threw up in it."

"I meant dark," Jesse said. "You have a tendency sometimes to be a little dark."

"Said the ghost to the mediator."

"Former ghost. And I like it. Both you *and* the room."

"Ugh, you would. You probably want to throw a few hunting prints on the walls."

"That would look very nice, actually. Anyway, the window seat is still the same." He bounced on the cushion once, then stretched a hand toward me. "Come here. There's something I've been wanting to try since the day I first met you."

There was no doubting his meaning by the decidedly sinful twist to his lips.

"What, *now*?" I slipped my fingers into his, and he pulled me down onto the window seat beside him. Our thighs were touching. This time, neither of us pulled away.

"The timing was never right until now," he said. "And you had your rules, remember?"

"What rules?"

"From when we lived here together." He slid a hand along my waist, his fingers curling beneath my tank top, even as his lips dipped to kiss the skin along my collarbone. "Rule number one, no touching."

I felt myself flush, and not because the press of his lips had caused goose bumps of pleasure to rise all along the backs of my arms.

"Oh, right," I said. "*Those* rules. Jesse, that was when you were undead, and I was in high school."

"I'm not undead anymore." He kissed me below my ear to prove it, the hand beneath my shirt rising. "At least, mostly not. And you haven't been in high school in a long time."

"You never followed my rules anyway. I always had to follow yours." I seized his wrist before his fingers could dip beneath my bra. "But I'm not going to do it anymore."

"Oh," he said with a laugh. "I think you are."

"Really? What about waiting until we're married?" I hated to spoil the moment, lovely as it was, but I didn't think I could take another stroke of his fingers, let alone another kiss, without leaping onto him and tearing his clothes off. "Do not promise me something you have no intention of delivering, Dr. de Silva."

"Have I ever, Miss Simon?" he asked, the eyebrow with the scar through it rising. "You're not the only one who's been keeping secrets."

I was so surprised by this answer that I forgot to hold on to his wrist, giving him the momentary physical advantage. He took it by yanking my tank top over my head.

"Jesse!" I cried, shocked. His training in dealing with uncooperative patients was in high evidence. "What are you—"

He silenced me by lowering first his mouth over my lips, then his entire body over mine, pressing me back against the window-seat cushion.

My mind spun. The sensations I was experiencing were not at all unpleasant—the lean weight of his body; the quick, light touch of his tongue and hands; his clean, soapy man smell (no trace of the Monterey County Jail that I could tell)—but I couldn't understand why they were happening here, now.

Then again, why was I wasting time thinking? How many nights had I lain in this very room, dreaming of this happening (though admittedly never on the window seat)?

And now it *was* happening, and I was questioning it instead of simply enjoying it, like the fact that he'd managed somehow to peel off my bra, and was tracing a hot trail with his mouth from my throat toward what the cups of the bra had revealed.

But what, I couldn't help wondering, in the part of my brain that could still think and not feel, if those things about the curse were true?

Then his fingers were undoing the zipper to my jeans, and I remembered what I'd said to Jesse the night before. I wasn't afraid of ghosts . . . especially this one.

I reached for the fly to his own jeans, and the sound of it popping open might have been the most satisfying thing I'd ever experienced in my life . . . at least until I felt, when he'd thrown his shirt aside, the sensation of the bare skin of his chest meeting mine. Then I decided no, *that* was the most amazing thing I'd ever experienced. He kissed me deeply, but after he peeled my jeans away from my hips, kissing wasn't ever going to be enough. We'd both seen and felt—for the first time—all of each other's secrets, and now nothing was going to stop us from fully exploring them, no matter what rules we ended up breaking.

A few heart-pounding, breathless seconds later, our clothes were in a tangled heap on the floor, and he was inside me. It was exactly how I had always imagined it would be, and yet unimaginably better. If evil was being unleashed, I couldn't see it, or feel it, either. What I felt was the opposite. I was flooded with playful joy, as if the dark blue walls around us were sweeping us up and rolling us into the peaceful blue Pacific beyond my windows, full of warmth and light. It washed over us again and again, leaving us spent and happy and full of gratitude and love. How could there be evil in that?

There couldn't. Only good.

Perhaps this was what Paul had somehow known and feared us discovering most of all.

Oh, well. Too late now.

I was so tired afterward I felt as if I could barely raise my head, but I did manage to notice something.

"Goddammit, Jesse. You didn't even give me a chance to take off my boots."

His head was resting on my shoulder as, with one finger, he drew lazy circles on my thigh. "I did try to remove them at one point, but you seemed more interested in my doing other things." His tone was teasing. "I was only trying to appease your wishes."

"Ha! If that were true, we'd have had sex a long time ago. What's changed all of sudden?"

His dark eyes gleamed. "You still don't know?"

"No, I still don't know. I mean, besides proving that you didn't turn into some kind of homicidal demon just from having sex with me, what happened to how we have to wait until we're married out of respect for what you owe to me and my family and the church and all of mankind? All this time you and Father Dominic—"

Jesse stopped drawing circles on my thigh and lifted his head to give me a disapproving look. "I really wish you wouldn't bring him up at this particular moment, Susannah."

"Well, I don't want to talk about him, either," I said. "But *you're* the one who dragged me to all those boring Pre-Cana classes. I'm certainly not complaining about how things have turned out, but what was the point of waiting if the entire time you were going to abandon all your religious scruples when—"

"I haven't *abandoned* them. I merely decided there was reason to be more flexible about them."

I grinned. "Would one of those reasons have to do with a certain person from our past who came roaring into town this week to declare his undying love for me, so you wanted to mark your territory?"

"It would not," he said, "though I feel as if I should add 'highly active imagination' to the list of your many assets."

"You can't blame me for thinking it after what happened last night."

"My reasons have more to do with what happened this morning. That's why I spoke to Father Dominic."

All feeling of postcoital lethargy left me. I sat up so abruptly I banged him in the head with my shoulder.

"You w*hat*?"

"Ow, Susannah. I'd ask if I hurt you earlier, but it's clear that you're feeling fine. If I were a less well-adjusted man, you might have wounded my dignity."

"Oh, don't worry about your dignity, I'll be walking bow-legged for a week. We're going to have to get a new cushion, as a matter of fact, or at least flip this one over. But why did you talk to Father Dominic? I get that he's your confessor, but he's my boss, too. I don't need him knowing *all* my personal business. You didn't tell him about *this*, did you?" I gestured to our clothes, which lay across the floor. "How could you confess something you didn't know you were going to do? Unless . . ." I gasped. "Jesse! You scoundrel! Was this premeditated sex?"

"I didn't confess anything," Jesse said. "I merely relayed to him the same good news I relayed to you."

"What good news?"

He sat up, as well, his hard abdominal muscles flexing as he hung his head in shame at my ignorance. "*Beca* in English doesn't mean bacon, Susannah. It means grant."

It took me a split second to remember. Then I gasped. "Jesse! You got the grant?"

He nodded. This time his grin wasn't lopsided. Both sides of his mouth slanted upward.

"They sent the congratulatory e-mail yesterday. But I didn't see it until this morning when the police gave me back my phone. I wanted to make some arrangements before I told you." The prideful glint in his eyes was adorable. He was no multimillionaire—yet—but every penny he had, he'd earned himself, through hard work. "One of them was with Father Dominic—he's doing much better today, by the way. It will still be some time before he'll be able to return to work, of course, but he might—just might—be well enough to marry us next weekend."

"Wait." I stared at him, not sure I'd heard him correctly. "Next *weekend*?"

He nodded again, looking almost apprehensive, his dark head ducked a little shyly. "Yes. I wasn't sure how you'd feel about it, especially after . . . well, everything that happened last night. But when I spoke to Father Dominic this morning, he felt you might like the idea. He was the one who suggested it, as a matter of fact. I don't know why."

Now I knew why Jesse hadn't wanted to see me that morning. It made sense. With Father Dominic's help, he'd finally put the past behind him, and had been busy making plans for the future—*our* future.

When I saw that priest, I was going to give him the biggest hug.

"It would have to be a very small private ceremony, of course," Jesse was going on. "And at such short notice, many of your parents' guests might not be able to attend. But David will be back in town for the holiday, and I think getting married over Thanksgiving weekend—well, what better way to show our thanks for finding one another, and for everything everyone has done for us? We can still have a formal ceremony in a year if you want to, but I thought since I finally have money, and you have this house—"

I'd already flung my arms around his neck.

"Thanksgiving weekend would be perfect," I whispered. "Just perfect."

treinta y siete

We had a church wedding after all.

It wasn't under the grand, sweeping arches of the basilica at the Carmel Mission, as we'd always planned. It was in the much smaller, more modest chapel at St. Francis Medical Center in Monterey.

But somehow I felt it was better that way. There were no statues of the Madonna (rumored to have once wept tears of blood because a virgin—me—graduated from the school) or Father Junípero Serra to gaze down upon us, only the familiar faces of friends and loved ones—our *true* friends and loved ones, because we'd invited only Jesse's colleagues from the hospital and my friends and family members who happened to be home for Thanksgiving.

Father Dominic was still there to perform the ceremony, but it was from his wheelchair rather than the intimidating altar at the San Carlos Borromeo de Carmelo Mission, which I preferred.

The ceremony went off without a hitch, with the exception

of the performance of the flower girls, who, in the tradition of flower girls throughout history, stole the show. Only Jesse, Father Dominic, and I knew, however, that their antics were due to the fact that a few additional guests had shown up to the ceremony uninvited . . . an elderly woman who'd passed away moments before in the cardiac ward and decided to stick around because, as she informed us, "I love a good wedding."

Then there was a forty-niner (the gold mining kind, not a member of the professional football team) who simply stood in the back, his battered top hat in his hands to show his respect for the bride.

Finding a venue for the reception afterward was simple. We invited everyone—minus the deceased—back to 99 Pine Crest Road for cake, champagne, barbecue, and beer.

"Well," my mother said as she stood with her arm around my waist on what had once been her back deck, but was now mine. "I don't know how you did it, Suzie. Or why. But I approve."

"Thanks, Mom." I clinked her champagne glass with my own. "Jesse and Jake worked really hard on it. David helped, too."

I didn't mention how David had arrived unannounced at Snail Crossing on the Saturday afternoon that Jesse and I had first made love, demanding to know where everyone was, and accidentally walked in on Jake and Gina having a romantic interlude of their own.

Then, upon discovering that I had somehow managed to procure ownership of our old house, and that there was no longer any danger from "the curse" he'd flown over three thousand miles to help break, David had proceeded to have a miniature nervous breakdown, from which we'd had to nurse him back to health with great quantities of brewskis and za.

"I don't mean the decorations," Mom said, indicating the party globes we'd strung across the backyard to light the picnic tables at which our guests were enjoying the barbecue Andy—ever the chef—had insisted on providing. "I mean the house. Suze, I had no idea this house meant so much to you. Why didn't you tell me? We'd never have sold it if we'd known."

"Oh," I said, sipping my champagne. "The timing wasn't right. Jesse and I had some things to sort out first."

What was I supposed to say? Well, the truth is, Mom, my husband—how I loved thinking, let alone saying, the word—died and was a ghost in this house for a while. He needed to work through that. And I needed to work through some crap that was haunting me.

But it's all good now. Well, all good *for now*.

"But how much did you pay Paul for it, if you don't mind my asking?" Mom looked around nostalgically. "Please tell me you didn't blow all your savings."

"Well, I won't lie to you, the taxes are going to be a bitch, but nothing I can't handle. I got a really good deal on the place, though." It wasn't hard to keep a straight face. "Paul practically gave it to me, as a matter of fact."

Mom seemed impressed. "Well, wasn't that sweet of him? See, I knew you two could work out your differences."

"Yeah," I said. "You weren't wrong about him."

"Simon!" A familiar male voice startled me from behind. I turned around to see Adam MacTavish, accompanied by one of my bridesmaids, CeeCee. "Or is it de Silva now?"

"We'll see," I said, and hugged him. "I haven't decided yet. Wow, don't you look like a young urban professional."

"You don't look so bad yourself, Simon. May I admire you?"

"You may." I handed CeeCee my champagne glass and curt-sied in my couture gown. Adam applauded.

"Love. Big fan of the sweetheart neckline and mermaid skirt, always have been, it's a classic for a reason. Now spin."

I spun. CeeCee pretended to be bored and studied the clouds overhead, which had turned orange and lavender as the sun sank into the western sky.

"Gorgeous," Adam said. "Love the lace, and the corset back does amazing things to your boobs, Simon. You look like a Victorian hooker."

"Geez, Adam." CeeCee handed my champagne glass back to me, then took his from him. "You're cut off. Her mother is standing right over there."

"I don't think she heard you." My mother had become involved in a conversation with Debbie Mancuso's parents, whom I'd noticed shaking their heads earlier at how little furniture Jesse and I possessed.

We didn't care. We had each other (and Spike and Romeo, who'd settled into an uneasy truce), and that was all we needed.

Plus the sizable gift certificate Mom and Andy had given us to one of the home-furnishing stores Andy represented. He'd said I could use his employee discount. I already had new curtains and carpets picked out.

"Mrs. Simon didn't hear me," Adam was saying. "And it was a compliment. By Victorian hooker, Suze, I meant, you know, one of those virginal-looking hot ladies from a vampire movie, or an old Western."

"Just the look I was going for," I said. "Will you two excuse me? I spotted some people I want to say hi to."

"Of course," CeeCee said. As I walked away from them, I heard a muffled thump, and Adam cry out in pain.

"What?" he asked CeeCee defensively. "I said it was a compliment!"

"You're such an idiot," CeeCee replied, but there was affection in her voice. Since the story on Jimmy Delgado's "suicide" broke, CeeCee had gotten a lot more confident about her professional prospects. The subsequent story she'd done on Father Francisco's arrest—and the arrest of the several other prominent Monterey Bay area residents who'd been members of Delgado's "private client list"—had been picked up by the Associated Press. CeeCee had been offered a promotion at the *Carmel Pine Cone* that she still claimed to be "mulling over."

This was a far greater gift than any I could have purchased for her online, although I was still looking for the perfect way to thank her.

She'd said, however, that my having had my wedding a year early—and in such a rush as to have no time to select bridesmaid gowns—was thanks enough.

I hurried down the steps from the deck, toward the newcomers I'd seen striding down the walkway from the front yard—or at least I hurried as quickly as someone in a tightly corseted, mermaid-skirted couture wedding gown could hurry.

"Becca. Kelly. Mr. Walters." I still could not bring myself to call him Arthur. "Hello. I'm so glad you could come."

"We wouldn't have missed this for the world." I saw Kelly's gaze flick quickly over my waist and abdomen. I knew she was trying to see if I looked pregnant, and if this could be the reason for my hastily thrown together nuptials. "Don't you look nice. Is that a Pnina Tornai?"

"No, Galia Lahav."

For once I had the pleasure of seeing Kelly struck speechless.

"I don't know if you girls are speaking English or what," her husband said in a jovial tone, "but you look stunning, Susan."

"Thank you, Mr. Walters." I smiled at Becca. "You look nice, too."

I wasn't lying, for once. Though it had been only a week since Lucia had left her, Becca looked like a different girl, standing with a newfound confidence, and wearing her dark hair away from her face. Her skin was clearing up, and the cream-colored dress she wore actually fit her. She still had a ways to go, but she no longer seemed frightened of the journey.

"Thank you, Ms. Simon," she said, giving me a shy look. The crowd in the backyard, which was considerably more sizable—and boisterous—than the one in the chapel, was seeming to intimidate her. Plus Jake had insisted on "treating" us to a live mariachi band—in full costume, including sombreros—and though talented, they were surprisingly loud. "Where can we put this?"

Becca was carrying a large, beautifully wrapped gift.

"Oh," I said. "On the table over there. Thank you so much."

"It's a tortilla maker," Kelly stated baldly. "You weren't registered anywhere, so we had no idea what to get you. I figured it's something *he'd* like." Her gaze flicked toward Jesse, who was radiating good looks and happiness in his tuxedo as he laughed with Brad and Dr. Patel at some mischief the triplets and the mini-Patels were getting up to over by the cake table.

"Well, how kind of you, Kelly," I said. I could afford to be gracious, since I was so happy. "Please help yourselves to a drink over at the bar. Oh, here's Debbie, she'll take you there."

Debbie had hurried over, having spotted her friend's arrival. "Kelly, oh, my God, it took you forever, was the traffic bad coming over? I'm so sorry. Arthur, come here, my dad wants to say hi. You, too, Becs, I want you to meet my adorable little brother-in-law, David. He goes to Harvard, you two are going to love each other."

Both Becca and David looked stricken, but only David, who'd been sitting at a picnic table next to Jake and Gina, turned nearly as red as his own hair. He'd invited his "good friend" Shahbaz to be his plus one at my wedding, then made it clear to all of us that they were more than friends by kissing under some mistletoe at Debbie and Brad's house during Thanksgiving dinner.

The Ackerman-Simon family did not shock easily, however.

Brad had remarked only, "Dude, we get it, you're gay. Now pass the gravy."

Shahbaz handled the Ackerman family and their many quirks with good humor. He'd even asked me, with a friendly wink, how my research project on ancient Egyptian curses was going.

"Go on, Becca," I said with a grin, giving her a little push. "Don't worry, he's taken."

"He's not," Debbie insisted. "He's just going through a stage."

I rolled my eyes. Debbie was the one person in the family who was resistant to change, but I knew she, too, would come around. She'd agreed to mediator school—and even vaccines—for the triplets, after all. "Did you have a good time at Sean Park's party, Becca?"

"It was okay, I guess. I didn't win at *Ghost Mediator*."

"You don't always win at *Ghost Mediator*, Becca. Trust me, I would know. Go hang out with David and his friend. They don't bite."

Fingering the horse pendant she still wore around her neck, she said, "Okay," in the grudging voice my stepnieces reserved for agreeing to try a new vegetable, and gingerly followed Debbie across the lawn, toward David and his boyfriend.

"Nicely done," said a voice at my elbow, and I turned to see a small, very elegantly dressed woman with bright white hair and even brighter red lipstick standing beside me.

"Dr. Jo! You came!" I leaned down to hug her. "I'm so glad."

"How could I not?" she asked, hugging me back. "I was so curious as to where you'd disappeared to these last few weeks. We all were." She released me and nodded at Jesse. "Now I know. He's the doctor I've heard so much about?"

"He's the doctor you've heard so much about."

"Be still my heart. And this is where the two of you are going to live?" She looked at the back of the house that, from behind, somehow managed to look even larger and more impressive than it did from the front.

"Yes. It's sort of a long story—"

"And I trust you're going to tell me about it someday. Well, as much as Suze Simon ever tells anyone."

I don't know what made me do it. Maybe it was because I couldn't believe she'd come. Maybe because we weren't in her office, but standing in the backyard of the home I'd come to love so much, and feel so safe in. Maybe because it was my wedding day, and I felt so happy.

But I found myself looking into her eyes and saying, "Dr. Jo, I'll tell you one thing, though I'm not sure you'll believe it. Your husband Sy has a message he wants me to give you. He wants me to remind you to worry less about your patients, and more about yourself. He says you need to remember to get the tires rotated on your—"

Dr. Jo stepped away from me so quickly I thought she might stumble, so I put a hand on her elbow to steady her. All the blood had drained from her face, except for the scarlet smear of lipstick across her lips.

"What . . . how could you possibly—?"

"I'm sorry," I said. "I didn't mean to scare you. It's just that you said you thought I suffered a trauma in my past, and I haven't. Not really. I just speak to the dead."

She reached out to clutch my arm. "I think I need to sit down."

Jesse chose that moment to come over. "Is everything all right?" he asked.

"Not really," I said. "Could you get Dr. Jo a chair?"

"Certainly." He disappeared, then reappeared just as quickly with a chair, into which he helped Dr. Jo. "Is that better?"

She'd closed her eyes, but once she sat, she opened them again and looked at him kneeling beside her in the grass, then back up at me.

"I'm assuming *he* knows about this . . . talent of yours?" she asked.

"Oh, yes," I said. "He has it, too. Way more than me, actually."

"Of course he does," she murmured. "Why did I bother asking? Well, go on. What did Sy tell you, exactly?"

"I'm sorry. It's just that your husband won't move on because he's so worried about you. He's very upset because you haven't remembered to have your tires rotated—"

"That's Sy, all right," she muttered. "That car. That damned car."

"I didn't know how to bring it up with you. But I see him almost every day in the faculty parking lot. One of my stepbrothers works at a car dealership, maybe he could—"

Dr. Jo wasn't listening. "That damned car. It was all he ever cared about."

"It's *you* he cares about, not the car," Jesse pointed out.

She reached out in a dazed way to pat his cheek. "You're adorable. But I think I need some alone time right now. And a drink. Would one of you mind . . . ?"

Jesse said, "Of course," and took me by the waist to physically steer me not toward the bar, but away from it. "Was that really the wisest idea? Isn't she your advisor?"

"And my therapist, yeah. But I think she needed to hear that. Why aren't we heading toward the bar? She said she wants a drink. I wouldn't mind another, either, after that."

"I'll have your stepbrother take it to her." Jesse signaled to Brad, who was acting as de facto bartender at the de facto bar, a couple of saw horses we'd placed a board between, then covered with a red-and-white-checked tablecloth. "If she's a therapist, he's exactly who should be speaking to her anyway. He needs a little career counseling. He's not going to be working for his father-in-law much longer, you know."

I sucked in my breath. "What?"

"No. He was telling me last night. He's hit up your parents for a loan so he can enroll in the police academy."

"A cop? *Brad?*" Somehow, preposterous as it sounded, it also seemed strangely right. Brad had thrived after the babies were born, loving the structure fatherhood brought to his life. A job on the police force would provide him even more structure. "Wow. Ackerman family get-togethers are about to get even more interesting."

"Yes. In the meantime, there's someone here who wants to speak to you."

"Who? I can't talk to anyone else, frankly. I'm in too much shock. Besides, I've already spoken to everyone, except the one person I most want to talk to. You." I turned to put my arms around his neck. "I've barely had a minute alone with you all day. What do you think of my dress? You're the only one who hasn't told me."

He reached up to take the empty champagne glass out of my hand and place it on a picnic table.

"I have an opinion on it," he said, "and you're definitely going to hear it, but not now." He removed my arms from his neck and spun me around to face Father Dominic a few yards away, still sitting tucked beneath a blanket in his wheelchair beside an outdoor heat lamp we'd rented.

"But I've already talked to Father D," I whispered. "Several times, as a matter of fact. And Sister Ernestine. She completely loves me since I got Father Francisco arrested. She says I'm hired . . . on conditional probation, of course, but that's fine by me. So since I've done all my obligatory chatting to the sweet old people, can we please just sneak—"

"Susannah," Jesse said, basically steering me until I was in front of a giant wearing a long black leather trench coat who was standing beside Father Dominic's wheelchair. "Do you remember *Jack Slater*?"

I had to crane my neck to look into the giant's face. When I did, I saw that it bore only the slightest resemblance to the child I remembered babysitting so many years earlier at the Pebble Beach Resort and Hotel.

"Jack?" I heard myself ask in a voice that sounded nothing like my own, it was so squeaky.

The giant smiled. "Hi, Suze," he said in a strangely youthful voice. He held out a massive right hand. He was wearing fingerless gloves in the same black leather as his trench. "Congratulations to you and Jesse."

I slipped my hand into the giant's and allowed him to pump my fingers up and down. Glancing surreptitiously at Father Dominic, I saw him grinning, though after such a long day—Dr. Patel had only granted him permission to leave the hospital for a few hours—I imagined he had to be feeling overwhelmed.

"Thanks, Jack," I said, feeling a bit overwhelmed as well. "You look . . . different."

"I know," he said with a chuckle. "Weird, right? Hey, it was really decent of you both to invite me."

This sobered me up even more quickly than the sight of his giant teenage hand. Jesse and I exchanged glances.

"Uh," I said. "No problem. We're so glad you could come."

But of course we *hadn't* invited him. I hadn't wanted Paul to discover we were getting married—we'd had enough trouble from him to last a lifetime.

So I'd taken care not to allow anything about the event to be posted online, and I'd *especially* not sent an invitation to Paul or his younger brother, Jack, though I'd felt badly about it.

"Er, yes, Susannah," Father Dominic said, looking slightly embarrassed. "Wasn't it nice of Jack to come? And all the way from Seattle, where he lives now."

I gave him a dirty look. Now I knew who'd invited Jack.

"Yes," I said. "So nice."

"I see that my brother isn't here," Jack said. "I asked him if he was coming, and he said he wasn't sure. Did he not get invited? He hasn't caused any more trouble, has he?"

"No, not trouble, exactly," I said, while beside me I saw Jesse set his jaw. I couldn't hear him grinding his teeth over the sound of the music, but I was sure that's what he was doing.

Now we knew how Paul had found out we'd moved up the wedding date, despite the care I'd taken.

The box had arrived via FedEx earlier that day, along with a card from Paul wishing us "many years of happily wedded bliss."

Inside the box was a framed notification letting the applicant know that, per their request, 99 Pine Crest Road had been determined eligible for the National Register of Historic Places, due to its being associated with "events that have made a significant contribution to the broad pattern of history" and with the "lives of persons significant in our country's past." As such, the property could never be torn down or altered in any way.

The request had been made by the Carmel-by-the-Sea Historical Society four months earlier. The notification was dated the day *after* Paul would have begun demolition on my house . . . if I hadn't stopped him.

I thought that Jesse and I had already had more than our fair share of miracles. But I was happy to take this one, too.

Jesse took a great deal of satisfaction in prominently displaying the notification over the fireplace in the front parlor. An official seal—the same as the one on the wall outside the Monterey County Jail, another historic landmark in which Jesse had spent time—would be following, according to the notification, as soon as it could be engraved.

To give Paul credit, I don't think he could have found a better wedding present . . . then again, the text he'd sent me later probably expressed his true feelings about my marriage:

> **El Diablo** Guess you don't have to worry about your something old, do you, Simon?

> When you're finally ready for something new, call me.
> Nov 26 1:24 PM

Insulting as it was, it was nice to know he was feeling better. It meant that while his jaw might have been broken, his heart never truly was—if he had one, which I wasn't sure.

I'd already decided, however, that it would be best not to reciprocate with a framed copy of the results of the paternity test I'd paid an extra thousand dollars (out of my own pocket) to have rushed during a holiday week.

Paul's probability of paternity for the triplets (or Child A, B, and C as they were referred to by the lab) had come back at a whopping 99.999 percent certainty . . . not that I'd ever doubted it, nor had any intention of telling anyone else, save Jesse. It was just a nice piece of insurance to have in case I ever needed it in the future.

"Yeah," Jack was going on. "Paul and I aren't very close anymore. Not that we ever were, really. I basically only see him at shareholder meetings."

"Oh?" Father Dominic asked. I could tell that the old man

was thoroughly enjoying himself. Bored from having been cooped up in the hospital for so long, even a normal wedding would have been very exciting to him. But this one was of particular interest to him. "Did your grandfather leave you a stake in his company?"

"Oh, no, not at all," Jack replied. "Gramps didn't leave me a dime. I bought into Paul's company with my own money. I design video games. Turns out I'm pretty good at it. Who'd have thought *I'd* be good at anything, right, Suze?"

He laughed at himself in a self-deprecating manner that was completely unlike his brother. The laugh, however, reminded me eerily of my stepnieces.

"Video games?" I echoed. "I thought you liked to write screenplays."

"What? No. Well, sort of. See, it's a bit stupid, actually. You've probably heard of one of them." Jack said the words aloud even as I mouthed them along with him. "*Ghost Mediator.*"

Jesse looked astonished. "That's *you?*"

Jack laughed some more, shaking his head as if he couldn't believe it himself. "I know. Weird, right? I mean, I know we're supposed to keep the mediator thing a secret, but I never expected anyone to see my game, much less take it seriously. I submitted it to a contest. Honestly, I never expected to win. They've even made a stupid TV show based off it."

"I've heard of it," I said woodenly.

"I know, it's really bad." Jack looked a bit deflated by my lack of enthusiasm. "It's taken off, though, internationally, and I get a ton of residuals. That lady who stars in it—"

"She's fake," I interrupted. "Her readings aren't real."

"Yeah, I know. But people really seem to like her. I try to give a lot of the money to charity. Animal shelters, mostly, but children's charities, too. Hey, I could give some to the hospital where you work, Jesse. That would *really* annoy my brother."

"That sounds wonderful." Jesse slapped Jack on the shoulder. "Keep up the great work."

Of *course* Jesse would say this.

"Thanks." Jack looked around shyly. "So, I don't suppose there are any, uh, girls my age here? It's cool if there aren't. I know it's asking a lot." His gaze was following Gina, who looked amazing, as usual, but had just finished dancing with Jake. Both were smiling at nothing. Gina had been doing a lot of that lately, not only because her romantic life was improving, but because she'd landed a plum role in Carmel's outdoor production of *Pippin*. Local theater wasn't exactly Hollywood, but it was better than nothing.

"Not her," I said to Jack. "She's too old for you. And I think she might be taken." I looked around, noticing that Adam and CeeCee were having one of their epic debates over by the cake table. Then I spotted Becca.

"You know what?" I smiled. "That girl sitting over there by my stepbrother David, looking bored? She actually likes *Ghost Mediator*."

Jack brightened. "Does she? Oh, great, maybe I'll go say hi. Thanks again for inviting me. I'll talk to you later." He was smiling as he made a beeline toward Becca, casually sidestepping his nieces, who were teaching Dr. Patel's children how to play "flower girl" (in their version, it was played by violently hurling pinecones at one another).

"So," Father Dominic said, hardly bothering to lower his voice. "The boy doesn't know those girls are his brother's children?"

"Shhh!" I glared at Jesse. "You really *did* tell him everything."

"Of course. You told *her* everything." He pointed at Dr. Jo, who'd recovered from her shock and was enjoying cake and champagne with Becca's father and stepmother. I couldn't tell if she'd met them before—perhaps because they'd set up an appointment for family counseling—or if their meeting was merely felicitous.

"Not *everything*," I said with a glower. "Thanks a lot for inviting assorted randos from my past to my wedding reception, Father D. Who else can I expect to show up? If you say the Backstreet Boys, I won't be held responsible for my actions."

"I have no idea what you're talking about, Susannah," Father Dominic said. "Jack Slater shouldn't be ostracized because of his brother's antisocial behavior. Now who is that lovely woman over there?" He gave Dr. Jo an appraising glance. "Why have I never met her before?"

I looked from Dr. Jo to Father Dominic and then back again. "Nope," I said firmly.

He had the grace to appear discomfited. "Oh, Susannah, please. I'm not interested in her romantically. I took a vow of chastity over sixty years ago and that's not something I'm likely to abandon, even if others in my profession seem to take it—and every conceivable limit of morality—lightly."

It was going to take him far longer to get over the revelations about Father Francisco than the injuries he'd sustained at the hands of Lucia.

"Whatever, Father," I said. "I'm not introducing you."

"Susannah, you do have a tendency to think the worst of people—even people you supposedly know and trust. I'm not saying she isn't a very pleasant-looking woman. I'm only saying it would be enjoyable to get to know someone my own age who isn't affiliated with the church or the school. This is a small town and I rarely meet new—"

"*Nope*," I said again, even more firmly, and took Jesse's hand. "You're on your own with that one, Father D. You wheel yourself over there and make your own introductions. We're going inside now. I need to have a word with my husband."

Husband! It was fun to say, and even more fun to drag Jesse from the party and into the house—the house that we owned— and not have anyone say a word about it. They couldn't, because we were officially a couple now, and it was officially our house, and we could do whatever we wanted in it.

It was quiet inside since everyone was gathered outside, drinking, eating, laughing, and listening to the loud, joyful music. Now that we'd had the chimney swept and the power transferred to our names, so that there was wood burning in the fireplaces at night, and air-conditioning cooling the rooms during the day, the house did not smell so much like "books" anymore.

But there was still a faint odor of them, and not only because Jesse owned so many, enough to fill all the built-in bookshelves, and then some.

I pulled Jesse by the hand up the stairs, using the other to hold the train of my very long dress, so I wouldn't trip.

"What's so important," he wanted to know as he followed me, "that we couldn't talk about it downstairs?"

"Nothing," I said when we got to our room. It really was our room now, not mine. Jake had helped move Jesse's enormous bed from Snail Crossing, and it now took up a tremendous amount of space—and had been nearly impossible to wrestle up the stairs. But it was worth it. "I just thought it was time for us to gracefully retire to the bedroom." I reached out to playfully tweak his bow tie as he lay down beside me. "I need you to unlace this corset so I can breathe, pardner."

"If that is another remark about me being a cowboy, you know I do not appreciate it." He traced a shape on the swell of my breast above the neckline of my wedding gown. "Do you really want to take off your dress? You haven't heard yet what I think of it."

I rolled over onto my back. "Oh, I have a pretty good idea what you think of it already."

He laughed and climbed on top of me. "Do you? You have a very high opinion of yourself."

"Healthy. I have a healthy opinion of myself."

He kissed me, laughing. "I think dresses like this are what you ought to be wearing all the time, Susannah. Although I suppose I'm lucky you don't, or I'd be in the Monterey County Jail every night."

"Ha! Are you saying I've finally done something of which your mother would approve?"

"I wouldn't go *that* far," he said, and kissed me some more.

A little while later the last slanting rays of the sun were creeping into the room, making bright gold splashes on the walls and wainscoting and occasional bare patches of skin—we'd been in too much of a hurry to bother to unlace the corset—and I was dozing in his arms. I'd discovered, after so many years, that I could fall asleep easily, as long as Jesse was in bed beside me.

Of course, I might also have been dozing because he was reading aloud to me from one of his innumerable ancient books, this one by the poet William Congreve.

"'*Thus in this sad, but oh, too pleasing state! my soul can fix upon nothing but thee; thee it contemplates, admires, adores, nay depends on, trusts on you alone.*'"

I heard him close the book, then lean over me.

"Susannah," he whispered. "Susannah, are you awake? We've been away from the party for too long. We should get back to our guests."

"In a minute." I reached to wipe the corners of my eyelids.

"Susannah." He sounded pleasantly astonished. "Susannah, are you *crying*?"

"No," I said with a smile. "It's my allergies again."

Jesse laughed and kissed me as the sun slipped beneath the sea.

about the author

MEG CABOT was born in Bloomington, Indiana. In addition to her adult contemporary fiction, she is the author of the bestselling young adult fiction The Princess Diaries and The Mediator series. Over twenty-five million copies of her novels for children and adults have sold worldwide. Meg lives in Key West, Florida, with her husband.

BOOKS BY MEG CABOT

"She is the master of her genre."
—Publishers Weekly

ROYAL WEDDING:
A Princess Diaries Novel

HEATHER WELLS MYSTERIES

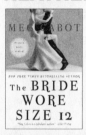

SIZE 12 IS NOT FAT
SIZE 14 IS NOT FAT EITHER
BIG BONED
SIZE 12 AND READY TO ROCK
THE BRIDE WORE SIZE 12

QUEEN OF BABBLE SERIES
QUEEN OF BABBLE
QUEEN OF BABBLE IN THE BIG CITY
QUEEN OF BABBLE GETS HITCHED

THE BOY SERIES
THE BOY NEXT DOOR
BOY MEETS GIRL
EVERY BOY'S GOT ONE

OVERBITE
INSATIABLE
RANSOM MY HEART
SHE WENT ALL THE WAY

For a complete list of Meg Cabot's books, available
in paperback and eBook, visit www.MegCabot.com